HEMLOCK

HEMLOCK

HEMLOCK

SUSAN WITTIG ALBERT

THORNDIKE PRESS
A part of Gale, a Cengage Company

LIBRARY OF CONGRESS CIP DATA ON FILE.
CATALOGUING IN PUBLICATION FOR THIS BOOK
IS AVAILABLE FROM THE LIBRARY OF CONGRESS.

ISBN-13: 978-1-4328-9037-7 (hardcover alk. paper)

Published in 2021 by arrangement with Levine/Greenberg Literary Agency, Inc.

Printed in Mexico
Print Number: 01   Print Year: 2022

A Curse on Book Thieves

For him that stealeth a book from this library, let it change into a serpent in his hand and rend him. Let him be struck by palsy and all his members blasted. Let him languish in pain, crying aloud for mercy and let there be no surcease to his agony till he sink to dissolution. Let bookworms gnaw his entrails in token of the Worm that dieth not and when at last he goeth to his Final Punishment, let the flames of Hell consume him forever and aye.

Edmund Pearson,
Old Librarian's Almanack, 1909

TABLE OF CONTENTS

CHAPTER ONE

There's hemlock — and then there is *hemlock.* The word refers to two very different plant genera, one so aggressively poisonous that you don't want to mess with it, the other harmless, helpful, and hospitable.

The bad guy first. Poison hemlock (*Conium maculatum*) and its cousin water hemlock or spotted hemlock (*Cicuta spp.*) are flowering plants in the carrot family. Infamous as the instrument of Socrates' death, poison hemlock is native to Europe and North Africa; humans carried it with them to the Americas and Australia, where it has made itself at home. Water hemlock — which looks enough like Queen Anne's lace to fool you — is native to North America. People have died when they mistook hemlock leaves for parsley, its root for wild carrot, or its seeds for Queen Anne's lace. In spite of its dangers, hem-

9

lock has traditionally been used to treat lung ailments, pain, and cramps. (Not recommended unless you know what you're doing and your insurance is up-to-date.)

Now the good guy, the hemlock tree, *Tsuga spp.* A majestic conifer native to the Americas and Asia, this tree is said to have earned the common name "hemlock" from the *Cicuta*-like odor of its crushed leaves. Rich in tannins, the bark has been used to tan leather, while a medicinal tea brewed of the needles treated kidney ailments, colds, coughs, and scurvy. Hemlocks can live up to six hundred years and are important forest trees. But in the Appalachian and East Coast regions of North America, they are threatened with destruction by the hemlock woolly adelgid, an aphid-like sap-sucking insect that is devastating whole forests.

China Bayles
"Hemlock"
Pecan Springs Enterprise

It was a Monday afternoon on a mild spring day in Texas. I was taking advantage of the fine weather to pull a few early weeds out of the Zodiac Garden, one of the dozen or so theme gardens that surround my herb shop,

Thyme and Seasons.

The shop is closed on Mondays, making it a good day for chores — checking inventory or ordering or repainting a shelf or gardening. If you have a garden, you know there is always *something* to do. And when it's done, it will need doing again. Sooner, rather than later.

The Zodiac Garden is a large, brick-bordered circle that my astrologer partner, Ruby Wilcox, helped me divide into twelve sections, corresponding to the twelve astrological houses. Each is ruled by a planet — for instance, Venus rules Taurus, Saturn rules Capricorn — and contains herbs that have been assigned (for many reasons, some obvious, some completely obscure) to that planet. This morning, I was on my hands and knees in the first house, Mars-ruled Aries, where I'm growing a variety of spicy and thorny herbs traditionally associated with the martial planet. Thistle and nettle, both of which are medicinal. And some tongue-searing culinary herbs: horseradish, hot peppers, garlic, and several kinds of mustard, including my favorite curled-leaf brown mustard, *Brassica juncea.*

Mustard reseeds itself with passionate abandon. Usually, I don't let these plants go to seed so I won't have many to thin out.

But last fall, I deliberately allowed several plants to mature so I could demonstrate how to collect and use the seed in a let's-make-mustard workshop. Nature did its usual fertile thing, and now, dozens of young plants were crowding their bedfellows. The fresh leaves would make a spicy dish of Southern-style greens for tonight's supper, with plenty of lemon and garlic — tasty alongside the pork roast I'd put in the slow cooker that morning.

I was enjoying this Monday garden chore, humming to myself and thinking of nothing more significant than tonight's supper menu and what I might do that evening. Work on my cross-stitch project? More likely: settle down with the mystery I'd picked up at the library on Saturday. I certainly wasn't planning anything out of the ordinary, anything like . . . well, like getting involved in a perilous situation in a faraway place with people I don't know.

Which is why I nearly turned down the invitation.

I was still pulling baby mustard plants when I heard footsteps crunching on the gravel and a light and bubbly voice.

"Hey, China. How are you?"

It was Penelope Paxton, the newly elected president of the Merryweather Herb Guild and one of my favorite people. Fortyish and energetic, Penny has long blond hair that frames her face and curls on her shoulders. She was wearing tan slacks and a green T-shirt that declared "Thyme in a garden is never wasted."

I tossed a plant in the bucket. "Hey, yourself, Penny." I lifted my trowel suggestively. "Happy to have you join me. The mustard got a little rowdy this spring. It wants Aries all to itself."

One eyebrow cocked, she glanced at my dirt-stained jeans, then stuck her hands in the pockets of her slacks. "Actually, I was hoping you might be about ready to take a break." She wore a serious look. "I have a question for you — and maybe a project, if you're interested. But it's a little complicated. Is there somewhere we can sit and talk?"

If I had known what was on the other side of this conversation, I might have said something like, "Oh, gosh, I don't think so, Penny. Not right now, anyway. I promised to —" And then make up some excuse to get out of whatever it was that Penny had in mind for me.

If I had known, I could've. But I didn't.

"We can sit on the deck." I pulled off my garden gloves and picked up the bucket of greens. "How about some tea?" Iced tea, the Texas state drink, which we serve even when there's a blue norther blowing and icicles hanging from the gutters.

"Sounds terrific." Penny grinned, probably relieved that I hadn't invited her to my solo weeding party.

A few minutes later, we were seated at a table on the deck outside Thyme for Tea, the tea room that Ruby Wilcox and I launched several years ago. I had filled two tall glasses with iced hibiscus tea and put a half-dozen of Cass Wilde's cookies on a plate. Cass cooks for the tea room, helps out with Party Thyme our catering service, and manages The Thymely Gourmet, a meal-delivery service for people who don't have time to shop and cook. All this is adjunct to my Thyme and Seasons and Ruby's Crystal Cave. We keep busy.

"Oh, lovely," Penny said, reaching for a cookie. She nibbled. "Chocolate chips and mint. Delicious. From your garden?"

"Right over there," I said, nodding at the patch of mint next to Thyme Cottage. That's the old stone stable-turned-cottage that I rent as a B&B. When it's not spoken for, Ruby and I teach our workshops there.

I added sweetener to my iced tea and leaned back in my chair, lifting my face to

14

the sun. In another month, I wouldn't be able to sit out here for more than a few minutes without sunglasses, a wide-brimmed hat, and sunblock. But today the sun was just right. There were early roses at the edge of the deck, mixing and mingling with late daffodils. A mockingbird poured a generous helping of song into the air, and an easy breeze teased the Texas mountain laurel blossoms, spilling their grape Kool-Aid fragrance into the air. It had been an unusually hard winter, with a pair of damaging back-to-back ice storms. Spring was especially welcome.

"So what's this about a project?" I asked. I contribute a lot of time to the Herb Guild, both because it's good business (I am, after all, in the business of herbs) and because I genuinely like the Merryweathers and believe in what we do together.

Elbows on the table, Penny leaned forward. She has blue eyes in a friendly face and she's normally all cheerful smiles. Just now, though, she looked troubled, like somebody who needs a favor and is afraid that it's too big an ask. She spoke slowly.

"I had a phone call this morning. A friend of mine has a problem — a rather hefty problem, actually. She wanted me to talk to you about it."

15

Uh-oh. I frowned. "What kind of problem?"

Penny hesitated, as if she were searching for the right word. She found it, and didn't look entirely pleased. "I guess you might call it a criminal problem. I mean, that seems to be what she's worried about."

"Ah." Every so often, somebody brings up my former career as a criminal defense attorney. This usually happens when the person (or a family member or a friend) gets into some kind of legal hot water and would like to hop out of it in a hurry. "Who's your friend?"

Penny reached for another cookie. "Actually, she's someone you know — Dorothea Harper."

Dorothea Harper. Of course. Over the years we have met a dozen times at various conferences and workshops around the country. Our acquaintance began when she gave an interesting presentation on English herbals from the sixteenth and seventeenth centuries — books that describe herbs and list their medicinal and culinary uses. We sat down to chat for a few minutes and wound up talking for a couple of hours. Dorothea taught courses in library and information sciences at the University of Wisconsin-Madison, where she specialized

16

in the conservation of old books. Herbs were a hobby for her, and she knew a lot about medicinal herbs in England during the Elizabethan era and through the eighteenth century, when almost all medicines came from plants and apothecaries had to know their herbs.

"I always enjoy talking to Dorothea," I said. "She's a treasure trove of historical information." I paused. "So what's up?"

"She has a new job. She's the director of the Hemlock House Foundation in North Carolina, northwest of Asheville. She moved there last September, after the previous director left." Penny hesitated. "Maybe you didn't know — Dorothea lost her husband a while back. Pancreatic cancer."

"Oh, gosh." I frowned. "That's terrible, Penny. I'm so sorry to hear that."

"It upended her life. She had to sell her house to pay some of the bills. Things were difficult for a while, and she felt that she needed to reinvent herself — although I'm not sure the Hemlock move was right for her."

"Oh, really? Why?"

"The house is in the mountains and quite isolated." With a thoughtful look, Penny sipped her tea. "The foundation manages a large estate that belonged to an eccentric old woman who collected rare garden books. There's a residence, a rather odd old house with a garden that's occasionally open to the public, as well as an extensive library. It was the library that enticed Dorothea, of course. It includes a valuable collection of botanical manuscripts and books, all of them old and some of them quite rare." Penny gave me a sidelong glance. "For instance, there's a copy of Elizabeth Blackwell's book, *A Curious Herbal.* A unique copy. And very valuable."

"Oh, really?" I said, sitting forward in my chair, suddenly attentive. "That's interesting."

Penny nodded. "Dorothea remembered that you once mentioned that book to her. She said you were fascinated by it."

Yes, fascinated — and for good reason. *A Curious Herbal* is recognized as simply the best of the eighteenth-century English herbals: books that contain drawings and descriptions of medicinal plants. But while her work is much admired and coveted by collectors of botanical art, Blackwell herself is curiously unknown to most modern herbalists.

In fact, I learned about her only by accident — on (of all places) the PBS television program *Antiques Roadshow.* Someone brought in a copy of a later edition of the book, in such wretched condition that it was literally falling apart in the appraiser's hands. Even so, he put an auction price tag on it of nearly $15,000, and for good reason. Besides the beauty of its illustrations, A Curious Herbal has the distinction of being the only English herbal, in any era, that was compiled, illustrated, and engraved and hand-colored by a woman. Little is known about its multitalented author, not even the date of her birth. More is known about her husband, Alexander, who seems to have been a first-class rascal with rather flexible moral scruples and a genius for causing trouble.

"I'm afraid it's the Herbal that's the problem. One of them, anyway." Penny waved off a yellow butterfly that wanted to perch on the rim of her glass. "The foundation's copy is unique. It seems to have been a gift from Elizabeth Blackwell to Sir Hans Sloane, the man whose collections were the foundation of the British Museum. It's signed. And valuable."

"How valuable?"

"Somewhere north of a hundred thousand dollars." She pursed her lips, looked straight at me, and said, "Unfortunately, it's turned up missing."

"Uh-oh." My skin prickled. "How?"

"That's what Dorothea would like to know. In fact, she's frantic about it, since whatever happened to it happened on her watch."

"Recently?"

"Ten days or so ago." Penny leaned forward. In a lower, more intent voice, she said, "She's afraid that she's about to be accused of stealing it, China."

"*She* is?" I was surprised. Dorothea is the kind of person who likes to follow the rules. If she can't find a rule to follow, she will make one — and expect you to follow it.

"Which is of course absurd," Penny said indignantly. "There appear to be other items missing from the collection, as well. The old lady died some months ago and her library is a mess. Dorothea can't be sure what they have. Or more to the point, what might be missing."

I asked the obvious. "The police have been notified, I suppose. Are they investigating?"

"Yes to both, but as I said, the house is isolated. It's in a rural county, and Dorothea says that the sheriff doesn't have much enthusiasm for an investigation." Penny pulled her blond brows together. "That's why Dorothea's afraid he may start focusing on her, for lack of other strong suspects

— and for other reasons. She wasn't very specific. I got the impression that she didn't want to go into it on the phone."

"Sounds like a difficult situation," I said.

"There's more, apparently. From time to time, Dorothea has mentioned odd goings-on at the house. And there's a board of directors that sounds like something out of a bad dream." Penny wrinkled her nose. "I don't want to be overly dramatic about this, China. But she's hoping you might be willing to . . . well, investigate."

"Me?" I asked, making sure the skepticism in my voice was clear. "Investigate? Really, Penny, I —"

Penny plowed on. "Dorothea says it needs to be somebody who can do it without attracting a lot of unnecessary attention. Sort of an undercover job. Under the sheriff's radar, at least. She says she doesn't want him to know. Or anybody else, for that matter. Including her board of directors."

I frowned. Including the board? Why would Dorothea not want the board to know? "There must be other people she could ask to help," I said. "People who know about rare books, for instance. I'm sure there's somebody who —"

"Maybe. But Dorothea is asking for *you,* China." As if in explanation, Penny added,

21

"Her sister worked at Mount Zion. Dorothea heard what happened there a few years ago."

Ah. Mount Zion Shaker village, in Kentucky. I had been visiting with a friend at a time when the historic village was facing a little problem of embezzlement — and murder. Dorothea's sister must have told her of my involvement in that sticky situation.*

But Penny wasn't finished. "She also knows that you used to work as a criminal defense attorney. And that you know and appreciate those early herbals."

I had to chuckle. "So you and Dorothea thought I could go to Hemlock House, take a quick look around, wave my magic wand, and come up with Elizabeth Blackwell's missing book. Is that it?"

"If you could," Penny said wistfully, "that would be wonderful." She cocked her head to one side. "I have the impression that investigating is something you especially like to do. That you are pretty good at it, in fact. If I'm wrong . . ." She let her voice trail off.

I considered. "No," I said slowly. "You're not wrong."

It's true. When I worked as a criminal at-

* The story is told in *Wormwood*.

22

torney, my favorite part of every case was the investigation. It was . . . well, I suppose you could call it fun. Or intellectually rewarding. It is certainly satisfying to go behind the reported events and find out what *really* happened. People forget things, accidentally and on purpose. Witnesses perjure themselves. Evidence gets misplaced or lost. A newspaper misreports. As a criminal attorney, I learned how important it is to build a legal team that conducts its own investigation into the alleged crime and ensures that *all* the facts are put in front of the jury, not just those that the prosecution chooses to bring into the courtroom. Digging up the details nobody else has bothered to find, interviewing people who aren't eager to tell what they know, asking questions that haven't occurred to anybody else, and then putting all these bits and pieces together to tell a believable, fact-based story — *that's* what I liked to do. That's what I was good at.

"So?" Penny asked hopefully. "What do you think? Want to find out what happened to that missing herbal? Spend a few days in a beautiful part of the country at a beautiful time of year? Dorothea says the foundation has an account she can tap for plane fare, if that would help persuade you to come. And you're welcome to stay at Hemlock House. There's plenty of room."

A blue jay hopped onto the deck, snatched up a crumb, and made off with it. I frowned. It sounded like Dorothea needed some help, but still . . .

"I can't just pack up and *leave,*" I said. I waved my hand at the gardens and shop. "I'm a working girl, you know, and there's never enough time around here to do what needs to be done. Plus, I'm also a mom, and Caitie has a concert coming up." Caitie, my niece and our adopted daughter — my husband McQuaid's and mine — is in junior high. She is also first-chair violin in the school orchestra, and keeping track of her doings is almost a full-time job.

"Hang on a sec." Penny raised her hand. "I happen to know that Caitie's concert isn't until next month. My Cindy has the seat next to her in the violins."

Caught. "But she needs encouragement now," I said defensively. "And anyway, I can't leave the shop. Spring is our busy time and —"

"Next week is spring break."

Caught again. "Oh. Yes, you're right. Spring break."

Spring break. Lots of people are out of town during spring break, and there'd be much less traffic in the shops and the tea room. I didn't think we had any catering events scheduled, and there were no classes or workshops. If I wanted to go to North Carolina, I suppose it would be as good a time as any, especially because Caitie was scheduled to spend the week with my mother and her husband Sam on their ranch near Utopia. My husband McQuaid (who teaches part time in the Criminal Justice Department at Central Texas State University and invests the rest of his working hours in his PI firm) was conducting a complicated investigation in San Antonio. But he would be home in the evenings and available to take care of Caitie's chickens, her cat, and her parrot. And Winchester, our basset, who hates it when his dinner is late.

Reading my expression, Penny gave me a crafty smile. "Besides," she said, "you owe me."

I sighed. I'd been waiting for her to bring that up. The previous fall, Penny and I had teamed up to manage the Herb Guild's table at Pecan Springs' Fall Fling. But I came down with a bad case of flu and was home in bed that weekend, leaving Penny to manage all by herself. I told her then that I owed her, big time, which made it difficult to say no to her now.

"I wouldn't ask if I weren't so worried about Dorothea," Penny added quietly. "I've known her for a long time, China. I've never heard her sound so . . . troubled." She put out her hand. "If you can make the time to do this, I would appreciate it. Very much."

"I'd have to ask Ruby," I said cautiously. "Just to make sure that there's not something on the calendar I've forgotten about." Ruby's Crystal Cave and my Thyme and Seasons are in the same building, side by side, with an open door between them. We like the arrangement because one of us can keep an eye on both shops if the other has to be away. Every now and then, it pays off.

Penny seemed to relax. "Thank you," she said with a smile. "I'm so glad you're willing to consider this, China. And I know Dorothea will be relieved to see you. I have the sense that she feels terribly beleaguered. She doesn't know quite what to do. She needs somebody on her side."

Somebody on her side. Don't we all?

But I couldn't promise anything without checking with McQuaid and Ruby. And even if I went, what could I do? The cops probably had the investigation well in hand and would likely resent anybody tromping on their turf. And the missing herbal could be anywhere by now — in some collector's European library, for instance. Getting it back might take a miracle.

I *was* intrigued, though. Was the *Curious Herbal* stolen simply because it was the most valuable book in the library — or was there another reason for making off with it? Who knew it was there? Who had access to it, besides Dorothea?

Penny's smile wavered just a bit. "Well, while we're talking about it, there's something I suppose I should tell you, just so it won't come as a surprise." She squared her shoulders. "I don't think it will daunt you, though. In fact, it might even entice you."

Entice me? I raised both eyebrows. "What is it?"

"It's . . . well, it's the house. The gardens are really spectacular — I've seen photos. But Dorothea says Hemlock House is supposed to be haunted. By the eccentric old lady whose family built it. She spent her life there. And died there."

"Dorothea doesn't strike me as the kind of person who sees ghosts," I said. "That's probably just the foundation's hype to lure tourists."

"Tourists can't visit. As I said, the gardens are open to the public only occasionally. The library has been open to a few researchers, while the house itself is private." She waved her hand dismissively. "But every old house in North Carolina has inspired some sort of ghostly legend — it only adds to the charm. And spring is the very best time of year there, with the dogwoods and redbuds and all the spring flowers in bloom. A great time for a little vacation."

I was silent for a moment. Finally, I said, "All right, then. I'll talk to my family. I'll call Dorothea and try to find out what's going on. Maybe she'll decide she doesn't need me." I paused. "I'm sure I have an email address for her somewhere, but she may have changed it. Do you have her phone number handy?"

"I do," Penny said promptly, digging into her shoulder bag. She took out a little notebook and tore out a page. "Here you go — both her new email and her phone number." She paused and looked me squarely in the eye. "She said you could call any time. She's anxious to hear from you."

Now was my chance to say no — and save myself from what turned out to be a dangerous and even deadly trip. If I had known where the journey was going to take me, I might not have agreed to go. I might have stayed home, gotten on with my work, and enjoyed spring break in Pecan Springs.

But I didn't say no.

Dorothea Harper had seemed relieved and very glad to hear my voice on the phone. I asked a few questions and learned a bit more about the strange disappearance of *A Curious Herbal*. The book — a unique presentation copy, beautifully bound and signed by Elizabeth Blackwell herself — had vanished from a locked display case in the library at the Hemlock House Foundation. Disturbingly, an inventory (begun some weeks before but nowhere near completion) had identified a number of pages missing from other rare books of botanical prints.

My first thought: This looked like the classic inside job, especially since there had been only a limited number of visitors over the past few months. At the risk of sounding like an officious Miss Marple, I suggested to Dorothea that she make a list of everyone who had been in the library since she assumed her position as director.

"But you've probably already done that," I added, "for the police."

No, she said. She hadn't. The sheriff hadn't asked.

Which told me something. And I learned something else, indirectly, from the tone of her voice. The Dorothea Harper I had known had been strong, self-assured, and poised. The woman on the phone sounded fragile, unsure of herself, apprehensive. And she made sure to tell me that, if I came, the real reason for my visit had to be kept secret.

"I can tell people that you're an old friend," she said, and then laughed a little. "Which is true, of course. although we've never been able to spend much time together. I will be very glad to know you better." She added "I really hope you'll come, China," in such a plaintive voice that I knew I had no choice. I couldn't back out now.

And then, after I agreed, Dorothea told me that one of her graduate students — a young woman named Jenna — was working as a library intern at Hemlock House. Jenna had done quite a bit of research into the life of Elizabeth Blackwell. She was writing a novel about her and would like to send me the first chapter.

"A novel!" I said, genuinely excited by this news. "I've often wondered just who Elizabeth was and how in the world she managed to carry out that mammoth project all by herself. I would love to read it, Dorothea."

"Excellent," Dorothea said. "I'll give her your email address and she can send it.

Jenna is a good writer, and she's sticking to the facts as closely as she can. Her take on the Blackwell story is intriguing."

Ah, technology. Fifteen minutes later, the chapter flew into my computer's inbox. I couldn't wait to settle down for the evening, open the file and read it.

When I did, I found that it was every bit as good as Dorothea had said. When I finished, I was eager for more and seriously looking forward to digging into the disappearance of the Hemlock House's copy of Elizabeth Blackwell's famous book.

And thereby hangs a tale.

Two of them, actually.

Elizabeth's curious tale — and my own tale of the theft of *A Curious Herbal.*

■ ■ ■ ■

Part One:
The Curious Tale
of Elizabeth
Blackwell by
Jenna Patterson

■ ■ ■ ■

January 4, 1735
Outside Newgate Prison, London
Since the fourteenth century, debtors could end up in prison for nonpayment of debts. In many cases, it was hoped that the debtors' families and friends would repay the debt. Generally, conditions in prison depended on your standing in society. The

warden of the prison would charge for accommodation — prisons were state-owned and subject to regulation, but were operated for private profit. If you could afford it, accommodation allowed access to a bar and shop. Conditions for debtors who could not raise money were appalling, with whole families cramped into overcrowded, cold, damp cells.

Andy Wood,
"In debt and incarcerated:
the tyranny of debtors' prisons."
The Gazette,
http://www.thegazette.co.uk/
all-notices/content/100938

Clutching her woolen cloak against the bitter wind, Elizabeth Blackwell turned to look at the forbidding façade of the prison where she had just left her husband. The despair that filled her was colored with anger and frustration, for her husband's imprisonment was of his own making. And even though he cheerfully acknowledged his faults, he was clearly depending on *her* to get him out of gaol — an accomplishment that would be nothing short of a miracle.

Alexander had been remanded to Newgate on the demand of his creditors and by order of the Commissioners of Bankruptcy. Elizabeth knew that it had been foolish of him to defend himself before the commissioners, for he made such an arrogant showing that it merely hardened the creditors' resolve against him. But all the attorneys of Chancery Lane could not have saved him — besides which, if there had been money for a defense it would have gone to pay off a creditor or two or put something toward the usurious court costs.

So there had been no money for a proper defense. There was, in fact, no money at all, which was why Alexander was being held in an unheated cell with a thin straw mattress and only a small table and single chair for furniture. For light, there was but one tiny window, very near the ceiling, and a stub of a candle in a saucer on the table. If there had been money, they could have paid the turnkey for a cell with a fire, a better mattress, more daylight, and meals.

As it was, Alexander would have to make do with the bedding Elizabeth had brought, as well as the rest of the supplies she had put together: candles, a plate and cup and cutlery; clean cravats, shirts, stockings and small clothes; a basket of bread, cheese, fruit, and sweets; a bottle of wine, tobacco, and the books he had requested. The air was foul with the stench of the prison and noisy with the prisoners' shouts, but Alexander would be more comfortable.

The Newgate warden — a man of large girth, with a bulbous nose in a pocked face — was still standing by the cell door with a heavy ring of keys in his hand and something on his mind.

"This cell 'twill not do for a family, o'course." He eyed Elizabeth. "How many little 'uns will ye be bringin' here, Missus? How large a room will ye need?"

Elizabeth felt an icy shiver of dread. The bankruptcy had forced them to forfeit their lease at the Atlas on the Strand opposite Catharine Street, where they had lived above Alexander's print shop. Their furnishings and presses and printing equipment and supplies — most of it purchased with her dowry — had been sold to satisfy their creditors. Alexander's living arrangements were now certain: he would remain in debtor's prison until she had scraped together the money to buy his freedom. Where she and the children should live — and how and with what funds — *that* was still an unanswered question.

When the head of a family was consigned to debtor's prison, the family often came too, with one or more "working out" to pay for the extra lodging and food and make payments on the debts. Alexander assumed that this was what they would do. In fact, he had told her as much.

But now, looking around, she thought of four-year-old Blanche's delicate constitution and two-year-old William's frequent earaches and nosebleeds. She didn't know where she and the children would live. But with a sudden strong conviction, she knew that this cold, damp, sunless place was no place for them, not for a single day.

She turned to face the warden. "The children and I shall *not* —"

"My wife and two little ones will be with me, of course." Alexander — as he often did — spoke over her. He cast a disdainful look at the brick walls and dirty stone floor. "We shall want a room much larger than this. With a fireplace and a proper window."

"I'll put you down for it, then," the warden said. "Thruppence a week for a place on the list of them waiting. One and six for the room, when it comes open. Fireplace for cookin', but no fuel nor furnishings," he added, with a cautionary look at Elizabeth. "Meanwhile, you and the children can stay here, but you'll have to provide your own bedding." He held out his hand and Alexander dropped three pennies into it.

Exasperated, Elizabeth shook her head. The Newgate wardens were notorious for charging exorbitant fees, but it was ridiculous to pay just to have a place on a waiting list.

The turnkey pocketed the coins. To Alexander, he said, "S'pose ye've already found yer way around. Billiards is in the second gallery. Taproom in the hall-gallery. Food and drink in the snuggery."

"Yes, thank you," Alex said courteously. "I have frequented all."

As the warden rattled his keys and made off, Alexander — a handsome man of slender build, with sandy hair and eyebrows and bright blue eyes — thrust his hands in his trouser pockets. With a smile he said, "Well,

38

Bess, my dear, since I don't have a bed to offer you, I don't suppose you'll want to pass the night. Next time you come, bring more candles. And do look through my things for the small chessboard and pieces. Surely I can find someone here who —"

"I will do that." Elizabeth straightened her shoulders. "But I am *not* bringing the children here, Alex. They're sickly enough already, poor things. I shall bring more food and wine and your chessboard when I can. But I shall have to find lodging elsewhere."

"Well!" Offended, he pulled himself up. "Just what sort of 'elsewhere' do you think you can conjure? And I shan't be in this place long, you know." With a confident smile, he put out a finger and touched her cheek. "I shall be out of here and in our own shop and house again in no time." He glanced around, as if to make sure that no one was listening, and lowered his voice. "I have stratagems afoot, Bess. One of them will come to fruition, I promise, and we will be together again."

I promise.

Elizabeth tightened her jaw. When they were married some six years before, she had been barely nineteen and smitten by Alexander's ebullient self-assurance, as well as by his handsome figure and easy speech.

No matter the difficulties, he was always charmingly confident that everything would work out for the best. *I promise,* he'd say, and she would believe him.

But her husband's cocky, never-a-care-in-the-world air had not worn well over the years. Unlike the provident Scots Elizabeth had grown up with in Aberdeen, Alex was financially irresponsible. Whatever he bought had to be the very latest and the very best, and his spendthrift habits were ruinous.

Added to that, he was impulsive. He had first studied botany, then medicine. Then, when a brief venture as a medical doctor had proved unprofitable (Aberdeen was oversupplied with doctors and he had not fully completed his training), they moved to London. There, with the help of Dr. Stuart, a friend of Elizabeth's family, he had found a place as a corrector — a proof reader — in Mr. Wilkins' print shop, where he became captivated by the printing trade and sure that it was a ladder to success. It might be, too, for the public's appetite for books, newspapers, and all kinds of printed material was already enormous and growing every day.

So it was that when Elizabeth's father had at last paid her dowry, Alex had set himself up as a printer, using all of her money and borrowing the rest. Hoping to ensure their success, Elizabeth had worked energetically beside him, dealing with authors who wanted their manuscripts printed, managing the accounts, and purchasing the paper and ink and other supplies. She had even done some of the work of a printer's apprentice. And she had enjoyed it all, for she was a tradesman's daughter and had a sharp entrepreneurial instinct.

Tragically, however, Alex had brought their enterprise to ruin. With his customary arrogance, he had decided to defy the statutory requirement to serve a seven-year apprenticeship before opening a print shop. He was challenged by the powerful printers' guild, fined, and forced to close. Had he taken a journeyman partner (as Elizabeth had pleaded with him to do), he could easily have avoided the ultimate catastrophe. But no, the shop and all its profits had to be *his*. The punishment was his, too.

And now she had to think for *them* — for the children and herself — and not for Alexander. He was still her husband, though, and however much she might rue the marriage, she would meet her obligation.

She managed a smile when she said, as calmly as she could, "Well, then, I shall look

41

for something to tide us over until your stratagems prove out." She cast an eye around the cell. "I shall come back when I can with more candles and food and your chessboard." She turned to go.

He put a hand on her shoulder and went with her to the cell door, remembering things he wanted her to do. "Be sure to visit old McCratchen to find out how much he cheated me on the lease of the Strand. And do have a frank talk with Stuart — I'm sure he can suggest the names of others in the London Scots community who might help."

"I won't beg for you, Alexander," she said sharply.

But she knew he was right about the Scots. Since the Union of 1707, nearly thirty years before, Scotland had been a part of Great Britain. England offered many opportunities, and scores of professional men — physicians, lawyers, merchants, scholars — had made their way south, to London. When they became successful, they held out a generous hand to those who came after and were in need. It was only logical that she should turn to them.

"And don't worry about me," he said, as if he had not heard her, as perhaps he had not. He did not always listen. "I'm sure I shall be quite comfortable." He leaned forward and dropped a kiss on her cheek. "I have Dr. Swift's 'Modest Proposal' to read and enough shillings for a few days' food and ale." He smiled. "I shall be glad of a nap, too."

Now, standing outside Newgate, Elizabeth thought of Alex's nap with a hard jab of resentment. He was treating this humiliating affair as if he were on holiday, while she was left to manage the children as well as raise the funds for his release. No holiday for her.

She gathered her cloak around her and stepped into the crowd jostling each other along Newgate Street. There were bewigged men in tricorne hats, boots, and greatcoats. Women bundled in cloaks and thick woolen shawls, some holding their skirts up out of the dirt, others holding nosegays of rosemary, mint, and lavender under their noses to sweeten the stench. Street children in ragged shirts and trousers, some of them barefoot, even though it was the dead of winter. And beggars of all descriptions, of course, as well as dogs and cats and the occasional escaped chicken or duck or young pig, sure to be snatched up and put in the pot or on the spit before the owner could reclaim it.

The damp, chill air was heavy with sooty

smoke from the countless coal fires that warmed the city and cooked its food, and noisy with the shrill cries of costermongers hawking their baskets and buckets and bags of produce. *Penny a bunch cabbage! This morning's mackerel, six a shilling! Fresh nuts, penny a pound, fresh nuts, only a penny!* Ahead on a corner stood a stout, jovial baked-potato man, his hot pot on the ground at his feet. *Hot baked potato-O. Hot baked potatoes, with butter and salt!*

Elizabeth thrust her hand through the slit in her heavy woolen skirt and pulled tuppence out of the pocket hung from a tie around her waist. Not stopping to ask herself whether there were any more coins in that pocket or what she would do if there were not, she pushed her way to the front of the crowd and traded the two silver coins for a smoking-hot baked potato — not so much because she was hungry but because it would warm her hands. The north wind was bitterly cold and it was a good two hours' walk to Bloomsbury, where the children were in the temporary care of one of the Stuarts' housemaids. In better days, she would have taken a hackney coach as far as Lincoln's Inn Fields, but shanks' pony would do for now. She was strong and not yet thirty, and she had grown up tramping the steep hills and deep dales of northeast Scotland. She didn't mind the walk.

And perhaps the exercise would clear her head of the stench of Newgate and help her face the irrefutable fact that she must find employment that paid enough for lodging and food with something left to pay toward Alexander's debt. While both Dr. and Mrs. Stuart seemed pleased to allow her and Blanche and William to stay as long as was necessary, she felt urgently that they must not impose. There were other friends who would be glad to offer temporary beds, but she couldn't spend the whole term of her husband's imprisonment — who knew how long that might be? — scuttling from one chimney corner to another like a housecat with kittens in search of a warm place to sleep. She would have to find money somewhere — but where?

Unfortunately, the usual recourse in the event of straitened circumstances was not an option for Elizabeth. It was true that her father, William Blachrie, was a Burgess of Trade for the city of Aberdeen and that he had built up a considerable fortune as a hosiery merchant, selling the handspun, hand-knitted woolen stockings that were produced in vast quantities by the women of the region. But aid from the Blachries was out of the question. Elizabeth's father had made that clear when, nearly two years after their elopement, he finally paid her dowry to Alexander, whom he knew well. *Too* well, indeed. The Blachries and the Blackwells were related.

"Your second cousin is a charming rascal," her father had said with his characteristic Scots bluntness. "You will certainly rue your choice, Elizabeth. He is handsome and glib but fickle, without an ounce of steadiness in him. He is an impulsive young man who has not one idea of what he wants to make of himself. He has no business taking a wife." Elizabeth's mother had opposed the marriage too, and when Elizabeth chose to follow her heart, both of her parents cut off all ties with her. She had written when the children were born, but there was no answer.

The Blackwells had gone even farther, not just opposing but forbidding the marriage. Alexander's father, now deceased, had been a prominent classical scholar and principal of Marischal College in Aberdeen. His brother, Thomas Blackwell, was well on the way to becoming a published (if dull and verbose) historian. Alexander himself was a brilliant young man who read several languages, studied some botany, and was destined for an outstanding academic career. Marriage before he'd completed his studies — and to a *tradesman's* daughter — had been unforgiveable.

Elizabeth knew that there would be no financial help from Aberdeen. But if not from parents or friends, where? Where was she to find the money to provide lodging for herself and her children and try to chip away at the mountain of debt that towered over her husband? As she trudged past the bleak gray hulk of St. Sepulchre Church, she was nearly overwhelmed by the heavy gray enormity of the tasks that lay ahead.

But in just a few moments, when she had crossed the bridge over Fleet Ditch and started for the top of Holbourn Hill, she would encounter something that would paint her future in much brighter colors.

CHAPTER TWO

Mugwort (*Artemisia vulgaris*). If you're looking for a magical herb to ease your travels, try mugwort. In medieval Europe, people didn't set off on a journey without it. Some early beliefs:

- If a footman put mugwort in his shoe in the morning, he may go forty miles before noon and not be weary.
- If mugwort be placed under the saddle of a horse, it will make him travaile fresh and lustily.
- If any propose a journey, then let him take in his hand this wort and then he will not feel much pain.

Minnie Watson Kamm
Old Time Herbs for Northern Gardens,
1938

I was deeply impressed by the chapter Jenna had sent me. Poor Elizabeth Blackwell! A foolish husband in prison, a mountain of debts towering over her head, small children to provide for, and nowhere safe and clean to live — in a city like London!

I closed the file with a knot in my stomach. What could Elizabeth do? And what was the "something" she would encounter at the top of Holbourn Hill that would color her future differently? I was hoping that Jenna would have another chapter or two ready for me by the time I got to North Carolina.

I wasn't exactly travailing lustily, and I rather doubt that mugwort in my shoe — even in *both* shoes — would have gotten me through Austin-Bergstrom International Airport any faster or more comfortably than my Adidas. But there is a very healthy mugwort growing in the apothecaries' garden at Thyme and Seasons. If I had tucked a sprig or two into my suitcase, maybe its magic would have eased some of the mischance I met before I got back home again. Maybe.

As I'm sure you know from your own experience, setting off on a journey isn't just a matter of grabbing your car keys and heading out. It's complicated. At home, I needed to pack Caitie's clothes before Leatha and Sam (my mother and her husband) drove from South Texas to pick her up — and Spock as well. Caitie had decided that her parrot was begging to go to the ranch.

"Boldly go," Spock announced. One of his previous owners had been a Trekkie and Spock is fluent in Trekese. "Final frontier. Where no one has gone before. Awk!"

Which settled it, as far as Caitie was concerned. Spock was going with her, which required a surprising amount of extra stuff.

I also had to make sure that the fridge was stocked and that there were heat-and-eat meals in the freezer for McQuaid, who if left to his own devices would subsist on beanie weenies until I got back. And remind him of how and when to feed the chickens and where the dog and cat food can be found. Little details.

At the shop, Ruby assured me that I wouldn't be missing a thing by taking spring break week off. She and Laurel, our helper, would keep an eye on the shop. Customer traffic would be manageable, there was only one group luncheon (Ruby's weaving guild), no catering events on the calendar, and no classes. It was a good time to take a few days off. Godspeed, safe travels, bon voyage.

And then she paused, thought for a moment, and said, "But I do have to tell you . . ."

Her voice trailed off and a small frown gathered between her eyes. She was wearing green today: green and purple striped ankle-length yoga pants, loose green scoop-neck tee over a purple tank top, a purple and green bandeau around her frizzy red hair.

"Excuse me a minute," she said. She tucked her right foot against her left upper thigh in a tree pose and closed her eyes, pressing her palms together in front of her chest. Ruby is tall, over six feet in her sandals. In the tree pose today, she didn't look like a tree. She looked like a red-crested green stork standing on one green and purple leg.

"Tell me what?" I asked. When I try to stand in a tree pose, I topple over after about ten seconds. Ruby is loose-limbed and limber. What's more, she has perfect balance. She can stand like a tree for hours, silently checking the messages the Universe has cued up for her.

I waited. Then waited a little longer. Then: "Earth to Ruby. Come in, Ruby."

Finally, she opened her eyes. "Sorry. I was trying to decipher it."

"Decipher what?"

"I can't quite make it out. There's too much . . . snow. All that's getting through is a warning message. Be careful."

"Like snow on an old TV set?" I refrained from rolling my eyes. "Somehow I thought that the Universe was too powerful to be taken down by a little local static. What do I need to be careful of?"

She blinked, dropped her hands, and lowered her foot. "I wish I could be more specific China, but I can't. All I know is that something will happen where you're going, and it won't be . . . what you expect."

As you probably know if you've spent any time with her, Ruby is psychic. The gift is not something she's exactly comfortable with, and she often tries to pretend that she's . . . well, normal. As normal as the rest of us, I mean. In a good sort of way, the Crystal Cave (still the only New Age shop in Pecan Springs) is a refuge for her, because it's a place where she can be just a little bit psychic, just for fun.

For example, when she uses the tarot cards and rune stones and the Ouija board, she can pretend that whatever she's telling you comes through them. I've heard her say it and maybe you have, too: "I'm only reading the cards." Or "That's what Ouija says. That's the message I'm getting."

The truth is more simple — and much more convoluted — than that. She doesn't need cards or a pendulum to tell her what she already knows. She just *knows* it. Which can weird you out, especially if (like me) you're not a believer in the strange and spooky. But I *am* a believer in Ruby. I've seen her get it right often enough to know that it's a good idea to pay attention when she has something to tell me.

I was paying attention now, wondering if she was going to say anything about the ghost who was reputed to haunt Hemlock House. But if she knew about that, she wasn't going to mention it. For which I cannot blame her, after her frightening scrimmage with Rachel Blackwood's ghost a couple of years ago.★

"So, okay," I said. "So this is an adventure. So I need to expect the unexpected. When the static clears and you get a better sneak preview on your psychic TV, please let me know. If something exceptionally bizarre is going to happen, I'd like to have some advance warning."

"Of course I will," Ruby murmured. She put both hands on my shoulders and pecked my cheek. "Just go and have a good time, okay? I'm sure it will be fine." She paused, and there was that little frown again. "But you might want to take a heavy coat and

★ You can read this story in *Widow's Tears.*

some woolies. Boots could come in handy, too."

"Boots?" I scoffed. "But the dogwoods and redbuds are all out. It's *April,* you know."

"I know." Ruby pursed her lips. "Just the same . . ."

I would wish I had listened.

As it turned out, the only really bad thing about flying east was the predawn start.

I was up at four on Sunday morning for the forty-minute drive to the airport just south of Austin. I caught a six a.m. flight to Charlotte, then a commuter flight to Asheville, arriving in the afternoon. My first stop: the rental car desk to pick up the car I'd reserved, a white Mitsubishi Mirage.

The guy behind the counter, a tall, skinny kid with a dark buzz cut and John Lennon glasses, asked where I was going. When I told him, he puckered his mouth and said, "Maybe you'd rather take a four-by-four?" He smiled. "Could be some weather in the mountains."

I hesitated. A four-by-four might be fun to drive, but the foundation was picking up the tab and they might not feel the extra cost was justified. "I'm good with the Mirage," I said.

He gave me his best salesman's you'll-be-sorry look and checked me out. Fifteen minutes later, I was heading out of the airport complex. The car took some getting used to. It had something called a variable transmission that continuously shifted for itself — silently, so I didn't know what gear it was in. Nothing like my old stick-shift Toyota back home.

My route took me north on I-26, in the direction of the famous Biltmore mansion, that huge, elaborate "mountain escape" built as a summer getaway by George Washington Vanderbilt. The Asheville area, I understood, had been the summer retreat for a number of East Coast bluebloods in the early part of the twentieth century. I was tempted to stop and visit the gardens — I've heard that the early azaleas are spectacular — but I had another sixty-plus miles to drive, and Dorothea was expecting me. Biltmore could wait.

So I drove west, marveling at the ever-varying, always-spectacular landscape. Fluid gray mists ebbed and flowed around green summits, cloud shadows constantly changed the apparent shapes of the valleys, and as I drove deeper into the mountains, the bright afternoon was darkened by drifting fog and finally by rain. I turned the windshield wipers on as I swung off the main highway and into a small, mist-cloaked town. Bethany (population 4,500) was nestled between two mountain ranges, on the bank of a boisterous mountain river. Picturesque and prosperous, it looked familiar, perhaps because it was an anywhere-America small town, with the usual antique shops, an art gallery, a bookstore (the Open Book), a couple of cafés, and a wide main street, washed clean by the rain and lined with pink-flowering crabapple trees.

I drove through town, then crossed a bridge over a fast-flowing river. From there, I followed the GPS's chirpy directions west and south through a series of valleys and along a tumbling creek that was in a hurry to get to the nearest valley. A half hour later and much deeper in the mountains, I was working my way up a ridge on a series of steep switchbacks that had to be thrillingly suicidal during a winter snowstorm or when there was ice on the pavement.

By this time, the road had narrowed to a two-lane blacktop with no shoulders. The forests crowded in on either side, tunnel-like and shadowy in the late afternoon gloom. The clouds had dropped out of the sky and were skimming the tops of the trees, trailing gauzy scarves of fog. The redbuds seemed to be finished blooming but Penny had mentioned the dogwoods and there they were, in abundance: wraith-like white shapes slipping through the dark forest like plaintive ghosts. The rhododendrons wouldn't be along for several weeks, but the native azaleas were in bloom, brushing the gray-scape with an optimistically rosy blush. The forest trees were mostly hemlock, I supposed, with white pine and oak and an occasional patch of maple, and all very dense and dark.

But occasionally the road crossed a clearing and I could see a ruffle of spring beauties and trilliums, a fringe of purple violets, and an emerald green clump of maidenhair fern bursting exuberantly out of a cliff. After twenty minutes of dizzying switchbacks, I crossed a narrow bridge over a frothy whitewater creek and turned right onto a graveled road.

I was there.

I had seen photographs and a history on the Hemlock House website, so I thought I knew what to expect. Maybe it was a trick of the evening twilight or the eerie tendrils of fog draped over the trees. But the house loomed much larger and more ominous in real life than it had on my computer monitor.

Hemlock House was built soon after the First World War by an American arms manufacturer named Reginald Carswell. A fervent admirer of then-popular French Châteauesque architecture, Carswell commissioned Richard Howland Hunt, the son of the Biltmore architect, to build a Biltmore-style house that would impress the friends and business associates he expected to entertain. Not quite as large as Vanderbilt's Gilded Age palace and lacking the expanse of Biltmore gardens, Hemlock House was still a quite sizable faux château, with thirty-some rooms, a stone gatehouse, and a scattering of outbuildings. It might have looked right at home in the Loire Valley in, say, the year 1400.

But not so much on this tree-clad Appalachian mountain, where its exaggerated, pretentious French Renaissance personality fitted about as well as a bejeweled matron dressed for opening night at the opera would fit into your neighborhood block party. The gray stone walls were studded with leaded-glass casement windows of various sizes and decorated with trefoils, flowing tracery, rosettes, and gargoyles. The steeply pitched slate roof was ornamented by towers, spires, parapets, and wrought-iron balustrades and crowned by a hodge-podge of chimney pots. It wasn't quite Shirley Jackson's Hill House, all ill-fitting angles and out of kilter, "never meant to be lived in, not a fit place for people or for love or for hope." But the effect was ominous and even threatening, especially shadowed as it was by the darkening light. It looked like a place where things might come out of dark corners or out of the walls. No wonder people thought it was haunted. It would be a surprise if they didn't.

I turned off the key and sat for a moment, looking at the house. If it hadn't been well after six and I hadn't been so tired, I might have turned around and driven back down to Bethany, where I could check into a cheerful B&B. But it was almost dark, I had spent most of the day on a cross-country flight, and I was too tired to negotiate those risky switchbacks. Anyway, what the heck. I was here for the adventure, wasn't I?

I got out of the Mirage, took a deep breath of the mountain air, and pulled my wheelie out of the trunk. As I lifted the heavy brass gargoyle doorknocker on the arched door at the foot of the main tower, I would not have been at all surprised if it were opened by the sinister Mrs. Danvers, straight out of du Maurier's *Rebecca.*

But there was nothing sinister about the willowy young woman who answered my knock. In her mid-twenties, she had an intelligent face, wideset gray-blue eyes behind owlish tortoiseshell frames, and dark, pixie-cut hair that gave her an impish look. She was wearing skinny jeans and a wooly gray cardigan over a dark purple T-shirt that displayed a tree-covered mountain peak and the words "Hemlock Rocks!" She was all smiles and easy welcome as she introduced herself.

"Jenna Peterson." She put out her hand. "I'm Dorothea's assistant."

"Oh, you're the author!" I had already emailed her my praise for the material she had sent me, but I repeated it. "I loved that first section, Jenna. Your Elizabeth is in a tight spot. I can't wait to see how she gets out of it."

"Thank you," Jenna said, beaming. "It's an amazing story, and I still have lots of questions about it. We'll have to make some time to talk." She took a breath. "Dorothea is on a conference call right now with some of the board members. She'll be super happy to know that you've made it safely. Hemlock House is a long way from Texas."

"And those last few miles up the mountain

61

are a challenge," I said. "I don't think I've ever had to navigate that many switchbacks. My arms are aching."

"It's even more of a challenge in the snow," Jenna said ruefully. "How long will you be staying?"

"I'm supposed to fly back on Thursday," I said. I could stay over for a day or so longer if there was a reason, but if I hadn't found what we were looking for by then, chances were that it wouldn't be found.

She nodded. "I hope you've brought some warm clothes. This big old place is hard to heat. If you haven't, no worries. We can fix you up." She reached for my wheelie. "Let's get you settled. Your room is up there." She pointed. "No elevator service, I'm afraid."

I looked. We were standing inside the stone tower that served as a kind of foyer, rising several stories over our heads. Somewhat bemused, I followed Jenna up the staircase as it made a three-quarter circle to a narrow second-floor balcony.

"Amazing," I muttered, peering down. If this were an Alfred Hitchcock movie, I'd probably be looking at a dead body sprawled on the stone floor some ten or twelve feet below.

"Isn't it?" Jenna replied blithely. "Parts of the house have been closed off for years,

62

ever since Miss Carswell's father died. Dorothea thinks it's depressing, not to mention spooky. But me, I always imagine it as a fairytale castle. I tell myself that Rapunzel must be hanging out in one of these rooms, braiding her golden hair at the window while she waits for her prince. I look for her sometimes, but I've never found her — so far, anyway. I keep looking. And of course there's a secret room here somewhere. There always is, you know."

"A secret room? As in an old Nancy Drew mystery?"

"Exactly," she said, and laughed. "Said to be on the third floor. But it's so secret that we haven't found it yet." She pointed to a corridor. "This way."

The hall ahead was long and dark and the doors were closed on either side. I tried picturing Rapunzel behind one of them, but it wasn't working for me. It was much easier to imagine something more ill-omened. I shuddered. Those creepy twins in the film version of Stephen King's *The Shining*, maybe.

Jenna was walking briskly and I hurried to catch up. "How long have you been here?" I asked.

"I came with Dorothea," Jenna said. "I'm studying library science at the University of

63

Wisconsin. My job is to help her sort out Sunny Carswell's library, which has never been catalogued. And as you know, I'm working on *A Curious Herbal*."

"Oh, dear," I said lightly. "The *Herbal*." Since I didn't know whether Jenna was clued in on the reason for my visit, I wouldn't have mentioned it if she hadn't brought it up. "It's gone missing, I understand. Has it turned up yet?"

"Not yet." Jenna gave an elaborate sigh. "Which means that my project is sort of up in the air right now. But I'm still working on the novel, which is part of my thesis project. And there's always the cataloging. It's a massive collection. I don't think we'll get finished with it — not in this lifetime." We had almost reached the end of the long hall. She stopped in front of the door on the left.

"Here we are," she said, putting her hand on the knob. "Dorothea wanted you to have a corner room. We hope you'll like it." With a dramatic gesture, she flung the door open.

The room was high-ceilinged, spacious, and elegant. The polished wooden floor was covered here and there with antique rugs, and gilt-framed landscapes hung on the walls and over the fireplace mantle. A lacy white canopy hung above the old-fashioned four-poster bed, which featured a colorful quilt and a generous scattering of cushions. A chintz-covered loveseat sat in front of the fireplace, and a desk and chair were arranged in front of one of the large casement windows that looked out into the surrounding trees. Some of the dark green hemlocks and pines were so close I could open a window, reach out, and touch them.

"Wow," I said, almost at a loss for words. "It's lovely. And those trees are spectacular."

"It's the nicest room," Jenna confided. "The rest are distinctly humdrum." She pointed. "There's a gas log in the fireplace, and you can adjust the radiator. It works most of the time. If you get chilly at night, there's an electric blanket on the bed, under the quilt. And here's the closet." She opened a door. There was a white terry robe hanging from a hook.

"The bathroom is the next door on your right — no entrance from here. The robe is yours to use if you didn't bring one. I've made some rosemary bath oil that's especially nice — there's a bottle for you on the shelf above the tub. My room is on the other side of the bathroom, and Dorothea's is several doors on the other side of mine. You won't be all alone up here. It can get a little . . . spooky at night." She slid me an inquiring, half-anxious look. "Have you heard about our ghost?"

"In general, but no details," I said. Was this the "unexpected" thing that the Universe mentioned to Ruby? "There really *is* a ghost, then? To go with the secret room, I suppose."

"Oh, you bet." Jenna sounded relieved, as if she'd been expecting me to scoff and was glad I hadn't. But her relief seemed mixed with a kind of bravado. "It's the ghost of Miss Carswell, the former owner. She killed herself in her suite on the third floor, above this end of the hallway." She jerked a thumb toward the ceiling. "Sunny — that's her name — isn't evil or anything like that, but she can be a bit of a nuisance, thumping around up there. She annoys Dorothea that way sometimes, although Dorothea prefers to pretend that she doesn't hear a thing. But Sunny will stop bothering you if she understands that you won't put up with her nonsense. Just tell her to go away. Be firm."

And then, as if she hadn't said anything at all extraordinary, she gave me a bright smile that did nothing to hide her obvious apprehension. Whether the Hemlock ghost was or wasn't real, Jenna accepted it. And feared it.

Full disclosure: I am by nature and education a skeptic where the supernatural is concerned. I do listen to Ruby, though, when she occasionally reminds me that there are things about the world that my "mega-logical mind" has to learn to accept. There is a certain skeleton in my closet, as well — or rather, in the closet at my shop: that is, the ghost of Annie, who lived there decades before I moved in. Still, although Ruby and Annie may have altered my skepticism, I'm not willing to extend belief to every ghost who happens along.

To give myself credit, I did not roll my eyes when Jenna said I should just tell Sunny to go away. Instead, I only said, "Thanks I will," and smiled.

Jenna turned toward the door. "Well, then, I'll let you get settled. When you're ready to come downstairs, go out in the hall, turn left, and take the back stairs — the servant stairs, in the old days when there *were* servants. It's a circular staircase, right out of one of Mary Roberts Rinehart's novels."

"Ah," I said. "*That* novel." *The Circular Staircase* was Rinehart's first bestseller. It featured a ghost. And a secret room. I smiled again, remembering my favorite line: *There's only trouble comes of hunting ghosts; they lead you into bottomless pits and things like that.* Things like that, yes.

"Be careful of the stair," Jenna added. "It's narrow and a bit dark, and the handrail is loose in places. When you get to the bottom, take the hallway on your right. You'll see our workroom, across from the library. The hallway on the left goes to the kitchen. You haven't eaten yet, I hope."

Barely waiting for me to shake my head, she rattled on. "Which would be good, because Rose has made shepherd's pie for supper, and there's enough to feed a small army. You can help us eat it." She hesitated, her hand on the knob, a serious expression on her face.

"Look, China. I know why you're here. I really hope you can find out what happened to Elizabeth's *Herbal*. Dorothea is pretty panicked over it." Her voice dropped. "Out of her mind with worry, actually. She's afraid that she's the prime suspect. Whether she is or not, I don't know. But it's a thing for her, a *big* thing. She won't be easy in her mind until that book is found."

I nodded, equally serious — but not ready to talk to her until I'd talked to Dorothea. "I'm no Miss Marple. But I'll do my best."

"That's all anybody can do." On her way out the door, over her shoulder, she said, "You'd better bring a sweater when you come down. There's a fire in the workroom, but it gets chilly when the sun goes down. And it goes down early, here in the mountains."

On the phone, Dorothea had told me that we wouldn't be fancy, so I had what I was wearing — a caramel-colored corduroy blazer over a red turtleneck sweater and black slacks — plus what was in my wheelie: jeans, tops and a couple of turtlenecks of various colors, a cardigan, and a denim vest. I unpacked, traded my blazer for a gray fleece cardigan, then visited the bathroom, which featured a huge claw-foot bathtub with gold-colored faucets, an old-fashioned marble sink the size of a washtub, and an ornate gold-rimmed mirror that looked as if it had been hanging on the wall since the house was first built.

I glanced into it quickly, wondering if I needed to comb my hair before I went downstairs. As I did, I saw the reflection of a furtive shadow hovering over my shoulder — not a shadow, exactly. An intense concentration of darkness, perhaps. I whirled, but nothing was there.

"Go away, Sunny," I said, remembering Jenna's advice. "I'm being firm."

And then I laughed out loud, to remind myself that I was play-acting. But I had seen *something,* and it was creepy.

The back stair truly was a circular staircase, narrow and with irregular pie-shaped metal treads that could be hazardous if you weren't paying attention. An iron handrail was anchored in the wall, but it felt flimsy and I hoped I wouldn't need to use it. The stair went up into the dimness, obviously to the third floor, and down, to the intersection of two hallways.

Following Jenna's directions, I turned to my right at the bottom and found the workroom near the end of the first-floor main hallway. It might once have been called a "morning room" and used by the lady of the house to receive early callers. Now, it served as an office for two people. There were two desks, each with its own computer (reminding me to ask about Wi-Fi). On the wall over one of the desks — Jenna's? — hung a framed five-by-six-foot map of eighteenth-century London, the Thames looping prominently through the middle. Against another wall, a worktable with a blue Selectric typewriter, a printer, a copy machine, a scanner, and a camera set up to photograph documents. Against a third wall, a ceiling-high bookcase jammed with books, and more books on a couple of rolling book trolleys like the ones you see in libraries. On the outer wall, French doors opened onto a stone-paved patio, bordered by blooming yellow daffodils. Beyond, a palisade of tall, dark trees. Hemlocks, I thought. Even farther beyond, the mountain fell away steeply.

There was no sign of Jenna, but Dorothea Harper was seated with a book in a wing-back chair beside the fireplace, where a small fire was burning brightly — more for the cheer it offered, I guessed, than for the warmth. I hadn't seen her for several years, and I was surprised. Now in her late forties or early fifties, she had grown thin and angular. Her dark hair was flecked with gray and there were worry lines between her eyes and across her forehead. She wore round granny glasses and a navy sweater, a pale gray silky shirt, and dark slacks.

She dropped her book when I came in, stood up, and held out her hand. "Oh, China," she said. "I am *so* glad you're here!"

And burst into tears.

CHAPTER THREE

Raven fell in love with a king's daughter, but the king refused to consider his suit. ("You are only a bird and undeserving of a princess. Go away.") Undaunted, Raven called on his supernatural skills to transform himself into a hemlock needle. The princess collected needles to brew a tea, swallowed Raven, and was changed into a lovely bird as black as night. Raven and his princess flew away and lived happily together for all time.

— Aleut legend, retold

"Well, gosh," I said gruffly, giving Dorothea a quick hug. "I didn't think my arrival would merit *that* kind of reception."

Dorothea swallowed, stepped awkwardly back, dug into her sweater pocket for a tissue, and blew her nose. "Of course it doesn't," she said in a low voice. "Sorry — I don't know why I did that. Just edgy, I guess. I've had a bad case of nerves lately. It is so kind of you to come, China. Thank you."

Well, there were certainly a few good reasons for nerves. I could understand why Dorothea had needed a change after her husband's death — an opportunity to put time and physical distance between her old life and whatever lay ahead. And Penny had said she'd had to sell her house, which suggested that she was dealing with major money issues.

But Dorothea had been a gregarious woman with many friends and interests. She had taught in the library program at the university, and she was active in the cultural life of her community. Hemlock House was hardly welcoming and not the easiest place in the world to get to. I wouldn't blame her for feeling terribly isolated. Add to that the theft of the *Curious Herbal,* the sheriff's investigation, and the inevitable fallout — plus the difficulties she apparently had with the board. No wonder she wanted somebody on her side, as Penny had put it.

The tears stopped quickly and she gestured to me to sit in the wing chair on the other side of the fire. On a small table was a decanter of sherry and several vintage stemmed glasses, silver-rimmed and etched with roses.

"Sherry?" she asked.

"That would be wonderful," I said, and she poured us each a glass before she sat down.

"You left Texas awfully early this morning," she said, retreating into small talk. "It must have been a tiring trip, and I'm sure you're hungry. Jenna's getting our supper together. It'll be ready in a few minutes."

"A little tiring, maybe, but interesting." I can do small talk, too, when I have to. "The drive from Asheville was spectacular. Mountains, trees, amazing views —" I smiled. "Quite a treat for somebody from Texas. I don't think I'd ever get used to the landscape."

"Yes, you would." She took off her granny glasses and put them on the table beside her. "We can get so used to happy days and beautiful things that we don't even see them — until they're gone. Then we miss them." She rubbed her eyes. "How long will you be staying with us?"

I told her what I'd already told Jenna. "I have a return flight on Thursday. It's spring break in Pecan Springs, and I'll have work to do at the shop when I get back home." I was ready to skip the rest of the small talk and dig into the subject of my visit. "So tell me about the Blackwell *Herbal* and how it came to be missing."

Wearily, she leaned back in her chair. "How much do you know?"

"Only that it disappeared from a locked case in the library. I poked around online, expecting to find an announcement of the theft and a few more details, but I came up empty." I sipped my sherry, adding in a neutral tone, "It might have been a good idea to warn other libraries that an active thief is out and about and could be a threat to their holdings."

"I'll show you the case and the room later," she said, setting her sherry glass on the table beside her spectacles. "And yes, I agree. It *would* be a good idea to publicize the theft, so booksellers and collectors could be on the lookout. The Antiquarian Book-sellers' Association has a page on their website where people — librarians, booksellers, collectors — can list stolen items. There's a new theft reported every few weeks." She sighed. "Rare book theft is big business these days."

"So I understand," I said. After Penny and I talked, I had done some basic online research. Recently, in Pittsburgh, a library archivist and a respected bookstore owner were charged with an eight-million-dollar theft of rare books, maps, and illustrations from the Carnegie Library. In Kentucky, four teenagers tied up a Transylvania University librarian and made off with two rare Audubon folios worth some five million dollars.

And on my ebook reader, I had a copy of *The Map Thief,* Michael Blanding's deeply researched book about E. Forbes Smiley III, an unlikely criminal important enough to have his own Wikipedia page. Smiley's weapon of choice: an X-Acto blade, which he used to remove maps from valuable library books and which he carelessly dropped on the floor of Yale's Beinecke Rare Book and Manuscript Library. The blade was spotted by an attentive librarian and Smiley was apprehended with a briefcase full of stolen documents. By the time the investigation was finished, Smiley had been charged with stealing ninety-seven rare maps worth over three million dollars.

Book theft not only grosses big money, it is an engrossing subject. But it's also a subject that many victims want to avoid, and for obvious reasons.

Dorothea pleated the fabric of her slacks between her fingers. "I'm afraid that the foundation's board of directors doesn't want the theft publicized. They're concerned that people — potential donors — will think we're negligent. The board hopes to raise funds to expand the library, and they don't want to scare people off." Another sigh. "I tried, China, I really did. A couple of members of the board sided with me, but the majority, no. They intend to keep the theft secret."

"Why don't you start at the beginning," I suggested. "Tell me about the foundation and the board and" — I waved my hand — "this place. How it all works. What you think of it. What your goals are here."

She settled back in her chair, sipped her sherry, and began.

Hemlock House and the surrounding estate of almost a thousand acres of native hemlock forest had been in the Carswell family for three generations. Reginald Carswell had made a sizeable chunk of money selling armaments during the First World War. When he died, the estate passed to his only son, Howard, who used the house as a hunting lodge and a setting for spectacular weeklong parties for politically well-connected friends. Howard died in the Reagan era, leaving everything to his only child, Sunny, who never married. She always hated the fact that the family money came from guns. So she turned Carswell Arms and Munitions over to a distant cousin, took up personal residence in the house, and spent her time gardening and indulging what had become her passion — or rather, Dorothea said, her obsession: collecting books about botany, horticulture, gardens, plants. Rare books, old books, new books, pamphlets, whatever. Not long before she died, she created the Hemlock House Foundation to manage her library and make it available to interested researchers — at least, that's what she hoped.

I broke into the narrative. "Jenna tells me that your resident ghost is named Sunny. Any relation to Miss Carswell?"

"Ah yes, Jenna," Dorothea said, with the first real smile I'd seen. "Isn't she a lovely girl? I'm so glad to have her here with me. She's good company, and she's done some quite remarkable research on the *Herbal* and on Elizabeth Blackwell's background. You'll have to ask her to tell you what she's discovered. Knowing your interest in herbs, I'm sure you'll find it fascinating."

Her smile faded. "But while Jenna is one of the most creative young people I know, she is also quite imaginative — and dramatic. There's no question that Sunny Carswell continues to inhabit this house, in more ways than one. When I'm being uncharitable — which is often, I'm afraid — I actually think of that woman as quite wicked, especially when it comes to her collection."

She frowned. "But whatever you may have heard, Miss Carswell is no ghost. That's Jenna's little dramatic fiction. The child is very curious about psychic matters, you see, and she wants her ghost to be real. She seems to enjoy being frightened — although I very much doubt that her fear is genuine." Her smile was almost maternal. "Jenna is a bit of a drama queen. She likes to play at being frightened."

Perhaps, although Jenna hadn't struck me as a child. I said, "Miss Carswell lived here until her death, I understand. How long ago was that?"

"Last summer. She killed herself, you know."

"No, I didn't know," I said, surprised.

"She used her father's gun — gruesome, really. She shot herself in the head." Dorothea's tone was studiedly neutral. "Howard Carswell killed himself with the same gun. *His* father, too."

"Her father's gun?" I shivered. "Oh, Dorothea, that's tragic!" It sounded like a kind of ritual suicide. Women don't usually shoot themselves in the head — the theory

is that they don't want to disfigure themselves.

"Yes, tragic. But she was nearly eighty, the
last of her family and suffering from breast
cancer. I'm told that she was a longtime
supporter of the right-to-die movement —
there's a local group, the Bethany Hemlock
Guild. From what members of the foundation's board have said, they weren't terribly
surprised when it happened. She had mentioned it more than once."

I filed that away for more thought. "What
can you tell me about her?"

"Sunny? She seems to have been a recluse
for most of her life, and very independent.
After college — Radcliffe — came here to
live and basically never left, except to visit
gardens and booksellers. She loved books
and plants above everything — and everyone — else. I never met her, but I understand that she could be hard on the staff
here, when she felt like it. Which was pretty
often."

"The staff?"

Dorothea put down her sherry glass. "Her
father had been in the habit of bringing
friends here for weeklong house parties, so
he kept a large staff — housekeeping,
grounds. That wasn't Miss Carswell's thing.
After his death, she lived in this wing, very

privately, and closed off the rest of the place. So she only needed a cook-housekeeper, a maid or two, and toward the end, a nurse. Rose and Joe Mullins, her cook and general handyman, are still with us. Rose cooks and does the laundry. Joe manages the garden, with help from a young man who lives down the road. When there's a public garden event, we bring in extra help. They're gone now, of course."

"Nobody to help with her book collection?"

"No. At least, not until the last year or so. She was quite private about her books. Secretive, you might even say. I don't think she wanted anybody to know what she had."

I studied her. "Doesn't that seem a little, well, odd?"

"Book collectors, especially the serious ones, are *all* a little odd. There's a reason it's called bibliomania."

I chuckled, and a smile ghosted across Dorothea's mouth.

"But as far as being secretive," she went on, "that may be justified. Someone who is collecting a particular author or subject is competing with other collectors for a finite resource. They might not want the world to know what they are looking for. And Miss Carswell liked to dicker. If she wanted a certain book, she *wanted* it — but she also wanted to get it at a good price. From what I've been told, she played her cards close to her vest. She never published a catalogue. In fact, so far as I can discover, she never even made a comprehensive list of her holdings."

"Which must be a problem," I said. "For you, I mean."

Dorothea nodded emphatically. "A *massive* problem. There are thousands of books in her library. Finding anything is like looking for a needle in a haystack — and sometimes you're looking for a needle you don't even know is there."

"Thousands? Really?" I was skeptical.

"Oh, yes. It's as if she got a visceral pleasure from surrounding herself with stacks of books. Maybe they were a kind of protection for her, a wall between herself and the world. Or between herself and others." She shrugged. "Books mean different things to different people. For Sunny, they were her refuge. For us, there are all kinds of problems, now that we're trying to organize the holdings. Lots of things are junk, pure and simple. Others . . . well, there are some serious jewels. Like *A Curious Herbal.*"

"Miss Carswell didn't catalogue the books

as she acquired them? Or put them on a list, or in a computer file?"

Dorothea laughed shortly. "That would have been too easy. She saved paid invoices and bills of sale, most of which have book titles and the amounts she paid. But she didn't file them in one place. They keep turning up, one or two at a time, here and there."

In the fireplace, a burning log broke in two with a fountain of sparks. Dorothea got out of her chair, picked up a poker, and pushed the log back into the flames, watching it for a moment.

"For a while, she worked with a bookseller down in Bethany. Jed Conway. But at some point, they had a disagreement and Jed — whom I've met only a couple of times — was out of the picture. He offered to help Jenna and me with the inventory, but since I don't know why Miss Carswell cut him off, I wasn't sure it was a good idea." She gave the log another nudge. "And sometime before she died, she connected up with a local woman named Margaret Anderson. Margaret writes a regionally syndicated book column and a quite popular book blog. Reviews and book news and the like. She's a little . . . unusual, perhaps. But she has always been eager to help out."

There was something in Dorothea's voice suggesting that she didn't altogether appreciate Margaret Anderson's eagerness to help. But I didn't want to interrupt the flow of her story with another question. She put the poker back in its stand and resumed her chair.

"The two of them hit it off and Margaret managed to persuade Sunny to begin organizing her collection. Unfortunately, they were just getting started on the project when Sunny was diagnosed with stage four breast cancer. She died six or eight months later. Margaret stayed on for a while after her death, but she wasn't trained in library management or in working with rare books. More importantly, she didn't seem to know or care much about book conservation, which — given the age and condition of most of the collection — pretty much disqualified her. The foundation's board of directors realized that they needed to know what they had here. They opened a search for a professional who could catalogue the library and appraise its value, as well as determine which items need special conservation and which ought to be disposed of. This information would give the board a better understanding of the collection and they could plan for its future. Which they presumably want to do," she added, in a drier tone. It sounded as if she thought the board wasn't exactly eager to undertake the task of planning for the collection's future.

I finished my sherry and put the glass on the table. "They rejected Margaret Anderson?" It might not take much to turn a disgruntled employee into a thief.

"She didn't apply. It was an amicable parting, I understand. She was in over her head. She was quite ready to leave."

I'd take that at face value — for now. "And that's when you got involved?"

"Yes. My husband was dead. I needed to do something other than teaching, somewhere other than Madison. I had already requested a leave of absence from the university. Through a friend, I heard about this position. I met with the foundation's board a couple of times and came to Hemlock House for a visit."

"And you liked it?" She must have, if she'd uprooted herself and moved here.

With a smile, she glanced around the room. "In some ways, you know, it's ideal. I was intrigued with the idea of working with an uncatalogued collection. For all its frustrations, it's rather like a treasure hunt. You never know what gems might be hidden on those dusty shelves. Every now and then we come up with something extraordinary. And I've always loved mountains, and gardens. So I came. Jenna came shortly after." She lifted her shoulders and let them fall. "I didn't count on the isolation, I'm afraid. I'm used to lots of people coming and going, colleagues dropping in to talk about their ideas, young people laughing and talking, stirring things up. There's not much of that here. We have a satellite dish, so we have television, cell service, and internet access. There's Wi-Fi in your room — no password, since we don't have any near neighbors. And of course, you're welcome to take books out of the library, although we'd appreciate it if you asked first and returned the items to my desk. We're trying to keep the shelves organized."

Spoken like a librarian. "Glad to hear about the Wi-Fi and cell service," I said, thinking that I needed to let McQuaid know that I'd arrived. "Who else is here, besides you and Jenna?"

"Now? Only Rose and Joe. Rose shops and cooks and keeps house for us, and Joe is our general handyman. After Sunny died, they moved out to the old gatehouse." She paused. "As far as visitors are concerned, there's Claudia Roth. She claims to have had some sort of tangential relationship to the Carswells, but I don't know if that's true. She lives up the mountain about half a mile and drops in every now and then, when she's not rescuing birds. One of the board members comes in a couple of times a week to help with —"

I stopped her. "Rescuing *birds*? As in wild birds? Hawks and eagles and such?"

"No, parrots. Apparently some people think they would love to have a parrot but the reality is . . . well, it's something they didn't quite bargain for."

"Tell me about it," I said wryly. "We have a parrot — or more accurately, he has us. Spock is quite an amazing fellow. It's a challenge to keep ahead of him."

It's also a lost cause. Recently, I heard the microwave beep and went over to take the food out — and then remembered that I hadn't put anything in. It was Spock, teasing me. He loves to imitate sounds that make us *do* something. It's a game for him, or a not-so-subtle form of the manipulation that makes parrots so human-like.

Dorothea nodded. "You'd probably get along with Claudia, then. She strikes most people as a little odd — bizarre, even. But she and Sunny appear to have been friends of a sort. And she's dedicated to those birds. Jenna and I don't see much of her, but the two of you would probably have a lot to talk about."

A little odd — bizarre, even? Well, given the exceedingly strange situation at Hemlock House, that hardly seemed out of line.

"I'd like to meet her," I said. "But I interrupted you when you were telling me about a board member. Somebody who comes here to work with the books?"

"Carole Humphreys. She's here a couple of mornings a week, lending a hand with the cataloguing. And of course there's Jenna."

I nodded. "She mentioned that she's writing about the *Herbal* for her master's degree. You're her supervisor?"

"Yes. She was my student, when I was still teaching. She's getting course credit for the work she's doing here — cataloguing and compiling finding aids. As you might guess, her work on the *Herbal* is on hold." She gave me a direct look. "Until we get it back."

I avoided a direct reply. "The cataloguing alone sounds like a huge job."

"It is. Jenna and I are doing our best, and we get a few hours' help a week from Carole. But there's just so *much*." She stood, went to one of the desks, and logged onto the computer. "Here. We'll take the tour later, but let me show you what we're up against first."

I went to stand beside her. On the screen was a photograph of a room about the size of my large bedroom upstairs, with windows along one wall. The other three walls were lined with floor-to-ceiling shelves, and more shelves filled the center of the room, with only narrow aisles between. The shelves were filled with books, some of them double-shelved. There were stacks of books in the aisles.

"This is one room," Dorothea said. "There are two others — plus dozens of boxes that have never been opened. Miss Carswell was a packrat. Sometimes she bought single titles, carefully. Other times she seems to have bought a box without knowing what was in it. Either way, when the books got here, she simply put them on the shelves, in no particular order. And then bought more."

I frowned. "It's pretty damp in these mountains, isn't it? I wouldn't think that high humidity is the best environment for books — especially old books."

Dorothea logged off the computer. "Oh, you're so right! A few weeks after I arrived, I brought in a couple of air conditioning people and asked them what it would cost to climate-control the book storage areas. It's not rocket science," she added. "It's a simple matter of buying and installing the right-sized units and doing whatever rewiring is necessary. The board has had my proposal for several months. They're still trying to make up their minds about it."

I could hear the frustration in her voice. The job was obviously very difficult and it was clear that Dorothea and the foundation's board weren't exactly made for each other.

She turned away from the computer. "Anyway, you can see the problem. We don't know what was here, so we don't know whether anything else besides the *Herbal* was taken. And even if the Hemlock County sheriff arrests somebody and his garage turns out to be full of antique botany books and nature prints, it wouldn't be easy to identify them as belonging to Hemlock House. Sunny didn't —"

The door opened and Jenna put her head in "Supper's on the table," she said cheerfully. "I thought we would eat in the kitchen, where it's warmer."

"Good idea," Dorothea said, with satisfaction. "The dining room is elegant, but it's as big as Mammoth Cave and about as cold. I'd rather be homey and comfortable than elegant and shivering." She made a face.

"There's certainly enough of that in *this* house."

"There's certainly enough of that in this house."

CHAPTER FOUR

American Indians used the cambium [the hemlock's inner bark] as the base for breads and soups or mixed it with dried fruit and animal fat for pemmican. Natives and white settlers also made tea from hemlock leaves, which have a high vitamin C content.

Eastern Hemlock, *Tsuga canadensis*
United States Department of Agriculture
Natural Resources Conservation Service

The kitchen still had the original stone floor and painted wooden cupboards, along with a walk-in pantry, an old-fashioned porcelain sink, and overhead racks for pots and pans and utensils. It had been built to accommodate a team of cooks plus the battalion of servants it took to produce and serve elaborate meals for the Carswells, a houseful of guests, and a sizeable household staff. But it had recently been modernized with a gas range, a microwave, a dishwasher, and a large refrigerator-freezer. One corner was furnished with a small round table and chairs for dining.

Jenna had laid three places at the table, which was centered with a pottery bowl of fragrant violets. Our meal began with a salad: fresh greens with avocado, tomato, cucumber, and feta cheese. Then the shepherd's pie, hot, with a flaky crust and a rich and savory beef filling. And a carafe of red wine. The pie was delicious, and after a day of travel-snacking, I was seriously hungry.

While the three of us ate, Jenna was mostly silent and Dorothea and I went back to our conversation. "Tell me about the foundation's board," I said. "How many members? Are they local?"

"Eight," Dorothea said. "Seven women, one man. Three of them live in Bethany, but the rest are in Asheville and Raleigh. They have lifetime appointments, and they can name their own successors." She wrinkled her nose. "Kind of an incestuous arrangement, if you ask me. But that's how it was organized in the bylaws of the trust Miss Carswell set up."

"Is it an active board?"

She chuckled wryly. "Well, they actively know what they *don't* want to do. They're not very involved with the collection, except for Carole Humphreys, who volunteers a few hours a week with the cataloguing. The full board is supposed to meet four times a year. I meet with them and report on our progress with the collection."

I glanced around the cavernous kitchen. The house was well over a century old, and huge. It must cost quite a bit to maintain.

"Is there enough income from the trust to keep this place going?" I asked.

Dorothea nodded. "Enough to pay current staff salaries, utilities, taxes, repairs, and maintenance. Better yet, there's enough to install the climate-control system and even to hire an additional one or two full-time people to help with the cataloguing — *if* the board could agree. So far, that hasn't happened. Worse, they can't agree on a long-term plan for the collection, or for the house and grounds, which is frustrating." With a sigh, she pushed her plate back. "There are factions. It's complicated."

I'll bet. Trusts and boards are always complicated and sometimes generate all kinds of bad feeling. I didn't envy Dorothea, having to deal with people who put board politics ahead of the job they were supposed to do. But that was an intractable problem and likely not relevant to the theft.

Changing the subject, I said, "How about that list I suggested? The names of people who have visited the library since you came."

"I mostly worked on it," Jenna said. "It wasn't hard, actually, because we haven't had that many guests. Just a handful of academic researchers — three from North Carolina, one from Georgia. They were already on the calendar."

"Opening to researchers was the board's idea," Dorothea said. "Eventually, it's what we want to do, but we're not ready for that yet. I've put a stop to visits until the collection has been catalogued."

"The garden was open to the public one weekend," Jenna added.

Dorothea nodded. "We don't have the names of all the people who came to that event because they didn't all sign the guest book. But that was in October, months before the *Herbal* disappeared. And none of those visitors came into the house." She frowned. "At least, they weren't supposed to. But anyway, yes — Jenna has the list for you. Names and contact information, where we have it."

"I also noted who has keys to this place," Jenna added. "There aren't many, but I thought you might want to know who they are."

"Thank you," I said. It probably wouldn't be of much use, though. Keys can be copied. And people don't always remember where they've put their key or when they saw it last. "When did the theft occur?"

"Hang on a sec." Jenna pushed her chair back. "If everybody is ready for dessert, I'll take your plates and bring coffee"

"And I'll get the dessert," Dorothea said.

We ended our supper with coffee and warm apple crisp topped with vanilla ice cream. I forked up a bite, savoring the cinnamon-and-nutmeg flavored apples. "Back to the theft," I said. "When did it happen?"

"Two weeks ago today," Dorothea said, stirring her coffee. "Jenna is the one who discovered it. She wanted to check something in the text, but when she went to the display case where it was kept, the *Herbal* was gone."

Jenna sighed. "I can still work on my project, but I have to rely on the online copies, like the one from the Raven Library at the Missouri Botanical Garden. Miss Carswell's copy is different. And special."

"Special how?"

Jenna hesitated. With a little smile, Dorothea said, "Go ahead, Jenna. It's *your* project. You know far more about it than I do."

Jenna leaned eagerly forward. "Elizabeth's book was first published as a serial."

I frowned. "You mean, installments?"

"Yes. Four pages every week, five hundred pages altogether, over a period of almost two-and-a-half years. After all the weekly installments were out, she published a two-volume set. The usual binding appears to have been morocco or calf leather, sometimes with gilt edges. Depending on what somebody wanted to pay."

"I saw quite a few copies online," I said. "Different editions, printed at different times. And even several modern reprints. In paperback."

Since I learned about the *Herbal,* I had done research on it and wanted to do more. Online, I had discovered plenty of photographs of the book, in various bindings. Most fascinating were a couple of sites where you can virtually turn the pages and study the plants and read Elizabeth's carefully hand-engraved descriptions. The one I like best is owned by the British Museum. It opens to a meticulously detailed, carefully hand-colored drawing of a dandelion in full bloom.*

Jenna picked up her cup and took a sip of coffee. "The Hemlock *Herbal* is special because all five hundred of the plates are bound in a single volume, with an ornately carved calfskin cover, eight silver corners, and a pair of ornate silver clasps. The book has Elizabeth Blackwell's signature and an engraved armorial bookplate signed and dated by Sir Hans Sloane, her sponsor and supporter. The illustrations are all carefully hand-colored, probably by Elizabeth herself. It's absolutely stunning."

"You probably know that the London apothecaries were trained in the Chelsea Physic Garden," Dorothea said. "The plants were grown there as medicinals and harvested for the apothecaries' laboratory, where herbal medicines were made. Elizabeth drew the plants from life — which means that she must have spent hours in the garden, sketching them, rather than copying the pictures from another book."

"Which is quite different from the way the earlier English herbals were produced,"

* You can see the British Museum's copy at http:// www.bl.uk/turning-the-pages/. It originally came from the library of King George III, who was an advocate of the study of botany.

Jenna added. "The herbals compiled by Gerard and Culpeper and Parkinson all contain stylized woodcuts that couldn't have been much help if you wanted to actually identify a plant. Elizabeth's copperplate engravings are highly detailed and *accurate.* They can actually help you find the plant you're looking for."

"That's important," Dorothea said with a little smile. "Especially if you're trying to tell the difference between look-alikes. Between Queen Anne's lace, which was used for birth control, and poison hemlock, for instance. Elizabeth's drawings were almost as good as photographs. The earlier woodcuts weren't much help when it came to identifying the plants."

Jenna nodded. "Plus, the earlier books were full of irrelevant and questionable information, including lots of superstition and old wives' tales. Elizabeth was succinct. She wrote down what doctors and apothecaries were actually prescribing the plants *for,* at that time. We wouldn't call her book 'scientific,' by the standards of our day. But that's what she's aiming for. That's why she calls it a *'curious'* herbal."

"I was wondering about that word," I said.

"Everybody does," Dorothea said. "Back then, it meant 'careful' or 'meticulously accurate,' something like that."

Jenna nodded. "*A Curious Herbal* was as good as it got in the seventeen-thirties. Gold standard. Amazing that Elizabeth could pull it off in the midst of all the politics and intrigues around the garden."

"And that husband of hers." Dorothea shook her head. "He certainly didn't help matters."

"I'd like to hear about him," I said, "but right now, I need to know more about the theft. When was the last time you saw the book?"

"Two weeks ago last Friday," Jenna said. "There's not enough light in the library, so I had brought the book to my desk in the workroom. Carole Humphreys, one of the board volunteers, came in. She's been interested in the *Herbal,* so we looked at it together for a little while. Then it went back where it belonged."

"I was returning a trolley full of books to the library," Dorothea said. "I took the *Herbal* as well, and put it in the display case."

"And locked it?"

"Of course. And put the key back where it's kept."

"Which is?"

"On a hook under a shelf beside the door.

Then Carole left and Jenna and I drove to Asheville to see a play. We stayed over to go shopping on Saturday and went to a movie on Saturday night. We drove home on Sunday."

"It was Monday before I saw that the *Herbal* was gone," Jenna said.

"That's when you phoned the police?"

Dorothea frowned. "I'm afraid it didn't quite work that way. I called Mrs. Cousins, the board chair, down in Asheville, and told her what had happened. She called the other members and they talked it over. The next day, she telephoned to tell me that the board thought I should report the theft to Sheriff Rogers, but they didn't want me to make a public announcement. Mrs. Cousins was quite specific about that. No public announcement."

"But that plays right into the thief's hands," I protested.

"I know. That's what I told her." Dorothea picked up her coffee cup, took a drink, and set it down again. "But she's the boss. I had to ask the sheriff to keep it quiet, and he agreed." She sighed. "Because he had to, I believe. Mrs. Cousins had a conversation with him."

I understood Dorothea's frustration. The board was obviously more concerned about the foundation's reputation than about getting to the bottom of the theft — or getting the *Herbal* back.

But I knew there was more. "Penny told me that you've found pages missing from other rare books of botanical prints," I said. "How many?"

"We don't know yet," Dorothea said. "We've surveyed only a few of the most important books. We keep looking, but we don't have the staff for a full inventory. We can't search every book. And even if we find a page or two missing, we have no idea when that happened. Maybe the book wasn't complete when Miss Carswell acquired it."

"And since we don't have a reliable inventory," Jenna added, "we don't really know what *other* books might have been taken."

"We gave the sheriff a list of what we think might be missing," Dorothea said. "But we told him it was a work in progress. We haven't found everything — we've barely got a start."

Jenna gave me a crooked smile. "And we haven't found the secret room yet, either. Who knows what treasures it holds?"

"You were serious about that secret room?" I asked quizzically.

"Every old house of this size has at least

one secret room," Dorothea said in a dismissive tone.

"But Dorothea," Jenna began.

"I wouldn't put too much faith in that old story," Dorothea said firmly.

"Who was here at the house when the *Herbal* was stolen?" I asked.

"Nobody," Jenna said, "Joe and Rose spent the weekend with Rose's parents — it was her mother's birthday."

"And Jenna and I were in Asheville, which we'd been planning for several weeks," Dorothea said. "We locked up when we left, and there was no evidence that anybody had tried to break in."

"Alarms?" I asked. "Video surveillance?" Surely, with a valuable collection . . .

"Cameras and an alarm system are on the list of things I proposed to the board right after I came," Dorothea said. "They haven't been approved yet."

I was feeling stymied. "How about the sheriff? Did he make a thorough investigation?"

"I don't know how thorough it was," Dorothea replied. "He questioned Rose and Joe, but I don't think he saw their nephew. Jenna, of course. Carole and Margaret, probably." She took a breath. "And me."

Jenna looked at Dorothea. "Poor Dorothea," she said sympathetically.

Dorothea winced. "He believes I did it. Since I didn't, he can't have any proof. But that doesn't keep him from *thinking* it was me. Or wishing it was me. Or something."

Earlier, I had noticed the worry lines between her eyes, and I wondered if they were the product of this threatening situation. If so, I certainly couldn't blame her. "Did he say why he suspected you?"

"No. Personally, I think it's because I'm handy." Her lips tightened. "And I'm afraid that Mrs. Cousins agrees with him. The two of us — Mrs. Cousins and I — didn't get off on the right foot. She thought my proposal for installing the alarm system was 'unnecessary.' The theft has strained things between us. I suspect that she thinks I took the *Herbal* just to prove a point."

"Prove what point?"

"To demonstrate that the cameras and the alarm are really necessary. Frankly, I wouldn't be surprised if I were fired." She nodded toward Jenna. "If that happens, it will mean a big interruption in Jenna's work."

"I wouldn't stay without you, anyway," Jenna said loyally. "But they'd be silly to fire you, Dorothea. You're just beginning to bring some organization to this collection.

And there's simply nobody else who could make sense of it."

"I'm afraid Mrs. Cousins doesn't agree." Dorothea gave me an apprehensive glance. "I don't suppose I need to tell you how unsettling this is, China. If I were charged with theft, that would be the end of my career."

"They can't charge you without evidence," I said firmly, and not entirely truthfully. I've seen plenty of charges based on easily challenged evidence.

"But even the suspicion of theft . . ." She bit her lip. "If the sheriff doesn't manage to find out who did this, the suspicion will linger."

"We won't let that happen." It's a lawyer's standard reassurance of an apprehensive client, and while I put the usual confidence behind it, I wasn't so sure. There were too many unknowns, too many players. There was very little security, as far as I could see. Anybody who knew that the *Herbal* was here could have walked in and taken it.

I pushed my dessert dish away and leaned my forearms on the table. "What are we talking about here? How much is the *Herbal* worth?"

"An auction estimate would probably come in at a hundred thousand dollars,"

Dorothea said. "Christie's and Sotheby's both have offered a couple of two-volume sets in the last two years. One went for forty thousand, the other for sixty. Of course, with interested bidders, this one would go for more, since it's Elizabeth's presentation copy to Sir Hans Sloane."

"Or the thief could take out the colored plates and sell them separately," Jenna reminded her. To me, she added, "I've seen those colored plates online for as high as three or four hundred dollars apiece, which means that there's probably a hundred and eighty or two hundred thousand dollars in the plates. It would be safer for the thief to sell it that way," she added glumly. "Once the plates have been removed, there's no way to tell which edition they came from."

I nodded, remembering that Michael Blanding's map thief had worked that way: slicing maps out of rare books and selling the single pages for thousands of dollars to eager collectors who never bothered to ask for provenance — where the plates had come from. And I, too, had seen colored plates from Elizabeth's *Herbal,* matted and framed, for sale on the internet. For the thief, this could be a low-risk, high-payoff enterprise.

"Where did Miss Carswell acquire the

Herbal?" I asked. "How long had she had it?"

Dorothea and Jenna exchanged looks. At last, Dorothea shook her head. "We don't know. She traveled to England several years ago, and we've found receipts for some things she bought at that time. But not the *Herbal.* We've asked Jed Conway, but he says he doesn't know." She lifted her shoulders and let them fall. "That's still a mystery to be solved."

"I read a couple of online biographies about Elizabeth," I said. "It appears that she's pretty much a mystery, as well. Which is strange, because her *Herbal* seems quite exceptional. I read that this is the only English herbal, in *any* era, that was written, illustrated, engraved on copper plate, *and* colored — by a woman."

"That's true," Dorothea said. "The male herbalists get all the attention. Nicholas Culpeper, for instance. And John Gerard. Everybody knows about them. Nobody remembers Elizabeth Blackwell."

Jenna spoke with a barely restrained passion. "And given the kind of pressure she was under — well, it's a wonder the work got done at all! Her husband had gotten himself thrown into debtor's prison. His own stupid fault, really. He was an arrogant

107

fellow who thought he could do exactly as he pleased and get away with it." She shook her head. "If Elizabeth hadn't spent three whole years of her life producing the *Herbal* and selling it, he might have spent the rest of his life locked up in Newgate. It was her persistence that bought his freedom. Plus her smarts. Not to mention her stubbornness. That woman just didn't know when she was beaten."

I had to smile at Jenna's intensity. This was obviously something she cared about. I said, "I read a nineteenth-century biographer who described the *Herbal* as Elizabeth's 'most touching and admirable monument of female devotion' to her husband. But I understand that Alexander only lived another ten years or so after she bailed him out. And wasn't there something . . . unusual about the way he died?"

Jenna and Dorothea exchanged eyebrow-arched glances. "You might say so, yes," Jenna said.

"He was executed." Dorothea said.

"They lopped off his head," Jenna said.

"In Sweden," Dorothea added.

"For treason," Jenna said, with a disgusted look. "If you ask me, he deserved it. That man was always trying to be somebody he wasn't. There aren't many details, but it seems that he was passing himself off as a physician to the Swedish king when he managed to get embroiled in some sort of palace conspiracy. And he plagiarized somebody's book, as well." She made a face. "That's Alexander for you. Always wanting to be a big-time player — and never quite understanding the game he was in. This time, though, Elizabeth wasn't there to bail him out. She had washed her hands of him. At least, that's what *I* think."

"Jenna doesn't believe that Elizabeth Blackwell was motivated by 'female devotion,'" Dorothea said matter-of-factly. "Her novel tells a different story."

"I've only read the first section," I said, "but I got that idea." I turned to Jenna. "The novel is part of your master's thesis?"

Jenna nodded. "Yes, along with an analysis of the printing history of the *Herbal*. I considered writing the usual biography. But I've dug up all this amazing stuff about eighteenth-century London and the apothecaries — the pharmacists of their day — and the way books were printed and sold. I think I've pieced together how Elizabeth got involved with the Physic Garden and how she produced the book, in spite of all the obstacles. I've begun to feel close to her, as if I *know* her. Know her personally, I mean. As a friend. So I didn't want to write just a biography. I wanted to get closer."

Dorothea put out a hand. "Jenna," she said gently, "you're on your soapbox again. China doesn't want to hear —"

"Yes, I do," I said.

But Jenna barely heard us. "And she's an incredible woman, really. Her husband had squandered her dowry and gone to prison and there she was, homeless, with two young children." She gave me an indignant glance. "Really, China. Don't you think she must have been just totally *disgusted* with Alexander? If he were my husband, I would have been ready to kiss him off." She made an impatient noise. "Female devotion, my foot."

"So what you wrote — that Elizabeth and her children had nowhere to go — that was really true? In real life, I mean."

"Oh, you bet. He had managed to lose their printing business *and* their house on the Strand. He was in prison and she had no money. Her parents had cut her off, his mother and stuck-up brother wouldn't have anything to do with them, and Alexander had squandered her dowry on his printing business, even though he didn't meet the seven-year-apprenticeship requirement. That man was always pretending to be

110

somebody he wasn't. Of course, Elizabeth —"

"Jenna," Dorothea said more loudly. But Jenna was going on.

"Of course, Elizabeth and the children could have moved into Newgate with him. Lots of women did. Or she could have sponged off friends. She and Alexander were both Scottish, and there was a big group of expat Scots in London. They looked out for one another. That's why Dr. Stuart was willing to give her a job and a place to live. But Elizabeth didn't go that route. Instead, she rolled up her sleeves and —"

She stopped herself, glancing from Dorothea to me. "Oops, sorry," she muttered. "I let myself get carried away sometimes. I can be a bore, chattering on about a story that mostly interests just me."

"That's okay," I said, admiring her passion. And her energy. "If you're writing a novel, I suppose you have to get carried away — or get carried *into* it — or you can't write."

"And you're never a bore," Dorothea said comfortingly. "I've already learned so much about the *Herbal* from you. And about Elizabeth, too."

A rueful smile hovered on Jenna's lips.

"Of course, she lived almost three hundred years ago, and a lot of her life really *is* a mystery. It's like a tangled skein that begs to be unraveled — the mystery of who she was."

"I loved the beginning and I'm ready for more," I said. "When can you send another chapter or two?" I wasn't just handing out an empty compliment. In her enthusiasm, Jenna had made me curious about Elizabeth Blackwell and that husband of hers. I doubted that knowing more about the author of the stolen book would take me further toward the thief, but you never know.

"How about tonight?" Jenna asked with a little laugh. "That is, as long as you don't mind reading a draft. This is very much a work in progress."

"That would be great," I said. "I have my tablet with me. You could email the sections. Or put them on a thumb drive."

Dorothea got up and began to clear the table. "Why don't you do that while I put the dishes in the dishwasher, Jenna. And don't forget the list you were making for China. The names of visitors to Hemlock House."

"I'll help with the cleanup," I volunteered. The kitchen chores were almost finished by the time Jenna got back to the kitchen. "I've emailed parts two and three of the novel," she said. "And here's the list."

"Wonderful," I said, taking the printout. "Bedtime reading."

I had gotten up early that morning in Texas, so I said thank you and goodnight and excused myself. I took the back stairs — the circular staircase — to the second floor, wishing for better lighting and being careful where I put my feet. As I came to the landing, I was tempted to go up and have a look around on the third floor, where Sunny Carswell was said to have died. And where her ghost presumably hung out, if indeed there *was* one. But I had no good reason to go where I hadn't been invited, and I was looking forward to my reading.

I was just opening the door to my room when Jenna caught up with me.

"I hope you noticed how worried Dorothea is about this thing," she said in a low voice. "This theft is really hard on her — the loss itself, of course, but also Mrs. Cousins' disapproval and the sheriff's suspicion. She doesn't believe that the police will find the *Herbal,* and I'm afraid I agree." She put her hand on my arm. Her eyes were intent, her voice taut, pleading. "Dorothea didn't steal it, China. I didn't, either. You *do* believe us, don't you?"

I hesitated. I did, didn't I? I had thought that Dorothea couldn't possibly be guilty of stealing a valuable book. But why did Jenna think she had to urge me to believe in her innocence? And how well did I know the woman, really? Money was obviously an issue for her. Was it possible that —

"You're our best hope, China," Jenna said urgently. "You've got to find it. Please don't fail us. *Please.*"

"I'll do what I can" was all I could come up with, and it didn't sound any too convincing, even to me. But I couldn't promise to find something that might be on its way to the shelves of some collector's private library — or a worktable, where it could be hacked to pieces by an enterprising thief with an X-Acto knife.

I liked Jenna, but I was glad to step into my room and close the door behind me. And I wasn't too tired to enjoy my lovely room. I opened the casement window and was rewarded by the inquiring *who-who-whooo?* of an owl in one of the nearby hemlocks and a whiff of April air, sweet with the scent of rich forest soil and new green leaves. I changed into McQuaid's old black T-shirt, two sizes too large and the most comfortable sleeping shirt I've ever worn.

Then I stacked up the pillows, crawled into bed with my tablet, and logged into the eighteenth-century world of Elizabeth Blackwell's London.

What Jenna had emailed me began where her first section had left off, with Elizabeth on her way up Holbourn Hill and into some sort of new adventure. I plunged in eagerly. Jenna's story might be fiction, but it seemed entirely plausible to me. It was fascinating.

And if the ghost of Sunny Carswell dropped in to read over my shoulder, I was too deeply engrossed to notice.

■ ■ ■ ■

PART TWO:
THE CURIOUS TALE
OF ELIZABETH
BLACKWELL

■ ■ ■ ■

January 4, 1735
Holbourn Street and Castle Lane
London

Street art provided something of a living
for chalk artists, who perfected a method
of portraiture not unlike caricature that
amused and entertained many. Some of
these street artists went on to employment
in the studios of artists who copied old
masters, for which there was a popular

market. Or they painted inexpensive land-scapes and portraits for the burgeoning merchant class.

Susan Blake,
London Artistry, 1700–1750

As Elizabeth began to climb steep Holbourn Hill, the wind blew away the clouds and a pale wintry sun brightened the grimy old buildings — most of them very old, because they had escaped the Great Fire of 1666, which destroyed almost everything from the Tower on the east to Whitehall on the west and from the Thames to the city wall.

Started by a careless baker on Pudding Lane (or so it was said), the fire had disastrously incinerated over thirteen thousand homes, eighty-seven churches, and St. Paul's Cathedral. The medieval city of narrow cobbled alleys winding among rat-infested wood-and-thatch tenements was destroyed. In the rebuilding, wooden structures and overhanging gables were forbidden and the use of brick or stone was mandatory. London was cleaner now, and with definite improvements in fire safety. Many streets had been widened and paved and open sewers abolished, creating more room for horses and wagons and people on foot.

But the fire had run into stiff winds and was halted before it could reach Holbourn. Here, the timbered buildings along the street were more medieval than modern, leaning forward over the cobbles so that their upper stories nearly touched. The smell of mold and damp timber, rotting rubbish, animal dung, and human sewage hung in the air, and women were well-advised to mind the hems of their skirts. Chick Lane, the next street to the north, was populated (as Elizabeth had recently read in the *Penny London Post*) by miscreants, street robbers, thieves, pickpockets, housebreakers, shoplifters, prostitutes, streetwalkers, and other monsters of wickedness, drinking and carousing in a most intemperate manner. It was altogether a dismal neighborhood.

The gloom of the scene so accentuated Elizabeth's despair about Alexander's plight that it took a drayman's sharp cry to rouse her. She had to step swiftly aside and out of the way of a draft horse laboring to pull a brewer's wagon up the steep hill to the summit. There, back in the day of King Henry VIII, was located the city's toll gate, Holbourn Bar. The Bar marked the northwestern boundary of the city, where a toll of a penny or tuppence was demanded of non-freemen driving carts or coaches into the city.

But the toll gate was gone. Now, across the way from the medieval stone towers of St. Andrew's, Elizabeth saw a cluster of people, jostling one another to get a better view of something on the pavement. Curious, she worked her way to the front of the crowd.

In front of her, on the pavement stones, was a gallery of drawings executed in colored chalks, while on hands and knees to one side of his work was the artist himself, a shabby young man with his brown hair tied neatly at the collar of his green jacket. As Elizabeth watched, he blew chalk-dust from the stern likeness of a man, softened the blush on a woman's pretty cheek with a scrap of leather, and with a stub of charcoal added an exuberant curlicue to the caption below his work: "Portrait Commissions humbly sought. Inquire of the Artist."

Beside the gallery was placed, hopefully, an upside-down hat. In it were several halfpence. As she watched, a man in a gray coat with a black velvet collar, a gold-headed walking stick tucked into the crook of his elbow, pitched a coin into the hat, then proffered a card to the artist. "Stop in at my office and ask for me," he said. "I should like a portrait."

The moment before, Elizabeth's attention had been fixed on her desperate need of money. Now, startled, she eyed the man with the walking stick and the young artist at work on his pavement.

Portrait commissions, she thought, *I could paint portraits, couldn't I? I could* sell *portraits.* She measured the boy's work with a critical eye, noting that some of the lines were not firm and that the likenesses rather tended to caricature. *I could make portraits at least as well as this fellow,* she thought. *No, I could do better. I know I could.*

And as she left the artist and his admiring audience and made her way to the top of Holbourn Hill, she considered this possibility with a growing excitement.

Her father had insisted that each of his daughters ought to have a firm grounding in the fine arts, so Elizabeth and her sisters had dutifully attended music classes, embroidery classes, and even dancing classes. But duty had nothing to do with her enjoyment of the art classes taught by a series of Scottish artists. She had studied drawing, landscape painting, portraiture, and (because one of the artists was also a printmaker) etching and engraving. She had proved to be an eager pupil with a considerable degree of skill. She had spent many happy hours sketching the plants in her mother's garden, then turning the sketches into engravings and then into prints.

Portraits, she thought now. She bent into the wind, making her way past Staples Inn, where a coach-and-four was waiting for passengers. *Yes, I could paint portraits.* Portraits were not her favorite form of art but she was certainly as competent as that fellow on his hands and knees. Of course, there was the difficulty of purchasing supplies — canvas, brushes, oils, watercolors were all expensive. And the challenge of getting commissions, unless she wanted to be a street artist, for which only chalk and an empty hat were needed but which seemed to her to present unacceptable dangers for a woman. And could she earn enough? After all, there were only a few ha'pennies in that hopeful hat.

But Elizabeth was the sort of person who felt better about her difficulties when she was actually *doing* something about them, even if the doing only amounted to planning. By the time she reached the Stuart home in affluent Castle Lane near Bloomsbury Square, she had arrived at a tentative scheme. She would look through the few belongings she had brought with her, find what she needed, and put it — and her scheme — to Dr. Stuart when he arrived home from St. George's Hospital, where he saw patients on Tuesday afternoons.

And she would also spend some time with the children. Blanche and William would not miss their father; he had been absent at work every day and out most evenings. They scarcely knew him. But the upheaval that followed the loss of their familiar home and the family's possessions had been even more difficult for them than it had been for her.

It was impossible for Elizabeth to assure herself that all would be well, but it was necessary to assure *them,* poor things.

Dr. Alexander Stuart took off his wig and rubbed his close-shaven head, puffing out his cheeks as he sat down in the leather chair beside the fireplace. It had been a trying day at St. George's Hospital, and the good doctor was tired. He took out a pouch of Virginia tobacco, lit his pipe with a coal from the tidy fire in the library grate, and settled back with a cup of hot China tea. The room was lit by the last pale gleam of the afternoon sun, which picked out the gilt on the bindings of the many leather-bound books on the bookcase shelves.

Dr. Stuart prided himself, as well he might, on his many medical successes. A Scot who had made a successful transition from the north to the south, he had earned a medical degree under the famous Herman Boerhaave at the University of Leiden. There, in the university's splendid botanical garden, he had studied the new pharmaceutical plants that were coming in from Asia and the New World.

Degree in hand, he returned to London, where with a calculating Scots shrewdness he chose the right friends and cultivated the right (that is to say, influential) patrons. On the basis of these choices, he built the right practice. He had cleverly specialized in female diseases and obstetrical care — important, for this was a time when wealthy women were beginning to turn to physicians for the births of their children, rather than (or together with) midwives. Within a very short time, he'd had the honor of being admitted to the Royal College of Physicians, as well as being invited to serve the royal household as one of Queen Caroline's physicians-in-ordinary.

But for all these vital assets, Dr. Stuart was possessed of one enormous liability: the man was up to his ragged brown eyebrows in debt. Like many of his friends, including that master of celestial mechanics, Sir Isaac Newton, Stuart had gotten swept up in the South Sea frenzy of fifteen years before. He had lost his frugal Scots head — had lost it completely and inexplicably, in some form (he thought) of socially induced insanity. He had borrowed heavily and repeatedly to invest in the stock as it rose from one hundred pounds a share to one thousand. At which point Sir Isaac was reported to have said, "I can calculate the movement of the stars, but not the madness of men."

When the bubble burst (as of course it did), Dr. Stuart lost all he had saved and borrowed. Given his flourishing practice and his standing in the medical community, his creditors elected to be patient, understanding that if they sent him to prison, they would never see a farthing of what he owed them. Over time and by careful management, he had managed to repay a portion of the debt, and he regularly paid the interest on the rest. But if it weren't for the fortune his wife Susannah had brought to their marriage, he would still be living in the cramped rooms he had rented from the apothecary Mitchell on Pall Mall, instead of this fine house in Bloomsbury. Susannah (the widow of a wealthy clothier) had graciously accepted him and had even paid the bulk of his debts, for which he was eternally grateful. It probably also explained his desire to offer whatever aid he could to those in distress.

So it was that he had been thinking what might be done for the Blackwells. There was no helping the man. Alexander would be in

Newgate (and deservedly so, in Dr. Stuart's opinion) until his creditors were paid, which would likely be a matter of years, not months. The doctor himself knew of at least one debtor who was still imprisoned after twenty years.

But young Mrs. Blackwell, who was left with two little ones and no means of support, did not deserve her fate. That was the awful tragedy of debt, which blighted not just the debtor but his entire family. A man's bad business decisions and extravagant spending habits could doom a woman and her children. Why, only recently, a destitute young wife and mother had leapt into the Thames with both her babes in her arms, preferring the mercies of the river to a life in the Fleet or on the streets.

And Dr. Stuart felt something of an obligation to Mrs. Blackwell. An Aberdonian Scot himself, he was a longtime friend of her father and had felt not a little consternation when he learned that she had eloped with young Blackwell, who had not yet completed his education and was in no financial position to support a family. Furthermore, while the young man's father (an academic of some local fame) liked to boast that his son was a prodigy, it was evident that Alexander suffered from a severe lack of diligence and discipline. He had not even finished his undergraduate studies when he took himself off to Leiden.

That was damaging enough, but worse was the lack of a professional credential. When the newly-married Blackwells arrived in London, Alexander was claiming to have earned a medical degree at Leiden. This seemed improbable in the extreme. When Dr. Stuart (remembering his own time with Boerhaave) had questioned him closely, it was evident that his degree was a fabrication and insufficient basis for the practice of medicine in London.

Still, because Alexander was genuinely bright and skilled in languages, Dr. Stuart had been able to help him find work as a proof corrector for William Wilkins. He excelled in that position and was encouraged to learn as much as he could about the technical business of printing, bookmaking, and bookselling. It was evident that he had a natural aptitude and a great enthusiasm for the trade. Dr. Stuart began to think that perhaps Blackwell had found a natural calling and urged him to stay on in the business.

But the foolish young man had made another rash decision. He would set himself up as a printer. And instead of entering a partnership with a journeyman printer, he decided to simply defy the printers' guild's requirement for a seven years' apprenticeship. To establish the business, he spent his wife's substantial dowry and when that was not enough, borrowed the rest, leasing a fine building over Somerset water gate in the Strand and purchasing three expensive presses and other printing equipment. It had to be the very best of everything, for Alexander Blackwell liked to present himself as an outstanding success.

Whatever else he was, Blackwell was adept as a printer. He had produced four commendable books when the predictable happened. He was haled into court and convicted of exercising the art and trade of printing without having served the requisite term of apprenticeship. He was fined and the business closed. Within two months, a commission of bankrupt was issued against him, and his printing equipment and household furnishings were sold. To complete his ruin, his creditors had him arrested and sent to prison. Those who knew Blackwell felt that this was a case where imprisonment was justified. Some might have said it was quite clearly deserved.

Mrs. Blackwell, on the other hand, was a brave young woman who had borne her husband's difficulties with equanimity and without complaint. Now, given his acquaintance with her family, Dr. Stuart felt — in a rather paternal way — that he ought to do something to help her. It was true that he and Susannah were providing her and the children a place to live, and many would say that this was enough. But was there something more he could do, some other way he could help?

Yes, there was, and in fact, an idea had occurred to the doctor that very afternoon. As he pulled on his pipe and thought how he might offer the suggestion to her, there was a knock on his study door and she came in, carrying a brown leather portfolio.

By the standards of the day, the doctor judged that Elizabeth Blackwell was not a pretty woman. But she had arresting dark eyes in an angular face, a fine head of thick russet hair, and a look of active intelligence that brought its own singular beauty to her face. Her dress was modest: a garnet-colored woolen bodice and skirt, simply styled and topped with a white lace kerchief pinned at the neck. She spoke with traces of a Scottish brogue, and her voice was low and firm. She was both direct and thoughtful, with none of the silly flirtatiousness of well-bred London ladies. The good doctor had found himself liking her, and now that he had thought of how he might help, he was eager to share his plan with her. But he did not begin there.

"Mrs. Stuart tells me that you have been to Newgate," he said, pulling on his pipe.

"Aye, that I have." Elizabeth's tone was grave. "I have just returned."

"And how is your husband?"

She managed a tight smile. "He was looking forward to a nap, and some time to read Dr. Swift's 'Proposal.' As long as he has a book, a candle, and his supper, Alexander will want for little else."

"Ah," said Dr. Stuart, thinking that this would be an accurate, if unemotional assessment of the man — not exactly what one might expect from a wife. He cocked his head. "And you, my dear?"

Her face darkened. "Well, I have decided one thing, at least. My visit to the prison today persuades me that I cannot take the children there. They cannot endure the cold and damp. And while you and Mrs. Stuart have been wonderfully accommodating, I don't feel that I can impose on you. I shall have to find some paying work for myself that supports us and pays something toward Alexander's debt. That is why I —" She held out the portfolio. "Please be so good as to look at these, sir."

Curious, Stuart laid his pipe aside and opened the portfolio. It contained a large number of pencil sketches, charcoal drawings, and water colors — portraits of people, of flowering plants, a drawing room scene, a street, boats moored along a wharf.

"Quite, quite nice," he said, in some surprise. "These are yours?"

"Yes. I studied drawing as a girl, and have continued over the years to pursue it." She gave him an intent look. "At the risk of presuming, I wonder if you think I might be able to earn money as a portraitist. If you do, might you be willing to introduce me as an artist to your friends?"

Stuart was somewhat surprised at the directness of her request, although he understood the necessity that compelled it. He laid the portfolio on the table beside his chair.

"I think it's entirely possible, Elizabeth, but I have another idea to advance to you. Would you agree to hear it?"

"Of course, sir." She folded her hands. "I will consider *any* kind of proposal. I don't think I need to tell you how desperate I am."

He picked up his pipe and puffed on it until it glowed. "As you know, I am in charge of obstetrical services at St. George's.

My work involves both attention to women in labor and to the training of midwives. It seems to me that you possess all the qualities of a good midwife: literacy, intelligence, strength, and energy." He regarded her through the cloud of fragrant smoke. "You have given birth to children, and understand women's pain and suffering. I am sure that you also understand that midwifery is a challenging profession. But it is a noble calling, an important service to women, and highly valued. I believe it would suit you."

Head cocked to one side, Elizabeth was listening attentively. "Thank you for your confidence. That's an excellent idea, and I shall be glad to consider it." She took a breath. "I hope you will forgive me for being direct, but I must know. What is the compensation? What will I be able to earn?"

Dr. Stuart resisted the urge to smile at her bluntness when it came to money. A true Scotswoman, indeed — her native habit perhaps strengthened by the painful dealings with her husband's creditors.

"During the six-month training period, I am afraid there is none. When that is complete, how much you earn will depend on the number of births at which you assist, your experience, and — to put it frankly — the kind of clientele you develop." He paused to be sure she was paying attention. "Mrs. Kennon, for instance, ministers to the royal family. She has a reputation that allows her to charge up to fifty guineas for a delivery. If you are introduced into the right circles, I think you should do as well as she. Not right away, of course, but in time." He intended to introduce her, and if she proved herself during her training period, he had the connections to ensure her success.

Elizabeth's eyebrows had risen at the mention of fifty guineas. "Indeed it *does* interest me, sir, and if I were responsible for myself alone, I should undertake it at once. But given my husband's situation, I fear that my need for funds is rather more urgent." She gestured toward the portfolio. "Please tell me truly. Do you think I can earn at least some money as an artist?"

Surprised at his disappointment, he picked up the portfolio.

"I should think so," he said slowly, looking again at her work. He turned over several pieces, admiring the colors in this one, the composition in that. Elizabeth Blackwell did indeed have some talent, although perhaps more in botanical illustration than in portraiture. Her renderings of roses, for instance, were outstanding. Vivid, detailed, delicately colored, and remarkably true to the life.

And as he considered her situation and mentally reviewed those of his friends who patronized the arts, an idea came to him.

A very *bright* idea, if he did say so himself.

PART THREE

■ ■ ■ ■

February 7, 1735
Number 3, Great Russell Street
Bloomsbury Square, London
Sir Hans Sloane, Baronet (born April 16, 1660, Killyleagh, County Down, Ire. — died Jan. 11, 1753, London, Eng.), British physician and naturalist whose collection of books, manuscripts, and curiosities formed the basis for the British Museum in London.

— The Encyclopaedia Britannica

Elizabeth looked at the copper nameplate beside the impressive door and pulled in her breath. The white stone residence was very grand in the pleasingly symmetrical style that was called Georgian, for the two King Georges. The park behind her — Bloomsbury Square — was also quite grand, with the Duke of Bedford's mansion on the north side, and just down the way, Montagu House, said to be the grandest private dwelling in all of London. As Dr. Stuart raised the ornate knocker and let it fall, a grand coach-and-four rattled over the cobblestone pavement, bearing a grandly bewigged footman in full livery.

The name on the nameplate was grand, too.

"Sir Hans Sloane?" Elizabeth whispered, not quite believing. Dr. Stuart had not told her whom they were meeting this afternoon. He said only that he had spoken to a patron of his — a wealthy doctor who took a personal pleasure in helping worthy and talented people who interested him.

Elizabeth was awestruck. She would be showing her portfolio to the legendary Dr. Sloane! This gentleman was reputed to have kept the dying Queen Anne alive long enough to allow the Elector of Hanover to scurry over from Saxony and mount the

Protestant throne, thereby dashing the hopes of the Jacobite Catholics. The new king, George I, had rewarded the helpful doctor with a baronetcy, while George II not only named him the royal physician but knighted him.

No doubt the honors were deserved. Throughout his long career, Dr. Sloane had shown himself to be a man of achievement. Born in Ireland to a Scots-Irish family, he had an immense botanical curiosity and an avid interest in plants that were novel and strange. At nineteen, he had come to London to study at Apothecaries' Hall and in the apothecaries' garden at Chelsea, gaining a wide knowledge of the plants that were the basis of all pharmaceuticals. In his twenties, he had served as the physician to the governor of the faraway island of Jamaica, where he observed the native practice of using an extract of the bark of the cinchona tree (what the French called quinine) to treat the eyes. For stomach ailments, he had observed Jamaican women mixing ground cocoa beans with sugar and milk; when he returned to England he brought with him a recipe for "milk chocolate" and advocated its medicinal use. He was one of the first to inoculate his patients against the smallpox, was a governor of the new Foundling Hospital, and in spite of his fame, still kept a daily free surgery for the poor. But Sir Hans was perhaps best known for the immense collection of curiosities he had assembled from around the globe, a collection that — it was said — rivaled any on earth.

Dr. Stuart lifted a gloved hand to ring the bell. "For many years, I have been privileged to count Sir Hans as a friend and colleague," he said. "I have explained your circumstance to him, and he is sympathetic. You could find no better, and certainly no more liberal, sponsor."

Elizabeth straightened her shoulders. "I trust he doesn't feel that I have come on bended knee," she said sharply. "I am not begging his charity." As Alexander's wife, it was her obligation to do all that she could to save her husband. But not that. Never that.

"He knows that you are a Scotswoman, and Scots never beg." Dr. Stuart rang the bell more smartly. "I have commended your artistic talents to him and told him why you are eager to apply them just now."

A few moments later, they were shown into Dr. Sloane's library, a room the size of a ballroom. It was filled floor to ceiling with bookcases and shelves that were crowded with the strangest assortment of rarities that

Elizabeth had ever seen, many of them labeled in a thin, spidery hand.

There was an odd-looking rock studded with tiny gold nodules, a ceremonial cup crafted from a carved nautilus shell, trays of assorted seeds and botanical materials, maps and manuscripts, tobacco pipes in various exotic shapes, a gilded rhinoceros horn, tiny figures carved from whalebone and labeled "Eskimo," a burning glass, an Indian drum from Virginia, a wooden medicine stick designed to induce vomiting, a rattlesnake's rattles, birds' eggs and feathers, glass boxes of beetles, a purse made of asbestos and sold to Sir Hans by a visiting colonial named Benjamin Franklin, and racks of thick green-bound volumes, each labeled Herbarium, containing pages and pages of dried plants collected from all over the earth. A stuffed striped donkey from the Cape of Good Hope sulked in a corner; an amazingly lifelike seven-foot yellow snake from Jamaica was draped over a large mirror, and a brilliantly colored tropical bird with a long tail perched on a chandelier. Above the fireplace mantel hung a silver-and-iridescent-blue fish as long as Elizabeth was tall, with a sword on the end of its nose. The floor was covered with a great variety of rugs, a Polynesian grass mat next to a

141

hand-knotted Persian carpet beside a tiger rug from India, its snarling fangs ready to snap at Elizabeth's toes.

"My gracious," Elizabeth murmured, drawing back her feet. "I shouldn't be at all surprised to discover a unicorn somewhere in this clutter."

Dr. Stuart chuckled. "Sir Hans finds himself interested in anything that he has never seen before." He cast a quizzical glance around the room. "It all rather wants organizing, doesn't it?"

It did indeed want organizing. It was such an extraordinary jumble of oddities that Elizabeth felt she was in a curiosity-dealer's shop. But she had always been deeply interested in the natural world, and there was more than enough here to hold her attention. She was studying a page in one of the herbariums when a short, portly gentleman wearing a full brown wig bustled into the room.

"Ah, my dear Stuart," he said with evident satisfaction. "How good to see you." In his seventies, he was dressed in brown breeches with a dark brown velvet coat, a lace-trimmed shirt, a ruffled cravat, and a heavy gold watch chain laden with gold seals draped across an embroidered waistcoat. His face was roundish, almost cherubic, and the gold-rimmed spectacles perched on the end of his nose gave him a professorial look.

Elizabeth regarded him with curiosity. His was a face that she would enjoy painting. She hoped he would agree to commission her to do his portrait — which was, after all, the purpose of this visit. She would paint him in the midst of his collection, an object or two in his hands. That African drum perhaps, or the rat skeleton over there. And the stuffed bird perched on his shoulder.

At the sight of Elizabeth, a smile relieved the severity of his face and he bowed over her hand as Dr. Stuart introduced them.

"Ah, yes," he said, rubbing his hands together. "And this is the Scotswoman you told me about, Stuart." He bowed again. "I understand, Mrs. Blackwell, that you are an artist. And I see that you have brought something to show me." He held out his hand for the portfolio she was carrying. "May I? I am most interested."

"Oh, indeed, sir," she said. Her heart thudding, she placed the portfolio in his hand.

He took it, gestured at chairs for his guests, and seated himself at a small table. For the next quarter hour, while she fidgeted, he leafed through her drawings. She had arranged her work so that the portraits would be seen first and the landscapes and botanical drawings after. He glanced rapidly through her portfolio, then, having a chatty conversation with himself, went back to examine her drawings of plants.

"Quite nice, quite nice, indeed," he mused, turning up a drawing of rosemary. "One of my favorite herbs, especially good with a joint of roast lamb. And look here — hemlock! Hemlock, the herb of Socrates and his choice for a noble death. The rest of us should have his courage." He held out the drawing, admiring it. "Delightfully pictured in all its parts, and very like. So accurately done that one could use this as a guide to instruct the ill-informed to distinguish it from parsley."

"Ah, yes," Dr. Stuart said, as if Sir Hans' remarks were directed at him. "I heard yesterday that another succumbed to hemlock, thinking it parsley." He shook his head. " 'Tis ever thus."

"And need not be." Sir Hans put down Elizabeth's hemlock and turned over another drawing. "What is this? Oh, to be sure. Ladies' mantle, *Alchemilla vulgaris* — from the Arabic 'alkemelych,' or alchemist — a name bestowed on the plant by old writers for its near-magical properties in the treatment of women's gynecological problems.

We have a specimen in the garden at Chelsea. Tragus describes it in his illustrated *Kreuter Buch* of 1539, but his woodcut is not nearly so accurate as this drawing." He looked at Elizabeth. "Where did you find the plant, my dear?"

"On a wild hillside, sir," Elizabeth said, "outside of Aberdeen. I have always enjoyed botanical excursions. I took my sketchpad with me and drew the plants that interested me most. It helped me to learn their many uses."

"You are a practicing herbalist, then?"

She laughed a little. "Only an amateur — but a dedicated one, sir." Early in her life, botany had been her favorite study, and she had imagined passing her days in a quiet cottage somewhere, surrounded by gardens. Marriage to Alexander had spelled the end of that modest dream. It still returned, especially in this last tumultuous year, but with it came the sad understanding that it could never be.

Sir Hans picked up another of her drawings. "And here . . . why, bless my soul, I believe you have drawn — and, yes, labeled — scurvy grass!" He lowered the paper and peered at her over the top of it. "Scurvy grass, Mrs. Blackwell!" he exclaimed. "*Cochlearia officinalis,* no less!"

Elizabeth nodded, although she was rather at a loss to explain Sir Hans' evident excitement. The drawing he was looking at was very simple, done on a long-ago day when she and her sisters had tramped through a seashore salt marsh in a drizzle. It was hastily drawn and not at all pretty. Indeed, it couldn't be pretty, for the plant was such a commonplace little thing, hiding itself among the marsh grasses like a bird with a broken wing.

She cleared her throat. Thinking that she ought to explain herself, she said, "The drawings of scurvy grass and ladies' mantle are two of a number I made of our native Scottish herbs." She paused. "I had it in mind to engrave and print a number of drawings, you see. They might have made a small herbal to be sold through the apothecary shops in Aberdeen. I thought it might be helpful to those with an interest in the many uses of our native plants."

"An herbal, you say? A book of Scottish herbs?" Sir Hans broke into a wide smile. "And of course it should include scurvy grass, certainly, certainly!" He cocked his head. "The Roman naturalist Pliny the Elder wrote about a scurvy-like disease which afflicted Roman soldiers in Germany. He recommended what he called *Herba bri-*

tannica, which I believe to be scurvy grass. Also called spoonwort, as I'm sure you know, from the shape of its leaves — not at all grass-like." He held up Elizabeth's drawing and waved it triumphantly in the air.

"And you have drawn it to the life! What a talented eye you have! And what a boon a picture like this would be, say, for seafaring ship captains who send sailors ashore to gather this plant so that it may be added to their shipboard diets!" His sentences were studded with exclamation points.

"I am glad you approve," Elizabeth murmured, allowing herself only the barest ironical tartness. She had hoped that Dr. Stuart's great friend might commission her to paint himself or members of his household and — much to be hoped — would recommend her to his wide circle of friends. But the man wanted to carry on about scurvy grass. How disappointing!

"Approve? Approve? Why, certainly I approve," Sir Hans exclaimed with a renewed enthusiasm. "Most certainly!" He turned to glance around him. "Somewhere here, although at the moment I can't think where, I have a formula sent to me by an old lady who lives in the West Country, in Cornwall, I believe. Yes, yes, in Cornwall. It consists of various plants — water cress, if I recall correctly, as well as scurvy grass, betony, wormwood, and brooklime — pounded together and mixed with white wine, beer, or orange juice. It is said to be an excellent medicine for preventing scurvy. If I can locate it, I will have it copied out for you. I am sure you will find it interesting. *Most* interesting — especially the use of scurvy grass."

"I'm sure I shall," Elizabeth said. By now, she had given up all hope of any help from this man. Perhaps she should set up shop as a street artist right here in Bloomsbury Square, where those who came and went would at least have a few coins in their pockets. She would be as likely to get work from them as she was from Sir Hans.

That gentleman was now leafing quickly through the rest of her drawings of plants, muttering under his breath, holding up first one and then another for a closer look. At last, he satisfied himself, and closed the portfolio. He took off his spectacles, polished them with his cravat, and put them back on again, peering at her.

"When you spoke a moment ago of compiling an herbal, I believe you said that you had it in mind to engrave and print your drawings." He looked at Dr. Stuart over the tops of his glasses. "May I take it, Stuart, that Mrs. Blackwell is also an engraver?"

"So I understand," began Dr. Stuart, but Elizabeth, by now quite impatient with both men, spoke up for herself.

"I am, sir. I studied engraving as a girl in Aberdeen. And until my husband was required to close his print shop, I provided engravings for books in his press, which I was most glad to do." She felt herself flushing and looked down. It was perhaps not wise to tell Sir Hans of the many duties she performed in Alex's shop — not just engraving, but dealing with customers and suppliers, managing the accounts, and marketing the books. He might think she was part of the reason it failed.

But he appeared to ignore the unfortunate reference and fastened instead on her experience.

"Engraving is a most useful skill for an artist. On one of these shelves, I have the *Metamorphosis* of Frau Maria Sibylla Merian, a delightful book which includes sixty of her life-size drawings of insects — engraved and also colored by herself. I should be glad to lend it to you, if I can find it. It would serve as an excellent model."

A model for what? Elizabeth wondered, but she didn't want to reveal her ignorance. "Thank you," she murmured.

"I speak of Frau Merian's work because it seems to me that you have a comparable skill," Sir Hans said, once again picking up her picture of hemlock. "The gift of close observation and the ability to draw what you see." He studied it for a moment, pursing his lips. "Dr. Stuart has informed me that you are in search of an undertaking — that is to say, a project by which you might earn some money. This is true?"

"Yes, sir. It is, sir." She took a deep breath, not certain what Dr. Stuart might have said but wanting to be sure that the full story, however shameful, was told.

"Perhaps you know that my husband is in Newgate gaol for nonpayment of a substantial business debt. Dr. Stuart and his wife have been generous, but my two children and I cannot continue to impose on their hospitality. He has offered the opportunity to train as a midwife. I am grateful and would be glad to do so if there were compensation during the training period." She drew in her breath and said what she had come to say. "I must support my children and myself and satisfy my husband's creditors. I was hoping most urgently that —"

"An honorable profession, midwifery." Sir Hans took out his handkerchief and noisily blew his nose. "I commend it to you. But it is not likely in the near term to provide the funds that you require." He tucked his handkerchief into his ruffled sleeve and folded his hands across his waistcoat, regarding her. "Therefore, I have a proposal to make. Will you consider it?"

Consider it? She was confused, but she could say only "Yes, of course, sir."

"Good. Allow me, then, if you please."

And she listened with a growing amazement while the celebrated Dr. Sloane told her what he had in mind.

And yes, it included scurvy grass.

CHAPTER FIVE

Scurvy Grass. *Cochlearia officinalis.*
Abundant on the shores in Scotland, growing inland along some of its rivers and
Highland mountains and not uncommon in
stony, muddy and sandy soils in England
and Ireland . . . The fresh herb was greatly
used on sea-voyages as a preventative of
scurvy. The essential oil is of benefit in
paralytic and rheumatic cases; scurvy-
grass ale was a popular tonic drink.

Maud Grieve
A Modern Herbal, 1931

I stared at Jenna's last sentence for a few
minutes, then closed my tablet with a strong
sense of exasperation. What *did* Sir Hans
tell Elizabeth? How did he propose to help
her? What did he want in return for whatever
he was willing to give? What would she have
to do? How much would she have to *risk*?
Why, oh why, did I have to wait to find these

153

things out?

I knew how the story ultimately ended, of course. That is, with an amazingly success- ful book that allowed Elizabeth to pay off her husband's massive debt and, two years later, bail him out of jail. I also knew that, in gratitude to Sir Hans, she had given him a custom-made copy — the very one that had been stolen from the Hemlock House library. Had given it to him with her own hands, most likely.

But when I finished reading, I had more questions than answers. I still couldn't guess how Elizabeth might have gotten from this moment in Sir Hans Sloane's library to the creation of the stolen book — and I very much wanted to know. If Jenna's email had included more pages, I would have kept on reading, straight to the end. Until daylight, if that's what it took.

But it didn't. I had never had the op- portunity to read an actual work in progress — a novel that was still in the making — and it felt like a special privilege. In the morning, I'd have to ask Jenna when I could read more. I was hoping she wouldn't leave me dangling for long, not knowing where the story was going next and just how Eliz- abeth had managed to do something no woman had done before.

I glanced at the bedside clock, remembering that North Carolina was an hour ahead of Texas, and that McQuaid was still up. I reached for my phone and called him to say goodnight. It was good to hear his voice, warm and intimate, like his touch. He'd spent the day in San Antonio, interviewing witnesses in the investigation he was working on for attorney Charlie Lipman. Caitie and Spock had arrived safely at her grandmother's ranch and she had called home to tell her dad, with great excitement, that they were going horseback riding tomorrow — Spock, too. Wearing his parrot harness and leash, of course, which he had to put on whenever he went outdoors. (You learn all sorts of new things when a parrot comes into your life.)

I also filled McQuaid in on what I had learned about Hemlock House and Elizabeth's *Herbal* and the situation here — that is, what little there was to tell. Tomorrow would be more productive, I hoped. But we didn't talk long, for the bed was a cozy nest, the room was quiet, and I'd had a long trip and a longer day. When I said "I love you" and turned out the light, I fell asleep almost immediately.

Sleep pulled me back into Jenna's vivid story. I dreamed I was walking up Holbourn

Hill to St. Andrews, where a street artist hawked his drawings. I bought a hot potato from the hot-potato man to keep my hands warm under my woolen cloak and when it cooled off, I ate it. But the hulking shadow of Newgate Prison darkened the London sky behind me, and I felt something of what Elizabeth must have felt that day: the bleak impossibility of redeeming herself and her children from her husband's reckless and costly mistakes.

And when I woke in the first pale light of dawn, I was startled. I wasn't in England in the eighteenth century or at home in my own bed, with McQuaid's body warm beside me and Winchester sprawled paws-in-the-air across our feet. I was in a strange bed in an elegant room in a faux French castle in the Appalachian Mountains. A new day in a strange place — and I had awakened with a plan.

The morning air was chilly, so my trip to the bathroom was as quick as I could make it. Back in my room, I hurried into jeans, a sweatshirt over a blue plaid flannel shirt, and blue wool socks with my leather sandals. Forget fashion. I was going to be warm.

It was too early to go downstairs, so I took out my pocket-sized notebook and began jotting down what I had learned since my arrival: general impressions of people and place, summaries of conversation, random observations, questions, concerns, names, and the inevitable to-dos. I didn't try to impose any organization on my haphazard notes — there would be time for that later, when it came to connecting the dots. I was operating on a theory I had built up in my years as a defense attorney: the more dots I could come up with now, the more connections I could make and the more conclusions I could draw later. All this notational urgency was probably premature, but the process gave me the feeling — a deceptive feeling, no doubt — that I had things under control.

I also glanced through the list of names Jenna had given me the night before and circled several. I intended to talk to people — at least three people today, if they could be located.

And I needed to come up with a cover story, a plausible explanation to account for the nosey questions I intended to ask. Who *was* I when I talked to these people? What did I want to know? How was I going to use their information?

After a few moments of putting my mind to it, I contrived a plan I thought would work. Then I folded the list into my notebook, tucked it into the back pocket of my jeans, and ran a quick comb through my hair. Dorothea had said that they usually ate breakfast around seven-thirty. It was nearly that now, and I was ready — more than ready — for coffee.

One of the people whose names I had circled was in the kitchen, frying bacon.

She was thin, narrow-shouldered, and almost gaunt, with high cheekbones and watchful eyes in a long, narrow face. Her graying hair was twisted into an untidy coil at the back of her head, and she was dressed in a dark sweater, baggy black slacks, and black sneakers, with a white bib apron tied at neck and waist. Bacon sizzled in a frying pan on the stove.

"Rose," Dorothea said, "this is my friend, China Bayles. She's come to stay with us for a few days. China, this is Rose Mullins. She and her husband Joe have worked at Hemlock House for — how long, Rose?"

There was a silence, as if Rose was deciding whether to answer. Her gruff mountain twang was dark with suspicion when she said, "Pert near thirty years now." She forked the bacon out of the skillet and onto a plate, drained some of the grease into a tin can, then began breaking eggs into the skillet, scrambling them.

Before Dorothea could explain who I was, I spoke up with my just-invented cover story, designed to give me the maximum latitude — and creative flexibility — in framing my questions.

"I'm writing a magazine article about Miss Carswell, Mrs. Mullins. She had such an interesting life, with her gardens and her books. Would you have time later this morning to talk with me?" If I was asked which magazine I was writing for, I would say that I was a freelancer and that I was querying several editors.

Rose put the plate of bacon on the table and returned to the stove to stir the eggs. She was frowning, but I wasn't sure whether it was a response to my request or a perpetual expression on her dour face.

"Reckon I can," she said at last, with obvious reluctance. "But it'll have to be later. I'm fixin' to commence on the wash." To Dorothea, she said, "The eggs'll be done in a minute, Miz Harper. There's biscuits in the oven, orange juice in the icebox, coffee in the pot."

And off she went. Was she just naturally brusque or was she avoiding me? I was about to ask Dorothea, but at that moment, Jenna breezed in, looking like springtime itself in a sunny yellow sweater over jeans. She was carrying a handful of Johnny-jump-ups from the garden.

"Oh, so pretty," Dorothea said. "So sweet and gay."

"In Elizabeth's time," Jenna said, "Johnnies were a remedy for children's tummy aches." She put the blossoms in a glass bowl in the middle of the table, where their purple, yellow, and white faces smiled, a cheerful sign of a mountain April. She stepped back, admiring the flowers. "In lotions, they were used to treat rashes and itching. In poultices, to heal cuts and scrapes. People have forgotten that."

"People have forgotten lots of things," I said. "In Elizabeth's time, plants were the only drugs. The trick was knowing which ones worked for what. Like scurvy grass."

"Which is exactly why Elizabeth's *Herbal* was so popular," Jenna said with satisfaction. "It was meant for apothecaries to share with their customers, and for ordinary people to use at home. Her drawings are easy to match to the plants — almost like photographs, which of course they wouldn't have for another hundred-plus years. And her descriptions are written in plain English, no Latin, no jargon. No superstitions, either, not like other herbals of her day.

160

Nicholas Culpeper, for instance, loads his with medieval astrology. He wants people to know that scurvy grass is ruled by Jupiter and that violets belong to Venus." She chuckled. "Elizabeth's was the first illustrated herbal to include just the facts, as they were understood in her day. Clear. Easy to understand. Almost photographic."

Dorothea took the biscuits out of the oven. "Jenna, could you get the coffee, please?"

As Jenna poured coffee, I thanked her for letting me read her first three chapters. "I admire the way you've drawn Elizabeth," I said. "And your descriptions of eighteenth-century London are incredibly detailed. You must have done tons of research."

"The research is the fun part," Jenna said with a grin. "You've seen that old map of London over my desk in the workroom? I use it a lot. And there are wonderful books and websites crammed with period details. But I just wish I knew Elizabeth better."

"Really?" I was surprised. "You write as though you know her very well."

Jenna shook her head. "For me, her character is full of ambiguities, especially her relationship to that ne'er-do-well husband of hers. There's no concrete evidence for it, but I believe that he spent her dowry before he racked up that mountain of debt. If she were like us — modern women, I mean — she'd be mad as hell. Wouldn't you be, if your husband went out and charged the family credit card past the limit — over and over again?"

Dorothea put the biscuits on the table, with a pot of strawberry jam. "But maybe eighteenth-century women were resigned to their husbands calling the shots," she said. "Maybe they thought that was the way it was supposed to be."

"Entirely possible." Jenna paused, reflecting. "On the other hand, Elizabeth was a Scotswoman, and they are said to have been more independent than Englishwomen." She went to the refrigerator for orange juice. "I'm making her up as I go along. It'll probably take me three or four drafts to get her right." As she took glasses out of the cupboard, she added, "Actually, I don't think I'll ever be sure what 'right' is. The men who wrote about her admired her wifely 'devotion' to Alexander and seemed to think that she did it all just for him. *I* think it was a lot more complicated than that. I think she was thoroughly out of patience with him. And out of love, to boot."

"I hope there are more chapters to come," I said.

She poured the juice. "I'll email you another batch. But I'm still doing research. I think Elizabeth's story will mostly stay the way I have it, but I may have to adjust the timeline. For instance, *A Curious Herbal* was originally published in weekly installments, four pages at a time. When she had produced sixty-three or sixty-four installments, she had it printed as a bound book. That was in 1737. Meanwhile, she kept on printing those installments until she had a total of one hundred and twenty-five."

"A persistent lady," I said admiringly.

"Absolutely," Jenna said. "But I haven't been able to find out exactly when the *first* installment appeared, which is important to the story." She put the glasses on the table. "And I don't know when she was able to bail Alexander out of prison. Even though he didn't deserve it," she added under her breath. She pulled out a chair and sat down.

"In your view," Dorothea prompted gently.

"In my view, definitely," Jenna replied. "If I'd been Elizabeth, that man could have stayed in Newgate the rest of his natural life."

As we dug into our breakfasts, I let Jenna in on my cover story: I was a freelance magazine writer working on an article about Miss Carswell — her gardens, her library, and the foundation she had created to carry on her work. I planned to use the story, with variations, when I talked to people in town. I was hoping to pick up some information that might point me in the direction of the missing *Herbal,* although I had to admit that it felt like a long shot. Still . . .

"If you or Dorothea are asked about me," I added, "please play along."

Buttering a biscuit, Dorothea said, "I'm glad you thought of that strategy, China. It will encourage people to talk. And you'll get a chance to hear different sides of Sunny's story. Some people liked her, others thought she was a tyrant — or a little bit nuts."

I looked down at my jeans. "I'll be going down to Bethany later this morning. Do I need to change into something dressier?" I glanced at Dorothea, who looked like a proper librarian in a silky white blouse, caramel-colored cardigan, and dark brown tweed skirt. "Silly me. I actually own a skirt, but I just didn't think of bringing it."

Jenna laughed. "Writers like to be casual. And Bethany is a down-home town. You'll fit in perfectly."

Breakfast over, Dorothea and Jenna took me to the library and showed me the glass display case, now empty, where Elizabeth's *Herbal* had been kept.

Apologetically, Dorothea said, "I know it's not much of a lock. I had suggested to the board that we get a proper display case with a real lock. Now, of course . . ." She let her voice trail off.

"Like locking the barn after the horse is stolen," Jenna said dryly.

"And where is the key?" I asked.

"Right here, on a hook." Dorothea took it out from under a nearby shelf. "I suppose I should have hidden it. As you can see, the lock isn't jimmied. Whoever did this had to have known where to find the key."

"Hiding it wouldn't have helped," I said. "That's a very simple lock. It can probably be opened with a paper clip." I noticed traces of fingerprint powder on the lock and the glass. "Looks like your sheriff dusted the box for prints. Did he say whether he came up with anything?"

"He found mine," Dorothea said with a sigh. "And Jenna's too — but mine were on top of hers because I put the book away on that Friday afternoon." She shook her head. "I imagine that's one of the reasons he suspects me."

"And me, too," Jenna put in quickly. "He suspects both of us."

"He even asked us both the same questions," Dorothea said, now sounding offended. "He wanted to know where I would try to sell it, if I had taken it."

"And he asked me to show him how the plates had been cut out of the other books and where I would unload them, if I'd done it." Jenna shifted uncomfortably. "He didn't come right out and accuse either one of us, but I'm sure he was thinking that we — Dorothea and I — might have teamed up to loot the library."

I looked from one to the other, wishing they could see this as the sheriff must have seen it. But of course they couldn't. Nobody could blame them for feeling nervous and uneasy about being accused, even if the accusation hadn't resulted in a criminal charge — yet.

And looking at it from the sheriff's point of view, I had to admit that this had all the earmarks of an inside job. A clumsy one, at that, marking the two of them as prime suspects. And what was that sheriff likely to think if he found out that Dorothea had called me in as an investigator? It now occurred to me that he might think I was here to divert his attention — and maybe even that I was complicit in Dorothea and Jenna's suspected theft. I was beginning to feel apprehensive. Why hadn't I thought of this before I agreed to come?

"I'm sure he's only trying to be thorough," I said, pushing my uneasiness away. "What about the door to this room? Was it locked?"

Dorothea shook her head. "The outer doors have locks, but not the interior doors. We're so far away from civilization that it never seemed to be an issue — not for Miss Carswell and not for us. Until *this* happened." She frowned at the case as though it were at fault.

I thought of something else. "Has the house been searched? Maybe somebody took the *Herbal* out of the case and put it in another room." I couldn't think why a person might do this, but I supposed it was possible. "Have you looked?"

Dorothea sighed. "That's the first thing we thought of, actually. All of us searched — Jenna and Rose and Joe and I. And after the sheriff arrived, he had the house searched, too." She chuckled wryly. "While they were at it, they looked for the secret room, but they didn't find it either."

"There really *is* such a thing?" The only secret rooms I have ever encountered are fictional, like the one hidden behind the fireplace mantel in Rinehart's *The Circular Staircase.* They add a nice twist to a mystery, but in real life, they must be few and far between.

"Rose swears there is," Dorothea said, "and Jenna thinks so. But I find it a bit Nancy Drew-ish. Don't you?"

"I find it . . . interesting," I said. "You discovered some other things missing, didn't you?"

"Too many," she said with a sigh. "Miss Carswell had one of Redouté's volumes of *Lilies.* Eight plates are gone from that book. And John Forbes Royle's rare 1839 book on the botany of the Himalayas — ten hand-colored plates are missing from that one. There are two or three others, including some valuable colored prints of fungi by Beatrix Potter — you know, the *Peter Rabbit* lady. Of course, we don't know *when* the plates disappeared. They might have been missing when Miss Carswell acquired the books."

"The value of those items?"

"Gosh, I don't know." She chewed on her lower lip. "Original prints from the *Lilies* are going for anything from a thousand to six thousand. And Christie's sold a copy of Royle's book last year for nearly seven thousand dollars, so I'm sure the individual plates are quite valuable." She did a quick mental calculation. "Somewhere in the neighborhood of seventy or eighty thousand, I would guess."

Which put the value of the theft — including the *Herbal* — at nearly two hundred thousand. I was remembering that under the federal Theft of Major Artwork Act, the theft of a cultural item stolen from a museum and more than one hundred years old or worth more than $100,000 was a felony, punishable by a hefty fine and up to ten years in prison. I'd have to look up the act's definition of "museum" to be sure that Hemlock House qualified, but I thought it did. The *Herbal* was certainly old enough and valuable enough to qualify.

What's more, it wasn't the local gendarmerie that had primary jurisdiction under the statute. It was the FBI. One of the things I might do here — maybe the *only* thing I could realistically do — was to make sure that this theft was properly reported. Which meant convincing Mrs. Cousins and the board to do the right thing, and if they refused, finding a way to work around them. If the FBI got involved, their art crime team might have a *real* chance of finding the thief. And *A Curious Herbal* might find its way back to Hemlock House.

"Of course we're still looking for other missing plates." Dorothea's frown deepened into a scowl. "The thief must have had a busy day of it. But since Miss Carswell didn't leave an inventory or even a shelf list, we have no way of knowing what *should* be here."

A busy day of it. There was another explanation, of course. "Have you ever thought," I asked, "that the missing *Herbal* might just be the latest in an ongoing *series* of thefts?"

Jenna seemed startled. "You're suggesting that this . . . this stealing has been going on for some time?"

"Well, think about it. Even when Miss Carswell was alive, there doesn't seem to have been much attention to security. There may have been even less after she died. There was someone else for a while —"

"Margaret Anderson," Jenna said. "Miss Carswell's friend. For three or four months."

I nodded. "And then you two came. But if someone was stealing from these shelves, you wouldn't have known it unless you happened to see them or some evidence that they'd been here. Or until they took something that was in frequent use. Something you *noticed.*"

"I'm afraid you may be right," Dorothea said grimly. "We realized that the *Herbal* was gone because Jenna was working on it. The pages cut from the other books — that might have been done at any time. Weeks ago. Months ago." She blew out her breath

170

in sudden despair. "He could have stolen *hundreds* of items."

"Or she," I said. "There's no reason a woman can't have done this."

Jenna stared at me. "Margaret? Are you thinking of *Margaret*?"

I nodded. So far, book theft has generally been a man's game, but there's no reason that this kind of thievery can't be an equal opportunity employment. "Do you have the books you identified as missing some plates?"

"They're on a shelf in the workroom," Dorothea said. She glanced at Jenna. "But maybe we'd better find a place to lock them up. Securely."

"That would be a good idea." *Fingerprints, maybe?* I pulled out my cell and checked the time. "I'd like to talk with Rose before I drive down to Bethany. It would probably be better if you and Jenna weren't there. Okay?"

"Fine with me," Dorothea said. She hesitated. "I have to go to town myself, to pick up some groceries." She turned to Jenna. "I forgot to tell you — Joe got the minivan running yesterday. He says it still needs work, but it's drivable." To me, she added, "I'd offer you a ride, China, but I have to make a quick trip, and you'll probably want to linger. We'd better take separate vehicles."

"That's fine," I said. "I'm planning to talk to Carole Humphreys and Margaret Anderson. And there's no telling who else I'll run into."

I was saying a true thing, although I didn't know it. I couldn't have predicted just who I would run into — or where it would lead.

Rose Mullins was slow to open up, which I thought might be due to a natural suspicion of outsiders who came into her mountains. But as we settled down at the kitchen table over a cup of tea and a toasted biscuit with jam, my questions were gentle and non-threatening. It wasn't long before the words were flowing easily.

The gist of Rose's story was that she and her husband had lived at Hemlock House since Miss Carswell's daddy was alive. When he passed, Miss Carswell kept them on, along with most of the others — a cook and a couple of maids and kitchen helpers indoors, as well as an outdoor staff of five. Now, she and Joe lived in the gatehouse, not the main house. And there was just Joe outdoors, doing his best to keep the roof and the old well pump repaired and the trees trimmed and the driveway and the lane plowed in the winter. They hired a few local people to spruce things up when the gardens were about to be opened. And now, indoors, there was just herself, Rose.

Yes, she remembered the names of the folks who had worked for Miss Carswell, at least the ones that had been here when Miss Carswell died. She spelled them out for me, all local folk, not hard to track them down. And some of them might tell me stories about Miss Carswell that I could use in my magazine article.

No, she and Joe had never had any children, although Joe's nephew Carter — a real smart boy, loved to read books — always came up from Charlotte every so often. Miss Carswell had paid Carter to unload book boxes for her and Joe paid him to help build shelves, because every time a box of books came in, Miss Carswell needed more shelves, which is how all those rooms got filled up with books. Yes, Carter still visited. In fact, he'd spent Christmas with them. But he was in college now at Appalachian State, over at Boone, and busy with girls and books and studies and such like.

Did she herself ever help Miss Carswell with the books? She rolled her eyes at that, with a firm shake of her head. Miss Carswell was particular about things in her library. And anyway, Rose didn't have time.

Even when there'd been maids to help, her days had been full of chores. When she got back to the gatehouse at night, she had chores there, too.

And in the last year of her life, Miss Carswell had Miz Anderson — Margaret Anderson — up from Bethany to give her a hand with the books. Miz Anderson had a way with Miss Carswell, and after a while she pretty much ran the place, like.

Oh, and there was that fellow who owned the bookstore down in Bethany, the Open Book. Jed Conway, his name was. Mister Jed. He used to come here a lot, bringing books for Miss Carswell to look at and maybe buy. But Miss Carswell had a falling out with him a while back, and he hadn't shown his face since.

Since when? Since before Miss Carswell died. What had he and Miss Carswell fallen out about? Rose didn't know. It was a secret, and she didn't listen at doors.

Which reminded me of another question. I felt a little silly asking, but it was on my mind. "I understand that there's a secret room in the house. Have you ever been in it?"

"Never." She gave her head a violent shake. "Don't know where it is. Don't *want* to know."

"How do you know there *is* one?"

Her eyes shifted away from mine. "Miss Carswell said so and she was the boss. That's all I know."

"Well, if there's time while I'm here, maybe we can look for it. I'm sure you know this house better than anybody else. Would you help me search for it?"

"I reckon," she said slowly. "If I have to. But I don't think we'll find it."

No help there, and I was already skeptical. The secret room had probably been invented to add to the romance of the place. I changed the subject to something that didn't seem to require speculation.

"I understand that Miss Carswell took her own life."

"Yup. Her daddy's old revolver, which was his daddy's before him. Had it all planned out for a while, I reckon," Rose said darkly. "She didn't take to bein' sick or people havin' the care of her. She was independent that way." She lifted her chin. "But how I was raised, life and death is the good Lord's doin'. So I don't hold with them that says we got the right to die whenever we feel like it. There's lots of folks down in Bethany that agrees with me, too. If 'n they could, they'd run Miss Amelia's and Mr. Jed's bunch outta town."

I was about to ask who Miss Amelia was, but Rose was pushing back her chair and saying that she had to put another load in the washer. I had already filled several pages in my notebook, so I thanked her for her help and left her to get on with the laundry.

Back in the workroom/office, I looked at the list of library visitors that I had been given. Conway, the bookstore owner, was missing, as was Rose and Joe's young nephew, Carter.

Important? Maybe not. Dorothea had mentioned Conway only in passing. He hadn't visited Hemlock House since Dorothea's and Jenna's arrival — or if he had, his visits had been clandestine. Still, he belonged on the list. I also added the boy, reminding myself that the four thieves who stole the Audubon folios from the Transylvania University library were teens from well-off families who had convinced themselves that staging a heist and stealing a couple of million-dollar books would give them something to brag about when they were old and gray. Instead, all four were sentenced to seven-plus years in federal prison; when they appealed, they ended up with nine. The rare book community was delighted.

The bookstore owner was local, so I added

him near the top of the list. I was hoping I could see him today, along with Margaret Anderson and Carole Humphreys. Sheriff Rogers was on my list as well. I could probably use my cover story with him, if I was careful.

Dorothea had already gone down to Bethany to shop, but Jenna was at her computer, staring intently at the screen. "May I interrupt you?" I asked.

She turned around. "Yeah, sure. I'm glad to leave it for a minute, anyway. I was thinking about what a tough couple of years it's going to be for Elizabeth and feeling sorry for all the calamities she has to face. Did you know that both of her children died while she was working on the *Herbal*? William died in 1736, Blanche two years later."

I tried to imagine losing two young children in the space of two years and felt the sad weight of it. "How in the world did she get through that?" I asked softly.

"I've wondered that myself." Jenna's tone was matter-of-fact. "But raising kids was a whole different story back then. A woman might have a dozen pregnancies during her childbearing years, with maybe three or four miscarriages and eight or nine live births. She had to expect that three or even four of her children would die before they were fifteen. There was typhus, smallpox, tuberculosis — consumption, they called it. And the plague, of course, and fevers and measles and bellyaches. So much illness — and no penicillin or antibiotics."

"Except for the antibiotic herbs," I reminded. "Garlic, oregano, thyme. I suppose that's where Elizabeth's *Herbal* came in handy. The medicines you were growing in your garden were every bit as good as the medicines you bought from your neighborhood apothecary."

"They might be even better," Jenna replied. "You wouldn't have to worry that the thyme in your sore throat gargle had been adulterated with something else. Or that some untrained apprentice mistakenly sold you some poison hemlock seeds instead of the Queen Anne's lace seeds you paid for."

I nodded. Back in the day, every woman of childbearing age knew that the seeds of the plant we call Queen Anne's lace were the most effective morning-after contraceptive available. But they looked a lot like poison hemlock seeds, or the seeds of *Thapsia villosa,* deadly carrot. It would be easy — and it could be fatal — to mix them up.

"Poor Elizabeth," Jenna sighed. "There she was, working her heart out to free that rascally husband of hers, and she had to cope with the loss of both her children. It just breaks my heart, China. Life was so terribly fragile back then. You didn't know what was going to happen, one day to the next." She bit her lip. "Sorry. Getting off track here. You wanted to ask me something?"

"Yes. A couple of things. I'll need an address and phone number for Margaret Anderson, if you have it. And Rose was telling me about a guy named Conway. He owns a bookstore in Bethany. You know him?"

She rummaged in the drawer, found a card, and jotted down an address and phone number. "Margaret has been taking care of her mom. I think you can find her here." She handed me the card. "Jed's store is called the Open Book. It's on the main street that goes through town. It's quite nice, actually. He has a good section of historical fiction." She paused. "He used to help Sunny with her collection."

"I was wondering why he wasn't on your list."

Jenna raised a dark eyebrow. "Dorothea told me to include people who have visited the library since we came, so that's what I did. Sunny used to order through Jed and I understand that he was here pretty often.

179

But they had a disagreement and he stopped coming sometime before she died."

"Not a problem." I nodded at the computer monitor. "Could we have a look at the store's website?"

"Sure." She brought up a search bar, typed in "Bethany" and "Open Book," and there it was: "The Indie Bookshop for the Blue Ridge," open Monday through Thursday from noon to five, Friday noon to nine, and Saturday nine to five. The photos showed a bright, open shop with carefully arranged bookshelves topped with trailing green plants and colorful new-title posters, reading spaces with inviting chairs, even a small coffee bar. The webpage advertised a monthly book club, a Saturday afternoon story hour for kids, a poetry reading by a pair of local ladies, and a visit from an Asheville novelist. There was an indie bestseller list and links to the shop's newsletter, a tab for Appalachian topics (including mountain music and a long list of books about moonshine), a contact page, and even a photo of the owner, a man in his fifties with gingery hair, pink cheeks, a cherubic smile in a round face, and a yellow-and-green polka-dot bow tie. Jedidiah Conway.

"Is there an online catalogue?" I asked.

Jenna brought it up and we studied it.

There were several pages in a variety of categories, but the catalogue seemed to be focused on Appalachian titles. If Jed Conway was selling pilfered Hemlock House books or botanical prints, he wasn't doing it on the shop's webpages. At least, not out in plain sight.

But that would be dumb, wouldn't it? That would be like putting up a sign in your yard advertising the stuff you stole from your neighbor's garage sale. You would take it somewhere else to get rid of it. And you wouldn't sell it under your own name. You'd have a different storefront, or a different website. Or you'd sell your ill-gotten goods to somebody else who would sell it to *his* customers.

And anyway, I was getting ahead of myself. The thief — whoever he was, or she — wouldn't likely try to get rid of the ill-gotten goods through a local bookseller. Chances were that Conway would prove to be just what he seemed to be: the enterprising owner of an attractive indie bookstore who was supplementing his onsite customers with online shoppers. The name of the game today.

"I also wanted to ask you about Sheriff Rogers," I said. "I'm curious about the kind of investigation he's made — if he's made one at all. Would it be worth my time to talk to him?"

"It might," Jenna said thoughtfully. "He's not a bad guy. It's just that, well, books are a little outside his territory. If we were talking about a stolen horse or a pot of missing money or somebody making moonshine, I'm sure he'd round up the usual suspects pronto. As it is, I'm not sure he knows how to deal with something like the *Herbal*. Which is why he focused on Dorothea and me." She made a little face. "Dorothea is sensitive to that, I'm afraid. It's just another straw on top of the other difficulties — working with Mrs. Cousins and the board, I mean. They don't know the first thing about rare books or library collections. But they always have an opinion."

I could certainly understand that. I glanced at the clock. It was well past ten. "I'm going to drive down to Bethany and drop in on Conway at his shop," I said. "I'm not sure when I'll be back, though. I have several people to see in town. And after that, I thought I might drive up to Claudia Roth's parrot sanctuary. We have a parrot at home — Spock, his name is."

"Oh, really?" She brightened. "Well, in that case, you might stop at Sam's and get a bag or two of banana chips. Sam's is a diner on the road into town," she added, "just past the Hemlock Mountain Inn. Here. I'll show you." She brought up a Google map.

"Shouldn't be hard to find." I studied the map. "Banana chips?"

"Treats for Claudia's parrots. Some people think she's a little bit loony for spending her life taking care of those birds. And the way she treats them — as if they're her kids." Jenna shook her head. "But she's an expert on parrots. You gotta give her that, crazy or not."

"Parrot people are all probably a little nuts," I said. "Parrots tend to inspire obsession."

Jenna shook her head. "It's not just parrots. Claudia is one of those people who overshare."

"Overshare?"

"She lacks a filter. I mean, she just pops out with whatever's on her mind, without thinking about who she's talking to or how it might sound if it's repeated."

"I've known a few people like that," I said wryly. A lawyer will tell you that the most dangerous client is one who doesn't know when to keep his mouth shut. Conversely, somebody with no filter is a gift from the courthouse gods when he's on the other side's witness list. You don't need a can opener. Just pop the top and he — or she — opens up.

Jenna nodded. "It gets Claudia in trouble sometimes. If she thinks somebody's being an idiot, she won't mince any words when she tells him so. And she makes stuff up."

"You mean she lies?" *Lie* is a perfectly useful word. I don't know why people are so reluctant to use it.

She gave a half-chuckle. "Maybe. But you can't be sure. For instance, she says she's Sunny's sister. That's what she seems to believe, so is it a lie?" With a shrug, she added, "You can't trust everything she says. But you're never in the dark about what she *thinks.*"

"Sister?" I raised both eyebrows. "Really?" I was remembering what Dorothea had said about Claudia Roth having a "tangential relationship" to the Carswells. Not quite so tangential, if she and Sunny actually shared a parent or two.

"Who knows?" Jenna replied. "Rose told me once that Claudia's mother was a housemaid at Hemlock House in the time of Sunny's father, so it's possible. He's even supposed to have left Claudia an annuity, although that could be just the local gossip. She drops in to see us occasionally."

I frowned. "Drops in? She's not on the list."

"That's because she's never visited the library — at least, not while we've been here. She mostly comes to visit Rose, and they sit in the kitchen and gossip over tea. She doesn't give a flip about rare books. But she'll bore you to tears about parrots."

"Sounds innocent enough," I murmured. But still, even somebody who wasn't a book person might have some insights on the theft. Had the sheriff questioned Claudia Roth?

"If you want to see her parrot sanctuary," Jenna went on, "you have to make an appointment. I could call and let her know that you're a parrot person and you'd like to drop in. Maybe late this afternoon?"

"That would be great. When do you and Dorothea usually eat in the evening?"

"Oh, six or six-thirty. Rose is making a pot of chicken and slicks for supper. It keeps, so we can eat whenever you get back. Or if Dorothea doesn't want to wait, we can go ahead and you can have a bowl when you get here. It's actually better after it sits for a while."

"Chicken and *slicks*?"

"Our favorite mountain dish. Flat dumplings, sort of like fat noodles. Rose's version

185

is extra tasty. You'll see."

But I already had my mind on my trip to Bethany, where I aimed to talk to Jed Conway.

CHAPTER SIX

Many plants thrive in the understory ecosystem created by mature hemlocks — among them ginseng (*Panax quinquefolius*). William Byrd II (1674–1744), a Virginia planter and amateur naturalist who corresponded with Sir Hans Sloane, describes his personal experience of the plant in a letter quoted by Wyndham Blanton in his ***Medicine in Virginia in the Eighteenth Century,*** reproduced here from the Lucy Meriwether Lewis Marks Gallery website:

"As a help to bear Fatigue I us'd to chew a Root of Ginseng as I walk't along. This kept up my Spirits, and made me trip away as nimbly in my half Jack-Boots as younger men cou'd in their shoes. Its vertues are that it gives an uncommon Warmth and Vigour to the Blood, and frisks the Spirits beyond any other Cordial. It cheers the Heart . . . helps the

187

Memory . . . comforts the Stomach, and Strengthens the Bowels, preventing Colicks and Fluxes. In one Word, it will make a Man live a great while, and very well while he does live. And what is more, it will even make Old Age amiable by rending it lively, chearful, and good-humour'd. However 'tis of little use in the Feats of Love, as a great prince once found, who hearing of its invigorating Quality, sent as far as China for some of it, though his ladys could not boast of any Advantage thereby."

https://www.monticello.org/sites/library/exhibits/lucymarks/gallery/ginseng.html

When I'd driven up the mountain to Hemlock House the afternoon before, the sky was a leaden gray and a mist trailed eerily through the dark trees. When I set off down the mountain this morning, the gray had vanished and the world had been recreated and blessed by sunshine. The air was fresh and crisp, the sky was so blue it made your heart hurt, and the mountains rippled against the distant horizon like the folds of a green and purple blanket.

But the switchbacks weren't any easier going down than they were going up, and I was glad that the brakes on my rental car were working. I breathed a sigh of relief when the narrow road delivered me safely to the foot of the ridge and more or less straightened out for its run along the frothy white river, which seemed as anxious to get downhill as I was. I buzzed the car windows down, loving the swift glimpses of the river's tumbling waters, the spiraling upward flight of a red-tailed hawk, the sharply resinous fragrance of fir and hemlock. Before I flew back to Texas, maybe I could find time to look for some ginseng. I could take photos to post on the Thyme and Seasons blog. Living in Texas, the only ginseng I saw came in the form of powder, capsules, or oil. I'd ask Claudia Roth — maybe she would know where to look.

But I could also see open corridors of downed trees and here and there the gaunt gray skeletons of dead hemlocks, victims of the hemlock woolly adelgid. I had read about this destructive aphid-like insect, which was accidentally imported into the United States from Japan in the late 1940s and has been sucking the sap out of hemlocks ever since. The environmentally safest chemical control is the same stuff you use to get rid of the aphids on your roses: a spray of insecticidal soap mixed with horticultural oil. As a biological control, there's the black lady beetle, also a Japanese import, that finds the adelgids especially tasty. But the situation is dire, for more than 90 percent of the eastern hemlocks in North America are infested. The beetles can't eat fast enough, and spraying a whole forest is a daunting (and expensive) task.

I tugged myself away from the sad thought that the hemlocks might be gone from these mountains in another decade and focused instead on what I intended to do in Bethany. Before I left Hemlock House, I had telephoned Carole Humphreys, who — as a board member and frequent volunteer — was on my list of folks to see today. You wouldn't think a board member would steal from the library she was responsible for, but stranger things have happened. I was to meet her at her shop, Blue Ridge Crafts and Antiques Gallery, at the corner of Main and Cypress, around one o'clock.

I had also done a quick check on the internet. Blue Ridge Crafts and Antiques Gallery proved to be an indoor mini-mall featuring several dozen craft vendors. According to its website, the gallery offered a variety of local arts and crafts, vintage wearables and collectibles, and antiques. One vendor even offered framed botanical prints, which caught my attention. I made a mental note to look for it when I got to the gallery, although I was pretty sure that a thief wouldn't try to sell locally stolen wares under the noses of the local gendarmerie. That would be tempting fate.

And I had no reason to suspect that Carole Humphreys had anything to do with the theft of *A Curious Herbal.* She was probably just a helpful, good-hearted member of the foundation's board, with a little extra free time that she generously donated to help sort out Miss Carswell's library.

Or she might be something else altogether.

Margaret Anderson, Miss Carswell's friend and helper, also lived in Bethany. She was included in the list because she had stayed on at Hemlock House after Miss Carswell died and had still been working there when Dorothea took over. She would have had plenty of opportunity to rummage through the shelves and take whatever she liked. Which didn't necessarily mean she had done that, of course. Or that she came back one weekend when the house was empty and made off with the *Herbal.*

But at the Anderson house, all I got was an answering machine. Instead of leaving a message, I clicked off. I'd try again in a couple of hours. In the meantime, I would talk to Jed Conway and Carole Humphreys and see if I could get an update on the case from the sheriff.

It was eleven-thirty by the time I got to town and I wasn't sure when I'd have time for lunch. So after I passed the Hemlock Mountain Inn, I pulled in at Sam's — the diner that Jenna had mentioned. In a few minutes I was enjoying a grilled cheese sandwich and a glass of iced tea, while the radio behind the counter poured out a toe-tapping rendition of "Foggy Mountain Breakdown." Good old mountain music.

When I finished the sandwich, I browsed the snack racks and picked up a couple of bags of the banana chips Jenna had mentioned. As I paid my tab at the cash register, I caught just the tail end of the local weather forecast. The last word I heard was "snow."

"No kidding? Snow?" I smiled at the blond, fresh-faced young woman sitting on a stool behind the register. "I'm from the Texas Hill Country. Snow would be a real treat for me."

The girl shrugged. "I'm not just real crazy about snow so late in the season." She got off her stool, leaned across the counter, and frowned down at my leather sandals. "If you're from Texas, how come you're not wearing cowboy boots?"

I might have told her that I don't wear my

cow*girl* boots when I fly because my feet sometimes swell and there's nothing worse than cramped toes in your cowgirl boots. But that seemed like too much information, so I handed her the money for my lunch and the chips.

As she gave me my change, she chirped, "Going to see the parrots, huh?"

"Actually, yes," I said, surprised. "I guess you know about the sanctuary?"

"All I know is that something up there is eating banana chips by the bushel," she said, and retired to her stool.

It was almost noon by the time I drove down Bethany's Main Street, but there was no noon-hour rush traffic. There were also no traffic lights and only a few pedestrians: an elderly lady with a two-wheeled cart filled with grocery sacks, a harried-looking mom with a pair of babies in a twin stroller, and a shaggy brown dog trotting purposefully on his way to a very important appointment.

There was also a clutch of cars and trucks around the courthouse square, which was centered by a white-painted neoclassical courthouse. The building's projecting front porticoes were supported by four stately Ionic columns, generally supposed to represent the reliability, durability, and stability

193

of the law — pretty much a cultural fiction, in my experience. The law is what happens inside the courtroom and in the judges' chambers, and it isn't always what you expect. It varies from trial to trial and judge to judge and depends more than you'd like on who the plaintiff and the defendant are.

Across the street from the courthouse, there were a couple of pickup trucks parked in front of a mom-and-pop grocery store. That's where I saw a gray Dodge minivan with a green Hemlock House decal on the rear window and remembered that Dorothea said she was driving to town to go shopping. Down the block, there were no cars in front of the Open Book, although the sign on the front door (above *Jedidiah Conway, Prop.,* in Old English letters) declared that the store was indeed open. I parked and got out.

I love bookshops, especially small indie shops, each as individual as its owner and as distinctive as its local community. The front window of this one artfully displayed a dozen regional titles, along with framed posters of mountain landscapes, mountain rivers, and mountain forests.

I lingered, thinking I would like to read about the Appalachians while I was here. There was an anthology entitled *Nature Writ-*

ing from *Western North Carolina and the Smoky Mountains,* a book called *Appalachia: A History,* by John Williams, a couple of books on hiking and fly fishing, and Phyllis Light's fine book, *Southern Folk Medicine: Healing Traditions from the Appalachian Fields and Forests.* There was also a book of photographs called *Twilight of the Hemlocks and Beeches,* by nature photographer Tim Palmer. Beside it was a large booklet called *Poison Plants of the Blue Ridge,* open to a dramatic color photograph of a hemlock plant in full bloom — the *bad* hemlock, the poisonous plant that Socrates had used to commit suicide. Across the open page was a generous scattering of small brown hemlock cones and some seeds that looked like they might be poison hemlock. Clever, I thought, to put the two hemlocks together for the display, although maybe not so clever to sprinkle those seeds around.

The shop was quiet and smelled of new books, that delicious blend of paper, ink, and bindings. On my right, the wall was filled, floor to ceiling, with regional titles. On the left was a similar wall of bestsellers. Also on the left, the sales counter was angled across the corner, at the far end of the display window. In the middle of the shop, on either side of a narrow center aisle, were shelves of romances, science fiction, mysteries (my favorite), nonfiction, biographies, reference books, and such, all set at angles to the center aisle. At the back was a section of used books. The Open Book was larger and more prosperous than you might expect for a small town in the mountains. A ready supply of summer tourists, maybe? Strong sales from that online catalogue? Likely both.

Standing here, surrounded by books, the idea that Mr. Conway could also be a rare book dealer seemed more plausible, and with that came another question. He might be able to tell me how and when Sunny Carswell had acquired the *Herbal.* Had he been involved with the acquisition? Had he arranged it?

I looked around, but there was no one at the sales counter, and nobody browsing any of the shelves. Was I the first customer of the afternoon? I stepped to the counter, looking for a bell I could ring. No bell. Well, okay. I would wait.

And while I waited, I could browse. On the counter, I saw a copy of Sharyn Mc-Crumb's *The Song Catcher.* I can get lost in McCrumb's evocative prose, and I hadn't read this novel about Appalachian music for . . . oh, a dozen years. It was one of her earliest. Maybe this was what I should buy and reread.

But as I reached for it, I happened to notice that the computer monitor at my elbow was displaying an online bookstore simply called Socrates.com. On the screen: a thumbnail image gallery of antique books and botanical prints. Two of those prints, displayed side by side, were from Redouté's *Lilies* — one for sale at an eye-popping $2,660, the other at $3,220. Dorothea had said that eight plates were missing from Miss Carswell's copy of *Lilies*. Were the other six pages also for sale on this site?

I sucked in a breath, the questions coming hard and fast. Why was the Open Book's computer displaying this website? Who did Socrates. com belong to? Somebody here in Bethany? Those last two question I thought I could answer when I got a chance to do some research on the internet. But the others . . .

I turned the monitor toward me and leaned forward for a better look. But that didn't help much. The image I was looking at was tiny. I'd have to enlarge it to be sure — and the computer keyboard and mouse were nowhere in sight. They must be under the counter.

Another breath. I'd been in the shop a

little bit more than a minute. Did I have another minute to step around the counter and grab the mouse? But even if I enlarged the image, I couldn't be sure about its source. The Blackwell prints were all over the internet. I wasn't going to prove a thing — and I might get caught. Wait until I got back to Hemlock House and ask Jenna to bring up the site?

"Hello," I called innocently, trying again to see if I was really alone. "Anybody, hello!"

I waited, listening for an answer. What I heard was something else. A moan, low but distinct, from somewhere near the back of the store.

The skin across my shoulders prickled. I dropped the book and took the center aisle toward the back, moving fast. The man was facedown on the floor behind the farthest bookcase at the rear of the store, one arm over his head, the other flung out to one side. He was wearing a white long-sleeved dress shirt, no jacket, and there was a neat round hole in his back, just one, a couple of inches below his collarbone. Blood was welling out of it, staining his shirt and soaking into the carpet beneath him.

I knelt beside him and pressed two fingers against the side of his neck, above what I could see was a red polka-dot bow tie. There was a pulse, faint and irregular. He took a breath, then another, both very faint.

"Hang on, Mr. Conway," I said urgently and reached for my cell phone.

The 9-1-1 operator was quick and crisp and when I said that the shooting victim was in the bookstore, she said, "They'll be there in three minutes, hon. They're right around the corner." And then, to remind me of my civic duty, she added, "Now, don't you go nowhere. You just stay right there, you hear? The chief'll be wantin' to talk to you."

"Yes, ma'am," I said. My heart was hammering. I was trembling. "Please hurry. I don't know if he's going to make it."

But as I clicked off, I could already hear a siren burp and rise to a wail, then another. Help was coming. I bent down, close to the man's face, which was turned toward me. His eyes were open and staring, unfocused. His skin was as white as bleached paper.

I put my hand over his, holding it tightly. Delicate hands, long fingers. Nails clean and nicely manicured, one gold ring, a college class ring. The hands of a man who handled books for a living, worked on the computer, met the public. I squeezed, but the fingers were unresponsive.

"Three minutes," I told him. "They're on

199

their way. Just hang on."

The seconds seemed to stretch into minutes, then hours, measured by the man's thin, reedy breaths. Bird breaths, sparrow breaths. His eyelids fluttered. His lips began to move. He opened his eyes and seemed to focus but only halfway and without any real recognition. Then he lost it again and his eyelids drifted closed. Outside the siren grew louder.

"Hang in there," I repeated, even though I wasn't sure he could hear me. "Stay with me. Jed. Don't give up."

And then his fingers moved in mine and he made a sound — was it a word? I couldn't quite hear. Was he trying to tell me something? I bent closer, and asked the question any cop would ask, or any lawyer.

"Did you see the person who did this? Do you know who shot you?"

He didn't even try to open his eyes. Instead, he seemed to reach down inside himself to pull up strength, or maybe he was just trying to get some breath behind the sounds so they could be heard.

"B . . . b . . . black," he whispered faintly. He grimaced. Bubbles of blood and spittle formed on his lips. A brighter, thicker blood was running out of the corner of his mouth.

Outside, the siren got louder, then cut off

suddenly in front of the store. Somebody shouted. A horn blared. Doors slammed.

His fingers suddenly flexed in mine and he pulled the word out of somewhere deep inside himself. Two syllables. "Black . . . well."

I stared at him, stunned. *Blackwell.* That's what I heard — but maybe I hadn't heard it right. Was that what he had said? If so, was it a confession or an accusation? Which?

But I didn't have time to reflect on this. Things were happening, lots of things, different things, all at once and fast. Another siren on the street out front. Vehicle doors slamming. The bell at the front of the shop jangling. Male voices, a female voice.

"Medic. Medic here! Where are you?"

"Back of the shop," I called, scrambling to my feet.

A pair of emergency medical technicians wearing navy-blue jumpsuits and carrying kit bags appeared around the bookshelf. I ducked back fast, getting out of their way. Deftly, they rolled Conway over. Yes, it was him, no mistake — the same round face and gingery hair I had seen in the online photograph, the same signature bow tie, the front of his white shirt soaked in blood from an exit wound. One of the med techs cut his shirt open and worked to stop the bleeding while the other spoke urgently into a shoulder mike. A moment later, a third tech appeared at a run, pushing a gurney.

The three men were well-trained and professional, quick and efficient. I didn't have a stopwatch on them, but I know it didn't take much more than a minute, ninety seconds at the outside. They heaved Conway onto the gurney, strapped him in, started an IV, and disappeared around the bookshelf — rushing him, I supposed, out to the waiting ambulance. If he made it, the credit belonged to them.

If. I didn't think his chances were good. He was ghostly white and he'd left a lot of fresh red blood in that puddle soaking into the carpet. What he'd whispered had been just a thin thread of breath with a couple of fragile syllables hanging from it — so fragile they might have been my imagination.

Black . . . well. Blackwell.

I have never cared very much for coincidences. It's been my experience that ninety-nine percent of real events have real causes and that if you look hard enough, you'll find the causes right where they're supposed to be, hiding in plain sight. It was difficult for me to believe that Jedidiah Conway just happened to have been shot by a random burglar whose name just happened to sound like Blackwell.

And I didn't really believe that I was making up the name I thought I'd heard. The shooting was somehow connected to the theft of Blackwell's *Herbal.* Conway hadn't wanted to die without passing that information along to somebody, anybody — even if they wouldn't know what to do with it.

But did he know that he was passing it along to *me*? Did he know who I was and what I was doing there? I didn't think that was likely. I had learned about him just that morning and he didn't know me from Eve. So the only coincidence in this spider's web of intersecting incidents was my happenstance blundering into the store just after Conway had been shot. Had the shooter made off with the *Herbal*? Had he —

But I didn't have time to dig any deeper, for another man had just stepped around the bookshelf. He was neatly uniformed: polished brown boots, dark brown pants, crisply pressed tan shirt with shoulder epaulets and stripes on the long sleeves, a full gear belt with a prominent sidearm on his right hip, and a police chief's gold shield on the left shirt pocket, above the name badge: Chief Jeremy Curtis.

"And you are — ?" Curtis asked. He was in his late thirties, early forties, dark hair, a jagged scar through his right eyebrow, an open, intelligent face, an attractive face. His eyes — a cop's careful eyes — were searching me, taking notes.

"I'm the person who found him and called 9-1-1." I fished in my bag for my driver's license and one of my minimalist business cards (name, email address, and cell phone number) and produced them for Curtis. He studied both for so long that I thought he must be looking for a secret code.

"Texas," he said at last, handing the license back and pocketing the card. "You're a far piece from home. Got business with the bookstore, or just browsing?" His voice was low and slow and deeply baritone, with a resonant mountain twang.

I gave him my two-sentence cover story. "I'm writing an article about Miss Sunny Carswell. I'm staying up at Hemlock House, and it was suggested that I might want to talk to Mr. Conway." I added a third sentence for good measure. "I understand that he did some book business with Miss Carswell."

I hate lying to cops. It can get you into tricky situations. About seventy percent of what I had just said was true, but I was realizing that (having just told this story to a police officer) I might have to actually write the article. Which I could, of course. Sunny Carswell's botanical library would make a nice piece for my column in the *Pecan Springs Enterprise* and for my Thyme and Seasons blog. And writing it would square my conscience.

"Did you see anybody when you came into the store?" Curtis asked. There was a muscle working at the corner of his jaw, and I wondered how many Bethany shopkeepers got shot during the year. Not many, I'd guess.

"No. There was no one up front when I came in. I looked around, then called out. There wasn't any answer, so I picked up a book and leafed through it for a couple of minutes while I waited." I didn't need to mention Socrates.com. What I had glimpsed on the computer monitor wouldn't mean anything to him. "After a minute or two, I called out, thinking that somebody must be around. That's when I heard him moan and came back here and found him. There." I pointed to the red bloodstain, already turning dark, in the carpet.

The chief was regarding me intently. "Hear anything? See anything else?"

I shook my head.

"Did anyone see you?" Curtis asked. "Anyone who might have noticed when you came into the shop? Somebody on the street, maybe?"

I didn't have to be F. Lee Bailey to see where he was going with this, and I narrowed my eyes. He was thinking that *I* was a pretty good suspect, first on the scene, no other witnesses. Well, I wasn't going to let him go very far down that road.

"Nobody saw me," I said. "But I would be glad to submit to a search. And a gunshot residue test, too, if that will make you feel better." I held out my hands. "If you're going to do that, please bag me."

Actually, I *wouldn't* be glad to submit to GSR testing, and if the chief intended to do that I wasn't climbing into a cop car without protection against contamination. Delicate gunshot residue particles can be transferred by contact, abrasion, even air movement. If I got into the back seat of a cop car or visited a police station, I could pick up residue and test positive. The FBI no longer conducts GSR tests for this reason (among others), but it is still a widely accepted evidence collection procedure. I figured it would be smart to anticipate a possible request.

"Oh, yeah?" He arched one suspicious brown eyebrow. "You know about GSR?"

"I do." I looked him straight in the eye.

206

"My husband is a former homicide detective. Retired."

No lie this time. Of course, I could also have said that as a criminal defense attorney (still true, because I pay my $235 annual dues to the State Bar of Texas) I had learned about the unreliability of the GSR test firsthand so to speak. However, as an attorney, I was also the chief's natural adversary. As the wife of a cop, even an ex-cop, we were colleagues, both on the same team. My statement, sub rosa, might also have conveyed a mild threat: *Don't mess with me, fella. I am a cop's wife, and my cop looks out for me.*

"Oh, yeah?" Curtis visibly relaxed. "Where?"

"Houston." I pulled down my mouth. "His name is McQuaid. Mike McQuaid." In case he took it into his head to check it out. "These days, he has his own PI firm — *not* in Houston."

The chief's tone was friendly now, even sympathetic. "I've been thinking about doing something like that. Thing is, there's not much business in a small town like this, only skip tracing, process service, stuff like that. I'd have to move over to Asheville or even —"

He stopped and let it go, smiling slightly.

207

"Don't reckon we'll need to do a search, Ms. Bayles. Or a GSR." He glanced at the blood puddle on the floor. "Good thing for you that you didn't get back here while the shooter was still on the scene. So the first you knew anything about this was when you stumbled over the victim?"

I nodded. "I wouldn't have come back here if I hadn't heard him moan."

The chief was silently checking things out, looking around at the floor, the shelves, the door, back at me. He wasn't missing much. "Did Conway say anything?" he asked. "Anything at all?"

And there it was.

I took a breath. I really, *really* hate lying to the cops. I had already done it once, not two minutes ago. But sometimes prevarication is required. And Conway's voice had been so bubbly with blood and spittle that I couldn't be absolutely sure of what I heard. The *Herbal* was on my mind, so it was entirely possible that I imagined it. Or that I'd made it up. Maybe he had said nothing at all. In which case, there was no sense in cluttering up the police investigation. Any investigator will tell you that no information is preferable to false information, which sends them down blind alleys and into dead-end searches.

And so I found myself doing it again.

"Nothing," I lied earnestly. "Mr. Conway is lucky that your guys got here so fast. I'm not sure how much longer he could have held out."

"Yeah." Curtis accepted my lie. "And lucky for him you came into the store when you did. He didn't look any too good when the guys wheeled him out. But the hospital is only five, six minutes away. Maybe his luck will hold." He reached for his cell phone. "Guess I oughta tell somebody to get in touch with his sister."

But instead of doing that, he glanced at me. "How long you fixin' to stay up there at Hemlock House?"

"Through the end of the week. I'm planning to talk to a couple of the Carswell foundation board members here in town. Carole Humphreys, for one."

His mouth tightened and he grunted.

I waited a beat. When he didn't explain, I went on. "And somebody else, Anderson, I think her name is. She used to work for Miss Carswell."

"Yeah. Margaret Anderson. Writes a literary column for the local paper. A blog, too." He pursed his lips. "I s'pose you heard about the missing book?"

I put on a blank expression. "Missing book?"

Did he look relieved? "Never mind. Just some little problem they had at the Hemlock House recently." He gave me a lopsided smile. "Before you head back up the mountain, I'd appreciate it if you'd stop in at the station and leave your statement. Okay? Won't take but a few minutes."

"Glad to," I said.

The bell over the front door jangled again, and a male voice called "Yo, Chief? You here, Curtis?"

Curtis raised his voice "In the back, Frazier." He reached into his shirt pocket, fished out a card and handed it to me. "If you think of something I need to hear, you phone me. Day or night. Got that?"

"Yes sir," I said. "Got that."

It was nice to know we were on the same team. At least for now.

CHAPTER SEVEN

Down through the years the May apple (*Podophyllum peltatum*) has had many common names, including wild jalap, hog apple, ground lemon, Indian apple, [and] raccoon berry . . . The medicinal dosage of podophyllin is very small and overdoses can kill, so do not eat the roots or foliage of the May apple (just as you should never eat the sprouts of the potato). The Penobscot Indians used the crushed roots of the May apple as a poultice for the removal of warts and the Menominee tribe considered the stems and foliage of the plant to be a good pesticide. They boiled those parts of the May apple in water and then applied the cooled liquid to their potato patches to repel the insects that attacked them.

Freddä Burton
"The Mighty May Apple"
Mother Earth News, July/August 1977

As I hesitated on the sidewalk, I looked first to my right, toward the grocery store where I had seen the Hemlock House minivan. The parking space was empty.

Then I looked to my left and saw Blue Ridge Crafts and Antiques Gallery, catty-cornered across the street at the end of the block. A woman was standing in the open doorway, watching the gaggle of cop cars and officers in front of the bookstore. After a moment, she went inside, closing the door behind her.

Carole Humphreys? I checked the time on my phone. Almost one o'clock, and she was expecting me. There was nothing more for me to do here, and no reason to follow the ambulance to the hospital. If Dorothea was driving the minivan, she had gone. Time to get on with it.

Humphreys' shop was located in an attractive old red brick rounded-corner building, with blue awnings over the display windows on either side of the blue double doors, one window featuring colorful quilts, the other handcrafted pottery and baskets. The sign on the door said closed, but I pushed and it opened.

When I stepped inside, I saw that somebody — Carole, I supposed — had invested plenty of money and time and creative energy making the old place into an attractive mini-mall habitat for Appalachian artists, crafters, and collectors of antiques, vintage wearables, and bric-a-brac. The brick walls were hung with a patchwork montage of colorful quilts, handwoven rugs, and various kinds of wall art. The large floor space was divided into corridors of booths and mini-booths, each its own little independent shop, creatively arranged, decorated, and lit. Traditional mountain music — a dulcimer playing the old hymn, "I'll Fly Away" — filled the air, which was sweetened with the scent of lavender.

The woman I had seen in the doorway was behind the counter, studying something on a shelf. She turned as she heard the door open. She was tall, with a graceful, willowy figure, her blond hair piled on top of her head in a messy do so that the curls came down around her ears and neck. She might have been forty, but she had a young face — and the air of a woman who knew who she was and felt good about it. She wore jeans, a green sweater, and a denim bib apron embroidered with "Blue Ridge Crafts & Antiques Gallery."

"I'm China Bayles," I said. "You're Carole Humphreys? We have an appointment at one."

As if I hadn't spoken, she said, very fast, "You were at the bookstore. What's going on over there? I heard the sirens and saw the chief's car and the ambulance and the gurney coming out of the store, but I couldn't see who was on it. Was it a customer?" Her voice thinned. "It wasn't *Jed,* was it?"

I paused. "Mr. Conway is a friend of yours?"

"We're in the Chamber together. We went to school together. We —" She looked away, then back again. "He's not sick, is he? His sister said something about an ulcer . . ."

"He was shot," I said bluntly, and watched her eyes widen, her jaw go slack. "I'm the one who found him."

"Shot?" she whispered. "But who would shoot Jed? Why?" Her voice registered shock and disbelief. "I'll bet it's that business with those Hemlock people. I told him it wasn't smart to do what he did. Kevin Maxwell —"

She bit off the rest of her sentence. "Jed's going to be okay, isn't he?"

Hemlock people? She must be talking about Dorothea and Jenna, but what "business"? And who was Kevin Maxwell? But I could come back to those questions later. There was something more important.

214

"I don't know if he'll be okay," I said. I wasn't going to make this easy or pretty. I had no idea whether Carole Humphreys had anything to do with what had happened to Conway, but I wanted to see her reaction to the news. "He was pretty close to dead when I found him. He was shot in the back."

"Shot in the —" she whispered, and her hand went to her mouth. Her consternation seemed genuine. "Oh, my lord, that's so *awful*. His sister will be wild! Has anybody called Kaye?"

"I think the chief was going to get somebody to call her. Is she a friend of yours?"

"We're all friends. Bethany is a small town. Everybody knows everything about everybody else." She straightened her shoulders. "Even when we don't want to."

Her last few words were tart, but I understood. Pecan Springs is a small town, too. Sometimes we know things about other people that we'd rather not — and vice versa. What did she know about Conway, I wondered. And what was the "business" with the people at Hemlock House? Did it have to do with books? With the Blackwell *Herbal*?

Carole closed her eyes and clasped her hands together as if she were saying a silent prayer for her friend — or simply trying to get hold of herself. When she opened her eyes again, her voice sounded steadier.

"I know that hospital. If I called there now, nobody would tell me anything. I'll wait until we're done." She took a breath and made a stab at sounding normal. "You're here because you want to talk to me about Miss Carswell and the foundation? For an article or something, I think you said."

"That's right." I reached for the notebook I'd stashed in my shoulder bag. "Is there somewhere we could talk? I know you want to see about your friend, so I promise not to take up too much of your time."

She came around the corner. "I was about to finish checking the vendor booths. We could talk while we walk, if you wouldn't mind following me around." When I agreed, she said, "But let me lock up the door. We're supposed to be closed." As she went to the door, she said, over her shoulder, "Does anybody know who shot Jed?"

"Not yet," I said. "It all happened before I got into the store. You might ask Chief Curtis, though. He looked to me like somebody who expects to get all the answers — fast." I meant it as a compliment, but that isn't how she took it.

"Oh, *him.*" Her tone was suddenly chilly.

"He wants all the answers, filled out and in triplicate, just so he can be better informed than anybody else." She locked the door and rattled the knob to be sure. "I suppose I should tell you that the chief is my ex."

That gave some useful context to her acidic comment about everybody knowing everything about everybody else. Cop spouses — even ex-spouses — are hardwired to the community grapevine. It's very difficult for a spouse not to know what a cop knows, which is not always a good thing. Believe me.

"I understand," I said. "I'm married to a cop. An ex-cop, that is."

"Poor you," she said. She was smiling at me as if we had just joined hands to make a great discovery. "You know exactly what I mean."

And there we were. Sisters under the skin. Funny how that works. Why, even the temperature in the room seemed a bit warmer than it had a few minutes before.

Carole started down an aisle with me at her heels, notebook in hand. After a moment, she paused in front of a booth called Glassworks, filled with stained glass art — wind chimes made of shaped fragments of colored glass, suncatchers to hang in a sunny window, lampshades that cast a colorful glow. There were several blown glass pieces, too. Bud vases, flowers, garden art.

"Lovely work," I said appreciatively.

"Husband and wife," Carole said, surveying it. "They have a studio just south of town. You should stop on your way back to Hemlock House." She picked up a vase, examining it. "I just can't get over what happened to Jed." She put the vase back on the shelf, shaking her head. "Domestic violence, yes. Somebody getting liquored up and shooting off a few rounds, yes. Bethany is an old mountain town, and this is moonshine territory. Stuff happens. But somebody shooting *Jed*? At noon on a weekday, in his shop? It's hard to get my mind around it." She glanced at me. "I'm sorry that you had to be the one who found him. It must be hard for you, too."

"It is," I said honestly, and opened my notebook, wanting to get to the reason for my visit. "About Miss Carswell. You knew her well?"

She seemed to take my question seriously. "I knew her as a book collector," she said, after a moment. "Other than that . . ." She let the sentence trail away. "I was surprised by her suicide, but I suppose I shouldn't have been. She was a very independent woman. Used to having her own way. I

218

guess I was more surprised by the way she did it. With that gun, I mean."

We moved on to another booth, this one full of artwork made from crocheted doilies. Vintage doilies framed for wall hangings. A doily draped over a dainty pink lampshade. Flowers made of doilies. Glass jars gaily clad in starched doilies. Paper doilies shaped into cones and stacked, so that they looked like lacy white trees. There was even a large crocheted doily rug in an arresting shade of apricot.

One of the paper-doily cones had fallen on the floor, and Carole picked it up and put it back on the shelf. "Sunny was a hermit and proud of it," she said without looking at me. "Who do you think is going to be interested in an article about her — especially now that she's dead?"

"Book collectors," I replied, making it up. "Librarians, gardeners. Donors to her foundation. And of course, people in North Carolina."

Carole moved on and I followed. She paused at a booth called The Village Herb Shop, where the rustic wood shelves were filled with dried herbs in jars, packaged culinary herbs and blends, a small selection of fragrance oils, and an interesting display called Native Appalachian Herbs. It featured several photographs of the May apple, a plant that thrives in the cool, damp eastern forests. I'll never find it growing around Pecan Springs. I've always wanted to know more about it.

But I didn't want us to be distracted. "Did you know Sunny very well?" I asked.

There was a silence. Being a sister under the skin apparently meant that Carole would give some serious thought to my questions — and maybe tell me more than she might have otherwise. But I wasn't betting that I would learn anything very revealing. I was wrong.

"Here's the thing," she said finally. "None of the Carswells — Sunny or her father or her grandfather — ever had much to do with Bethany. I mean, it was like our little town was beneath them, you know? Other wealthy people who live on the mountain usually show up for the Fourth of July fireworks or the August bluegrass weekends. They like to mingle with the masses. Act like they're one of the local folks."

Her voice sharpened. "But not the Carswells. Joe drove Sunny over to Asheville to do her doctoring. Sunny sent Rose down here to do the grocery shopping. And she always made Jed go up to Hemlock House to do their book business. She rarely showed her face here in town." At the mention of Jed, she winced but straightened her shoulders and went on with her story.

"So that's the way it was, you see. Folks down here know that she lived up there, but most have never seen her. Except for Jed and Margaret, of course, because of the books. That's how the two of them were connected. And Amelia too, although that was different. It didn't have anything to do with books." A small frown creased her forehead. "You'll definitely want to talk to Margaret." There was an acerbic edge to her voice. "I'm sure she'll want to talk to you."

"That would be Margaret Anderson?"

"Right. She's the one who took me up to Hemlock House for the first time."

"I've left a message for her." I made a note. "When was that? When you first met Miss Carswell, I mean."

"Maybe two years ago." Carole paused in front of a booth full of handwoven items, wall hangings, rugs, throws, shawls, a couple of vests. "Margaret said that Sunny had cancer and the doctors were telling her she didn't have long to live. So she was trying to figure out what to do with that ginormous book collection of hers. Her lawyers were telling her that she ought to set up a

221

foundation to manage the library and the house and the garden. They suggested that she ask a few local people to serve on the board, as well as some people she knew in Asheville and over in Raleigh. Margaret suggested my name and took me up there to meet her." She laughed shortly. "That was *before*. When Margaret and I were still friends."

I made a mental note, but her tone didn't invite me to ask what she meant. "Ms. Anderson blogs about books, I've heard. Is that right?"

Carole waved her hand. "And organizes literacy programs for kids. And was the president of Friends of the Library for several years, and runs a couple of book groups at Open Book and has a podcast and —" She pointed to a door in the back wall. "That's the break room. Let's get something to drink." Over her shoulder she added, "I'm sure she'll be glad to give you all the splendid details."

"She sounds like a busy lady," I said neutrally. I was remembering that Dorothea hadn't much liked Margaret, either. As we went into the break room, I asked, "Do you know why she thought you'd be a good fit for the foundation board?"

She opened a compact fridge. "Well, I

know what she *said.* It was because I worked in the Bethany Library before I opened this shop. And because I love books, which is certainly true. I do. All kinds of books — new books, old books, fiction, nonfiction. Real books and ebooks, too. I think books are the most wonderful things in the world." She held up a soft drink can. "Diet Coke?"

"Yes, please," I said, and she handed it to me.

"If I didn't have this place, I'd have a bookstore." She got her own drink and led us to a small table set against a wall under a calendar with a large photo of the Bethany courthouse. "I wonder what will happen to the Open Book if Jed . . ." She shook her head. "I don't want to think about it."

Others might have been a bit more suspicious, but I didn't believe that the chief's ex-wife's desire to own a bookstore would have driven her to murder the bookstore owner. Or maybe I saw it that way because we were sisters. Under the skin.

I opened my drink can. "You must have felt a kind of kinship with Miss Carswell. She was a book lover, too."

"Yes, but for somebody who had all that money, you'd think she'd be better organized." She popped the top of her soda can and sipped it thoughtfully. "I mean, if I didn't keep my accounts straight, and all the cash register receipts and the expenses and the taxes and stuff, I'd be out of business next week. You've got to be *organized.*"

"And that wasn't Miss Carswell's thing?" I had already heard this from Dorothea, but it was good to have it confirmed.

"Miss Carswell didn't give two hoots about that end of it. She left it up to Jed to keep track of what she bought, at least until they had their falling out. All she cared about was the books. Some she didn't like, and she'd just stick them on a shelf and forget about them. Others were like a new adventure for her. She couldn't stop talking about them. I guess that's what we had in common."

So Jed Conway may have kept some records of Miss Carswell's book purchases. Well, that would make sense, if he had been doing most of her buying and selling. If Dorothea knew this detail, she hadn't mentioned it. Why?

Carole sighed. "You know, there are a gazillion books up there at Hemlock House, some of them very rare and costly — and beautiful. Some of those botanical drawings are just incredible, when you look at them closely. But most are hidden away on the shelves in those damp, dark rooms where

224

nobody can find them." Her voice became earnest. "Really, now. What's the good of a beautiful book if nobody sees it? Don't you think it ought to be someplace where people can at least have a look at it? That's why I volunteered to help Dr. Harper with the cataloging. It gives me a chance to actually see and appreciate the books."

I raised an eyebrow, thinking that it also gave her a chance to decide which books to loot. "Did you tell Miss Carswell how you felt? About the books being hidden away, I mean."

"Well . . ." She dragged it out. "Not really. She wouldn't have wanted to hear my opinion. After all, I'm just one of those *Bethany* people." She gave the word a mocking emphasis.

"But after she died? After the foundation got underway? You were on the board. Did you tell the other board members how you felt?"

She shifted uncomfortably. "I'm not sure where you're going with this." She frowned. "What kind of an article are you writing?"

I was pushing her, and I backed off a little, giving her my standard dodge. "I'm just trying to understand the big picture." I picked up my can for a sip. "If you like, we can consider all of this deep background." I put

225

my drink down and gave her a reassuring smile. "In other words, I won't quote you." I wasn't exactly sure if that's what "deep background" meant, but she looked relieved.

"That's okay, then," she said. "I just don't want to cause any more trouble than I have already. On the board, I mean." She sounded frustrated. "I'm the one who rocks the boat, and Mrs. Cousins doesn't like me very much. I was even thinking of resigning. But Jed said I ought to stick it out, at least as long as Dr. Harper is there. That way, I'd know what's really going on up there."

"So you told the board what you thought?"

"Yes, after Miss Carswell died, when they were trying to figure out what to do with all those books. What kind of person they should hire as the library director, I mean." She bit her lip. "It was sticky, though. Because of Margaret."

"Oh? How was that?"

"Well, nothing against Margaret, of course, except that she wasn't qualified. Of course, *she* would never say that. She thought because she had been Miss Carswell's right-hand-girl for a few months, the board would just fall into line and hand her the director's job. But that's not what happened."

I looked up quickly. "No?"

"No. Jed helped. He put in his two cents and they listened because he's in the book business. Between the two of us, we persuaded the board to open a search for somebody who was qualified to actually work with the books — catalogue them, conserve them, figure out what should be done with them. We had several good candidates, I'm glad to say, but it was unanimous for Dr. Harper, who was exactly what we were looking for. That's why it's so unfortunate. The way they reacted when the *Herbal* disappeared. Since then . . ." She let her voice trail off.

I raised both eyebrows. "They think Dr. Harper was somehow at fault?"

"Well, what would *you* think?" she challenged. "After all, she had to know how much it was worth. And she'd probably have a pretty good idea of who might want to buy it. Not that *I* think she stole it," she added hastily. "Just sayin' what others think. Especially Mrs. Cousins. She's the board chair."

It was an interesting little aside, but I wanted to pick up on something else.

"How did Ms. Anderson feel when she

was passed over for Dr. Harper? Was she . . . disappointed?" It sounded as if Margaret's departure from Hemlock House wasn't quite as "amicable" as Dorothea thought it was. Or *said* it was, although I couldn't think why she would want to deliberately misrepresent what happened.

"Disappointed." Carole chuckled dryly. "That's one way to describe it. Or you might say that she was super ticked off. She blames Jed and me. She says we bad-mouthed her to the board." She stopped, remembering that we weren't *really* sisters, and backed up a little. "Which of course I never did. I mean, I might not be her biggest fan, but I wouldn't do a thing like that. And I'm sure Jed didn't either. He's a gentleman."

Ah. I thought of the other valuable items that were known to be missing — plates from Redouté's *Lilies* and from Royle's book on the Himalayas, as well as Beatrix Potter's fungi prints. And *A Curious Herbal,* of course. Altogether, we were looking at thefts that could add up to a couple of hundred thousand dollars, with not nearly the risk of walking into a bank and asking for the day's deposits.

And if Margaret Anderson was "super ticked off," as Carole said, she could easily be much more of a player than Dorothea imagined. She had been at Hemlock House from the time Miss Carswell died until Dorothea took charge — with no attention paid to security. She would have had ample opportunity to pilfer anything she felt like pilfering, from individual pages to whole books. Why didn't she take the *Herbal* until some months later? Maybe she had waited until the new director was in place, so Dorothea would be the prime suspect — as it seemed she was, at least in the sheriff's mind. That would net her two birds with one stone, so to speak. She would settle accounts with the board for letting her go while she got even with her rival for being better qualified. Plus, there was all that lovely money.

Well, then. Assuming that Anderson had done this, how would she have disposed of her ill-gotten goods? Did she have a book-seller connection in Asheville or Raleigh? Or maybe she didn't have to go that far. Maybe her fence was closer to home. Jed Conway, for instance. Or Socrates — or whoever owned Socrates.com. It might even be Carole.

Carole? Yes, Carole. In her website, I had seen that at least one vendor in her mini-mall offered framed botanical prints. Maybe that was Carole herself?

But we weren't there yet, and I didn't want to raise any suspicions. I took us back a step or two.

"And the rest of the board? Were they in favor of doing a search for a librarian? Or a curator or a director — whatever you were calling the position?"

"Director." Carole made a face. "To tell the truth, they weren't exactly keen on the idea. A search is a lot of work and the chances of finding the right person might not be very high. In fact, Mrs. Cousins would have been perfectly content to let Margaret stay on — less trouble, you know. Plus, they liked her. I have to say that she does her best to be likeable, even though —" She broke off.

I wanted to ask *even though what, please?* But I didn't want to remind her that we had wandered pretty far outside the topic I was supposed to be interested in.

"Anyway, Jed and I knew we had to find someone else." A smile flitted across her mouth. "His first choice would have been *him,* of course."

"Jed Conway wanted the job?"

Dorothea hadn't said anything about that. But then, she hadn't said much at all about Jed Conway. What I knew about him had come from Rose and Jenna. Was there a reason for Dorothea's silence on the subject? I shivered, remembering Conway's ghost-like whisper.

Black . . . well. Blackwell.

Was he trying to say that he'd been shot because of Blackwell's *Herbal*? And then I thought of something else. Hadn't Dorothea driven to Bethany today? Yes, she had. In fact, I had seen the Hemlock House minivan in front of the grocery store — just down the block from the Open Book. A sudden shiver ran through me. But Carole was going on and I filed the question away to deal with later.

"Well, of *course* he wanted the job. And with his book background and his acquaintance with the collection, I'm sure there would have been an argument in his favor. But everybody on the board knew that he and Miss Carswell had had a disagreement."

"What did they disagree about?"

My question was more blunt than it should have been. She looked away for a moment and when she looked back, she spoke hesitantly.

"Well, I don't suppose there's any harm in telling you. It's not really a secret. Jed thought that some of the books ought to be sold. He made a list — a long list, actually. And in a couple of cases — the *Herbal,* for one — he'd identified potential buyers."

Buyers? Now, that was interesting, especially in view of the fact that he had just been shot. "Do you know why?" I asked. "Why he thought they should be sold, I mean."

She gave a little shrug. "He said they ought to be held in collections where they could be properly conserved and displayed, rather than stuck away on a shelf. Sunny was offended by the suggestion that she wasn't taking proper care of her books. And the idea of selling *A Curious Herbal* . . . Well, as far as she was concerned, that was completely off the table." She frowned. "I really hope you're not going to —"

"I won't," I said reassuringly. "It's just helpful background for the paragraphs where I'll cover Dr. Harper." I moved on. "I hope you're satisfied with the job she's doing."

Her expression cleared. "Oh, yes. Dr. Harper is a real library person, with training and credentials. Just what we need. And Jenna — the graduate student who is working with her — is a perfect jewel." She raised an eyebrow. "Did she tell you she's writing a novel?"

"I've read the first three chapters," I said. "They're very good. It's a great beginning. Leaves me wondering what's going to happen next."

"Jenna and I have talked quite a bit about Elizabeth Blackwell," Carole said. "She probably knows more about the way the *Herbal* was compiled and published than anybody else in the world, so I hope she'll be able to publish her novel. The story is even more interesting when she gets into how Elizabeth Blackwell made enough money to bail her husband out of jail. And then there's the big mystery of what happened after that. Anybody who loves books will be interested — especially a writer. Like you."

I ducked my head, feeling a little guilty at my deception.

"Anyway," she went on in a practical tone, "both Dr. Harper and Jenna know what has to be done with the library and I'm behind them a hundred percent. If anybody can get that collection whipped into shape and catalogued and open to researchers, they're the ones. Or get the books moved to another library — a university library, for instance — where the collection would be much more accessible. That's *my* idea."

"Move the books?" I was surprised. "You

think that might happen?"

"Probably not." She sighed. "I mean, it's one of the board's options, if they could only agree. Half of them don't want Hemlock House open to the public, because that will cost too much. Not just completely cataloguing the books, of course, but we'd have to hire more staff and upgrade all the facilities, including parking. Plus, there's a lot of deferred maintenance on that ugly old house that has to be managed — a new roof, just as one example. And we'd probably have to close in the winter. That road can be treacherous when it snows. That old place is one huge bundle of liabilities."

She smiled grimly — a sisterly sort of grimness. I had the feeling that Carole would have said none of this if our comradeship had not been so opportunely established. And I could see the problem.

"Where the library is concerned, it's either, or?" I asked. "There's no middle ground?"

"There might be. Dr. Harper says we could digitize the best part of the collection and put it online, so people could read the books without coming to the library. Then we could keep a skeleton staff and just open the library to only a few visiting researchers who need access to the actual documents.

But digitizing would cost a lot of money. And the house would still need maintenance." She regarded me for a moment, her expression darkening. "Actually, I'm wondering why you're asking all these questions."

"I think it's important to have a balanced view of the situation, don't you?" I was making this up as I went along. "I mean, the Hemlock collection is an important one, and the board is facing a lot of challenges. I'd like to represent as many sides of the issue as I can. And a little more publicity for the Hemlock library — done in the right way, with a positive perspective — might encourage a few donors to take a closer look." I assumed a cautious expression. "I understand that the board has been concerned about the possibility of actually *losing* donors — when they became aware that the *Herbal* had been stolen, that is."

Carole cocked her head, frowning. "Dr. Harper told you about that?"

"Yes. As I said, I've known her for a while — we share a common interest in old herbals. When the Blackwell *Herbal* went missing, she told me she wanted to send a heads-up to rare book dealers and collectors so they could keep an eye out for it. But the board wouldn't let her."

She sighed. "Another of our disagreements. Some of the board members feel that the thefts make us look sloppy and unprofessional. I don't think they're going to move off that position." She shifted in her chair. "Are we done here? I really need to find out what's going on with Jed."

"I think we're done, thank you." I was paging through my notes. "Oh, hang on, here's something. You mentioned Kevin Maxwell. And Amelia somebody. Are they on the foundation board?"

"Amelia sells real estate," Carole said tartly. "She would love to be on the board, but she isn't."

"Her last name is —"

"Scott." She was impatient. "Amelia Scott. She and Jed are the cofounders of . . ." She looked away. "They used to be friends. That's all."

I frowned. *Cofounders of what? A readers' group? An arts program? A business enterprise?* I glanced down at my notebook again. "How about Maxwell? Kevin Maxwell?"

But I wasn't going to get any more out of Carole. She was looking up the hospital number on her phone.

I closed my notebook. "Thanks for taking the time to talk to me," I said. "I appreciate it." It had been an instructive conversation. It was beginning to seem that Margaret Anderson might know more than anybody else about the thefts at Hemlock House. And what did she know about the shooting of Jed Conway?

"Glad I could help," Carole said, but her mind was already on her call. A moment later, she had reached the hospital and was being put through to a nurses' station. A moment after that, she was saying, "Hi, this is Carole Humphreys. I'm calling about Jedidiah Conway. Can you tell me how he's doing?"

I watched her face. There was a moment's silence, then her shoulders relaxed a little and she closed her eyes in relief.

"Thank you," she said. "I'll check again later."

I didn't have to ask. Jed Conway was still alive, and his whispered syllables were — perhaps — no longer his last words. But they still trebled in my mind, an acoustic ghost.

Black . . . well. Blackwell. Was that what I had heard?

The conversation with Carole had been unexpectedly instructive. I was beginning to think that Margaret Anderson might know more than anybody else about the thefts at

Hemlock House. What might she know about the shooting of Jed Conway?

And there was yet another question. The Hemlock House minivan had been parked only a half-block away from the Open Book when Jed was shot. Where was Dorothea?

CHAPTER EIGHT

[Born in Athens c. 470,] Socrates was one of the most respected thinkers of the age, acting as a teacher and mentor to the equally famous Plato. When he was seventy years old, Socrates was sentenced to death by a jury of five hundred. [He chose execution by] a simple drink of hemlock, which was a revolutionary new manner of delivering death for Athenians. . . .

Hemlock had been used by ancient physicians as a remedy for ailments like joint pain and arthritis. Minuscule amounts were always used, since an overdose could result in paralysis of the entire body, including the lungs and heart. Hemlock belongs to the same plant family that includes carrots and parsnips, but it derives its deadly force from the fact that it contains eight piperidine alkaloids, which are compounds that can have a strong physical effect on the body. The two main alkaloids in hemlock are coniine and g-coniceine, and they are almost singularly responsible for its fatal results. . . .

The story of Socrates' death has long been an inspirational tale of a man who refused to abandon his principles and greeted death cheerfully.

"Hemlock, the Drug of Socrates"
http://bestdrugrehabilitation.com/articles/
hemlock-the-drug-of-socrates/

I wasn't going to talk with Margaret Anderson that afternoon.

I tried again to reach her on the phone, but with an irritating cheerfulness, the robotic voice repeated, regretfully, that Ms. Anderson was not available and advised me to leave a message.

Conceding defeat and now strongly motivated by what I had learned from Carole Humphreys, I offered a quick recap of my cover story and left my cell number. My call might put Anderson on her guard and give her time to come up with a set of alternative facts about the situation at Hemlock House. On the other hand, it might make her nervous, and nervous people sometimes say things they don't intend to say. I would drive by her house before I left town. At least I could get a look at where she lived.

But before I started my car, I sat for a moment, thinking about Dorothea. I called her cell phone number and when she came on the line, I said brightly, "Dorothea, are you still down here in Bethany? If you are, maybe we could get together for a quick cup of coffee."

"Sorry," she said. "I've just gotten back to Hemlock House." She paused. "Did you get to see Jed Conway?"

I hesitated. It sounded like she'd already driven off before the cops and the ambulance arrived, but I wanted to see her face when I told her the news. "I'll fill you in when I see you this evening," I said, and hung up.

Chief Curtis had told me to stop by the police station and make my witness statement. This was easier said than done, as it turned out.

There were two desks in the main reception area, one of them empty. I dutifully reported at the other, behind which sat a harassed young female officer, neat and trim in a crisply pressed tan uniform. She was doing her level best to field a barrage of incoming calls about the shooting at the Open Book. Jed Conway was obviously a popular member of the Bethany community. Word was getting around fast.

In a brief interval between calls, I managed to get the officer's attention long enough to tell her that I was the one who had found Mr. Conway and that I was there, at Chief Curtis' instruction, to leave my statement. Could somebody help me, please?

The phone rang again. "An officer will be with you in a few minutes," she said breathlessly. "Just have a seat."

Cops came and cops went, all of them in a hurry. After three or four had cruised into the reception area and cruised out again, I got out of my chair and accosted one.

"Excuse me. Chief Curtis told me to come here and make a statement about —"

"Sorry," he said brusquely. "Can't help. I'll see if I can find somebody. Have a seat."

Ten minutes later, tired of sitting and with plenty of other things on my to-do list, I took the matter into my own hands. On the empty desk was a typewriter, an old but absolutely gorgeous blue IBM Selectric, which you hardly ever see now that the world is completely computer-driven. I went to the desk, sat down, took a clean sheet of paper out of the top desk drawer, rolled it into the machine, and began to type.

The officer at the other desk glanced over at me, did a double-take, opened her mouth, and started to say something. But her phone rang again and she closed her mouth and rolled her eyes as she reached for it. I gave her a sympathetic smile and a quick thumbs-up to show her that I was on the level and had only the best intentions and kept on typing while more cops came and more cops went, paying me no never-mind. A woman at a typewriter. In a man's world, what's so unusual about that?

At the end of ten minutes, I was finished with my statement. I hadn't mentioned Conway's whispered word when I talked to the chief and I didn't mention it now — a lie by omission I hoped I wouldn't regret. I had not mentioned the Hemlock House minivan parked just down the street, either.

Otherwise, I was as truthful as I knew how to be. I included everything I could remember, except Socrates.com, which would have required a much longer explanation than I was able to offer at the moment. When I finished, I was left with only questions.

Who? Who had tried to kill Jed Conway? Why?

And why "Black . . . well"?

But there was nobody here who could answer these questions, and I didn't think

243

Chief Curtis had a clue.

I had said all I had to say. I rolled the page out of the machine, signed and dated it, and added my cell phone number. There was a copy machine on a shelf across the room, so I made a copy for myself. I took the original to the officer at the other desk, who was once again on the phone. I peeled a yellow sticky note from the dispenser on her desk, wrote FOR CHIEF CURTIS in block capitals on it, added a smiley face, and stuck it to the page.

"Have a good day," I said, waggled good-bye with my fingers, and left. I had two more errands in Bethany, and it was time I did them.

You can tell a lot about people by the house they live in.

The address that Jenna had given me for Margaret Anderson was on a tree-lined residential street in a well-kept and prosperous section of town, just off the ninth fairway of the local country club. The house was a substantial-looking white Southern Colonial with a trio of dormers stationed across the roof (the one in the middle was larger and positioned directly over the central entrance) and a matched pair of windows with white shutters balanced on either side of an impressive front door behind a lineup of symmetrical white columns across the front. Privet shrubs were pruned in geometric precision on either side of the walk that led out to the curb.

Through a screen of trees, I could see the country club's tennis courts and hear the *thunk thunk* of balls in play. There weren't many visible cars, but those I could see were of the Lexus, BMW, and Buick Regal varieties. The neighborhood and the Anderson house were upscale, orderly, traditional, and — obviously — politically conservative. Margaret's career as a columnist and book blogger either paid very well (which I seriously doubted) or she was married to a local doctor, lawyer, or merchant chief. I could envision her greeting me at the door — in her late forties, a little overweight but not too much, with frosted hair and wearing an expensive gray skirt and a pink twinset. Oh, and pearls, of course.

I was glad I had done the drive-by. It had given me an important glimpse into the life of Margaret Anderson.

My next errand turned out to be even more productive. On the main highway into town, I had spotted the Hemlock County sheriff's office, a red brick building next door to the larger community center. There were several sheriff's cars in the parking lot, which gave me heart. At least they weren't all out chasing Jed Conway's killer. If I was lucky, I might even get to talk to Sheriff Rogers. I had prepared a little twist in my cover story for just that possibility.

I was lucky. The uniformed deputy at the front desk nodded when I asked if Sheriff Rogers was available, took my name, and picked up the phone.

A few minutes later, notebook in hand, I was introducing myself to a heavyset, square-built man with a sheriff's badge pinned on his shirt. His gray hair was buzz cut. He had thick gray eyebrows, shrewd gray eyes in a leathery face, and a gray walrus moustache across his upper lip. He could have been Wilford Brimley's twin brother.

"I'm writing an article about Miss Carswell's library up at Hemlock House," I said, seating myself on the other side of his paper-littered desk and handing him one of my unrevealing business cards. "I intended to include some photos and several paragraphs about the Blackwell *Herbal,* but Dr. Harper told me that it was stolen several weeks ago. She says you're looking into the matter. I'm wondering if you could bring me up to date on the investigation. Off the record, of course, and just for background. I understand that the board still doesn't want any announcement of the theft."

Without looking at my card, the sheriff tossed it onto the general litter on his desk. "Oh, yeah — that rare book thing." He leaned back in his chair and gave me an appraising look. "Well, now, I'm just gonna level with you, Ms. Boils."

"Bayles," I said politely, not wanting us to get off on the wrong foot.

He picked up my card, peered at it, and tossed it down again. "Bayles. Old books is a little out of my line, you see, and there was nothin' up there at the scene that could give us much of a lead. But I'll tell you what we did, for what it's worth. We lifted some prints, which didn't do us much good. We did a search of the place and came up with zero, although that old hulk is so big, you could stable an elephant in there and nobody'd be any the wiser. Since the ladies on the foundation board nixed any announcement of the theft, we couldn't work on it from the fence end, way we'd do with a jewelry heist, say." He looked at me to see if I understood and added, "By which I mean the places where the thief might've tried to sell the book. As a consequence, we haven't done much of anything except wait for a lead. Sorry to say that nobody's come up with one. Or if they have, they haven't bothered to tell me."

I felt seriously lucky. This was a man who liked to talk, and I was hearing more detail about his investigation than I expected. Nothing new yet, but we were just getting started.

"I suppose you checked out all the people at Hemlock House," I said helpfully.

He blew out his breath, riffling his moustache. "Yes, especially since Miz Carswell was shot and killed up there not so long before."

Was shot? Wasn't she the shooter? I ventured, "That was officially ruled a suicide, I understand."

"Yep. Coroner kinda waffled about it for a while, but that was how he finally came down." He picked up a pencil and spun it around his thumb. His fingers were gnarly but surprisingly dexterous. "About the book, I had it figgered for an inside job from the get-go, which pretty much narrowed it down to Dr. Harper and her helper plus the hired help. So that's who I interviewed, which didn't turn up anything much, except to make Dr. Harper think I was gonna haul her off to jail."

"Did you come to any conclusion about her?"

"Nope." He eyed me. "Case is open, so she's still a possibility, same as that girl — Jenna, her name is. I also talked to some folks here in town who've been connected with that place up there. Humphreys, Anderson, Scott, Conway." He ticked them off on his fingers. "Even talked to that crazy parrot lady up the road from Hemlock House. Claudia Roth. Didn't get much out of her, but those parrots of hers, they're a sight to see. Real smart birds. Gotta watch 'em, though. They'll poop on your head."

Crazy parrot lady. The woman I was planning to see later this afternoon. I tilted my head. "Did you consider any of those people as possible suspects?" It was a nosy question, but since he was in a mood to talk . . .

"In my business, ever'body's a suspect 'til they ain't. Seemed to me that any of that bunch could've done it and got away with it, no problemo. Dang thing is worth a hunk of money, too." He pulled a cigar out of a breast pocket. "And that's where I am on this. You write what you feel like, Miz Biles, or whatever that board will let you. And if you got any bright ideas, I'll be glad to take 'em into consideration."

"I don't, actually," I said. The sheriff

249

seemed to have covered all the bases. "The fingerprints — did you find anything useful?"

He grunted. "Come up with some matches, if that's what you mean by useful. Dr. Harper's, the girl's, Miz Anderson's —"

"The girl's. Jenna's?"

He nodded. "And a couple more we couldn't identify."

"Miss Carswell's?" I hazarded.

"Prob'ly not. She's been dead for a good while now, and that book has been in and out of the display case pretty often since then. Not Conway's, neither. He said he hadn't been up there since before Miz Carswell died." He regarded his cigar hopefully, shot a glance at me, and thought better of it. He put it back in his pocket. "Best chance for recov'ry is to put the word out to book dealers down in Asheville and over in Raleigh, same as we'd do to pawnshops and known fences when we're dealing with stolen property. Prob'ly not much chance of it now, so long after the fact, but if you got any sway with the ladies on that board, you might tell 'em what I just told you."

There was a moment's silence. He was regarding me. "Speakin' of book dealers . . ."

"Yes," I said quietly.

250

"Yeah. Heard you was in the shop when it happened. And your man's retired from Houston PD."

News travels fast in a small town. But if I had wondered why the sheriff was so unusually informative, his remark about McQuaid gave me the answer. Sheriff Rogers, Chief Curtis, and I. We were all on the same team.

"I just came from the police station," I said, to encourage this perception. "I left a statement."

He grinned, showing one gold-capped tooth. "Typed it yerself, I heard. Even made a copy."

"Everybody was pretty busy. I didn't want to be a nuisance."

"Bad day at Black Rock. My deputies are all over at the bookstore, helping Curtis' boys. Ever'body's on the job. Nobody's got time to sit at a typewriter. You done good."

"Thank you," I said modestly. "Any word from the hospital on Mr. Conway's condition?"

"Critical is all they'll say." He pulled down his mouth. "Life-threatening."

I paused, wondering if I should, thinking I shouldn't, deciding to ask it anyway. "Any reason to think the shooting might be connected to the theft at Hemlock House?"

There was a long silence. He regarded me

narrowly. His voice was sharper when he said, "I don't have a reason to, not right now, no." He paused. "You?"

I shook my head. "Except for the fact that it was a book that was stolen, and Mr. Conway is a book dealer." I couldn't very well tell him what I hadn't told the chief: about a critically wounded man's whispered word and a website called Socrates.com that displayed what looked like prints stolen from Hemlock House.

"Well, there's a coinkidink for you," the sheriff agreed, and I smothered a smile. Cops don't believe in coincidences any more than lawyers do. Both are capable of building elaborate connect-the-dot theories to explain almost any imaginable connection.

He pushed his chair back, ready to stand up. We might be on the same team, but he had given me enough time. "I understand that you're from Texas, so maybe you don't pay attention. But if you're gonna be around the next couple of days, I'd advise you to keep an eye on the weather."

"The weather?" I was surprised.

"Yeah. You ain't heard about Virgil?"

I shook my head. "Who's Virgil?"

"That's the name the folks at the Weather Channel are giving to the big storm that's moving in. A humdinger, they're saying. Polar jet pushing down from the north, Pacific jet shoving in from the west, Gulf air riding up from the south on the rump of a big old low-pressure area." He used his hands to illustrate this complicated meteorological choreography. "Last time we had a setup similar to this was the blizzard of '93 — storm of the century. Middle of March. You heard of it?"

I shook my head again.

"Yeah. Well, that time, we got three-plus feet of snow dumped on us. Fourteen-foot drifts. We was better'n a week diggin' out. Where you're staying up there on the mountain, Miz Carswell lost her barn roof. Caved in from the weight of all that snow."

"Actually, I wouldn't mind seeing some snow," I said. "We don't get much of it where I'm from."

"You don't say." The sheriff eyed me ironically. "Now, ain't you got something better to do than stand around and talk to an old man?"

I was dismissed.

But I wasn't quite done here. On my way to the car, I paused in front of a community bulletin board plastered with flyers, notices, and advertisements. Belle's Quilting Bee Quilt Shop was opening its spring classes.

The Thursday night First Baptist choir welcomed all voices but was particularly looking for tenors, regardless of religious affiliation. Meals on Wheels needed volunteers with their own cars. The Hemlock Guild was holding a get-acquainted meetup tomorrow at the community center.

And there, right in front of me, was Amelia Scott's name. She was president of the local right-to-die organization, the Bethany Hemlock Guild, and Jed Conway was vice-president. At the bottom of the flyer, in capital letters: Urge Your State Legislators to Support Death with Dignity.

I didn't have to look back at my notebook for a reminder of what Carole Humphreys had said when I'd told her that Jed Conway had been shot. I remembered it word for word.

I'll bet it's that business with those Hemlock people. I had assumed that she was referring to Dorothea and Jenna, at the Hemlock House. But Carole had more likely been talking about the people of the Hemlock Guild.

I had been lucky again.

CHAPTER NINE

Herbs for Your Birds. Here are three herbs that parrot lovers should know:

- Ginger — planning an auto trip with your bird? If your parrot suffers from motion sickness, offer fresh thinly sliced ginger root or steep fresh ginger slices in a cup of hot water for tea and use it (cooled) to replace the water in the cage cup. Ginger is a time-tested remedy for nausea.
- Aloe vera (the "Band-aid plant") — promotes skin cell growth. It can treat cuts and bites, prevent infection, and ease itchy skin. Feather picking? Try spraying a mixture of aloe gel and water (one part gel to three parts water). And yes, your parrot can safely nibble your aloe plant, although too much may have a laxative effect.
- Chamomile — traditionally known as a soothing sleepy-time relaxant, chamo-

mile has been used for centuries to help relieve stress, calm restlessness, and ease minor stomach discomfort. Keep a supply of purchased teabags on hand. Add 1/4 cup of your regular-strength tea to 1 cup of warm water and share with your birds at bedtime.
"Herbs to Keep Your Bird Healthy"
https://susanalbert.com/herbs-for-your-bird/

The drive back up the mountain was easier than it had been the day before. I knew where I was going and what to expect of the twists and turns, more or less. I could keep my attention focused on the road instead of being distracted by the mountain landscape.

Now that the sheriff had alerted me to Virgil's coming, I thought it would be good to listen to a weather forecast and see just when the storm was due to arrive. I was still more than a little skeptical, because the sky was a cloudless blue, the spring air was mild, and the understory trees were flaunting their flirty green leaves against the darkness of the hemlocks. If snow was on the horizon, there was no sign of it yet. I punched the car's radio buttons, looking for a local station with a weather report.

But all I seemed to get was mountain

music — "Rambling Boy," "Handsome Molly," "Barbara Allen." And then, dolefully, a traditional ballad by a group of local musicians that called themselves the Mountain Songcatchers. I remembered it from the movie *O Brother Where Art Thou.* In a minor key and a capella, the song was so eerie it made me shiver.

Death, oh death,
How can it be
That I must come and go with thee
For death, oh death
How can it be
I'm unprepared
For eternity.

Now, I'm not somebody who looks here and there for omens — that's Ruby's department. But as I drove through a dark tunnel of hemlocks growing close to the road, the song seemed so ominous that I hurriedly turned the dial. All I could find was the national news out of Washington, though, and it was as dark and unnerving as the song lyrics. I was glad when my cell rang, in a holder on the console, and I turned the radio off.

"Just checking in," McQuaid said. "I'm headed back to Pecan Springs from San

257

Antonio. Where are you?"

"Driving up a mountain," I said, negotiating a hairpin curve to the left, with a hundred-foot drop-off on the downhill side. "A *steep* mountain. On a twisty road. Forest on one side, sheer cliff on the other and 'Death Oh Death' on the radio. A thrill a minute. How are you?"

"Fine. 'Death O Death' here too, actually. I'm risking life and limb on I-35." McQuaid likes to say that he had enough excitement with the Houston PD to last for two lifetimes, although I notice that he seems to relish the occasional dangerous investigation that walks into his PI firm. "You? Besides cliffs and trees and twisty roads, I mean."

"Does a shooting count?" I filled him in on my discovery in the Open Book.

He whistled. "Jeez, China, how do you *do* it? I let you out of my sight for a few hours and you're stumbling over dead bodies!" I imagined him rolling his eyes.

"This body wasn't dead," I said. "At least, last I heard." I followed with a quick rundown of my meetings with my two pals, the chief of police and the county sheriff, and Carole, my sister under the skin. "I'm hoping to see Margaret Anderson tomorrow, if we don't get snowed in. And there are the

Hemlock Guild people, too. I have to find out how to connect with them — and who to talk to." *Amelia Scott?*

"Snowed in?" McQuaid asked incredulously. "What snow? It's spring break already! We're in the eighties."

"It's spring break in Texas. Here in North Carolina, we're expecting Virgil."

"Who's Virgil?"

"A blizzard. The sheriff says he's the storm of the century, reincarnated."

"Huh," he grunted. "Sounds like you're living dangerously. Please tell me that you're staying out of the line of fire."

"Doing my level best." With a shiver, I changed the subject. "You've heard from Caitie?"

"Yeah. She and Spock are settled in for a weekend of ranch fun. Caitie says Spock has a crush on your mother's horse. She's teaching him to ride. And say "Hi-yo Silver, away!"

"Uh-oh," I said. "Next thing we know, Spock will be asking for his own horse."

"Brian is coming for supper tonight," McQuaid said. Brian is his son by his first wife, bad-penny Sally, who turns up every now and then and turns us all upside down. He's a student at the University of Texas. "I was thinking that I could stop for a pizza,"

259

McQuaid added. "Or . . ." He left the sentence dangling.

"Or there's a quart container of beef stew in the freezer," I offered. "And a loaf of sourdough bread. I think there's a tub of garlic butter in the fridge. Is he bringing Casey?" Casey is Brian's live-in girlfriend.

"Casey's moved out," McQuaid said quietly. "Lotta angst, I'm afraid. Which is probably why he's coming. Man-to-man about women. That, and his laundry. The washer at his place appears to be inop. I need to get up there and see if I can fix it."

"Oh, dear," I said, but not about the washing machine. Brian and Casey have been together for quite a few months now and I genuinely like her. She is smart, athletic, and beautiful. But she is also pre-med and competition tennis, and there isn't a lot of room in her life for a boyfriend. Still . . .

"Tell him not to give up just yet," I said. "She may reconsider."

"Love is hard on the young." McQuaid sighed. "I wouldn't be that age again for a million dollars." There was a moment's silence. "You'll be at the Hemlock House tonight?"

"That's the plan. I'm told we're having chicken and slicks for supper."

"Chicken and . . . sticks?"

260

"Slicks. Chicken stew with flat dumplings. Traditional Appalachian dish."

"Doesn't sound like it would go good with beer," McQuaid said. "Here's my off-ramp. Looks like I survived another drive through the death trap. Talk to you tonight." His voice became stern. "No more dead bodies. Hear?"

"Love you too," I said, and clicked off, glancing at the clock on my cell. Not quite four, and supper was a couple of hours away.

Plenty of time for parrots.

A hundred yards beyond the Carswell mansion, the road narrowed, made a hairpin left, and rose at an even steeper angle. I had to navigate several more switchbacks in the next mile or so before I saw the wooden sign: Hemlock Forest Parrot Sanctuary. Appointment only.

The sanctuary was located on the side of the mountain, well above the road and surrounded by forest. It took me a moment or two to figure out what I was looking at, for all I could see when I got out of the car (bags of banana chips in hand) was a screened enclosure that turned out to be an outdoor aviary. It was built on three sides of an open grassy square in front of a large A-frame house with a steep green metal

261

roof. A mini-jungle of bushes and small trees grew inside the enclosures, and I could hear the musical splashing of a waterfall. Next to the A-frame was a large storage shed with a snowmobile parked off to one side.

Sometimes when you set things in motion, you don't know where they're going to end up or what's going to happen along the way. Ruby, with her intuitive gifts, could probably have guessed that this was one of those times. But I'm usually so focused on what's directly in front of me that I don't give much thought to what's around the corner.

The same thing was true today. I wasn't expecting much from this visit except for a few interesting parrot closeups. I got that — and more. Much more.

I found my way to the front door and rang the bell. From the slightly open window beside the door came a strident voice: "Don't want any."

"I'm China Bayles," I said. "Jenna Peterson called about my visit. I'd love to see the parrots."

"Don't need no more parrots," the voice said. "Got enough parrots."

"I'm not bringing a parrot," I replied, beginning to agree with the people who thought that the woman who lived here was a little nuts. "I'm China Bayles. I'm staying down the mountain at Hemlock House and I'd like to meet —"

The door opened about three inches. The woman peering out was in her sixties, short and wiry, with a lined, leathery face and snappy blue eyes behind oversized red plastic cat-eye glasses. She wore a beaded Indian headband and a pair of long steel-gray braids tied off with red yarn, an ankle-length blue caftan heavily embroidered with bright colored feathers, and scuffed brown loggers' boots. Perched on her shoulder was an African grey parrot with a black beak and a fan of bright red tail feathers.

"Hello, cutie," the parrot said, and made kissing noises. "Don't need no more parrots."

I felt foolish for mistaking the parrot for Claudia Roth. "Hello," I said to the bird. "What's your name?"

"Pipsqueak," the parrot replied, holding out one light-gray foot. "Got something for me?"

"Don't be pushy, Pippy," the woman said. She squinted up at me. "China Bayles? You're the one with the parrot?"

"That's me," I said cheerfully. "His name is Mister Spock. He's an Eclectus, and boss of the house. Keeps us on our toes." I held out the bags of banana chips I'd bought at Sam's. "This is for your parrots."

She snatched the bags from my hand before Pipsqueak could get them and opened the door just wide enough for me to squeeze through. "Be quick. I just got my guys rounded up. I don't want them making a break."

As I squeezed through the door, I heard a raucous squawk and a bright blue and green parrot swooped over my head, wings flapping noisily. I ducked and looked up as the parrot landed next to a large blue macaw perched in the A-frame's rafters. With a shriek, Pipsqueak lifted off Claudia's shoulder and flew to join them. One of them dropped a fat wad of poop onto the floor below, where a pile suggested that the rafter was a favorite perch.

"I thought they lived in the aviary," I said. "It's gorgeous, by the way. I wish we had something like that for Spock." I was thinking that maybe I could talk McQuaid into building one. After all, he'd built Caitie's chicken coop. Spock could spend the day out there when we were at work and Caitie was in school.

"Most do live in the aviary, when its warm," she said. "They're indoors now because of Virgil. They'll go back out when the nighttime temp stays above forty." She peered at me. "You look agile enough. How handy are you when it comes to catching birds?"

"I've had a fair amount of practice," I allowed. Spock likes to play hide-and-seek-the-parrot. "You need some help?"

She nodded. "I got most of them. But there are still three stubborn birds out there, and it's easier with two. You're just in time." She turned and began clumping across the room. "This way."

Maybe it was the tricks I'd learned catching Spock, or just a round of good luck. But when I tossed a towel over the last bird, a bright orange conure, Claudia nodded shortly.

"You're a pro. Let's put these boys up and have a cup of coffee."

The birds I'd caught were returned to their own large, bright bird rooms, three separate indoor aviaries built against one side of the A-frame. The size of small bedrooms, they were equipped with cages against one wall; perches, swings, ropes, and toys hanging from the ceiling; feeding stands on tables and shelves. The floors were covered with newspaper. Large birds, such as the macaws, lived in one room, cockatoos in another, and Amazons and African greys in the third. There was another smaller room lined with cages for birds that, for a variety of reasons, couldn't go cage-free.

Altogether, Claudia said, she was taking care of twenty-five birds at the moment. "I'm down a few," she added, pouring coffee. A bright blue parrot — Tick-Tock — flew down from the rafter and landed, teetering, on the back of a chair, where he began to preen, cooing. "Fostered some out last month," she added. "Due to get another two or three this week. One of them has a broken wing. I also do rehab."

I thought of multiplying Spock's mischievous energy by twenty-five or thirty and decided that "a little bit loony" wasn't quite the right word. *Certifiable* might be more like it, or *unhinged* or even *stark staring nuts.*

Claudia put the cups on the table and we took chairs on opposite sides, as Pipsqueak returned to her shoulder with a loud squawk and a flurry of wings. She opened a bag of banana chips and began sharing them with him and Tick-Tock. In a moment, the other two parrots, an Eclectus (like Spock) and a large red macaw with gorgeous blue and yellow wings, flew down from the rafters to join the party. When the four of them had finished the banana chips, Claudia shook the bag to show them that it was empty. Tick-Tock gave a frustrated screech and Pipsqueak wailed "All gone!" so despairingly that I had to laugh.

I gave her my cover story, but Claudia didn't seem very interested in my magazine article about Sunny Carswell. While the parrot quartet chattered and clucked and cooed and recited scraps of parrot ditties, the two of us swapped parrot tales, sipping our coffee and enjoying the bond that forms between people — even between strangers — who share a common passion.

When I met Spock and was offered the chance to adopt him, I knew I couldn't bear to see him go to yet another unhappy or sterile home, where he would be locked up in a cage in the corner and neglected. Claudia understood that impulse, and I understood why she couldn't turn down a bird with a broken wing or one that just needed security, structure, and somebody to pay attention. She might be unfiltered and a little loose with the truth, but she knew her parrots — what to feed them, what toys keep them occupied, how to deal with parasites, what books are helpful. She told me about *The Parrot Who Owns Me* by Joanna Berger, and I told her about a list of parrot-friendly herbs and spices I'd written for my newspaper column. Put a pair of parrot people across a table from one another and they will talk parrots for hours on end.

Parrots weren't the only thing on my mind, though, and after ten minutes or so, I shifted the subject.

"You must know Jed Conway," I said. When she frowned and nodded, I told her what had happened in Bethany. I didn't, of course, tell her about Jed's whispered word. "He could be dead by now, I suppose," I said regretfully.

Her lips tightened and she turned her head away — but not before I saw that the news of his shooting didn't seem to surprise her. It certainly didn't distress her, either, which was interesting.

"The police don't have a suspect yet, as far as I know," I added. "I talked to Carole Humphreys afterward, and —"

"Got what he deserved, after the way he treated Sunny," Claudia broke in abruptly. I saw what he was doing and I know why he did it. If he's dead, that gets three cheers from me." She clapped her hands in slow-motion applause. Joining in, the red macaw gave a loud police-siren whistle. Tick-Tock flapped his wings and cried "First down!

Goal to go!" Pipsqueak bobbed his head and clicked his beak.

Well. Now we were getting somewhere. Jenna had told me that Claudia was an over-sharer who lacked a filter. She said whatever she thought without considering who she was saying it to. What else might she say?

"How *did* Jed Conway treat Miss Carswell?" I asked.

An ordinary person would surely have thought twice about answering this blunt question, especially when it was asked by a stranger who claimed to be writing a magazine article about a dead neighbor. Someone else might even have said something like, "And just why are you asking?" or "What the hell business is it of yours, anyway?"

But Claudia didn't ask. The answer to my question was at the top of her mind so she let me have it. She didn't pull any punches, either.

"Jed Conway is responsible for the way Sunny died," she said flatly. "He introduced Sunny to that pal of his, Amelia, and after that, all Sunny could talk about was that Hemlock Guild stuff about death with dignity. Oh, I could understand her suicide — after all, she was going to die of cancer. What I couldn't understand was the gun. She had plenty of pills she could have used

269

if she'd wanted to. I just can't believe that she would have used that gun. The same gun that killed her father and grandfather." Her face grew dark. "*Our* father and grandfather. Has anybody told you that Sunny was my sister?" If she was lying about the relationship, it sounded as if she had managed to convince herself.

"I've heard it mentioned," I said.

In fact, as I sat here and listened, I could easily imagine it to be true. Jenna had said that Claudia's mother had been a housemaid, and it wasn't unheard of for a man to impose *droit du seigneur* on the women who worked for him. Sunny and Claudia might have a passel of siblings scattered across the mountain. And Jenna had mentioned an annuity. Had Carswell money paid for Claudia's aviaries?

But Claudia wasn't finished. "Guns reminded Sunny of all the bad things our family has done over the decades, selling arms and munitions, making money off of wars. She stayed as far away from the business as she could. She *hated* guns."

I frowned. This was news. I had thought that the gun — the same gun that killed her father and grandfather — might have been her first choice. A kind of ritual hara-kiri.

"Are you saying she didn't kill herself?"

Claudia shifted uncomfortably. "Sunny believed that everybody has the right to die when and how they choose. But when I heard she'd used a gun — and *that* gun, to boot — you could have knocked me over with a feather." She put up her hand and stroked Pipsqueak, on her shoulder. "Somebody must have talked her into doing it that way. I've even wondered if maybe somebody picked up that gun and shot her. Not sayin' who," she added hastily, "and not sayin' for sure. Just sayin'."

The death had been ruled a suicide. But according to the sheriff, the coroner had had questions. "Who might have suggested it?" I asked.

Claudia laughed harshly. "Well, it wasn't the Hemlock ghost, that's for damned sure. Amelia told Sunny it was the quickest way. Told her it would make a statement. A *statement*! I ask you!" She shook her head disgustedly. "But that wasn't all. There's what Jed did about the books, too — especially after he found out that Sunny had cancer."

I wanted to ask Claudia how she knew all this. And about Amelia — Amelia Scott, I assumed — and the gun, too. But Claudia was pushing the conversation forward, too fast for me to keep up. I tried to slow her.

"Wait," I said. "The books? You mean, Sunny's books? What did he do about —"

"Hell, yes. Sunny's books. Who else did Jed know who owned thousands of pricy books and never read any of them? He kept telling her that she should sell the whole lot before she died. He said he just wanted the books to be safe and cared for after she was gone and the idea of the foundation wasn't going to work." She narrowed her eyes. "But what he really wanted was to get the commission on the sales, especially the best ones. And maybe more. Maybe a lot more."

"A lot more?" I was fishing. "A lot more . . . what?"

She didn't answer directly. "The thing is, Sunny wasn't worldly, not in the least bit. She had a lot of money and she didn't bother to keep track of it. What's more, she liked Jed so much that she couldn't see what he was doing."

The words were coming fast and the bitter jealousy in them was unmistakable.

"Jed's bookstore was about to go under, and Sunny was keeping it afloat. He got her to buy good stuff she didn't want and bad stuff that nobody wanted and took every penny of commissions he could. Then he'd get her to sell and take a commission on that end, too — pumping up the value as high as he could. Bless her heart, Sunny never asked a single question. She just told her accountant to pay whatever he asked. She was a cash cow. He just kept milking her."

Ah. This was beginning to make sense — a *different* kind of sense. "So you think Conway might have —" I didn't get to finish.

"When I tried to tell her that Jed was pulling the wool over her eyes, he turned her against me." Claudia's voice broke. "That hurt, believe you me. She didn't want to see me — her own sister. Told me I wasn't welcome, when I was the only one who had her interests at heart."

He turned her against me. So Claudia had a personal reason — and a strong one, a realistic one — for disliking Jed. I was hearing some potentially useful information that nobody else had given me, from somebody who seemed close enough to the situation to know what she was talking about.

I leaned forward on my elbows. "How long had this been going on? Conway pumping up items from Miss Carswell's collection so he could dump them."

Pumping and dumping is the term that's used in securities fraud cases. It describes what happens when a fraudster buys a cheap stock, mounts a big PR campaign to inflate the value, then sells it at a higher price. Something like that also goes on in the art market. I had read recently about a well-known European art dealer who was charged with arranging for fraudulently high evaluations from a prominent auction house on several collectible paintings so he could charge a higher commission. I could see how this strategy might work for a collection of rare books — with or without the collusion of the books' owner. And primarily for the benefit of the dealer, who might also be the owner of Socrates.com.

"How long did it go on? Years and years." Pipsqueak was nibbling at Claudia's braids and she flipped them both over her shoulder. "But the worst of it was the way he badgered her about the *Herbal.*"

My pulse quickened. We were getting at what I most wanted to know. "Badgered? Badgered her how? Why?"

Claudia's expression was fierce. "He just kept after her about selling it. He'd say he had a buyer, or that there was a really great auction coming up, and now was the time. He kept telling her how much it was worth — six or seven times what she'd paid for it — and that it would be a shame to leave it at Hemlock House with nobody but Margaret Anderson to take care of it after she was dead." Her laugh was gritty. "Sunny liked Margaret because Margaret likes books. But Margaret only likes to *write* about books. She doesn't know the first thing about taking care of them. Cataloging and conserving and stuff like that." Claudia snorted. "She's like Jed that way. Both of them care more about how much they're worth than anything else."

How much they're worth. Dorothea had estimated that the plates in the *Herbal* could be worth two hundred thousand — and there were plates missing from other valuable books as well. Margaret Anderson had worked at Hemlock House for several months after Sunny died. She obviously had ample opportunity to take whatever she wanted, whole books as well as individual prints. And if she had joined forces with book dealer Jed Conway, deciding what was worth stealing and how to dispose of it could be a piece of cake.

I cleared my throat. "A minute ago, you mentioned the ghost. There really is one, then?"

"You bet your sweet boobs there's a ghost," she snapped. "More than one."

"You've seen it?"

She nodded. "Could be our dad, our

grandfather, maybe both." Pipsqueak was after her braid again and she pulled it away from him. "Dorothea doesn't believe, but Jenna does." She gave me a knowing look. "Just you wait, you'll see it too. Sunny always said it appeared on stormy nights. Said that anybody could hear it but you had to be a believer to see it."

"I suppose that's why Jenna sees it," I ventured. "She believes."

"Sunny, too." Claudia grinned and her eyes glinted behind her red-rimmed glasses. "The difference is that Jenna is scared of it. Sunny actually liked it, because it seemed like a member of the family. If people came around bothering her, she made sure they knew all about it. Told them to be on the lookout for it. Made it sound really scary. She said it was a sure-fire way to keep them from coming back."

I had more questions, but Claudia was dealing with the parrot. Denied access to her braids, Pipsqueak jumped off her shoulder to the table and strutted toward me, clicking his beak and goose-stepping with the comic precision of a Prussian soldier. When he reached me, he stopped, put his head on one side, and studied me curiously, as if he were deciding whether I was worth knowing. Then he fluttered up onto my left shoulder and nibbled my ear.

"Nice," he said softly, and cooed.

"Pipsqueak is usually standoffish with strangers," Claudia said. "He must like you."

I held out my finger and after a moment Pipsqueak jumped off my shoulder and onto my hand. Murmuring that he was a lovely boy, I scratched his neck. He ducked under my fingers, letting me scratch his head, too. After a few moments he gave another soft coo, turned and sidled up my arm to sit on my right shoulder and nibble that ear. I turned to face him, making kissing noises. A little parrot lovefest.

After a moment, I turned back to Claudia and asked, "Do you think Jed Conway might have stolen the *Herbal*?" I wanted to surprise her with the question, with no lead-in. "If he did, could his shooting have been somehow involved with the theft?"

On the back of his chair, Tick-Tock clicked his beak, squawked, and then lifted one foot and began nibbling his toes. From one of the rooms came the tinny clang-clang of a bell being rung by a parrot. Pushing her lips in and out, Claudia eyed me. Perhaps she was actually filtering her answer, I thought. Perhaps she was better at that than she was given credit for.

"Well, maybe," she said warily, after a moment. "Maybe somebody helped him steal it. Margaret, maybe. And then the two of them got into a disagreement about something." She sounded tentative, as if she was trying out possibilities. "Or maybe somebody thought Jed must have the *Herbal* and they wanted it. But he couldn't give it to them so they shot him."

I was startled by her mention of Margaret. It was as if she had plugged into my thinking. "What makes you say that Margaret might have helped him?" I asked. But she disregarded my question.

"Or maybe it was Kevin Maxwell who shot him," Claudia said. "In fact, that seems a lot more likely to me."

"Kevin Maxwell?" Who was this? Somebody new? Oh, wait. I had heard the name before. He was the guy Carole Humphreys mentioned in the context of "those Hemlock people," which — at the time — I had found puzzling.

"Kevin Maxwell is Wanda Sanger's older brother," Claudia said. "Wanda had ALS for years. She was toughing it out — until the Hemlocks told her it was okay to decide that she'd had enough. Nobody's going to say this out loud, but she was encouraged. It was Jed who coached her, same way

Amelia coached Sunny."

Of course nobody would name a suicide coach out loud. Assisting suicide is a crime — manslaughter, at least — in all but seven states. You can't provide the drugs or tools, or advise or persuade somebody to commit suicide. And even where assistance is legal, it's restricted to physicians.

"When did this happen?" I asked.

"Oh, maybe three, four weeks ago." Claudia pushed her red cat-eye glasses up on her nose. "Kevin says Jed should be in jail and has been making a lot of noise about it, but Jeremy Curtis — he's the police chief in Bethany — says there's not enough evidence. What's more, Wanda left a tidy pot of money to those Hemlock people, which rubs Kevin the wrong way." She shook her head. "Can't say I blame him, either."

Those Hemlock people. When I first heard the phrase, I had thought Carole Humphreys was referring to Dorothea and Jenna at Hemlock House, and I dismissed what sounded like an unfounded accusation. But Carole hadn't meant the Hemlock House. She'd meant the Hemlock Guild. I had been mistaken.

Now I wondered about Jed's whisper. Had I been mistaken there, too? I'd thought he had said *Blackwell.* But what if he had said

Maxwell instead? Was he accusing *Kevin Maxwell,* whose sister he might have helped to kill herself? I didn't think so, but I couldn't rule it out.

And now that I knew about this possibility, I also knew I had to tell Chief Curtis what I'd heard. Which would not be a pleasant task. I had withheld potentially important crime-scene evidence. The chief would be justifiably angry. He might even decide to charge me. I couldn't blame him. And I had no defense.

But at the moment, I needed to figure out just where Claudia was coming from. How much of her evident animosity toward Jed Conway and Amelia Scott was based in fact and how much was conjured up out of a grudge against the Hemlock Guild — or even more personally, out of jealousy toward Conway for getting between her and Sunny? Was she just guessing? How much did she actually know? How much was *true*?

There were several ways to go about this, but I elected a straightforward question. "A minute ago, you said something about the gun that Sunny used. You seemed to suggest that Amelia prodded Sunny into using that gun to kill herself. Did I hear that right? Is that what you meant to say?"

"Well . . ." She hesitated, frowning. "Jed

280

had a hand in it, too. After all, he wanted that *Herbal.* His store was in trouble, you know, and he had to have money."

"His store was in trouble? The place looked pretty well stocked to me." But appearances can be deceiving. Things can look totally shipshape, and suddenly the ship starts to sink. "How do you know?"

"His sister Kaye fosters parrots for me. She told me about it. That place bleeds money and Jed's in hock up to his ears. If he took the *Herbal,* he did it for the money. And because Sunny wouldn't let him sell it." She wore a cagey look. "But Amelia's a totally different story. For her, Sunny was a trophy."

"Trophy?" I frowned. "Is that why you said the gun was a 'statement'?"

"Yeah. You know, here was somebody who actually *did* it. That bunch down in Bethany talks a good game. But Sunny was the first — and she was somebody important. There was that damned *gun.*" Her grin was mirthless. "Of course, now the Hemlocks can claim Wanda as well, which is why Kevin Maxwell is out for blood." Her eyes glinted behind her red cat-eye glasses. "Sounds like he might've got it, too. I —"

But I didn't get to hear the rest of it. Tick-Tock chose that inconvenient moment to

281

lift off his chair-back perch and fly to the kitchen counter. He landed next to an unstable stack of bowls, knocking three or four to the floor with a loud crash. He peered over the edge of the counter.

"Offsides!" he squawked cheerfully. "Penalty!"

"Damn it, Tick-Tock! Just look at that mess." Claudia went to get the broom.

Clearly, we had arrived at the end of the conversation. I lifted Pipsqueak onto the back of my chair, told him he was a good boy, thanked Claudia for sharing her parrots with me, and promised to keep in touch. On the way out, I remembered about the ginseng and asked, off-handedly, where I should look for it.

"Wild ginseng?" She snorted. "Come back in about six weeks. Maybe it'll be putting up leaves by then — berries in July and August." Another snort. "But don't bother to bring a shovel, unless you want to get arrested. Not legal to dig it until September."

"Oh," I said. Embarrassed, I thanked her again and headed for my car. Claudia Roth was definitely unfiltered. She hadn't given the answers I'd expected and surely some of what she said was not factual — or at least unsupported. But she had given me a different, and very interesting, view of

Sunny Carswell and her relationships with Jed and the Hemlock people.

And now I knew a little more about ginseng.

CHAPTER TEN

In many cultures, herbal baths are an important ritual. The bathers believe that when certain herbs are added to the bath water, they release not only their scent but their special energies. A bath using the protective herb rosemary, for instance, was thought to make the bather safe from the forces of negativity and evil. Bay, basil, and fennel are other protective herbs.

To recreate this ritual for yourself, put a cup and a half of crushed rosemary leaves and one-half cup each of crushed bay leaves, basil, and fennel into a quart jar. Pour boiling water over the herbs and let them steep. Strain into a warm bath. An alternative, using essential oils: blend six drops rosemary oil with two drops each of bay, basil, and fennel oils. Mix with one tablespoon of carrier oil, such as grape-seed, jojoba, or almond. Add the oil blend to the bathwater just before you climb in,

so you can enjoy the scent before the essential oils evaporate. Rub the droplets of oil onto your skin as you relax in the bath.
"Personal Herbal Rituals"
https://susanalbert.com/
personal-herbal-rituals/

I got back to Hemlock House in time for a civilized sherry before dinner, which gave me an opportunity to tell Dorothea and Jenna what had happened at the Open Book that afternoon. As I did, I watched Dorothea closely to see how she reacted to the news about the shooting.

"Oh, no!" Jenna exclaimed. "Oh, God, China, that's awful!"

Dorothea was silent for a long moment, looking stunned. "Who would do a thing like that?" she whispered finally.

I relaxed a little when I learned that Rose had gone to Bethany with Dorothea that morning, and that the two of them had been together at the grocery. I even felt a little silly for suspecting that Dorothea might have shot Jed Conway.

But neither she nor Jenna could come up with a possible assailant and they looked at me blankly when I mentioned Claudia Roth's candidate — Kevin Maxwell.

"Kevin Maxwell?" Dorothea was puzzled.

"I don't think I know him. Do you, Jenna?"

Jenna shook her head. "But that's no surprise, really. We haven't spent much time in Bethany."

I didn't share the rest of Claudia's unfiltered confidences with them, and when they asked whether I had made any progress in the search for the stolen *Herbal,* I put them off with a shrug and an apologetic "To be honest, not much."

Which was, if anything, an overstatement. I had made no progress at all. If Jed was our thief and if he died, we might never know what had become of the *Herbal.* And I certainly didn't want to tell them that as far as Sheriff Rogers was concerned, they were both still under suspicion. And while Dorothea was off the hook for Jed Conway's shooting, I understood where the sheriff was coming from. I had thought I knew her, but I had to admit I didn't know her all *that* well. The theft of the *Herbal* certainly looked, as the sheriff had said, like an inside job, and Dorothea and Jenna were the two most logical insiders.

But I hadn't come to the end of my to-do list. First thing tomorrow I had to confess my sin of omission to Chief Curtis who — I hoped — would see his way clear to pardoning me for my crime. I hoped to see Margaret and drop in on the Hemlocks' get-together, to meet Amelia Scott. And I should probably have a telephone conversation with the president of the board, Mrs. Cousins, and try to convince her to announce the theft. If she and the board continued to refuse, there wouldn't be much left for me to do here. I might even see if I could bump my flight from Thursday to Wednesday.

Rose had cooked a marvelous dinner for us, as I discovered when we sat down at the table. I polished off two bowls of chicken and slicks — a thick, rich, flavorful chicken soup studded with carrots and celery and afloat with flat, slippery, slurpy dumplings. A chicken soup to top all chicken soups, forever. I found it every bit as delicious as Jenna had predicted, as was the cabbage salad and the warm apple pie.

While we were eating, I asked Jenna if she happened to remember which of Redouté's lily plates had been taken from the Carswell library.

She brightened. "Funny you should ask, China. I was working on that list just before supper. I haven't typed it into the computer yet." She reached into her jeans pocket and pulled out a handwritten list. "This is what I've got so far. It's incomplete, of course."

I ran a glance down Jenna's penciled list. My skin prickled. The blackberry lily and the Barbados lily were both on it. I pushed it back toward her. "May I have a copy?"

"Sure." She repocketed the list. "Can I ask why?"

"Just wanting to be on the lookout," I said. I had more work to do on this. Time enough to loop them in when I found out who owned Socrates.com. "Hey, did either of you hear the weather forecast?"

They hadn't, and my news about a possible snowstorm was a surprise. The past winter had been mild, with only a couple of light snows. They had no experience of mountain snowstorms and no idea what to expect.

"I suppose I should find out if Joe is ready to plow the drive," Dorothea remarked, when I told her what the sheriff had said about the Carswell barn roof. By that time, we had finished eating and were beginning to clear the dishes. "I've often wondered whether the county plows the main road up here," she added, "since we're so near the end. The road doesn't go any further than Claudia Roth's place. I suppose it's possible to get snowed in." She smiled at me. "But I wouldn't worry, China. It's spring already.

If we get some snow, it'll probably just melt."

Jenna turned from the dishwasher, a bowl in her hand. "I proofread more of my novel this afternoon, China. I took the liberty of emailing the next section to you. But please don't feel obligated. You don't *have* to read it, you know."

"Of course I'll read it!" I said. "I thought of Elizabeth several times today. I wondered what she would make of Jed Conway's bookstore."

"She would be blown away by the electric lights, for one thing," Jenna said with a laugh. "Can you imagine lighting a bookshop with oil lamps and candles? On a dark day, you wouldn't be able to see the books on the shelf — and London had plenty of dark days."

I planned to spend some time that evening reviewing the notes I had made after today's interviews. So when the kitchen cleanup was done — quick work, with three of us on the job — I excused myself and went upstairs. I had just propped myself against the generous pile of pillows on the bed and opened my notebook to the Humphreys notes when my cell phone rang.

It was Margaret Anderson, apologizing nicely for having missed me earlier that day.

She had gotten my message, understood that I was a writer doing a piece on the Hemlock House Foundation and the Carswell collection, and would be glad to talk to me at any time. Apparently, she had just gotten back from the hospital, where she had tried to see Jed Conway.

"But of course I couldn't," she said. She sounded younger than I had expected, and I mentally subtracted about ten or twelve pounds, changed the color of her pink twinset to red, and gave her a pair of red Manolos. "What a horrible thing! And so hard to believe." She took a breath. "I understand that you found him. It must have been a terrible shock."

"Yes," I said, wondering how she had managed to learn that little detail. But she was hurrying on.

"Well, do come over tomorrow and let's talk. I was a great admirer of Miss Carswell and I know a little about her collection. And of course I'm always glad to talk books."

"Thank you," I said. "What time tomorrow would be convenient for you? And where?"

"Oh, let's do it here." She rattled off the address — the one I already had. "It'll have to be first thing, though," she added. "Is nine-thirty too early?"

"Sounds right." I paused. I didn't want to put her on her guard, but there was one more thing. "I had hoped to interview Jed Conway, but . . ." I hesitated. "When you went to the hospital this evening, did you hear anything about his condition?"

"They're saying it's touch and go. He's still critical. If he makes it through the night . . ." She hesitated, took a breath, and said, "I wonder — when you found him, was he able to talk?"

"He was barely conscious," I said, evading. I owed my *mea culpa* and a report of what I had heard to Chief Curtis. I wasn't going to share it with anybody else. And why was she asking? Was she worried that I might have heard something from him? The name of his assailant, maybe? *Her* name?

She tried again, more insistently this time. "But did he *say* anything? Was he able to identify —"

At that moment, my phone beeped and I looked down to see that McQuaid was calling. "Oh, gosh, I'm sorry, Margaret," I said quickly. "My husband is on call-waiting. We've been playing phone tag all day and I really have to talk to him. I'll see you at nine-thirty in the morning."

I clicked off. Every lawyer learns how to duck questions she doesn't want to answer.

And it wouldn't hurt Margaret Anderson to twirl her pearls and stew about what Jed Conway *might* have said to me before the medics showed up.

McQuaid had just sent Brian back to Austin with a load of clean laundry. They had opted for takeout pizza from Gino's instead of my beef stew (pizza goes better with beer) and spent the evening commiserating about how hard it was to keep a relationship going when two people are so busy that they barely see one another except in bed. And when seeing one another mostly in bed just isn't enough.

"Real-world stuff like that," McQuaid said. "Hard lessons in love." He paused. "So how about you, Sherlock? Stumble over any more dead bodies?"

"Not funny," I said darkly. "Not to joke about."

"Sorry. Starting over." In a faux sprightly tone, he said, "So how did the *rest* of your day go, dear?"

"I met a flock of parrots," I said. "And I have an idea for an aviary for Spock, out by Caitie's coop. He can keep an eye on the chickens and report any troublemakers."

"Refer it to the buildings and grounds committee." McQuaid chuckled. "Maybe Spock would be willing to settle for an aviary instead of a horse. Caitie says Spock thought it was great fun and wants to go riding again tomorrow."

"I hope she remembers to put his harness on him." When he goes outdoors, Spock wears his parrot harness and a leash, which is attached to Caitie's wrist. "He'd probably come back if he got loose — *if* he could find his way. But he might get lost, especially on the ranch. It's a wilderness." I paused. "Listen, I wonder if there's something you might do for me."

"Within reason," he said. "What did you have in mind?"

"I need to find out who owns a website called Socrates.com. I'll take a quick look at WhoIs, but I'm sure I won't find it there." WhoIs enables you to look up the owners of domain names and IP addresses on the internet. "I'll bet you have ways of digging up the ownership information even if it's privately registered, which this one probably is."

"Sure thing," McQuaid said easily. "I'll check it out tomorrow and get back to you. Oh, almost forgot. I ran into Ruby when we stopped to get the pizza. She wanted me to tell you something. She said it was urgent."

Uh-oh. I was instantly worried. Something must be wrong at Thyme and Seasons or the Crystal Cave. We've had our share of calamities over the years and any one of them could happen again — or two or even three of them could happen at the same time. A water pipe could break and flood the kitchen. Somebody could trip on the tea room doorsill, break a leg, and sue us. Big Red Mama, our shop van, could have blown a valve. A catering client's check for a very large party could bounce. The old pecan tree out front could —

"China?" McQuaid said. "You still there?"

I realized I was holding my breath. "What did Ruby want to tell me?"

"She said, 'The Universe says boots.' "

"Boots? What's that supposed to mean?"

"I have no clue," he said. "I've done my job. I've *told* you. Boots. Cowboy boots, maybe? Riding boots? Hiking boots? Chukka boots? Combat —"

"Thank you," I said.

He changed the subject. "Any word on the condition of that guy who got shot today?"

I told him what Margaret had told me. He reminded me to stay out of the line of fire, blew me a telephone kiss, and went off to watch his favorite political talk show on TV. I opened my notebook and began going over the notes I had taken during my conversations that day, summing up what I had learned about the mysteries — two of them, now, instead of just one. Who stole the *Herbal*? Who shot Jed Conway? And there was a corollary: Are the two events related, and if so, how?

I hadn't gotten much from Rose, except for some background information about the people who came and went at Hemlock House and her reluctant confirmation that there *was* a secret room. Not that it had anything to do with the theft of the *Herbal.* It was just an interesting side note about this place.

From Jed Conway, I'd heard a whispered word suggesting that he might have some connection to the Blackwell *Herbal,* or that his assailant might have been Kevin Maxwell, or something else entirely — how was I to know? As for Socrates.com: I went online and did a quick search of WhoIs. But I had been right. The site's ownership was privately registered. I'd have to wait and hope that PI McQuaid could dig up the registration.

And when I went to the website and looked at the images of the sale items, I realized that I would need Jenna's list of the prints and pages that were missing from the Carswell collection. Even then, without some distinctive physical characteristic that tied each item to a particular book, it might be next to impossible to match them so that they could be used as evidence of theft. As a for-instance: one of the detectives in *The Map Thief* had related how hard it had been to prove that the maps in the thief's possession were the same maps that had been stolen. Maps aren't like cars, he'd said. They don't come with VIN numbers. (He had traced one of the stolen maps by matching wormholes — *bookworm* holes! — in the pages.) This was a research project that would take some time and would require inspection of the physical evidence. Which meant that the chief or the DA would have to subpoena the inventory of Socrates.com.

From Carole, I had learned that Margaret Anderson's departure from Hemlock House had not been entirely amicable and that she — Margaret, aka Ms. Twinset — might have grudges against the board and especially against Dorothea. She'd had plenty of opportunity to identify the most valuable books and steal prints from them. Had she also made off with the *Herbal*? Were all these things being fenced through Socrates.com, which might or might not be owned by Jed Conway?

If so, that could link Twinset to Jed and

make her a serious candidate as the shooter. To my image of the frosted hair, red twin-set, and Manolos I considered adding a concealed-carry Smith and Wesson 9mm handgun.

From the talkative Sheriff Rogers, I'd gotten the lowdown on his investigation of the theft, including his frustrations and his evident suspicion of Dorothea. Oh, and a warning against Virgil, for whatever *that* was worth. And from the bulletin board outside the sheriff's office, the information about the Hemlock Guild meeting, with Amelia Scott's name and phone number.

But it had been Claudia the Unfiltered who had given me the most to think about, starting with her claim to a wrong-side-of-the-blanket family-tree connection to the Carswells, her sisterly friendship with Sunny, and her information about Jed Conway's precarious financial situation and the pump-and-dump scheme that he used to inflate his commissions. Plus the fact that the phrase "those Hemlock folks" had likely referred to the local right-to-die group, rather than the current occupants of Hemlock House — and Claudia's revelation that Jed had been threatened by Kevin Maxwell, angry about Conway's alleged role in his sister's suicide. I had to add Maxwell to my suspect list.

Which led me to confront the awkward fact that the whisper I had withheld from Chief Curtis might be the name of Jed's assailant. *Damn.* In legal terms, I was guilty of obstruction, which is a very bad thing. First thing tomorrow morning, I would have to visit the chief, eat a big helping of crow, and hope that he would find it in his heart to overlook my sin of omission.

And for tonight, one more thing. Ms. Twinset's upscale, golf-club-neighborhood residence had already told me something about her. Now I needed to look for her website and her Facebook and Twitter and Instagram accounts. I wanted to see what kind of online persona — professional and personal — she had created for herself.

But when I tried to get onto the internet, there was no signal. I went back to the sign-on popup and tried again. Nothing.

I cocked my head, listening for the first time to what was happening outdoors. It was raining buckets — a gully-washer, we call it in Texas. As I looked up, a blue-white flash of lightning lit the hemlocks outside the windows and I saw that a wild wind was lashing the trees.

My first thought, regretful: Rain, and lots of it, messing with the satellite signal. My online research would have to wait until the storm passed.

My second, snarkier thought: Rain? What happened to big, bad Virgil and the blizzard he was supposed to bring us?

My third thought, more like a silent prayer: Please don't let the power go off. I had already downloaded the chapter Jenna had emailed me and my tablet's battery was charged, so I could read, electricity or not. But I'd hate to have to grope for the bathroom in the dark. Why hadn't I brought a flashlight.

Oh, wait. There was a flashlight on my cell phone, wasn't there? I took a moment to find it and make sure I knew how to use it, just in case.

Then I looked back down at the scribbles in my notebook, feeling frustrated. I'd made a lot of notes but I wasn't any closer to identifying the thief who had stolen the *Herbal* than when I began. The theft had been the main target of investigation, but it was now overwritten by the attempted murder of Jed Conway. All things considered, the question of who had tried to kill him and why was now more important — and more urgent — than the question of who had stolen the *Herbal.*

Unless, of course, the two questions were

opposite sides of the same coin, and the answer to one turned out to be the answer to the other. In which case, both were equally urgent.

If Conway lived, he might solve this duplex riddle for us. If he died . . . I shook my head. If he died, we might never know *either* answer.

Wearily, I rubbed my eyes. Enough. Maybe this muddle would look clearer after a good night's sleep. Meanwhile, Jenna said she had sent me the next section of her novel — and there it was, in my phone. Hadn't she also said that she had made some rosemary bath oil and left it for me on the shelf in the bathroom? It would be lovely to take my book and climb into a hot, rosemary-scented bath.

That's what I did. The water was hot, the bath delightfully fragrant, the oil soothing to my dry skin. I opened Jenna's chapter on my phone and began to read.

Within minutes, I was so deep in the eighteenth century that it would have taken a very determined ghost to pry me out. But the ghost let me read, and if anything unusual went on at Hemlock House that night, I didn't know a thing about it.

■ ■ ■ ■

PART FOUR:
THE CURIOUS TALE
OF ELIZABETH
BLACKWELL

■ ■ ■ ■

February 7, 1735
Number 3, Great Russell Street
Bloomsbury Square, London

Apothecary. The earlier name for one who prepared and sold drugs for medicinal purposes — the business now (since about 1800) conducted by a druggist or pharmaceutical chemist. From about 1700, apothecaries gradually took a place as general medical practitioners.

The Oxford English Dictionary

In addition to dispensing herbs and medicine, the apothecary offered general medical advice and a range of services that are now performed by other specialist practitioners, such as surgeons and obstetricians. Apothecary shops sold ingredients and the medicines they prepared wholesale to other medical practitioners, as well as dispensing them to patients.

"Apothecary"
https://en.wikipedia.org/wiki/Apothecary

What Sir Hans Sloane wanted, it turned out, was an entire book of carefully detailed botanical drawings, and quite a substantial book, at that — the most substantial of its kind ever imagined.

The three of them — Sir Hans, Dr. Stuart, and Elizabeth — were seated in front of a pleasant fire in Sir Hans' great library-cum-museum.

"To explain why this book is needed," Sir Hans said, "I must tell you about the Society of Apothecaries and the garden of medicinal herbs that the society maintains at Chelsea. I studied botany there when I first came to London some fifty years ago."

He paused, glancing half-apologetically at Dr. Stuart. "I fear that this is a rather long story and for you, Stuart, one that you already know well. I shall try not to ramble, and when I have done, we shall have some tea."

"Ramble as you like, sir," Dr. Stuart said, bending over to pick up a pair of ember tongs from the hearth and lighting his pipe with a glowing coal. "It is a most interesting story."

Elizabeth felt a twinge of nervous anxiety, wondering where and how and why she might fit into this great man's scheme, whatever it was. She listened intently, which was not hard to do, for Sir Hans spoke with a compelling conviction and energy.

His story went like this. As the practice of medicine grew and developed in London, the importance of apothecaries increased, and with it the commercial trade in medicinal plants. Over a hundred years ago, during the reign of King James I, the apothecaries broke away from the Grocers' Company to which they belonged. They formed their own professional society: the Worshipful Society of Apothecaries of London. Then, just thirty years ago, they had won the legal right to act as doctors and to prescribe medicines, as well as make and sell them.

With the new privileges came new responsibilities, and the society set new goals for itself. It pledged to educate and train apprentice and journeymen apothecaries, ensure the quality of the medicines its members made and sold, find and punish frauds, and raise the professional standards of its members. It established a laboratory adjacent to its meeting hall in Blackfriars Lane, where medicinal herbs grown locally or imported from overseas could be prepared and wholesaled to apothecary shops. It conducted "herbarizing" expeditions led by trained botanists in the area around London, to identify and gather native medicinal plants where they grew in the wild. Since the medicines that were prescribed were mostly plant-based, these expeditions were important. Every apothecary had to learn to correctly identify every medicinal herb. A misidentification might mean that somebody died.

The apothecaries also purchased a lease on a three-and-a-half-acre plot of land in Chelsea, a Thames-side hamlet some three miles west of the city. There, they created a teaching, demonstration, and experimental garden, where they began to cultivate not only the familiar English herbs but the new and unfamiliar exotics that explorers were bringing in from Asia, Africa, and the Americas. They hired gardeners, laid out plots and paths, and constructed conservatories and heated greenhouses — "stoves," they were called, built over networks of subterranean fire pits and brick-lined flues that allowed tropical plants to be grown in English winters. The focus in this garden was not on a plant's beauty or exotic nature but always on its *usefulness,* particularly its use as a medicine.

As part of the society's educational program, the garden was open to the public, and to visitors it was a source of wonder. Exotic plants and trees such as had never before been seen in England flourished there, including a Peruvian bark tree (chinchona, used to treat malaria), a great acacia, and four cedars of Lebanon. Collectors such as John Bartram of Philadelphia introduced plants from faraway places, and many people like Carl Linnaeus — the Swedish botanist who was creating a new method of naming plants — came to see these novelties.

The garden quickly became an important part of the apothecaries' educational programs, but maintaining it proved a daunting challenge. It was miles away from Blackfriars, and the roads could be impassable in wet weather. It cost a good deal to keep a knowledgeable and trustworthy gardener, who required both a salary and a house. (Trustworthiness was important. A gardener of the untrustworthy sort had made off with a thousand valuable plants and was never heard from again.) Building and maintaining the glasshouses was expensive, as were the rare plants brought from far places by botanical explorers.

And then a challenge of another magnitude arose. Lord Cheyne decided to sell Chelsea Manor, which had once been the home of Princess Elizabeth and of Anne of Cleves. Obligingly, His Lordship first offered the garden to the apothecaries, but they couldn't afford the £400 he was asking. They were faced with the very real prospect of losing their garden — until a contributor took care of the matter and they were able to carry on.

Sir Hans paused at that point to ring for tea, and while they were waiting, Dr. Stuart spoke up.

"If you will pardon me, Sir Hans, I fear you are too modest. I should like to tell Mrs. Blackwell who saved the garden." With a smile at Elizabeth, he went on before Dr. Sloane could object.

"It is a fact, Mrs. Blackwell, that without Sir Hans, the garden would have been lost. He has always been a patron and staunch friend of the apothecaries, generously helping them with building expenses and laboratory equipment. But he saved the garden by buying the *entire manor* — its houses and surrounding estates. That done, he leased the garden to the apothecaries for an annual five pounds. Five pounds, mind you, and a promise to send a few distinctive plants every year to the Royal Society. It was a generous, *most* generous gift."

Sir Hans had put up his hand to object, but Dr. Stuart vigorously shook his head. "No, no, sir, it must be said. If you had not intervened, the garden would have been lost, and with it several thousands of rare plants of inestimable pharmaceutical value. It is now said, in fact, that the Chelsea Garden rivals the botanic gardens of both Paris and Leiden."

At that point, tea arrived — a silver pot and a crystal platter of frosted raisin teacakes — and there was a brief silence while it was served, with Elizabeth wondering all the while what this bit of apothecary history had to do with *her*. She was not a trained botanist and had little interest in working in a garden. Unless, of course, she should be paid enough to reward the time spent.

Then Sir Hans took up the story again. The garden, he said, was currently under the direction of Mr. Isaac Rand, with Philip Miller as gardener. Rand was an apothecary and an ardent botanist. He had recently published a catalogue of over five hundred of the garden's plants. Mr. Miller was not only a master gardener but the author of the popular *Gardener's Dictionary* and more recently, *The Gardener's Kalendar.*

"Excellent works, and very thorough," Dr. Stuart said, munching on a cake. "The catalogues especially are much in demand among the apothecaries, for they list all the plants that can be obtained from the garden."

"Yes, much in demand." Sir Hans emptied his cup and put it down on the table. "And that is why I have it in mind to commission another book."

"But, sir," Elizabeth said. "If there are already several recent books about the garden, I cannot see that another will serve. Won't it simply duplicate what Mr. Rand and Mr. Miller have done? How will it distinguish itself?"

"Ah, Miller and Rand," Dr. Stuart said in a low voice. "That may present some difficulties, I fear."

"But we need not confront that now," Sir Hans said briskly. He smiled at Elizabeth. "Your questions are very good, my dear Mrs. Blackwell. Excellent, in fact! A new book *must* distinguish itself. And this one certainly shall, for the simple reason that both Mr. Rand's and Mr. Miller's books are botanical. While they are fine in their way, there is not enough attention to the medicinal properties of the plants." He put down his teacup and gave her a direct look. "And — most importantly — they are not illustrated. A reader who does not already know what the plant looks like will remain unfortunately unenlightened." He put a hand on her portfolio. "What is needed is an *illustrated* manual of the plants of Chelsea."

"Ah," Elizabeth said softly, beginning to understand. She took a deep breath. "Ah, yes. I see."

"Indeed!" With enthusiasm, Sir Hans went on. "The book I have in mind will be a work of engraved and colored plates of the major plants in the garden. These are not woodcuts or casual drawings, but plants drawn from life, labeled, and described briefly in an accompanying text. The book will serve as a manual for apothecaries and their apprentices, assisting them in identifying the medicinal plants with which they work. They can use it in their consultations with their patients and customers. It can also be sold to the general public, which would very much benefit from more knowledge about plants and their uses as medicine."

Elizabeth swallowed hard. "And how many of these engraved and colored plates are you thinking of?"

Sir Hans made a vague gesture. "Mr. Rand's handbook contains just over five hundred plants, I believe. I should think there would be that many illustrations." He paused, watching her closely. "I should, of course, be glad to advance some monies to

310

see the artist well into the project."

But she had stopped listening when she heard the number of illustrations the man expected. "Five hundred?" she whispered. *"Five hundred?"*

Elizabeth was no stranger to the making of books. She knew what such an undertaking would cost — the hours and the labor — and her stomach muscles knotted at the thought of it. There would be preliminary sketches followed by final drawings, followed by engravings on copperplate. There would be the descriptions to compile and engrave or typeset. There would be the printing and binding. And then the whole business of marketing the book, which was crucial to its success. She had seen fine books moldering in warehouses for lack of adequate marketing.

But this was no time for timidity. Although she was not entirely sure she could actually *do* the work, she knew how it should be done. She needed the money, and it seemed that Sir Hans was willing to provide something by way of an advance — perhaps even something in the way of living expenses for her and the children as the project got underway. She needed a new start, desperately. Daunting as it might be, she could not let this opportunity go by.

Her pulses hammering, she took another breath and sat straighter in her chair, hoping she looked like a woman who knew whereof she spoke.

"Well, then. A publication of the size you're considering should best be done in two volumes." She pursed her lips thoughtfully. "It might even be useful to first publish the plates in serial form — say, one issue each week, by subscription and by single sales."

"Serial?" Dr. Stuart asked, frowning uncertainly.

"Yes, published first in numbers. By installments, that is." She was thinking of a serial publication that had come from Alexander's press. "At the shop, we published Peter Hardy's *Travels through Holland and Germany* in just such a manner, weekly, in fifty-two issues, by subscription. Then it was to be published in a single volume." She omitted to mention that the volume had to be turned over to another printer when the creditors had closed the shop.

"You've had some experience with this," Sir Hans said with satisfaction. "How incredibly fortunate. Tell me, my dear — what sort of weekly publication would it be?"

Elizabeth did not find this question difficult, given her experience with the Hardy book. "Four plates per issue," she said, "together with a page of descriptions, bound in the usual thin blue covers. The issues could be sold uncolored for perhaps a shilling, with colored offered at two." She paused, thinking rapidly. The creation of such a book would be a huge undertaking, more than two years, by her quick calculation. She added, "The bound volume could also be sold as both uncolored and colored, of course."

"The bound volume," Dr. Stuart said thoughtfully. "You envision both the sale of serial installments *and* a bound volume."

"Two bound volumes," Elizabeth corrected herself. "Five hundred plates would best be managed in two volumes. They need not be published at the same time, of course. The first volume might appear when half of the serial installments — say, a hundred-twenty-five plates — have been published. Which would increase the demand for the second installments *and* the second volume, I should think."

"I see," Sir Hans said. "Yes, I see. What a clever idea, Mrs. Blackwell."

"And," she added, "if the installment sales are not high enough to merit the publication of a bound volume, there is no need to go to that expense." She looked from one to the other. "It's always best to be cautious and try out the market."

"An excellent point," Dr. Stuart said approvingly. "Quite shrewd."

Sir Hans brought them back to something Elizabeth had said earlier. "You mentioned subscriptions, I think," he prompted.

Elizabeth nodded. "Since the work is intended for the use of apothecaries and physicians, subscriptions could be offered to them, not just in London but in all the major cities of England, Scotland, and Ireland. Paid in advance, that could create a cash reserve large enough to subsidize the initial printing costs. Booksellers, of course, will prefer to take the numbers on consignment."

She was feeling the excitement beginning to tremble in her, and she made fists of her hands in the folds of her woolen skirt. The more she thought about this, the more she thought she might have stumbled into something that would actually be profitable enough to redeem Alexander's freedom. And — if she managed it adroitly — something that could support herself and the children in the interim.

But still, *five hundred illustrations!* That would require hundreds, no, thousands of hours in the garden and at the drawing table. She was a practical woman of some experience. She knew that those hours — and days and weeks and months — would cost her dearly, especially with her children. She should have to find someone to look after them while she spent all day working on the book. But how else could she produce enough earnings to support them *and* buy Alexander's freedom? She made herself relax her hands, but her insides were knotted so tightly that she could scarcely take a breath.

Dr. Stuart did not appear to notice. He leaned toward his patron. "Sir Hans, I believe that Mrs. Blackwell understands what is needed here far better than you or I."

Sir Hans nodded vehemently. "Before George, I believe she does!" He turned to Elizabeth. "Mrs. Blackwell, what do you say? Are you willing to undertake the project?"

Elizabeth managed a slight smile, but she was still thinking of the work — and the years. Little William would be nearly five before it was done, Blanche past seven. And what if she failed? What if she invested all that time in compiling the book and still couldn't earn enough to pay Alex's creditors?

She took a deep breath. Sir Hans had mentioned an advance. How much did he have in mind? How far could she trust him — or his lawyers? What if he promised support and then reneged? She could think of a half-dozen ways in which such a project could go awry. She was tempted to say yes on the spot, but she knew it would be foolhardy to jump into a scheme like this without a written and signed agreement.

"I am interested," she conceded, "but there are things to discuss. I should wish to own the copyright, for instance, and the plates. I should also prefer to manage the project myself, set its schedule, choose the printer, and so on." In this, she knew she was departing from the usual author's course. She would make more money if she retained control of her work and didn't assign the rights to a publisher, as was usually done. She would be assuming the greater risk, of course — but Sir Hans' backing would cushion that, at least a little.

"And I must settle the matter of my children's support," she added. "To be quite frank, sir, I am in need of money. I cannot take on a project for the love of the garden or for the sake of the apothecaries. I am obliged to meet my husband's debts. And I must find a nest for my chicks and myself." Another narrow smile. "I hope you will forgive me if I suggest that we first give some careful thought to the matter of an agreement."

"A Scotswoman through and through." Sir Hans looked pleased. "I am quite ready to consider your terms, Mrs. Blackwell. Since this is clearly an area in which you are experienced, I suggest that you draft an agreement that covers the issues you judge to be crucial to the success of the project. When we have that, we can discuss it and see where we are." He held out his hand. "Will that suit?"

"Very well, sir," she said primly, taking his hand. But her breath was coming short and her heart was leaping within her. It scarcely seemed possible — but had she happened on the means to set Alex free?

Only time — and her best efforts — could tell.

CHAPTER ELEVEN

The Hemlock Society was an American right-to-die and assisted suicide advocacy organization which existed from 1980 to 2003. . . . . The group took its name from *Conium maculatum,* a highly poisonous biennial herbaceous flowering plant in the carrot family. The name was a direct reference to the method by which the Athenian philosopher Socrates took his life in 399 BC, as described in Plato's *Phaedo.*

"Hemlock Society"
https://en.wikipedia.org/wiki/Hemlock_Society

Just before I woke the next morning, I dreamed that Elizabeth Blackwell and I were dashing pell-mell through the Physic Garden at Chelsea, around and around a huge stone statue of Sir Hans Sloane that sat in the middle of the garden. Pursuing us through the chilly gray mist was Sunny Carswell, dressed in a burnt-orange tracksuit, waving her arms and shouting that we were making off with her precious *Herbal.* A large white gull circled overhead, crying *thief thief thief.*

But I had awakened in Hemlock House, not the Chelsea Garden, and the cry of *thief thief* wasn't a gull but the *beep beep* alarm on my cell phone. I got out of bed and went to the window. It must have been raining all night, for the hemlocks were bowed with the weight of water, a light rain was still falling from a leaden sky, and an antic west wind was whipping the trees and bushes. I opened the casement a few inches and pulled in a quick lungful of damp April air — *warm* air, pleasant spring air.

Well, so much for Virgil, I thought as I closed the window. The meteorologists had missed the forecast by a country mile. If it weren't for the wind's shrill howling, it would be just another balmy spring day.

After a few minutes' debate, I decided that the plaid shirt, jeans, and sandals I had worn the previous day might be too informal for this morning's interviews with the police chief and Ms. Twinset and the afternoon get-together with the Hemlock Guild. I settled for a caramel-colored corduroy blazer over a red top and black slacks. I had brought a pair of red and black striped woolly socks that Ruby had knitted for me and I put those on, with black loafers.

While I dressed, I found myself wondering — worrying, really — about Jed Conway. Had he survived the night? If he was able to talk, would he confirm what I heard him whisper? And what *had* I heard, anyway? Had the man said *Blackwell* or *Maxwell*? I didn't know. I honestly didn't know. That's what I had to tell Chief Curtis. And hope he didn't throw the book at me.

I pulled a quick comb through my hair, decided I didn't need lipstick but definitely *did* need coffee, and took the back stairs to the kitchen.

Aside from the dream, I had slept well all night. Jenna hadn't.

We met in the kitchen, where she was huddled over a plate of the breakfast Rose had left for us — pancakes, spicy sausages from a local farm, and fried red (not green) tomatoes. Dorothea's place was empty. She had apparently already eaten and disappeared into the library.

Jenna looked up at me. Her face was pale. "Did *you* hear it?" she asked anxiously.

"Hear what?" I glanced at the clock as I poured myself a glass of orange juice. Rose's breakfast looked too good to miss. But if I wanted to have time for a full and contrite confession to the chief before I saw Margaret Anderson, I would have to eat fast.

"The ghost." We were alone, but she lowered her voice to a whisper. "The thunder woke me up about three. The ghost was in the room over mine, moving around. I heard a really loud thump, like something falling over. And then scraping, as if somebody were dragging something across the floor — a coffin maybe. And rustling noises. Hideous rustling noises — not just upstairs, but out in the hall. Right outside my door." Remembering, her eyes were huge, with dark smudges under them, and she put her fist to her mouth. I could see that she had been terrified. "I've heard the ghost before, China, but never like that. I wanted to get up and wake you. I wanted you to hear it, so you'd know what I've been talking about."

"My goodness," I said mildly. Remembering what Claudia Roth had told me about the ghost showing up on stormy nights, I pulled out a chair, sat down, and helped myself to pancakes and sausages. "Did you get up and take a look? Did you go upstairs?"

"Are you *kidding*?" she demanded. "I was so scared I couldn't —" She reached for her coffee cup and took a sip, her hand visibly shaking. "I was afraid that if I got out of bed, I'd faint. And upstairs is where Sunny killed herself. You wouldn't catch me dead up there."

"I certainly hope not." I poured syrup over my pancakes.

She stared at me for a moment before she got it. Her lips trembled and she sounded almost despairing. "You don't believe me." With a clatter, she set the cup into its saucer. "You and Dorothea. You think I'm imagining all this. Hallucinating. You don't believe in ghosts."

"It's not that I don't believe," I said, wanting to explain. "In fact, I —"

This is complicated. I am a practical person, a believer in what's real and can be proven. Until the past few years, I had never believed in ghosts. However, my adventures with Ruby and more lately with Annie, the original and long-deceased occupant of my herb shop, have altered the way I think about these things.*

But while it is fair to say that I believe in the ghosts with whom I have a personal acquaintance — Annie, for instance, who is

* Ruby's adventure story is told in *Widow's Tears*. Annie, the ghost in China's herb shop, appears in *Queen Anne's Lace*.

altogether benign — I won't lay claim to a generic belief in unspecified spirits. One woman's ghost is another woman's shadow on the blind or an owl in the chimney or a tree branch scraping against the roof.

I didn't want to share this with Jenna, though. She was quite obviously frightened — no, terrified — by the noises she had heard in the night. Hemlock House was over a century old, and not in the best repair. There could very well be a real-world explanation.

"It's not that I don't believe," I said again, reassuring now, "and I apologize for sounding snarky. If it'll help, you can wake me up when you hear something that scares you. Or if you'd rather, I'd be glad to spend the night in your room."

Jenna brightened immediately. "Oh, would you, China? There's a fold-out sofa bed, if you're willing to do a sleepover. I would be so grateful."

A sleepover. I hadn't done something like that in a while. "Fine. Let's do it, then." I attacked my sausage. "I finished the pages you sent."

She slid a glance at me. "I hope you're going to tell me that you thought they were okay."

"More than okay, Jenna. In fact, your

novel is really good. You've answered most of my questions — such as how Elizabeth managed to earn the hundreds of pounds it took to get that ne'er-do-well husband of hers out of jail. I hadn't thought about the possibility of her selling the book as a serial — *and* selling it in the apothecary shops. Makes perfect sense."

"Of course it makes sense. It's what happened. I'm sure she had street vendors selling those weekly serials. The women who peddled herbs could have hawked them, too." She smiled. "I'll have some more pages for you this evening. And maybe, after that, we can talk about where the book needs to go. I'd really like some feedback."

"Perfect." I finished my pancakes, glanced up at the clock, and pushed my chair back. "I need to be on my way down the mountain. I have a couple of interviews in Bethany this morning and a meeting this afternoon." I looked out the window to see that the drizzle had almost stopped but the wind was still blowing a gale. "All I have is this corduroy blazer, and that wind is pretty impressive. Do you suppose I could borrow a coat?"

"Of course. I'm not going out, so you can take my parka." Jenna stood and began picking up her dishes. "You might want a pair of boots, too."

I thought of Ruby's recommendation of boots and smiled. There's no denying that my best friend is psychic, and it looked like she had scored once again. But I shook my head. "Thanks," I said. "I'll mostly be in town. I don't think I'll need them."

In a moment, Jenna was back with a chocolate-brown fleece-lined North Face parka. "This ought to keep you warm," she said, handing it to me. "Tonight, if the ghost comes back, we can play ghostbusters." She looked hopeful. "Dorothea thinks it's all silly stuff, and I'm too seriously chicken to do it on my own."

"Sure." I grinned. "Just us chickens. Sounds like fun."

Had I but known . . .

It felt cooler than it had when I got up that morning. The clouds had thickened into a dense gray porridge, and the wind was definitely blowing harder. I didn't need the parka and probably wouldn't, I thought, but it was good insurance.

When I got into the car and started down the mountain, I tried again to get a local weather radio report. No luck this time, either. But that was okay, because I needed to pay attention to the road — the switchbacks were, if anything, more terrifying going down — and I had plenty to think about. I wasn't looking forward to confessing my wrongdoing to Chief Jeremy Curtis, believe me. But I had done a bad thing and I wanted to get it off my conscience before it ate a hole in my grimy soul.

Cell phone service on the road was intermittent, but just as I completed the last zigzag, McQuaid called. He had dug up the information we had discussed the night before. By the time we said goodbye, my conversation with the chief was looking even more complicated.

There was much less coming and going in the police station this morning, but the same young female officer who had been so busy the day before was at the front desk.

"Any word on Mr. Conway's condition?" I asked. An appropriate question, I thought, coming from the person who had probably saved his life.

She actually smiled. "They're saying he's off the critical list."

I let out my breath. "Has the chief been able to talk to him yet?" I needed to know, but this was an impertinent question. I doubted that I'd get an answer.

She fooled me. "The hospital said they thought he could be questioned this morning," she said, which I took to mean "not yet." The red light on her phone blinked. "You can go in now." She pointed in the direction of a door marked chief.

Chief Curtis sat behind his desk and listened gravely to my confession of hearing Jed Conway's whispered word. *Blackwell? Maxwell?* Not a dying declaration, now that Conway was on the survivor's list. But in the scheme of things, perhaps just as important.

Then he read me the riot act, scathingly and at length. He left nothing out, but I took the scolding meekly. I deserved every word of it.

He finished with "You might get away with that in Texas, but not in North Carolina. I could arrest you for obstructing justice."

I was tempted to point out that I *had* gotten away with it in North Carolina — until I confessed, which I had done voluntarily and of my own free will. But I was at fault and I knew it, so I ate more crow, with a hefty garnish of *mea culpa.* I said I was sorry (which was true), and that my husband (the ex-cop, remember him?) had been very, very, *very* angry when I told him what I had done (which was a lie, because I didn't tell him). But I thought it might make the chief a little more sympathetic. I even offered to amend my witness statement to include my best guess as to what I might or might not have heard. His staff was probably pretty busy this morning, so I would be glad to retype it myself. I would be willing to sign it in blood, if he liked.

His mouth twitched but he managed to frown instead of smiling. "Well, okay," he said, drawing it out grudgingly. "Amend your statement. Apologize to your better half. And don't do it again."

"I won't," I said contritely. "I've learned my lesson." I waited a beat. We weren't done here. "I suppose you've already talked to Kevin Maxwell." The impertinent question again.

He pushed his lips in and out, deciding whether he wanted to answer. But we were on the same team once more, so he said, "Okay. I don't know what you've been told, but Bethany is a small town. Everybody's heard that Kevin was pissed off at Conway and his Hemlock friends over something that happened with his sister. Sure. Maxwell was the first one I thought of. Figured he had a damned good motive, although I was a little surprised that he didn't finish the job."

"Okay." I pushed my luck. "And?"

He leaned back in his chair. "And it turns out that when Conway was shot, your boy Kevin was over at the Bull's Head, way to hell and gone on the other side of town. Three of his coworkers were with him. They were sitting down to brisket and beer about the time you called 9-1-1. No way he was at the Open Book."

Not my boy, but whatever. I nodded. "So my first impression — that Conway had said 'Blackwell' — is probably correct."

"Maybe," he said, drawing it out. "I'll have to check, but if there are any Blackwells in town, I can't think of them right off."

I took a breath and dove in. "It happens that Blackwell is the name of the author who compiled the rare book that was stolen from the Hemlock House a couple of weeks ago. The one you mentioned yesterday," I added helpfully.

"Whoa." He narrowed his eyes at me. "You're telling me that the shooting had something to do with that book?"

"The possibility did occur to me," I admitted.

He thought about this for a moment.

"That theft wasn't my case," he said finally. "Hemlock House is outside my bailiwick. However, I routinely see the county's log of ongoing investigations. And

Sheriff Rogers and I sit down together every couple of weeks, just to catch up. He told me about that book. He also said it looks like some other things are missing from that library. Rare books, maybe. Pictures of flowers, stuff like that."

"Yes. The Carswell collection has never been catalogued, so it'll take some serious work to determine just how much might be gone. An initial guesstimate puts the loss at seventy or eighty thousand. But it could be a lot more than that, not including the Blackwell book. The auction estimate on *that* is a hundred thousand dollars."

Both eyebrows went up and Curtis whistled softly. "Mucho dinero."

"Plus, there's this." I told him about standing beside the counter at the Open Book and noticing Socrates.com on the shop's computer. The website offered a couple of prints from an antique book about lilies, maybe from the book in the Carswell library. The two I had seen — the blackberry lily and the Barbados lily — were priced at nearly $6,000.

"There are thousands of botanical prints for sale on the internet," I went on, "so the site itself isn't any great surprise. I struck out when I tried to trace the owner, though — the domain name is privately registered.

My husband's PI firm has the software to do forensic web searches, and he had better luck. He thinks I ought to tell you that it's owned by Jed Conway. The prints for sale on that site may have been stolen from the Carswell library."

I made eye contact with the chief, wanting to be sure that he understood that the information I was giving him came via a legitimate, card-carrying detective — one of his tribe — and was hence credible and trustworthy. Yes, I admit it. I was shamelessly draping myself in McQuaid's borrowed authority. But whatever works.

"Jeez." The chief sat up straight and swiveled his desk chair to the computer on his right. "Socrates.com, you said?" He typed it in. As the site came up, he opened a desk drawer, pulled out a pair of black-framed glasses, and put them on, peering at the screen.

"I'll be damned," he said softly, scrolling down the page. "A ton of stuff here. Pricy, too. Three grand for a picture of a freakin' peach!"

I waited for a moment, then said, "There's something else you should know."

He turned away from the computer, frowning. "Something else like what?"

"I talked to Claudia Roth yesterday —

she's a neighbor and relative of Miss Carswell."

"The parrot lady." He was dismissive. "About as loony as they come."

"Not so much," I said. "She confirmed something I had already heard from the cook-housekeeper at Hemlock House. Conway had a serious dispute with Carswell several months before she died. He had come up with a scheme to sell items from her collection for her — including the Blackwell *Herbal.* According to Roth, Conway needed the commissions from those sales to offset the serious losses at his retail shop."

"Losses?" The chief gave me a sharp look. "The store was in trouble?"

"Online bookstores are giving brick-and-mortar bookstores a hard time everywhere. You might check with his bank to see what kind of deposits and withdrawals he's been making." I paused. "Anyway, Carswell was planning to create a foundation to turn her collection into an accessible library, and she wasn't keen on selling pieces of it. They argued, and she sent him packing." I paused. "He had already introduced a couple of other people to her, and her edict didn't apply to them, apparently. They got along with her. They continued to visit. Frequently."

"Who would that be?"

"Margaret Anderson, for one. She worked at the library for months, both before and after Carswell died."

"Margaret —" His jaw tightened. "You're not saying she . . ." He shifted uncomfortably. "Who's the other one?"

His reaction made me curious, but I filed it away and went on. "Amelia Scott. Anderson was there to help organize the collection, which had never been catalogued. Scott was there —"

"Scott was there on Hemlock Guild business," the chief put in.

This was getting interesting. "Hemlock Guild?" I played dumb.

"Named for a poison plant, not the tree. It's a right-to-die support group. It came up when I was investigating Wanda Sanger's suicide."

I raised an inquiring eyebrow and he went on. "Seems that there were questions when Sunny Carswell shot herself. Was the suicide assisted? Who helped? Sheriff Rogers — it was a county investigation — was skeptical. So he took a look at the Hemlock Guild. For a while, he had his eye on Amelia Scott."

Hmm. We were back to Sunny's suicide now. I was interested to know what triggered the sheriff's curiosity, and Curtis was willing to talk about it.

His story went like this. Amelia Scott had been at Hemlock House on the day Sunny died. The housekeeper had called 911 after Amelia discovered the body. But Sheriff Rogers couldn't find any evidence of assistance. At least, nothing that the DA was willing to take to a grand jury. Doc Peters, the county coroner, had ruled it a suicide. Carswell had used the same gun her daddy and granddaddy had both used for the same purpose — a 1911 .45 automatic, a one-off prototype made by the Carswells for a military contract before World War I. There were a couple of her clear prints, yes. But the gun had been wiped very clean, so there wasn't the usual smudging you'd find on a weapon somebody had been handling — no smears or partials, just several very clear prints, Carswell's prints. But as a prototype modification of the Browning patent, the gun was worth quite a bit of money on the collectors' market. Maybe it had been cleaned with the idea of selling it.

Curtis shook his head, speaking half to himself. "Think of that. Very same gun her daddy and granddaddy used. So yes, the coroner ruled it suicide, but there were still a few questions. And not much in the way of answers."

Answers. I thought bleakly of Sunny, the last of her family, alone with her books in that monstrosity of a house, with nothing to look forward to but a lingering and painful death. She couldn't be blamed for wanting to make a ritualistic end to it. But I also understood why the sheriff had questions. And why the questions had no answers.

There was a silence while Curtis chewed on his lip, going back to the thefts. Then he said, "Did Scott have access to the library, before or after Carswell died?"

I noticed that he hadn't asked about Margaret Anderson. "I don't know, but it seems likely. There was no security — no alarms, no video surveillance. There still isn't. And it would have been easy to duplicate a key."

He was thinking out loud. "So Scott could have been taking valuable stuff out of the library and handing it over to Conway to sell."

"Scott or Anderson," I said. "Or both. Conway may have had access, too, even after Carswell sent him away." I held up my hand, cautioning.

"But this is all speculation, Chief. I haven't talked to either of the two women. What's more, it hasn't yet been confirmed that any of the items on Jed's site came from the Carswell collection. That task may take

336

a while. And Socrates.com may not be the only website he owns." For good measure, I added, "The state sales tax people and the IRS may be interested in this, too. If he's running the website off the books, he's likely not paying taxes."

The chief pulled on his lip. Thinking out loud, he disregarded my caution about speculation. "And then Conway and his partner got crosswise — probably over money — and she shot him."

If that's the direction we were going, I'd go along, although I was still wondering why he seemed to discount Anderson as a possible partner.

"You might want to start with Conway," I said. "He's in a tight place. On the one hand, he surely knows the identity of the shooter and should be more than happy to tell you. On the other hand, if they were working together in a criminal enterprise, he's weighing the likelihood that whatever they were up to will be exposed and he'll be implicated. He definitely doesn't want to incriminate himself. Still, since it appears that he's going to recover, it's in his interest to cooperate." I smiled thinly. "You might want to get to him before his lawyer does."

The chief digested that, then reached for the phone. "Phyllis," he said, "call Mary

Jean over at the hospital and find out when's the soonest I can talk to Conway." He put the phone down and looked at me. "*You* a lawyer?"

The question put directly like that, I couldn't evade. "In a former incarnation. Licensed but no longer in practice."

"What flavor?"

"Criminal defense attorney."

"Figures," he said, turning back to his computer. "Probably easier to stay married to an ex-cop if you're not in the business of defending crooks." He typed for a moment, then turned the monitor so I could see it. "This your husband's outfit?"

We were looking at the website of Mc-Quaid's PI firm. "That's it," I said, smiling a little. It looked good. Black background, white lettering, red accent lines, a photograph of the scales of justice. Mostly Mc-Quaid's work, but I had offered a few suggestions.

"The firm's investigators," he read aloud from the site, "have considerable experience working alongside state police agencies as well as federal agents of the FBI, ATF, DEA, IRS, and the US Postal Inspection Service. The firm's founder is a graduate of the FBI National Academy in Quantico, Virginia."

He cocked an eyebrow at me. "All true? No hype?"

"Every word," I said. That paragraph came right straight out of McQuaid's résumé.

"Impressive. Hope business is good." He took his glasses off and dropped them into the drawer. "You an investigator with the firm?"

"No, I'm not." Which is also true. I have occasionally been on the perimeter of McQuaid's work but I've never been fully involved with it. Still, this seemed like the right time to come clean about who I was. "The truth is that I am a longtime friend of Dr. Harper. She asked me to see what I could learn about the theft of the Blackwell *Herbal.* She was deeply frustrated that the foundation's board refused to publicly acknowledge that it had been stolen so that collectors and booksellers could be on the lookout. If nobody's looking, it's not likely to be recovered."

"Yeah, well, she has cause to worry. The case is still open, and Rogers considers her a suspect."

"Exactly," I said dryly. "Under the circumstances, if the thief isn't found and charged, it may be impossible to clear her name. And salvage her professional reputation."

The phone rang. The chief picked it up, listened a moment, then said, "On our way." He hung the phone up and stood. "We're going to the hospital."

I stood too. "You want me to come along?"

"Yeah. Conway wants to thank the woman who saved his life. And when I question him, I may need someone who can back me up with book stuff, art stuff — details I've got no way of knowing." He cocked his eyebrow at me. "You're that person. Or as close as I can come. So get a move on."

"Yes, sir," I said.

I wasn't surprised. We were on the same team.

CHAPTER TWELVE

I have presented to view divers forms or
plots, amongst which it is possible you
may find some that may near the matter
fit, and shall leave the ingenious Practi-
tioner to their consideration and use.

Leonard Meager
The English Gardener: Or, a Sure Guide to
Young Planters & Gardeners, 1688

In the time I'd spent with the chief, the
temperature had dropped ten or fifteen
degrees and snow had begun to spit from
the leaden sky. When I came out of the
police station, the wind ran icy fingers down
my collar, grabbed fiercely at my hair, and
ripped my breath away. Virgil had arrived.

I was wearing only my corduroy blazer, so
I ran to the car and grabbed Jenna's parka
from the back seat, although when I put it
on, it was like folding myself into an ice
pack. When I put a hand into a pocket, I

was glad to find a pair of mittens.

At the hospital, I parked as close as I could to the entrance. When I got out and yanked the parka hood over my head, something cold and wet hit my cheek. I looked down as a large white snowflake splatted onto my cocoa-brown sleeve. In Pecan Springs, it snows only once or twice a decade, so I was as thrilled as a kid with a new sled.

The chief, not so much. When I caught up with him outside the entrance, he was glaring up at the sky. "I'm ready to be done with this winter crap," he growled as he opened the door. "Hard on the city's snow-plow budget." Which isn't a topic I had given much thought to, so I followed him without reply.

Inside, the small community hospital had a sharp antiseptic smell. The hallways were bright and busy, and the people wore that look of focused intensity you see on the faces of those who are working on important — perhaps life-altering — tasks. Conway had been moved out of the ICU into a private room, and a uniformed cop was parked on a chair outside the door. The day-shift cop, Curtis said. He hadn't been taking any chances that Conway's assailant might come back to finish him off.

The charge nurse — Mary Jean — and the chief were first-name acquaintances. She sniffed her displeasure when she saw that he had brought somebody with him. But he was firm, so she directed us to Conway's door and told us we had fifteen minutes. The room was small, with one window in the outer wall so the patient could watch the snow falling onto azaleas covered with pink blooms and one on the hall so the nurses could watch the patient.

Conway was flat on his back in the narrow bed, his head elevated a couple of inches. His left side was heavily bandaged, an IV drip was taped into the back of his right hand, and he was hooked up to several monitors strategically stationed at the head of the bed. He was pale and deflated, as if the life force that pumped him up had seeped away, along with the blood he'd lost. An oversized florist bouquet of orange and yellow lilies sat on the wheeled table over the foot of the bed.

We took off our parkas and dumped them on the room's only chair. "Hey, Jed," Curtis said in a friendly tone. "How you doin' there, man?"

"Not just real well." Conway's voice was a hoarse whisper and he cleared his throat and tried again. "But they're saying I might live." He managed a wan smile.

"Glad to hear it," Curtis said. "When I saw you on that gurney, I figured you for a goner." He gestured to me. "Hey, this is the pretty lady who found you and called nine-one-one. China Bayles. An investigator all the way from Texas, on the hunt for that big old book that got stolen from Sunny Carswell's library. She happened to walk in the front door of your store about the time you were going down at the back. Kept you from leaving any more blood on your carpet."

Conway's eyes focused on me and he tried for another smile. "I really can't thank you enough. You being there — lucky thing for me." His forehead puckered. "An investigator?"

I returned the smile, murmured the obligatory "So glad I could help," and moved back against the wall without answering his question.

Curtis stepped closer to Conway. "I guess you know why I'm here, Jed. There are things I've got to know, and the sooner the better." He reached up and flicked the switch on the black body cam he wore clipped to his uniform shirt. "For the record, we're on camera. Let's start with who did this. Who shot you?"

I approved. Some cops object to body

cams, but they work for both cops and citizens. The protection goes both ways. And in this circumstance, it was an unobtrusive way to document the interview.

Conway turned his head. "I don't feel like —"

"Come on, man," Curtis said impatiently. "You and me, we go way back. But this is not a social call and I don't have time for games. You give me what I need and I'll see what I can do to keep you out of the worst of the trouble."

"Trouble?" Conway turned back again, alarmed. "I'm the victim here. Somebody came in through the back door of my shop, looking for money." His voice got squeaky. "Big bald biker-type white guy with a tattoo on his neck and a —"

"Stuff it, Jed," Curtis snapped. "You sure the hell are in trouble. Don't make it worse with obstruction." He glanced at me and leaned closer. "Blackwell," he said distinctly.

Conway's eyes widened. "No, no. He was white. Biker. Snake tattoo on his neck."

"Socrates dot com."

Conway sucked in a breath. "Means nothing to me. I —"

"Sunny Carswell."

"Sunny —"

The chief held up a finger, then another.

"Amelia Scott. The Hemlock Guild. That expensive book that's gone from the Carswell library. Those high-priced flower prints you're pushing. Socrates dot com." He was holding up five fingers. "All this shit is tied together in one big plot. I want to know how, and you're going to tell me."

"I'm calling the nurse." Conway felt for the call button that was on the bed, close to his hand. "I need to get some sleep."

"Forget it." Curtis shoved the button out of reach. "You know I won't quit on this, Jed. And if you won't talk to me, the next person standing here will be the DA. You don't want to deal with her, do you? Marlene won't care how bad you hurt. She'll haul your ass out of that bed and plant you in front of the grand jury so fast it'll make your head swim. She'll ask you about those pricy pictures you're hawking on that website of yours. How you got 'em, who's buying them, what kind of taxes you've been paying on the income. She'll haul Amelia in there, too." His cell phone rang and he reached into his pocket to silence it. "Your gal pal is in it just as deep as you are. And whoever shot you is in deeper." His voice grew rougher. "Who was it? Amelia?" His voice altered. "Margaret?"

Conway closed his eyes. "Not Margaret,"

he whispered. "Margaret had nothing to do with any of this. I want . . ." He stopped.

I was waiting for him to say "I want my lawyer." Actually, that's what he *should* have said. If I'd been a member of the North Carolina bar I would have felt obligated to step forward and say, "This cop may be a friend but you don't have to answer his questions, Mr. Conway. Whatever you've got to say, you need to say it to your attorney first."

But I wasn't and I didn't and Conway didn't either. Instead, he lay there in bed and thought about things. When he opened his eyes again, he said, "It's complicated, Jeremy."

"It's always complicated," Curtis said flatly. "That's the hell of it. Mary Jean will be booting me out in a few minutes. So start with whoever it was who put the gun to your back and pulled the trigger. We can get to the rest of the plot later."

There was a long silence. "Shit," Conway said finally. He took a breath. "To tell the truth, I'm pretty damned sick of living like a criminal. I want my life back." Another breath. "It was Amelia. It was Amelia all the way."

"Amelia Scott?"

"How many other Amelias do we know?"

Conway was wearily ironic. "But the shooting wasn't her fault. I'm sure she only meant to threaten me." He gulped a breath. "The gun must have gone off . . . you know, accidentally."

"Got it. Amelia Scott tried to shoot you. Accidentally. So how did you work this little operation? She lifted the stuff out of the Carswell library and gave it to you to fence?" Curtis' voice took on an edge. "And Margaret? What about her? Is she any part of this?"

"No, *no*," Conway said again. "*Not* Margaret. She worked at Sunny's library, yes. But she had nothing to do with this. Jeez, Jeremy, you of all people ought to know that. Margaret wasn't in on this."

Something about the way he said that caught my attention. Why should Curtis know what Margaret was involved in?

The chief grunted. "So okay. So how did this cottage industry work? Amelia stole, you fenced? Is that it?"

"Fenced." Conway winced at the word. "Yeah, basically. I'd tell her what to look for, what I had a buyer for, what I knew would sell. She'd get it out of the library. Had to do it that way, after Sunny shut me out. But then the new director — Harper, her name is — said she was closing the

348

library to visitors and wouldn't let Amelia in. As far as I was concerned, that was the end." He coughed, painfully. "I told Amelia I was calling it quits."

I suppressed a wry chuckle. I'd often wished I had a hundred bucks every time I heard a crook claim that the crime he'd been caught in was his *last* crime. I had the feeling that there was more to this plot than Conway was telling us. Much more.

"Calling it quits?" the chief asked. "Ending the partnership, you mean? Closing down the website? What?"

"All of it. I wanted out. I was ready to . . . go straight, I guess you'd say. When the book went missing, Dr. Harper started tightening security at the library. She told the foundation board they had to have cameras and an alarm system. I told Amelia we were done." Another cough, harder this time. He lay back, pale and wasted-looking. "That's when she lit into me about the Blackwell book."

"Lit into you?"

"Yeah. Yesterday. We were in the shop and she was loud and pretty wired. I told her I had to open the store and I walked her to the back door to let her out. But she was screaming and —" His jaw was working. "I kind of pushed her out the door and turned to go back into the shop and . . . and, that's when it happened. When the gun went off. I don't think she meant to do it."

"You said she lit into you about the book. You're talking about the big one that was stolen from Hemlock House a couple of weeks ago?"

"Yeah. *The Curious Herbal.* Amelia believes I took it. She wanted her half."

"Wait a minute. Amelia *believes* you took the book? You're saying you didn't?"

"I didn't." He looked up, his eyes on Curtis' face. "Swear to God I didn't, Jeremy. In fact, when I heard it was gone, I figured *she* had taken it. Amelia." He dropped his eyes. "I may have given her a pretty hard time about that."

Oh, he had, had he? I could imagine the two of them, fighting over who had stolen the *Herbal,* each one accusing the other. I could see the argument escalating until it finally ended with a gunshot.

He was going on, as if he were glad to get this off his chest. "I don't have a clue where the damned book is, and I kept telling her that, over and over. But I couldn't convince her. She just kept saying she knew I'd taken it out of the library and sold it to that collector in Brussels who wants it. She said she had to have the money and I had to hand it

350

over. She's got money troubles." His smile was a grimace wobbling with exhaustion. "Like me. Like you." He closed his eyes and his voice dropped to a whisper I could barely hear. "Like everybody. Money troubles."

I was squirming. If this were a movie, we'd just had our confession moment — taped on the chief's body cam, start to finish — and the end titles soundtrack was coming up while the closing credits rolled. But in real life, the Hemlock County DA would be a lot happier if Curtis would break off the interrogation right now and do two things.

One, subpoena Conway's bank account records, to see if there were any recent large deposits.

And two, question Amelia Scott. It was time to confront her with Conway's accusation. Get her denial or her explanation. Or that of her lawyer.

But most important, get the weapon Scott had used to shoot Conway — before she chucked it in the river and they had to pay a dive team to look for it. Which was probably not in the city's budget.

And he ought to have a talk with Margaret Anderson, too. I could think of several reasons why Conway might want to convince the chief that she wasn't involved in his scheme. The most likely: that she had taken the *Herbal,* he had sold it for her, and the two of them had split something close to a hundred thousand dollars.

I had thought about this earlier, after I'd heard from Claudia Roth that Anderson was angry when the board replaced her. Stealing the *Herbal* would settle accounts with the board for essentially firing her and at the same time get even with her rival for being better qualified. Plus, of course, there was all that money. I had even considered Margaret as a candidate for Conway's shooter. Now, I mentally subtracted the Smith and Wesson from my image of the frosted hair, the red twinset, and the Manolos.

Next questions: If Margaret had stolen it, did she still have it? Or had Conway already fenced it for her? And why had the chief so deliberately evaded any discussion of Margaret in our conversation earlier that morning? What did he know that I didn't?

Meanwhile, Conway was not going anywhere. He would no doubt get a lawyer with whom the DA could dicker. If he returned the unsold items and helped to recover those he had sold, he might get the charges reduced from felony larceny to —

Mary Jean appeared at the door. She

frowned at me and gave Curtis a starchy smile.

"Time's up, Chief. And Phyllis just called the nurses station — says to tell you that you need to pick up your cell. It's urgent."

"Thanks." Curtis put a hand on Conway's arm. "I'm going now, Jed. After I've got a few things straight with Amelia — with Margaret, too — I'll be back and we can start getting this mess cleaned up. You hang tight for now. LeRoy Hatch is sitting right outside the door. Need anything, just ask him."

This sounded generous, but I knew what it was: a warning that there was a cop standing guard. Take one step out that door, you'll be wearing cuffs.

Conway knew it, too.

Outside, the snow was coming down fast and fierce now, blown almost sideways by the whipping wind. Virgil had arrived in earnest. Through the blur of its shifting white curtain, I could see the time/temperature sign on the red brick bank building across the street. I shivered. Thirty-two degrees — a full twenty-five degree drop since I left Hemlock House that morning. The calendar had flipped back to winter in just a few hours.

Behind me, the chief was on his cell. He ended the call and pocketed the phone, lips tight. "You're coming with me." He jerked his thumb toward the intersecting street. "Six blocks south on Pine, big brick house, middle of the block on the right. Meet me there."

"What's going on? Who —"

But I was talking to the back of his black parka. He sprinted to his car, turned on the flasher and the siren, and pulled out of the parking lot fast, fishtailing on the icy pavement. Wherever we were going, he was aiming to get there in a hurry.

I was slower. Somebody had spread salt pellets on the sidewalk, but the footing was still treacherous. Bent against the wind, I had to struggle to keep my balance. In the car, I saw that it was now nearly nine-thirty and I was supposed to be at Margaret Anderson's house, so I called and told her I was running late. "I should be able to make it in another hour," I told her.

And maybe, by that time, the chief could go with me. But he seemed to have some sort of information about Margaret that I didn't have, and we would have to discuss my plan to meet with her before I kept the appointment. I would cross that bridge when I came to it, though.

The streets were already glazed and treacherous, and where I'm from, we don't get a lot of practice in driving on ice. It was definitely a challenge, especially since the windshield wipers of my little Mirage were having trouble keeping up with the blowing snow. I could see the chief's flasher ahead but I didn't even try to catch up to his car.

Midway down the block, several squad cars were angled into the curb in front of an impressively porticoed brick house. An EMS ambulance was there too, the med techs huddled with their backs to the wind, hands in their pockets and watch caps pulled down over their ears. As I got out of the car, I saw the chief hurrying up the snowy driveway toward the double garage. Yellow crime-scene tape was stretched across the driveway and the front walk. The snow had been blowing hard enough to create a small drift in front of the garage door. It had stayed in place, like a low white curb, when the door was lifted.

A uniformed officer in a heavy navy-blue parka, her blond hair skinned back into a ponytail, had come out of the garage and was talking with the chief. When I joined them, I saw that the officer's name badge said *Chris Bojanov.*

"When?" the chief was asking.

"Last night, seems like. A neighbor found her this morning and called it in —" Bojanov glanced at her watch. "A half hour ago. Doc Lawrence just got here. He's in there now." She jerked her head toward the garage. "With her."

"A note?"

"In the car, along with an empty bottle of Lunesta and a Glock 9mm. The car ran until it ran out of gas. Most of the night, probably." She added, "I bagged the note, the gun, and the bottle and left them where I found them. The note is kinda long and rambling, but it explains the gun."

"Stay here," Curtis told me.

I stayed. I've seen suicides. I didn't need to see another.

"I know who you are." Bojanov frowned at me. "You're that woman from Texas who found Jed Conway after he got shot yesterday. The one who was typing." There was a faint note of accusation in her voice. "At the police station."

I nodded. "I just can't resist those Selectrics, you know? Every time I see one, I have to sit down and put my fingers on it. And then before I know it, I —"

She rolled her eyes.

I should behave. "Anyway," I said penitently, "it looked like y'all had more than enough to do."

She eyed me, remembering I was there with the chief, and decided we must be on the same team. "We're understaffed," she agreed. "Ask the chief, he'll tell you. Every budget, it's the same. City council never gives us enough positions. Or overtime."

I nodded sympathetically. I'd heard the same complaint from my friend Sheila Dawson, the Pecan Springs chief of police. But I was thinking of Amelia Scott and wondering what had driven her to kill herself. Was it the prospect of going to prison for attempted murder — or for murder, if Conway had died? Was she repenting her role in the library larceny that the two of them had dreamed up? Or was there something else? Something like . . .

I turned my back to the wind and pushed my hands into my pockets. My fingers were cold inside my borrowed mittens. My feet were even colder. "I understand that Ms. Scott was the president of the Hemlock Guild."

"Yeah. The right-to-die folks. Not all that popular in Bethany. I guess she decided to practice what she's been preaching." Another frown. "Except that I thought they were supposed to use hemlock. No shortage of that around here." She pointed a leather-

357

gloved finger toward a tall, conical tree beside the garage, now frosted with snow. "There's one right there."

"Hemlock poison doesn't come from the hemlock tree," I said.

"It doesn't?" Bojanov looked surprised. "No kidding?"

"No kidding," I said.

"Where does it come from, then?"

"Poison hemlock is a plant, maybe yea tall." I held my hand waist-high. "Looks a lot like Queen Anne's lace, blossoms like little white umbrellas, lots of green, ferny leaves. Doesn't take much to kill a person — a hundred milligrams, just eight or nine fresh leaves, will do the job. It was the go-to poison for centuries, if you had a mind to do yourself in. Not so much now, though." Now, there's carbon monoxide, as near as your closest car and garage. And a lot less painful way to go.

"Queen Anne's lace? I see that blooming along the road all summer." Bojanov shook her head. "Jeez, I always thought hemlock poison came from the tree. Like, if you boiled a bunch of cones, maybe. How about that? All these years, and I was wrong."

"I think somebody told me she sold real estate," I said. "Ms. Scott, I mean."

"Yeah. Commercial real estate." Feeling

the cold, Bojanov stamped her feet. "Market hasn't been any too good here and the chances for recovery don't look great. I heard her company bottomed out a couple of months ago, after some bad investments. Filed for Chapter Eleven. Folks said she might lose her house, too." She looked up at the place speculatively. "Maybe she decided she couldn't live without it. Some people are like that, you know."

"Could be," I said, remembering Conway's remark about money troubles. Looting the Carswell library must have seemed like an easy way to make up the difference. And once the money began coming in, it would have been an incentive to more looting. The loss of it could have been an motivation for suicide. "Family?"

"Divorced last year, no kids. All wrapped up in that Hemlock Guild stuff, I understand. You know how it is with some people. They get a tribe, they don't need anybody else."

The chief stepped out of the garage, his eyes flinty. To Bojanov, he said, "Miller is taking over for you and you're coming with me. Bring your car. This may take a while and I may need you to stay after I leave." To me, he said, "I'm bringing in a team to search this place for that book you keep talking about. Can you describe what they're looking for?"

"I can likely get you a photo," I said, taking out my phone. Pointedly, I added, "while you get a search warrant." Back in 1973, North Carolina had been the last state to abolish the common-law crime of suicide. Which meant that no crime had been committed here, and there were no exigent circumstances. It wasn't my job to remind him he needed a warrant, but I did it anyway. I was on his team, wasn't I?

He narrowed his eyes at me. "The warrant is coming." His cell dinged, and he looked at it. "It's here. You got a problem, Bayles?"

"No problem at all," I said cheerfully. "Just being helpful."

I put in Jenna's cell number. The chief pulled Bojanov off a little distance to talk to her. Bojanov went to her squad car, and he came back. By time, my phone was displaying three photos of an impressive calf-bound, gold-embossed, silver-clasped copy of *A Curious Herbal*. Jenna had sent them.

"Forwarding to you," I said.

It took just a moment to transfer the photos from my phone to his and from his to the search team's. He pocketed his cell.

"Follow me," he said, and started down the drive.

"Where to now?" I asked, trying to step in his footprints. The snow had been falling hard and drifting while I'd been talking to the officer. My loafers were soaked. Ruby's hand-knitted wool socks were soggy. And cold.

Over his shoulder, he said. "Margaret Anderson's. I want you there, too." At the foot of the drive, he stopped abruptly and turned. "Something else. When you were interviewing folks for that so-called article of yours, did anybody come up with the idea that maybe Carswell hadn't killed herself?"

I stopped too, pausing to answer his question. "The parrot lady couldn't add it up," I said. "Her thing was the weapon. According to her, Sunny would never have used a gun to kill herself — and especially not *that* gun. Because of her father and grandfather, that is." I hunched my shoulders against the wind. "Are you going to tell me what was in that suicide note?"

The chief scowled. He was deciding whether I deserved to know. At last, he said, "It was a confession. Scott claims she killed Sunny Carswell."

"O-kay," I said slowly. I wasn't surprised. Even the sheriff had said that the death

361

raised more questions than they had answers for. And murder can be made to look like suicide — if the murderer is smart. And lucky. "She give details?"

"How she did it, why she did it. Says Sunny caught her stealing pages out of books. Says she knew where that old gun was kept. She got it, met Sunny in her room, shot her, wiped the gun and put it in Sunny's hand." He paused. "Says she shot Jed as well, and left us the gun to prove it. A Glock nine."

I whistled between my teeth. "She say why she shot Conway?"

"Yeah. Says that he knew how Sunny died and threatened to tell. When she found out he wasn't dead, she figured he'd turn her in." Another pause, this one longer. "But she claims she had nothing to do with the big book. The one you're looking for." His voice was oddly flat. "She says Margaret Anderson must have stolen it."

And there it was. An accusation made in a dying declaration was considered an exception to the hearsay rule and was therefore admissible in court.

But this revelation wasn't much of a surprise to me, either. I had already moved Anderson to the top of my suspect list. "You're going to search Anderson's house?"

Silly question. Of course he was going to search Anderson's house. Scott's suicide note provided the probable cause he needed to get a warrant. He wanted me to be there to identify the *Herbal* if he found it. Well, I supposed I could do that preliminarily. He would need to bring Dorothea or Jenna down from the mountain for an official identification.

"Yeah," he said briefly. There was more coming, and he opened his mouth to tell me what it was.

But it didn't come. He cleared his throat, tried again, and gave it up. After an awkward moment, his glance fell on my loafers and he found something he wanted to say.

"In weather like this, anybody with a lick of sense would be wearing snow boots."

CHAPTER THIRTEEN

"There's rue for you, and here's some for me — we may call it herb of grace o' Sundays. Oh, you must wear your rue with a difference."

William Shakespeare
Hamlet (IV, v)

The herb rue has many complex meanings, often contradictory. Its bitter taste symbolizes regret and consciousness of guilt; at the same time, it has a cleansing and purging effect, symbolizing repentance and forgiveness. Its use as an abortifacient linked it with fornication and adultery, while in other instances it is the emblem of virginity. "Rue in time is a maiden's posy" was a favorite Scottish saying that linked these disparate meanings.

Susan Wittig Albert
China Bayles' Book of Days

The chief had left Scott's suicide note for the crime-scene team to collect. But I didn't have to read it to know the legal steps that lay ahead. The note would be authenticated and accepted as a dying declaration in a hearing on Scott's death. On the basis of her written confession, Sheriff Rogers would reopen his investigation into Sunny Carswell's death, which could result in a new ruling in that case: murder, not suicide.

In a separate matter based on the same confession and his own, Jed Conway — a victim of his partner in crime — would be indicted as an accomplice in the theft of rare documents and with the sale of stolen property. He would be out on bail while his lawyer and the DA dickered over a plea, a fine, and his prison sentence. All of which takes time, of course. It might be a year or more before he was sentenced. He would likely lose his store and Bethany would lose its bookstore. Unless somebody bought it, that is. Carole Humphreys?

This left only the *Herbal,* but we now knew the identity of the thief and were on our way to apprehend her. As I got in the car and pulled out into the snowy street, I found myself getting excited about the very real prospect of recovering the book. Soon. Today, possibly. Maybe even this very morning. I thought of holding it in my hands, of feeling the rich leather binding and running my fingers over the silver clasps, of opening the cover and turning the pages. The *real* pages, not the pixel-perfect but unreal pages on my tablet screen. I took a breath. I could feel the excitement mounting.

And if Margaret (or Jed) had already sold it?

We could still get it back. The buyer would be traced, discovered, and questioned. He likely wouldn't be charged but was required by law to return the book to the Carswell library. If he wanted his money back . . . well, he'd have to try to shake it loose from the thief or thieves, which might not be so easy. Excuse me. I have no sympathy. That's what you get for buying stolen goods from a shady fence with sketchy morals.

And there it was, all the loose plot threads neatly wrapped up and tied with a flourish. Dorothea and Jenna would be ecstatic. The foundation board would (presumably) be pleased. I could go back to Pecan Springs with a feeling of accomplishment.

If it all fell into place, which was a long shot. I got that. But there was something else here I wasn't getting — something the chief wanted to tell me but hadn't. What was it?

I brought up the rear of our three-car caravan, the chief and Bojanov in their squads, and I in my little Mirage — slowly. The street was a skating rink and gusts of blowing snow closed down visibility to less than a block. I get to practice driving on ice maybe once every three or four years and I was determined to get where we were going without banging up the rental car.

But the country club neighborhood had a Christmas-card charm and when we pulled up in front of the Anderson house, the snowy white blanket softened its severe symmetries. Last night, I had decided that Margaret must be somewhat younger than I had thought, and I had mentally exchanged her pink twinset for one that was lipstick red. Now, looking forward to recovering the *Herbal,* I removed the pearls from her neck and substituted a snarky pearl-studded gold book on a gold chain. But the frosted hair and red Manolos remained.

Our little parade pulled into what looked like a snow-covered curb, behind another squad car. I turned off the motor and was about to get out when the chief opened the passenger door and slid into the seat.

"Ms. Bayles," he began, and stopped.

The snow was glistening on his brown hair. The jagged scar that sliced across his eyebrow gave his face a rakish look.

"Yeah?" I prompted, and he tried again, awkwardly.

"I need to tell you something. In the interest of transparency."

He was finally getting around to it. "Okay," I said. "Tell me what?"

He stripped off his gloves, delaying another minute. "Margaret Anderson and I have been . . . dating." He stuffed his gloves in the pockets of his parka, one glove in each pocket. He wasn't looking at me.

"Whoa," I said softly.

This was something I hadn't anticipated, but it certainly explained his hesitation. It might also explain the edge of animosity I had heard in the voice of Carole Humphreys — Chief Curtis' ex — when she'd talked to me about Margaret Anderson. Had her husband been cheating on her before their divorce? In a small town like Bethany, that could have been a public humiliation for Carole.

The chief ran a hand through his hair. "I know it . . . complicates things." His voice was rueful.

You bet it did. It complicated things considerably. Here we were, about to interview a woman who was accused of walking off with a rare book worth a hundred grand or more, and the chief of police had been *sleeping* with her? (If "sleeping with" was speculative, it was informed by the guilty expression on the chief's face.)

To make things worse, this particular interview was crucial to the investigation. Not only did it take us one step closer to getting our hands on the *Herbal,* it gave the chief a chance for a flip. Flipping — getting a crucial witness to come over to *your* side and tell you where the bodies are buried and who put them there — is a critical investigative tool that I've used more times than I can count. Amelia Scott, God rest her soul, was now beyond the reach of the law. Nobody was ever going to flip her. But Jed Conway was still here. And as a co-operating witness, Margaret Anderson might be willing to trade her testimony against him for a lighter sentence.

There's another thing, too. No matter how good your documentary and data-based evidence is, it can sometimes put a jury to sleep. A cooperating witness, on the other hand, could wake them up and make them see the crime as it was committed. Believe me. I've been there and watched the jury. I know how this works.

The chief was obviously not a happy camper. "I have to tell you that I don't for one minute believe that Margaret took that book," he said, spacing the words for emphasis. "She has lived in this town her entire life, she has an excellent reputation, and I know her to be as honest as . . ." He struggled for a suitable simile, gave it up, and settled for "totally honest."

"But I realize that she has to be questioned," he added gruffly, "and questioned now. I've explained the situation to Bojanov, and she's going to take the lead. I'll be there in case of . . . well, difficulty. Which I don't expect," he added with emphasis.

He jerked his head at the squad car parked ahead of our little convoy. "A couple of officers will assist Bojanov with the search for the book. You're here to authenticate it, if it turns out that Margaret has it — which I don't expect, either." He narrowed his eyes at me, remembering that I had confessed to being a lawyer. "I don't want you interfering with the questioning, Counselor. Got that?"

"Got it," I said, and looked at him with some sympathy. His jaw was set, his eyes were dark. It looked like he was thinking that Margaret had played him for a fool.

The path to the house hadn't been shoveled yet and was drifted ankle-deep — more snow in my loafers. The two officers stayed in their squad car while the three of us trooped to the front door, Bojanov looking about as glum as the chief.

He punched the bell, and after a moment, the door was opened by a slender, very attractive young woman. She might have been eighteen or twenty-eight or anywhere between. Her face was narrow, with high cheekbones. Her dark hair was short and strikingly asymmetrical, cut high and shaved over her ear on the right side, cut on a sharp slant and cupped under her jaw on the left. On the high side, a flowery vine tattoo climbed up her neck and under her ear. She wore a loose, drapy top, ivory, over tight jeans tucked into lace-up suede boots with three-inch stiletto heels. *Red* boots. Ms. Twinset's younger sister, maybe? A visiting niece?

No. Not.

The chief snatched off his cap. "Good morning, Margaret," he said, his voice formal and so strained it nearly cracked. "We need to come in and talk to you, if you don't mind."

Wait — what? *This* was Margaret? The chief's number-one girlfriend? The number-one felony-larceny suspect, credibly accused by a self-confessed larcenist in a dying declaration?

371

It was time for a rapid reset. I hastily erased the twinset, gray skirt, gold chain, and extra pounds. But those sexy suede boots were fire-engine red. I'd probably been right about the red Manolos.

"Come in?" Margaret looked startled. "Well, of course, Jeremy." Her eyes, questioning, went to Bojanov. "Hello, Chris." To me. "And this is —"

"Hi, Margaret." I leaned forward. "I'm China Bayles. We have an appointment this morning."

"Oh, you're the writer," she said. "Weren't we going to talk about your article on Sunny?" She looked puzzled. "I didn't know you'd be bringing . . . reinforcements."

"Ms. Bayles is here as an investigator working for the Hemlock House board of directors," the chief said. "She's looking into a few problems having to do with the Carswell library."

Not quite accurate, I thought, but I didn't want to correct him.

"The . . . board?" Margaret's eyes came back to me. "So you're *not* a writer." It wasn't a question.

I shook my head ruefully.

She thought about that for a moment, surveyed the three of us, then stepped back, holding the door open. "Well, I guess it won't do any good to say no." She glanced past us to the squad car. "Maybe your buddies want to come in, too?"

"They can wait, thanks," the chief muttered.

We went in, hanging our parkas on a hall tree inside the door. There was a piece of green carpet on the polished wood floor and we diligently wiped our feet, then followed Margaret past the stairway and down the hall. Her angled hair swung loose on one side and a spicy scent trailed behind her. She moved with a sure, swingy ease, even in those heels. I sneaked a look at the chief's face. It was grim.

Margaret hesitated at the double-door entrance to a spacious living room, its walls and carpet and furnishings every bit as bland and monochromatically traditional as the house itself. Above the sofa hung a lake-and-trees landscape that might have come from a starving-artist assembly line. Its twin — this one a lake-and-mountain scene — hung over the fireplace, on either side of which symmetrical walnut bookcases displayed a couple of years' worth of Book of the Month Club releases, along with a hodgepodge of trinkets and decorative stuff. I glanced at it curiously. This was the home of somebody who wrote about books? Who wore her hair lopsided?

"No," she decided, and turned to go down the hall. "I've got a fire going in the den. It's full of boxes and stuff, but let's go there anyway."

Boxes and stuff, indeed. A red brick fireplace burned brightly in one corner, and the walls were hung with trophy fish, mounted deer and bobcat heads, and dozens of framed photos and certificates. Through a large bay window, I could see the country club's tennis court drifted with white, its sagging net heavy with crystalized ice. A Siamese cat sat on the red-cushioned window seat, staring out at the falling snow. The floor was littered with stacks of dinner china, boxes of silver, crystal, and kitchenware, along with piles of newspaper and balls of twine. A larger box, prominently labeled *Goodwill,* was filled with sweaters, purses, and shoes, with an umbrella sticking rakishly out of the top. Another was heaped with what looked like curtains and draperies, a stack of folded scatter rugs on the floor beside it. A dozen U-Haul cardboard cartons, still flat, leaned against the wall.

Margaret added another stick of wood to the fire and pointed the chief and me to a pair of denim-slipcovered chairs at one side of the fireplace. Bojanov pulled up a cushioned bench and perched on the edge.

"Can I get you anything?" Margaret asked, hesitating beside a worn brown corduroy recliner. "Soft drink? Coffee?" Her eyes went to Curtis. "I think there's some of your Bud in the fridge." It was a declaration of their relationship — deliberate, I thought. Done in order to stake a claim, or to let Bojanov and me in on the secret? Or to remind Curtis of their friendship and ask him to go easy?

Coloring visibly, the chief got the point, whatever it was. "We're fine, thanks," he said brusquely. Bojanov nodded. I did too, with some regret. I wasn't on duty, and coffee would have warmed me up. My feet were wet. And cold.

Margaret sat in the recliner. With a gesture at the boxes, she said to me, "In case you're wondering, this is my mother's house. Dad died a year ago and Mom has moved to an assisted living facility. The house will be sold. My brother is working in London, so I'm the one who gets to deal with this stuff."

So that explained it. Some of it, anyway. I glanced at Bojanov, but she was getting out her notebook. Into the pause, I said, "I understand you're a blogger. And that you write a book review column." The chief was frowning, reminding me that I wasn't supposed to talk. I ignored him.

Margaret nodded. "I work with a couple of major online blogging organizations. For one, I review steamy romance, book and film. For another, I write about nontraditional relationships in the kink culture. Plus, I also do general reviews for regional newspapers. I was working in Raleigh, but when my folks got sick, I came back to Bethany to help out. That's when Jed — Jed Conway — introduced me to Sunny Carswell."

Well. I had been way out in left field on this one. Steamy romances and nontraditional relationships? The real Margaret was far more interesting than my fictional Ms. Twinset. I wanted to ask her to tell me about the kink culture, but the chief had cleared his throat and was now looking pointedly at Bojanov, who opened her notebook and made an obtrusive gesture that called attention to the fact that she was turning on her body cam.

"Margaret —" She stopped, started again. "Ms. Anderson, I don't know if you've heard this, but Amelia Scott died last night."

"Amelia?" Margaret's hand went to her mouth and her eyes opened wide. "Oh, my god, Chris. Really? I mean, first Jed and now Amelia? I can't believe it! I mean, who would do something like —"

Bojanov cut in with, "The investigation is still ongoing, but it looks like suicide."

Margaret gasped. "Suicide! But . . . but Amelia wasn't sick, was she? How did she —" She stopped. "Why did she —" She broke off again, leaning forward now, her face intent. I could see the wheels turning. She was getting to the *why.* "This doesn't have to do with what happened to Jed, does it?"

Without waiting for an answer, she turned to the chief. "How is Jed, Jeremy? I called the hospital this morning and Mary Jean told me that you were with him. She said he was better but —"

"We can come back to that later," the chief interrupted in a gruff voice. He nodded curtly at Bojanov, who cleared her throat and got on with it.

"Ms. Scott left a note. In it, she addressed the issue of some materials that are missing from the Carswell library. Among them is a rare book, called —" She looked down at her notebook. *"A Curious Herbal."* She looked back up at Margaret. "In the note, she says that you have that book in your possession."

The accusation was delivered without inflection. I studied Margaret's face, searching for her response. But if I'd been expecting a sudden *mea culpa,* I would have been disappointed.

"Me?" She looked blank. "*Me?* Why would Amelia think that I have the *Herbal?* It was stolen, wasn't it? That's what I heard, anyway. Somebody broke into the library a couple of weekends ago and took it. They've never caught the guy who —"

Her mouth hardened as the situation began to dawn on her. "Wait a minute. You're telling me that Amelia says *I* stole it?" She pointed at Bojanov's body cam. "Is that why you're recording this? You're here to accuse me?"

Bojanov was stone-faced. "We're here to find the book."

"Well, you're just out of bloody luck," Margaret shot back angrily. "And if anybody here in Bethany took it, it would have been Amelia herself." She turned to the chief, holding out her hands in a half-defiant, half-pleading gesture. "Jeremy, tell Chris it wasn't me. I didn't steal it. You know me better than that. And anyway, that happened the weekend I moved Mom to assisted living, didn't it? I was with her all day, every day, Friday, Saturday, and Sunday, getting her settled. I even *stayed* with her on Saturday night!"

In my days in the courtroom, I've watched plenty of liars plead innocent, and I've even defended my share. If this one was a liar, she was doing a pretty good job of it. I felt sorry for the chief, who obviously wanted to intervene but knew that he could only cause trouble for himself if he did. If he didn't, he was causing trouble for himself with Margaret, so as far as he was concerned, it was pretty much a lost cause.

"You're aware of the book, then?" Bojanov asked, studiously making notes. "About what it is, I mean."

Margaret rolled her eyes. "Don't be silly. Of course I'm aware of the book. It was a treasure, the most important thing in Sunny's library. She loved to take it out of the case and study the drawings. She couldn't stop talking about Elizabeth Blackwell and the way she saved that absurd husband of hers. I walked past the book every day when I was working there. It was gorgeous."

"But you don't have it now?" Bojanov persisted.

Margaret pulled herself up. "No, I don't have it *now*," she said indignantly. "I have never had it, and I don't know who does. Period. Paragraph. End of story."

Bojanov glanced in mute appeal to the chief and I could see that she had reached the end of her string of questions. She was going to pull out the warrant and that would likely be the end of this subject's cooperation. Next thing, Margaret would telephone her lawyer. It was up to me to deescalate this situation.

I smiled. "One of the things I've been curious about is the way Jed and Sunny worked together to build that really stunning collection," I asked mildly. "What can you tell us about that?"

For a moment, I didn't think she was going to respond — which would pretty much put an end to my questions, since I had no authority to require any answers. The chief looked puzzled, and irritated. He'd told me to keep my mouth shut. Bojanov was peering down at her notes.

After a moment's silence, Margaret said, a little stiffly, "Sunny usually had a pretty clear idea of what she wanted. Jed kept her supplied with catalogues, and she would go on the internet and do the research. Then Jed would make an offer for the item she was after, or if it was being sold at auction, he'd bid on it, in person or on the phone. She wasn't involved in that at all. In the buying, I mean."

"So he actively participated in building that collection," I said, remembering my conversation with Claudia about pump-and-dump. It was also possible that he might have been colluding with the seller to increase the price of what he bought — for a share of the extra. "Is it fair to say that he was acting as her agent?"

"Sure. Sometimes it meant buying individual titles, sometimes he'd buy lots — batches of books or prints, whatever. So we might get a box of miscellaneous stuff when Sunny was interested in just one item. Jed would dispose of the rest."

I glanced at the chief to see if he would like to jump in here, but when I caught his eye, he gave me an imperceptible nod, signaling me to go on.

Back to Margaret. "Through Socrates-.com?"

"Yes." She nodded, appearing now to be interested in my questions — or perhaps relieved to be talking about Jed and Sunny, not about herself. And I wasn't a cop, so I might have seemed a little less threatening. "He launched that website especially to help Sunny get rid of books she didn't want. He told me once that he sold everything he posted, so I guess he was doing pretty well." She laughed a little. "The logo for the site is a poison hemlock graphic. Socrates, hemlock. Get it? Jed helped to found the

381

Hemlock Guild here in town."

I got it. I also got that the dates and amounts of those online sales transactions could be retrieved via a subpoena from Conway's merchant bank. I pushed this line just a little farther, glad that Bojanov had turned on her body cam. She was taking notes now, too.

"And when he was buying or selling for Sunny, he worked on commission? Any idea how much?"

She cocked her head, thinking about that. "Well, once I heard him tell Sunny that rare book shops got as much as fifty percent when they sold a print or a book for a collector. He said he thought that was exorbitant. He'd be happy to do it for thirty."

I'll bet he would, I thought. If Sunny had let him sell the Blackwell *Herbal* for, say, a hundred thousand, he would take thirty of it — at zero risk.

Margaret was going on. "I'm sure that Jed would have sold more if Sunny had let him. He was always trying to get her to let him have an online clearance sale. That's what he called it — a clearance sale. Sometimes, when he bought a couple of boxes, there was stuff that didn't belong in her collection. She'd let him take that. And after she got sick, he put books into crates and took them out, just to help her get rid of them."

There were several important implications here for the case against Jed. Pressed, Margaret might have more information about what had gone into the boxes he filled for his "clearance sales" and how valuable it was. She might also be able to say more about his efforts to get Sunny to sell the *Herbal.* What else did she know that a prosecutor might be able to use?

Outside the window, the light had become a little grayer. The snow was coming down harder now, drifting against the tennis net like a miniature skateboard ramp. The cat leapt lightly down from the window seat and stalked across the room and out into the hall, tail twitching.

"Jed said it would be easier to manage the collection if it was organized." Margaret crossed her arms, tucking her hands inside her sweater sleeves as if she were chilly. "Of course, Sunny wasn't interested in organizing books — just in *having* them. Jed used to say that she was an 'accumulator' rather than a real collector. Once she got what she wanted, she'd look at it, enjoy it, then put it on the shelf and go on to the next thing. That's why I was there. To get the books sorted out. To catalogue them, if I could."

She shook her head. "But there was just so *much*."

"How long did you work there?"

"Oh, seven months or so. I'd make a little progress, and then some new stuff would come in. It was overwhelming. I was glad when Amelia began to take an interest in the collection. She enjoyed the sorting and that kind of thing a lot more than I did. She'd spend hours browsing through the shelves, just looking."

Margaret lifted a hand to brush her dark hair out of her eyes. If she was aware of Amelia's pilfering, she wasn't letting on. But we could get into that later.

"Amelia was there because of Sunny's interest in the right-to-die movement?" I asked.

Margaret nodded. "Amelia and Jed founded the Hemlock Guild here in town. They've been trying to get the legislature to change the law to allow assisted suicide. It's a heavy lift, of course. But you have to give them an A for effort. They worked at it."

"And that's when Amelia began coming to Hemlock House?"

"Yes. Sunny had been interested in the movement for some time. She became more interested after she was diagnosed with cancer." She sighed. "I was sad when she died. I told the board chair — not a nice person, I'm afraid — that I would stay on until they found somebody to take over and make a real library out of it. I've got to hand it to Dorothea and Jenna. They're doing a great job."

I wasn't finished. I wanted to find out what Margaret might know about Sunny's death. But the chief was shifting in his chair. Bojanov noticed and leaned forward, intervening.

"So you know nothing about the theft of that book?" she asked.

I sighed. Bojanov had brought us back to the accusation, which was only going to result in more antagonism.

"Of course I know nothing," Margaret said indignantly. "You're welcome to search this house if you want to. I gave up my apartment six months ago, when Mom got sick. I've been living here ever since. So go ahead, search if you want to."

"Actually, we're planning to do that," Bojanov said. She pulled out the warrant and handed it to Margaret. "This copy is for you." Getting up, she said to the chief, "I'll go tell Officers Murphy and Roberts that they can come in now."

As Bojanov left the room, the chief shifted in his chair again. "Sorry, Meg," he muttered, half under his breath. "Had to do this."

"Of course you did," she said sarcastically. "Well, unless you want to handcuff me, I'll go make some hot chocolate. Your guys must be half frozen, sitting out there all this time."

The chief stood as Margaret left the room. I felt sorry for him. He was trapped in one of those inescapable damned-if-you-do-and-damned-if-you-don't cul-de-sacs. "I'm sure you have other things to do this morning, Ms. Bayles," he said. "We're done here."

I didn't need to be told twice that he wanted to get rid of me, but I wasn't quite ready to go.

"You have my card," I said. "If your county prosecutor has any questions for me, she can call or email. Glad to help if I can."

"Yeah." Remembering his manners, he said, "Thanks for coming."

I held his eyes. "I suspect that Ms. Anderson knows more than she thinks she knows about what might have led up to Sunny Carswell's murder. And both you and your prosecutor may want to talk to Claudia Roth. She might have some useful witness information on both Conway and Scott."

Cops don't like it when a lawyer suggests what to do, so I didn't wait for him to respond. Anyway, it wasn't my business — he was going to handle this case the way he wanted to. My only concern at this point was the *Herbal,* and that felt like a lost cause. I put out my hand, he shook it automatically, and I turned to go.

But before I put on my coat and saw myself to the door, I went to the kitchen, where Margaret was turning on the burner under a saucepan of milk on the stove.

"Could I ask you a question?" I ventured. "It doesn't have anything to do with the Blackwell *Herbal* or the Carswell library."

She went to a cupboard and got out several cups. "What do you want to know?"

I cleared my throat. "When you were telling us what you do, you mentioned that you write about nontraditional relationships in the 'kink culture.' That's a term I'm not familiar with. What is it?"

She found a spoon, went to the stove, and began to stir the milk. From her sidelong glance, I guessed that my question was the dumbest one she'd heard all year.

"It refers to sexual tribal communities," she said. "BDSM."

"BDSM? Sorry. I'm not —"

Her angled hair swung against her cheek. She didn't say *dork,* but I was sure she thought it. "BDSM is an umbrella term for

387

certain kinds of erotic behavior between consenting adults."

"Certain kinds of . . ."

"Bondage, dominance, sadomasochism."

After a moment, she added, impatiently, "*Fifty Shades of Gray.* Not a good movie, not even a good book. But one you might have heard of."

"Oh," I said. "Oh, right. Well, thanks. I can see myself out."

"Hey." She was looking down at my wet loafers. "I'll bet my mom's snow boots would fit you. They're in the box in the den — the one that's going to Goodwill. I think there's a couple of pair of wool socks, too. Take what you want."

I didn't hesitate. "Thank you," I said fervently. "Thank you very much."

She went back to stirring the milk.

CHAPTER FOURTEEN

In the Victorian language of flowers (an elegant means of communication between nineteenth-century friends and lovers), hemlock conveyed a poisonous message: "You will be the death of me."

Susan Wittig Albert
China Bayles' Book of Days

The snow boots had never been worn. They were fuzzy inside, and only a half-size too large — a perfect fit, after I pulled on a pair of thick gray crew socks that came almost to my knees. I stuffed Ruby's wet socks into my loafers and carried them with me as I saw myself to the door.

Stepping outside, I saw that the neighborhood had taken on a Christmas-card beauty that tempted this Texas girl to just stop and gawk for a moment or two. I welcomed a cleansing breath of pine-scented air into my lungs, holding out a mittened hand to catch a few snowflakes. I pulled up the hood of my borrowed parka, thrust my hands into its pockets, and drew another breath, a deeper one. Some deviant part of me wished she knew whether Margaret and the chief were involved in the kink culture, but my better angel shoved that thought away. Their private lives were their private business, not mine.

Still and all, the morning had been informative. Margaret's answers filled in at least some of the blanks. Amelia's note explained her role in Sunny's death and her attempt on Conway's life. From Jed's Socrates.com sales, an investigator could piece together a list of what Amelia and Jed had stolen from the Carswell library. Jed's commissions were a different matter — that information was likely available but it might take a forensic accountant to dig it up, under the direction of the prosecutor.

But there was still no sign of the *Herbal,* and I had done everything I could. It was time for me to go back up the mountain, which might not be as easy as it had been the day before. Virgil was here, with a vengeance.

I looked out toward the street. The blowing snow was so thick that the cars parked along the curb were not much more than shadows. The path was drifted and I deeply appreciated Margaret's mom's boots as I trudged out to the Mirage and brushed the snow off the front and rear windows. I opened the hatchback and checked for tire chains, although I wasn't sure I'd know how to put them on if I found them. I didn't, of course, and I doubted the tires were snow tires. I'd better get going before the roads became impassable. I thought of the switch-backs up the mountain and shuddered.

It wasn't so bad in town, once I got out of the country club neighborhood and onto Bethany's Main Street. As I drove past the bank, I saw that the temperature had risen just above freezing, and there was enough traffic to melt the worst of the ice and turn the street-snow to a muddy brown slush. But the few pedestrians on the sidewalks were bent double against the wind, which was blowing the snow nearly horizontal and ripping thin white ribbons off roofs and drifts. Brave blooming tulips, azaleas, and forsythias shivered, the new leaves on the trees were heavy with snow, and several branches had already snapped. Spring was suffering a serious setback.

It was past lunchtime by now, and I thought I'd better get something to eat before I attempted the mountain, so I pulled off at Sam's, the diner where I'd stopped for lunch the day before. Just the day before? Surely it had been at least six weeks ago. This time, I had a BLT and a side of coleslaw, neither of which taxed the cook's skills. Coffee, too, figuring I could use the caffeine.

When I paid the check, I picked up three bags of banana chips for Claudia's parrots. The fresh-faced blonde who had told me yesterday that she wasn't crazy about snow so late in the season said the same thing again today. But I didn't repeat what I'd said yesterday: "Snow would be a real treat for me." I was done with snow.

Back at the car, I had to brush off the windshield again. Then I phoned Jenna and told her I was about to leave Bethany.

"It's snowing like a sonofagun down here," I said. "There's already maybe four or five inches on the ground, with deeper drifting. How is it up there?"

Jenna's voice was tinny and sounded so far away that she might be on another planet. "It's a blizzard." She sounded excited. "The lights keep going off and on. The county hasn't plowed the road yet, but Joe has cleared the drive once already, and he's got the emergency generator set up and ready to go. Looks like we're going to need it." She dropped her voice. "Did you see Jed? How is he?"

"He's going to be all right." I didn't want to break the news of Amelia Scott's suicide over the phone, and the rest of it was too complicated to go into. "There's more. Tell you when I see you." I glanced up. Through the gray-white curtain of snow, I glimpsed a grocery store on the corner. A very small garden tractor armed with a big snowplow was attempting without much success to clear away the snowdrifts between the cars in the parking lot. "Is there anything you need from town? Milk, bread?"

"We've got what we need," Jenny said. Now she sounded urgent. "Just get yourself up here in one piece, China. Even on a good day, that road can be bad."

Bad on a good day, my smarter self growled as I pulled out of Sam's parking lot. And a couple of blocks farther on, when she saw the sign for the Hemlock Mountain Inn, she had a better idea.

Hey, instead of driving up that mountain, how about if we check into that comfy-looking B&B? We can kick back, look out the window, enjoy the snow, and find a nice place nearby for dinner. We can drive up the mountain tomorrow." She began to coax. *"Come on, China. Let's do it. What do you say?*

393

"No," I muttered stubbornly. I hate it when part of me comes up with something that's clearly better when the rest of me has already committed herself to something that isn't. "It won't be so bad. I just have to pay attention."

But when I turned at the next left — the narrow two-lane that zigzagged up the mountain — I knew I should have said yes instead. The visibility couldn't be more than twenty yards. The road hadn't been plowed yet and while some patches were scoured bare by the wind, elsewhere the snow was bumper-deep and it was difficult to be sure that what I was driving on was actually *road.*

To make things worse, the Mirage was a front-wheel drive that hugged the pavement. Did it have enough clearance to plow through the deep stuff or would it stall out? Cell phone coverage was spotty on this road. If I got stuck, would I be able to get help?

And as I had noticed when I drove out of the Asheville airport, the car didn't act like my stick-shift Toyota. I had no idea whether its variable transmission would have enough power to manage the steep grade and the drifts at the same time. I definitely didn't want to get into a situation where the car lost power and slid off the mountain. That would be a killer.

And now, as the road snaked through the tunnel of trees, the daylight darkened into an eerie snow-filled twilight. The wind cranked up a couple of notches, pummeling the car first from one side, then the other, then straight ahead, the snow funneling directly at my windshield. At one point, a sixty-foot hemlock had lost its grip on the rocky soil and come down onto the road, leaving barely enough room for me to snake past. It was white-knuckle, adrenaline-fueled driving, and every now and then I had to remind myself to stop holding my breath or I was going to pass out.

My smarter self was on top of things, of course. *Bet you wish you'd listened to the skinny kid with the John Lennon glasses, she snarked. You could be driving a four-by-four right now — more weight, more power, better traction. Think of that when you're sliding off the mountain, why don't you?*

And as the wipers struggled to clear the clotting snow from the front and back windshields and I used Jenna's mittens to wipe the fog off the inside, Ms. Know-It-All remarked significantly, *A bigger vehicle would have better wipers. Bigger defroster, too, huh?*

She also remembered odds and ends of

advice she had picked up over the years and now offered in a running commentary.

Don't jam the brake, just tap it gently. No sudden moves, now — easy does it.

No, that is not a bear over there, and even if he is, he's not a problem unless he runs out in front of you. Keep your eyes on the road.

Accelerate slowly — no, no, SLOW, you idiot! And keep your eyes on the ROAD!

"Knock it off," I muttered as I maneuvered around the second sharp dogleg, then sped up to tackle the steep grade that followed. But she wasn't finished.

Don't you know there's nothing worse than accelerating on an icy hill? You'll spin out and lose control. You need to get your speed up on the flat before you make the next corner and take on the grade.

Yeah, right. Well, if I drove this road every day, I would know when the switchbacks were coming, wouldn't I? I would know whether the road flattened out or a hill loomed around the next blind corner.

But since I'd only driven it twice before, I had no clue — especially since I could barely see past the front bumper. I had to hold the speed down, which meant that as I climbed through one switchback and then another and the road got steeper, the car didn't have the traction it needed. I knew it

396

was going to stall, so I accelerated and the back tires spun and I started fishtailing.

Turn into the skid! my smarter self shrieked, now in full-throated panic. *Turn into the skid, you dolt!*

So I turned into the skid while my heart jumped into my throat and stayed there. My mouth was dry and my throat was parched. My knees and calves ached from the strain of managing the accelerator and the brake. But turning into the skid straightened me out and I could breathe again.

It had to be the longest twenty minutes of my life. But at last, through a curtain of blowing snow, I saw what I remembered as the last sharp switchback in the zig-zaggy road. Beyond it was a longish flat stretch and then the Hemlock House gatehouse.

I let out my breath in a rush. I'd made it.

The electricity was off when I got back but came on not long after and stayed on for the rest of the afternoon, which all three of us spent huddled in front of a blazing fire in the workroom, keeping warm.

Jenna had made a pot of hot chocolate for us, and I reported what had happened in Bethany that morning: my talk with the chief, our visit to Jed Conway in the hospital, the grisly find in Amelia Scott's garage,

397

and the conversation with Margaret Anderson. Some of it was a confirmation of what they already knew. The rest was news, and unsettling.

"Amelia shot Sunny?" Dorothea whispered incredulously, her eyes wide, her hand to her mouth. "But that was ruled a suicide!"

I nodded. "She must have wiped her prints off the gun and put it in Sunny's hand. Sunny was an old woman with a terminal illness *and* a right-to-die supporter, so the suicide seemed to fit."

It must have looked like such a sure thing that the sheriff hadn't bothered to test for gunshot residue on Sunny's hand. The only one who didn't seem to accept it was Claudia Roth, who could live with the idea of suicide but couldn't believe that Sunny would use a gun, and especially not *that* gun.

"And Amelia tried to kill Jed Conway, too?" Jenna asked, disbelieving.

"Yes. She thought that he stole the *Herbal,* sold it, and owed her half of the money — which she needed. Her real estate business was going under and she was about to lose her house. Jed said he thought she didn't mean to shoot him, and he was probably right. Apparently, she heard that he wasn't expected to make it through the night. That's when she decided to put an end to it."

"So hard to believe," Dorothea murmured.

Jenna was looking excited. "Maybe that's the reason for the ghost," she said.

"Reason for the ghost?" Dorothea frowned. "What are you saying?"

"Sunny's ghost. Maybe she hasn't been able to leave this place because nobody knew the truth behind the way she died. Maybe now that the truth is out and people understand that she was murdered, she can rest in peace."

"I don't know about that," I said, remembering what Claudia had told me: that Sunny herself had claimed to see the ghost, which meant that it predated Sunny's murder. "But I'm sure that Chief Curtis is going to want to talk to you two. The case is now in his hands, not the county sheriff's, since Conway has admitted to fencing some of the library's prints through his website and Scott confessed to being his accomplice."

I turned to Jenna. "You would probably earn Chief Curtis' undying gratitude if you would go to your computer, bring up Socrates.com, and make screenshots of Conway's current listings. Then check to see if these correspond to items missing from this library. It's possible that he and Amelia were pilfering other collections." I didn't say so out loud, but I thought it was possible that Margaret had been involved, as well. I wasn't entirely convinced of her innocence.

"That's a great idea." Jenna's eagerness suggested that she thought this would be fun. "I'll do it this afternoon."

"But there's still no word about the *Herbal*?" Dorothea's tone was not hopeful.

"It hadn't turned up by the time I left," I said. "The storm may slow things down, but I'm sure that the chief has already gotten a search warrant for Jed's place and has a team searching there. The bookstore, too." I paused. "And even if he's sold it, there's still hope."

"You think?" Jenna's question was tinged with sarcasm.

"It's possible," I said. "Not long ago, the Carnegie Library got its four-hundred-year-old Geneva Bible back. It had been stolen by the library's archivist and sold by a local bookseller to a museum in Germany. The museum director saw it on a list of stolen rare books and returned it."

Dorothea's forehead wrinkled. "But to make that happen, the board would have to . . ." Her voice trailed away.

"Publicize the theft," Jenna said firmly, topping off my hot chocolate and then her own. "Dorothea, you're just going to have to push them."

"Absolutely," I said. "In a few weeks, the county attorney will announce charges against Jed Conway. The board could announce the theft then." I gave Dorothea a direct look. "Of course, it would be much, much better if they publicized it earlier — like today. Tomorrow wouldn't be bad, either."

"I'm sure you're right." Dorothea pulled her sweater around her. "Well, I have a trolley-load of books to catalog. I'd better get to it."

I sighed. It didn't look like Dorothea was ready to challenge her board of directors. Which meant that if the police didn't find the *Herbal* at Jed's house or his shop — and if he didn't name the person he sold it to — it would likely never be found.

Jenna got up. "I'll work on those screenshots," she said. "Oh, and I've emailed you another part of the novel, China — the last one that's finished."

I opened my tablet to look for her email with the file attachment. "How many more after this one?"

"I wish I knew." She looked troubled. "Actually, I'm kind of stuck. There are a couple of ways the book could end. I have my preferences, but I'm not sure I'm right. Maybe you'll have some ideas."

I looked up. "Far as I can remember, nobody's ever asked me how a book should end. And anyway, this is biographical fiction, isn't it? Don't you have to stick to the real story?"

Jenna chuckled. "You're assuming that we *know* the real story, which may not be entirely true. There are facts, yes — or what seem to be facts. But there are ambiguities, too. After all this time, it's not easy to know what really happened."

I thought of Amelia's suicide. "It's not easy to know what really happened even when all the facts are right in front of you," I said.

I pulled my chair close to the fire and propped my feet on the brass fireplace fender. It was a perfect place to read, with my tablet on my lap and a cup of hot chocolate on the table beside me. Outside the French doors, the patio was knee-deep in snow, completely blanketing the fringe of spring wildflowers that had bloomed so promisingly just the day before. Beyond, the palisade of tall trees loomed darkly behind a curtain of blowing snow.

A few minutes later, Jenna put on a CD and the sounds of Pachelbel's "Canon" filled the room. After the events of the morning and the high-tension anxiety of the drive up the mountain, I was glad for the soft music, and I dove into Jenna's chapter with pleasure.

■ ■ ■ ■

PART FIVE:
THE CURIOUS TALE
OF ELIZABETH
BLACKWELL

■ ■ ■ ■

July, 1738
Number Four, Swan's Walk
Opposite Chelsea Physic Garden
The Undertaker being desirous to make this Work more useful to such as are not furnished with other Herbals, is resolved (for their Sake) to give a short Description of each plant; the Place of Growth, and Time of Flowering with its common Uses in Physick, chiefly extracted from Mr. Jo-

seph Miller's Botanica Officinale, with his consent; and the ordinary Names of the Plant in different Languages.

Elizabeth Blackwell,
Introduction, *A Curious Herbal*

Elizabeth put down her engraving tool and flexed her stiff fingers. The clock on the mantel told her that it was nearly midnight. The calendar on the wall over her drawing table told her that it was the fourth night she had worked late this week, driven by the desire to see the final installment finished.

And now, on the desk in front of her, lay the engraved copper plates for Number 125 of *A Curious Herbal.*

This last installment, the very last, contained detailed drawings of the native herb bugloss, yellow and white water lilies, and water lily tubers. Like the 496 plants before it, each of these was pictured on its own page, and there was a separate page with brief descriptions of all four. When this installment went to subscribers and to the booksellers and vendors and news agents who sold it on the street, her work would be done. She had reached a milestone. *A Curious Herbal* was finished.

All that remained was to hand over the engravings to the printer — Samuel Harding, at the sign of the Bible & Anchor in St. Martin's Lane — and arrange the printing and sale of the second volume, which Mr. Harding was already advertising in newspapers across England and Scotland.

And there was one more task she was looking forward to with great pleasure: the creation of the large presentation copy she had decided to make for Sir Hans. It would contain both volumes — that is, all five hundred plates. It would be bound in the finest calfskin and would have eight decorated silver corners and a pair of elaborate silver clasps. She had already found a silversmith to make the corners and clasps and they had agreed on a design. She would color every plate herself, with the greatest of care. It was to be a very special book that would please and impress Sir Hans and be preserved for generations to come.

The journey had been an epic one and — if Elizabeth weren't so exhausted — she would be celebrating. Three years, five months, and ten days ago, she had handed her draft agreement to Sir Hans. It retained the copyright and the ownership of the plates to herself and named a substantial advance to be paid by Sir Hans and repaid to him from the sale of the books. Sir Hans had added the stipulation that the book would include no fewer than five hundred herbs, described in plain English and drawn from life or from plants preserved in his herbarium.

The title was Elizabeth's idea. It was to be

called *A Curious Herbal* — "curious" in the sense of minutely accurate, exact, precise. In other words, scientific. It would not include any of the traditional old wives' tales that clustered like flies around herbs, or the outmoded astrological attributes that Nicholas Culpeper had included in his popular *The English Physitian* and which still appeared in its many piracies. *A Curious Herbal* would be up-to-date, accurate, and specific, befitting the new age, which a Frenchman had recently called the *Era of Lumières,* or Enlightenment.

After Elizabeth and Sir Hans had signed the agreement, things had moved rapidly, for he was eager to see the work underway and she was desperate to begin earning money. As soon as she could, she had gone to the Physic Garden to meet Isaac Rand, the director, and Philip Miller, the head gardener, on whose botanical help she had to depend.

And the two of them *were* helpful. Mr. Rand offered to make a list of the plants she should draw for the first dozen numbers. Mr. Miller, who had something of a combative personality, treated her as a nuisance at first. But he grudgingly agreed to help with Mr. Rand's list. He also took her to the garden's new orangery to show her the collection of botanical reference books that she could consult for the descriptions of plants.

The next week, Mr. Rand — a skilled botanist and widely-admired apothecary with a shop between Piccadilly and Pall Mall in the Haymarket — introduced her at a meeting of the apothecaries' guild, where he stressed Sir Hans' sponsorship of the project. She showed four colored drawings (dandelion, poppy, melon, and cucumber), described the book, and began enlisting subscribers. Dr. Stuart, ever helpful, arranged a meeting with members of the Royal College of Physicians, whose endorsement she needed. Elizabeth even sent advance copies of two installments to her uncle, John Johnstoun, professor of medicine at the University of Glasgow. He responded by enlisting subscribers — apothecaries, physicians, and booksellers — in Glasgow and Edinburgh.

She was surprised and delighted when the subscription list passed the hundred-mark before the first number was published, most of them for the more costly hand-colored pages. She added another fifty after she met with the doctors. There were nearly two hundred booksellers in London and even more news agents. She couldn't talk to each of them individually, but she visited the largest and left an advance copy with each, soliciting regular consignment sales. Of course, there would be cancellations, but with this kind of early support, she could hope that she might earn enough to pay Alexander's creditors at least a pound a week, perhaps more.

Elizabeth's most important meetings, however, were with the printers, where her experience in Alex's shop stood her in good stead. She interviewed and considered several men and one woman before she settled on Samuel Harding. She had worked with him earlier — he and Alex had referred print jobs to one another — and knew him to be experienced and reliable.

She needed someone who was both, for this project would continue for over two years. To include all five hundred of the herbs that Sir Hans wanted would require 125 numbers, as they were usually called. They should be published weekly, on the same day (she thought Friday best). Once published, the installments had to be delivered, either by courier or, if going a distance, by the post. Mr. Harding made the arrangements and saw that they were carried out.

Also, experience in Alex's shop had taught Elizabeth that supplies of paper and ink could be unpredictable. For a job like this both should be purchased ahead of time so all was at hand when needed. Since she knew the suppliers, it made sense to buy these herself (thereby increasing the profit) and have them delivered to Mr. Harding. Planning ahead, she had included this in the initial advance she had requested from Sir Hans.

Elizabeth paid Mr. Harding to place advertisements in the newspapers, and as the replies came in they were added to the subscription or consignment lists. But while the subscription list provided some predictability, it was hard to know how many more copies might be sold on consignment to booksellers and street vendors. And when it came to vendors, there were (in addition to hundreds of London newsboys and broadsheet and pamphlet sellers) the many herb ladies as well, selling fresh herbs in the markets and on the streets.

When Sir Hans paid over his agreed-to advance, Elizabeth and the children had moved into a rented three-room apartment to the west of the Fleet Ditch and not far from Newgate, so Sunday afternoon family visits to Alex could be managed. She had hired a maid-of-all-work to live in — a sensible young woman named Janet Proctor — who cared for the children while she was working. Between the organizing meetings and the sketching, drawing, engraving, printing, and coloring — not to mention the brisk foot travel required to manage all of this — the demands had been unrelenting. Elizabeth ended every day footsore, bone-weary, and always with a stack of sketches on her worktable, still to be turned into finished drawings and engravings.

And then something quite wonderful happened. Mr. Rand met her one morning when she came to sketch and told her that the house at Number 4 Swan Walk, just across the lane from the east gate of the Physic Garden, was to let. He had the key and would like to show it to her.

Isaac Rand, a stout, gray-wigged man of sixty, had been reserved at their first meeting. But he had unbent when she brought the children to the garden with her. Blanche amused herself by making full-skirted dolls of frilly pink hollyhock blossoms and green ferns, while William, on his hands and knees at the edge of the mint bed, collected shiny beetles in a small box.

"They will be my friends and live under my bed until I am big enough to go to school," he told Mr. Rand gravely. "And then I shall bring them back and they can be *your* friends."

The towheaded little boy had won Mr. Rand's heart, and he asked Elizabeth how far she and the children had come that morning. He frowned when she said that they had walked from their apartment — a good three miles, through a very muddy lane.

"So difficult for the children," he murmured.

On her next visit, Mr. Rand had met her with the key. Number 4 was one of a block of narrow red brick row houses, set back a little from the lane, with a walled garden for the children and an expansive north window that let in the purest and most wonderful light, perfect for her drawing and engraving. There was even a bedroom for Janet, so she would no longer have to sleep in the scullery.

The children had taken great delight in their new home. On a quiet lane, away from London's smoke-laden fogs, the air was cleaner and healthy. If they went south, Swan Walk led them to the busy Thames, where they could wave to the boats moving slowly along the river, fully laden as they moved downstream, empty as they made their way back upriver. Small boats with one or two fishermen, out to catch tonight's supper. Large boats heavy with coal or sacks of milled flour and butts of beer, or crates of live chickens and ducks bound for market.

If they went to the north, Swan Walk led them into the quaint little village of Chelsea and beyond, where they could wander in the quiet orchards and market gardens that supplied the city with fresh fruits and vegetables. They could fill their baskets with apples and pears that Janet would turn into fruit pies and potatoes and peas and carrots and cabbage that would become soup. Along the lane, Elizabeth could point out wild herbs — mullein and wood sage and nettle and plantain — and tell the children how they were used. Overhead, they could watch the harriers and fork-tailed kites as they dipped and turned and soared and listen to the raucous cries of the gulls that fished along the river.

Just across the way, the garden offered many delights. There was the daily pleasure of drawing, the work she liked best and which she enjoyed in the early morning, when the plants were at their freshest. Plants arrived every week, so many that there was always something new to notice and admire and puzzle over — unusual and exotic plants from the Americas and Africa and the Orient. There were interesting books to be read in the library and discus-

415

sions with the gardeners, especially Mr. Rand and Mr. Miller, who (now accustomed to her regular visits) seemed to appreciate her questions and observations, for there was always something more to learn. And there were visitors from everywhere in England and Europe, many of them naturalists or explorers who were bringing plants.

But perhaps the most important visitor was the accomplished Swedish botanist Carl Linnaeus, who was engaged in the extraordinary work of identifying, naming, and classifying every living thing in the entire world. Each plant and animal received two Latin names: for example, *Homo sapiens* for the human species, *Rosa gallica* for the French rose, which in the garden was variously called "the apothecary's rose" or sometimes the "damask rose" or "the red rose of Lancaster." Linnaeus' system was based on the sexual structures of plants: the number and arrangement of stamens and pistils in the flowers. If it was widely adopted, it could clear up a great deal of confusion. Elizabeth wished that he were far enough in his work so that she could use his classification system in the *Herbal*.

For the sake of the children, she also wished that Alexander could be with them. Did she wish it for her own sake, too? Did she miss him and the always dramatic twists and turns he had brought into her life, or had she grown content — and even happy — with the quietness of the days and nights without him? Although she resented the recklessness that had created his debts, she was certainly bending all her efforts toward repaying them. But was that because she truly loved him or because she was his wife and therefore obligated?

Search her soul as she might, she couldn't find the answers. And since she didn't know what she would do with the answer if she found it, she felt she might fare better if she did not know.

But now she could at least glimpse the end of that journey. The first half of the *Herbal* had been bound and published as Volume One, and the sale of those copies had allowed her to pay off the larger and most demanding of Alex's creditors. If this had been a usual case, the rest might have relented and freed him on condition of future payment. But they had been offended by what they saw as his arrogant flouting of the Stationers' Guild apprenticeship rule and intended to see him pay whatever price they could exact.

Fortunately (or unfortunately; Elizabeth was not sure which) his confinement had not troubled Alexander overmuch. He had settled comfortably into Newgate, where he had become the hub of a group of educated, well-read bankrupts, professional men and a few gentry who had spent themselves into debt. Elizabeth gave him a portion of the weekly book sales that enabled him to pay for his meals, his wine and ale and tobacco, and his laundry. In return, his nominal task was to provide the names by which the plants were known in various languages: Greek, Latin, Italian, Spanish, French, German, Dutch. This allowed him to proudly tell people that he was one of his wife's "chief contributors," which he did, without reservation. He even gave them to believe that he was expert in the subject of medicinal plants and that the project had been his idea from the beginning.

The truth was, however, that Alex was not as much of a botanist as he liked to claim. He had known only a few of the names, so Elizabeth usually went to the orangery and looked them up in the garden's library. That's where she also found the botanical descriptions of the plants and their preferences for light and soil. Mr. Joseph Miller (no relation to the head gardener) had given her permission to use descriptions from his recent book, *Botanica Officinale.* She always asked Mr. Rand to read what she had done to be sure it was correct, and he was glad to comply. He also looked over her drawings and made suggestions.

Thus, with or without contributions from Alex, the work had gone forward successfully. When it began, Elizabeth had been a modestly skilled artist; she became more skilled as time went on and she grew to love her subjects, which seemed always patient and cheerful and ready to share their small green secrets with her. Already an engraver, she learned how to do the work more expertly — and her copperplate handwriting improved. The weekly issues of the *Herbal* had sold well, exceptionally well, according to Mr. Harding's accounting. Fifteen months after the very first issue was released, Elizabeth arranged to have the first sixty-three issues printed, bound, and published as a book. In another few months, she would arrange for the publication of the last sixty-two issues in Volume Two. She was still a troubling distance from repayment of her husband's full debt, and one of the creditors was getting restive. But she would have to deal with that later. Her first task was to complete the book and to do it *well.*

If Elizabeth had thought that life without Alex would be grim, she was wrong. Janet had become a friend and companion as well as a helper. The house was a calm retreat, the green and ever blooming Physic Garden a daily delight, and the children the joy of her heart. Elizabeth's life was so blessedly full and busy and comfortable that she sometimes wondered if such contentment could last.

It didn't. There was a cruel sweep of disease across the land during the wet early weeks of May, and little William had died of a fever — just one of many children who died that month. Blanche followed her brother two years later, almost to the day. The only blessing was that they had been taken suddenly, both of them lively and laughing one day, feverish the next, and gone the day after that.

The sadness still sat in Elizabeth's bones, like a fatal infection that could be neither banished nor born. She thought of William and Blanche constantly, even allowing herself to pretend that they were simply asleep in their little beds just down the hallway from her drawing studio, telling herself that tomorrow they would walk to the river and wave at the boatmen or across the lane to the garden, where she would sketch while Blanche played with the hollyhocks and William made friends with the beetles. But these were just sweet stories, to comfort her grief. The children lay in the sweet green quiet of the parish churchyard, near enough that each Sunday she and Janet could take fresh flowers and herbs to them.

And now she had thought of a way to manage the publication of the second volume *and* the rest of Alexander's debt, both at the same time. There was still £150 owing — a debt that might take her another year to repay. But she had discussed the matter with John Nourse, a bookseller and printer near Temple Bar. Mr. Nourse had agreed to publish the second volume of the *Herbal* and she had agreed to sell him a one-third share of the book for £150.

The money from the rights' sale would go to pay off the debt. There was enough coming in regularly from the book to allow her to keep the Swan Walk house, which she loved. Alexander would be home at last, and they could pick up their life together. Elizabeth was still young and had been quite fertile: Blanche was conceived within a few months of their marriage and William even before Blanche was weaned. There would likely be more children to fill the empty space in her heart.

But how would she *feel*, sharing her life again with her husband? Before the New-

421

gate years, he had been headlong and impulsive, unwilling to do the hard work of preparation or the mundane work of routine tasks. One of his closest friends had said that while Alex was a "natural genius," his brilliance was marred by "want of principle and unsoundness of judgment" — and Elizabeth agreed. Had he changed? Had he learned the importance of patience and persistence? Would he be willing to take up the task of earning the family's living?

But if Alex hadn't changed, *she* had. The years she had worked on the *Herbal* had given her a new confidence in herself. She made her own decisions, conducted business as she thought best, earned enough to support herself and the children, spent money carefully, incurred reasonable debts and promptly repaid them, and developed a group of helpers, allies, and friends that she could count on. While the years had been full of challenge and darkened by grief, there had been joys, too, and the satisfaction of recognized achievement. And she had grown accustomed to living alone, with only Janet to keep her company. Would Alex step back into her life and attempt to direct it, as he had before?

And what would he do for a living, once he was released? He couldn't go back to the printing trade — no one would hire him. With the bankruptcy on his record, it would be difficult to start any new business. He had become intrigued with her reports of the new plants coming in from around the globe and had said that he might like to work with some kind of agricultural project. He had asked her for books about estate and farm management and had been reading about modern methods of drainage and the improvement of soils.

This puzzled Elizabeth, for Alex had no firsthand understanding of plants or farming. But she didn't doubt that he could turn his hand to anything he wanted, *if* he wanted it badly enough and if he had the patience to prepare himself.

Anyway, it wasn't up to her to decide what her husband would do. He had rarely taken direction or suggestions from her, even when it was her dowry they were spending. Thus, she executed the agreement with Nourse, took the money he paid her, and handed it over — with a great deal of satisfaction — to Alex's last two creditors.

There. That was done. She had achieved what she set out to do: earn enough money to buy her husband's freedom from debtors' prison. No one could say she had not done her wifely duty.

At last, on a bright day in late September, Alexander walked free. In celebration, she met him at Newgate's entrance, and they went to a small tavern where they had dined often when they were first married. And then hired a coach to take them to Chelsea, where they would begin their life together, again.

And then . . .

CHAPTER FIFTEEN

Elizabeth Blackwell remained in London with her son until at least July 1747. There is no further record of her, although one historian claims she died in 1758 and was buried in Chelsea Old Church. Her work was acclaimed long after her death and was translated into Latin [and German] in 1773 as the *Herbarium Blackwellianum,* by the Count Palatine, Dr. Christopher Jacob Trew, and Christian Ludwig. It was unusual for a woman of her time to produce such a book, as it was intended for and used by a professional medical audience.*

— *Biographical Dictionary of Scottish Women*
Edinburgh University Press, 2007

* The subtitle of the German translation: *The Masterful Book of Plants by the Extraordinary Elizabeth Blackwell*

And then? And then? I looked up from my tablet.

"And then *what*?" I asked aloud. "I've come to the last page. Elizabeth has paid her husband's debts and bailed him out of jail. She is about to finish the book. They're starting over. So what happens next? When can I read your next chapter?"

Jenna got up from her computer and went to put another couple of logs on the work-room fire. She wore a half smile. "What do *you* think happens next?"

"But you're the one telling the story," I objected. "Do the two of them live together? Are they happy? Does Elizabeth have other children? Can they manage on the sales of her book, or does Alex have to go to work? He obviously doesn't have a very good reputation. Who is going to hire him? To do what?"

"Whoa." Jenna lifted her hand. "Wow. So many questions. I wish I could answer them all."

"You can't? Why not? It's your novel, isn't it?"

"Yes, it's my novel. But it's Elizabeth's *life.*"

Oh, right. I had momentarily forgotten. "That's true," I said. "Well, okay, then. Tell me what happened to Elizabeth after she finished the Herbal."

"It's easier to tell you what happened to Alexander," Jenna said. "There's still a lot of mystery but I've found at least some documentation on him."

She sat down in the chair on the other side of the fireplace, pulling it closer to the fire. "After Elizabeth got him released from prison, he lived in the Swan Walk house with her for at least a year or two. We know that, because he's listed on the tax rolls. Elizabeth did get pregnant — at least once." She bent toward the blaze, warming her hands. "We know that because they baptized a son named Alexander in 1742. The baptism took place in St. Paul's Church, in Covent Garden, so I'm guessing that Elizabeth wasn't living in Chelsea at the time."

"At least once?" I calculated. "You think she might have had a miscarriage before Alexander was born?"

"Or a baby who died." She sat up and crossed her legs. "That wouldn't have been unusual at a time when nearly half of the children didn't live to celebrate their first birthday. We also know that somebody — most likely Alex himself — published a book under his name about how to drain clay lands and improve the soil. That was in 1741. The Blackwells had sold more shares of the *Herbal* to the printer John Nourse, so maybe they were using part of the money from the sale to finance the printing of that book."

"Under his name? You're suggesting that he didn't actually *write* it?"

Jenna looked grave. "I am. I've read this book — in fact, I own a facsimile copy that I bought online. It's called *A New Method of Improving Cold, Wet, and Barren Lands.* It's quite evidently written by somebody who had spent decades improving the soils of Northern England. There's absolutely no evidence that Alexander even traveled there or that he had any farming experience whatsoever."

"You're saying he *plagiarized* this book?"

"I think he somehow acquired the manuscript, perhaps when he was still in the printing business. He had it printed and then claimed authorship — or let people believe that he was the author, which amounts to the same thing. The title page has no author's name and the dedication signature is missing. Even so, the book is still sold under his authorship, almost three centuries later. I saw it for sale recently for nearly eight hundred dollars. It's said to be quite rare, so perhaps he had only a few copies printed and handed them out himself, rather than putting it in bookshops." She grinned bleakly. "I can just see him, holding it out with a modest, 'I thought you might like to have this little trifle of mine.' "

I was puzzled. "But why would he do such a thing?"

"To bolster his credentials." Jenna's mouth tightened. "Don't you see, China? He was inventing himself all over again. This book turned him into a bona fide agricultural expert — which would be quite understandable, since his wife was now an internationally recognized expert in medicinal plants. He used it to leverage himself into what might have been a very good job, if he'd had any ability at all."

"What kind of a job?

"Around this time the Duke of Chandos, probably on the basis of that book, hired Alexander to manage the gardens at Canons, near Edgeware. It was a prestigious post, because the gardens were thought to be among the loveliest in England. Some historians say that Alexander laid out the gardens — but that simply isn't true, for the gardens were designed in the early 1720s, long before Alexander arrived on the scene." A burning log shifted in the grate and she took a poker and pushed it back. "The duke's estate was north of London about ten miles, a half-day by coach and too far to commute in those days of bad roads."

"Then I suppose he must have lived on the estate," I said. "Did Elizabeth make the move with him?"

"We don't know." Jenna returned the poker to its rack. "But we do know that Alex wasn't at Canons very long. When he left, it was 'under a cloud' of some sort, as one of his friends diplomatically put it."

"No details?"

She shook her head. "I think he had stretched his credentials with that book and couldn't deliver. He was found out to be a fake, word got around, and he packed up and left England for Sweden. That would have been about 1742. Elizabeth didn't go with him."

"*Sweden?*" I blinked. "Isn't that rather . . . odd?"

"I thought so, but maybe not. Maybe Sir Hans helped. Or he knew somebody who knew somebody. Anyway, he was invited by the Swedish prime minister to serve as an agricultural consultant — on the strength of that book, it seems. He must have talked a good line, for he was given an annual stipend, a house, and the supervision of a Swedish model farm. He also somehow managed to get himself named a court physician."

I chuckled. "Another reinvention." But it wasn't funny.

"Exactly. But things must have gone downhill pretty fast. He wasn't well liked — he was said to be self-important, arrogant, and 'conceited of his own abilities.' He made a mess of the model farm and people began to wonder whether he had actually written that book. Then he got involved with a woman and was implicated in the death of her husband."

"Wow," I said, transfixed by the story. "Really?"

"Really. Carl Linnaeus writes about it. It appears that he didn't think much of Alexander, either."

"Carl Linnaeus? The Swedish naturalist who invented the binomial classification system? You mentioned him in the section I just finished. Did Elizabeth meet him when he visited the garden?"

"I'm sure she did," Jenna said. "Linnaeus wrote to a friend about Alexander's scandalous behavior. As he tells it, Alexander was 'intimate' with the wife. The husband got sick. Alexander treated him. When the man died, it was apparently easy — and perhaps convenient — to blame Alexander, either

431

for poisoning him or for being such a poor doctor that he couldn't save him. Who knows?"

"It could have been just gossip, couldn't it? It sounds like he got a lot of preference from the Crown. People must have been jealous."

"I suppose. And it may have just been Carl Linnaeus who was jealous. But after that, things went from really bad to horribly worse for Alexander. He got involved in a political intrigue in the royal court, something to do with a plan to poison the heir to the Swedish throne and put the Duke of Cumberland — the youngest son of King George II — in his place. Alexander claimed to be acting for the British Crown, but King George called him a 'liar and an imposter,' so that explanation never went anywhere."

"Sounds like a spy thriller," I said. "Like something out of a novel by Le Carré."

"You're so right," Jenna agreed. "The thing is that nobody ever knew whether Alexander made the story up — working for the British Crown, I mean — or whether the Brits actually put him up to it and then abandoned him. Whatever, he was convicted of plotting against the monarchy and beheaded."

"Beheaded?" I yelped. "Yikes!"

Jenna leaned back in her chair, stretching her feet toward the fire. "He's said to have made a joke about it. He apparently laid his head on the wrong side of the block and then apologized. He said it was an honest mistake — it was the first time he had ever been beheaded."

"Oh, God," I said softly. "Oh, poor Elizabeth!"

"Can you imagine?" Jenna was shaking her head again. "One account — the one that depicts her as a devoted wife — says she was on her way to join him in Sweden when she got word that he was dead. Personally, I doubt it." She lifted her chin. "*My* Elizabeth probably gave that jerk his walking papers when he got fired by the Duke of Chandos and left England. After all, she had a continuing income from sales of the book. She could support herself and her son with that — or she could do something else. But no matter how she felt about Alexander, she had to deal with the fallout from what he had done. There were reports about his execution in all the London newspapers and magazines, in Scotland too — it was a huge story. And since nobody knew the details, there must have been dozens of rumors floating around. Can you imagine how difficult that was for her?"

I thought of the elaborate copy of the *Herbal* that Elizabeth had signed and presented to Hans Sloane — the book that had disappeared from the library at Hemlock House. She would have been proud of what she had achieved and treasured the recognition of her work. So she must have felt horribly embarrassed and even humiliated by Alexander's irresponsible behavior, especially since it was out there in full public view. All the men she had come to respect would have known about it — would she have had to answer their questions? But could she? How much did *she* know about what her husband had been up to in Sweden?

After a moment, I thought of something else. "In one of your early chapters, you mentioned midwifery. Is there any evidence that Elizabeth might have gone in that direction?"

"According to a nineteenth-century account, that's what happened. The *Herbal* had given Elizabeth plenty of connections in the medical community. She was still a young woman, educated, adaptable. But nobody knows for sure. She probably stayed on in Chelsea. When she died in 1758, she was buried in the graveyard at the Chelsea Old Church. Her name is on a plaque there, along with three other notable women." She eyed me. "So what do *you* think, China?"

I considered for a moment. "Your Elizabeth — the one you've already created in your novel — is a woman who knows her mind. She's smart, gutsy, and able to make her own choices. I'm betting that she didn't cut that husband of hers any slack at all. When he left England, she probably told him not to bother coming back. Not to her, anyway. I'm also betting that she wouldn't have wanted to sit around twiddling her thumbs, living off her book sales. She would want to be doing something *useful.* So I would vote for midwifery." I paused. "Since there's lots that isn't known, you can make it up, can't you?"

"Yes, of course," Jenna agreed. "But that's the problem with biographical fiction, isn't it? I can tell a story that fits with the recorded details of Elizabeth's life. But it's impossible to know her inner life. What she hoped, feared, loved, hated. I wish she had left a journal, some letters, a trail of breadcrumbs, something that would tell us more about her."

"Well, it's Elizabeth's story but it's yours, too," I said. "You have a right to tell it your way." I sighed. "I'm just so sorry that I haven't been able to put a happy ending to the search for her *Herbal.*" I pointed to her computer. "Have you been able to match any of the items Conway has listed on his website with things you know to be missing from this library?"

"Actually, yes," Jenna said, brightening. "I've identified five definites and two possibles. I'll know for sure when I get a look at the items themselves. And I just looked at a few webpages. There's lots more."

"That's a good start," I said. "The chief will be delighted to get your list, I'm sure." I sighed. "Jed is going to have to come clean about the whereabouts of the *Herbal.* He must know *something.*"

"Well, you've given it your best shot," Jenna said in a comforting tone. "And if you didn't find the herbal, you've uncovered so much else. If you hadn't been in the bookstore when Jed Conway was shot, he would probably have died. And if he had died, Amelia might never have revealed the real story of Sunny's murder." She stretched her arms over her head. "When are you going back to Texas?"

"Day after tomorrow." I glanced out the window, where the snowfall seemed to have stopped. "I'm glad it isn't tomorrow. I'm not sure I'd want to drive those switchbacks until the road is plowed."

"I heard the snowplow go past a little while ago." Jenna got up and went back to her computer. "But it's good that you'll be here one more day. If you like books about plants, there's lots to look at in the library." She turned to give me a sober glance. "And we were talking about a sleepover tonight — playing ghostbusters. Remember?"

"How could I forget?" I asked. "We'll have a party."

I wasn't being snarky. As I said earlier, my attitude toward ghosts was changed when I was introduced to Annie, a benign spirit who likes to ring the bell over my shop door and — when she has something to say — communicates via the magnetic letters on the announcement board behind the counter. So who am I to question the existence of a ghost at Hemlock House?

And while Dorothea had described her as a "bit of a drama queen," Jenna struck me as a highly imaginative but commonsensical young woman. I didn't question her claim that she had been deeply frightened by what she had heard the night before. And that she genuinely believed it was Sunny's ghost.

Was it? The ghost of Sunny, I mean.

Well, there was Claudia Roth's testimony that Sunny believed that Hemlock House was haunted with the ghosts of her father and grandfather, both of whom had died in this place. Claudia claimed to see the ghost too, so something spooky had apparently been going on here long before Jenna arrived. And there was plenty of room for another spirit — especially that of a woman who had been robbed of her life by someone she liked and trusted.

On the other hand, the place was old and not very well maintained. There could be any one of a number of explanations for the noises Jenna had heard and the ghost that Claudia and Sunny had seen.

As Ruby says, the Universe asks us questions. It doesn't give us answers.

The snow stopped in late afternoon, leaving the house surrounded by white-draped hemlocks in a sculpted winter wonderland landscape. Jenna was right. The snowplow had cleared the road. The switchbacks might be scary, but I was sure I could manage them on my way back to the airport, even in my small car.

As if to apologize for the late-season snowfall, the sun came out and smiled contritely across the mountain, so Jenna and I decided to go for a walk. Dorothea loaned me her parka and I wore Jenna's mittens and the snow boots I had borrowed from

Margaret. The snow was a special delight for this Texas girl — someone who doesn't have to live with it all winter long. It crunched deliciously underfoot, the air was crisp and fresh, and the valley below stretched out like a scene from an Alpine postcard. I had wanted to look for ginseng and Mayapple, but they were buried under inches of snow. The view was spectacular, though. I took photos on my phone and emailed them to McQuaid and Ruby. Ruby replied with two words and a string of exclamation points:

SNOW BOOTS!!!!!

We followed the road uphill in the direction of Claudia's parrot sanctuary, and when we got tired, we turned around. Back at Hemlock, I called Chief Curtis to ask about the outcome of his searches. He said that his officers had come up empty-handed. They hadn't found the *Herbal*. He was satisfied that Margaret Anderson didn't know anything about the theft, but they hadn't closed the book on her and he was going to continue to question Conway.

"It's possible he's still concealing that information," he said. I shrugged. The investigation was in his hands now. I had done all I could.

Our walk had made us hungry, which was a good thing. For supper, Rose had left us a big pot of Hoppin' John soup — black-eyed peas, ham, and rice — served with warm chunks of skillet cornbread.

The soup, Dorothea said, was one of those Appalachian New Year's traditions that's good all year round. It's said to have taken its name from Hoppin' John, a street soup-peddler in Charleston, South Carolina, who walked with a cane. The black-eyed peas are supposed to bring luck, especially if you leave three of them on your plate for financial fortune, good health, and romance. Served the next day — a sign of the household's frugality — Hoppin' John leftovers are known as Skippin' Jenny. For dessert, we had something called stack cake with an old-fashioned homemade apple butter filling. It was scrumptious. I was going home with a couple of extra pounds, I was sure.

Over our soup and cornbread, we talked about the day's events. Dorothea was trying to think of the best way to break the news about Sunny's murder to the Hemlock Foundation's board and to anticipate the questions they would ask. They had been Miss Carswell's friends. They were bound to want answers.

"I just don't understand why Sheriff Rogers couldn't see that it was murder and not suicide," she said, shaking her head. "He must have done a really sloppy investigation."

"I wondered that too," Jenna said. "You'd think a trained law enforcement officer could tell the difference — especially because Amelia was in the house when it happened."

"It's not always that simple," I said. "If somebody phones 9-1-1 and says, 'I'm reporting a suicide,' the responding officers may arrive on the scene with that mindset. They'd tend to treat the situation from the first as a suicide, rather than look for clues to a possible homicide." I paused, remembering. "The sheriff did say that the coroner had some questions, apparently about fingerprints on the gun. But even he was eventually satisfied. Yes, it's a mistake, and one that the cops are supposed to be alert to. But it's still an easy mistake to make."

"Rose told me that she was the one who called," Jenna said. "She heard the gunshot, then Amelia yelled from somewhere upstairs that she should phone 9-1-1 and tell them that Sunny had just shot herself. Rose said that she didn't even go up to Sunny's room until her body was gone and she had to clean up the blood." She shuddered. "That's something *I* could never do. Even a few drops of blood make me feel faint."

"So Amelia would have had plenty of time alone with the body before the deputies got here," I said. "She could have moved it or wiped her prints off the gun and imposed Sunny's. And there were other factors that made suicide seem plausible. For one thing, everybody knew that Sunny didn't have much longer to live."

"Lots of people knew about her interest in the Hemlock Guild, too," Dorothea said.

"And the gun," I added. "It had killed her father and her grandfather. Maybe it reinforced the idea that this was some sort of ritual suicide. All of that could have outweighed the absence of a suicide note."

In fact, I thought, it was probably all too easy for the sheriff's deputies to assume that Sunny had killed herself. Now, though, the case would be reopened. Amelia's suicide note would be entered into evidence. Jed Conway would be called to testify — and maybe even charged as an accessory after the fact. The coroner's ruling would be changed from suicide to homicide. The case would be big news in Hemlock County.

"Amelia must have figured she was home free," I said, "until Jed Conway threatened to tell what he knew."

"So she shot him to keep him from spilling the beans," Jenna said thoughtfully. "About Sunny's murder. And the thefts as well."

"But her suicide note said that she didn't take the *Herbal,*" Dorothea pointed out.

"And that Margaret did," Jenna said.

"Which apparently isn't true," I reminded them. "At least the cops couldn't find it when they searched the house where Margaret had been staying. Her mother's house." I didn't think it was necessary to tell them about Chief Curtis' romantic involvement with his suspect. That was his own particular can of worms.

Dorothea turned to me. "Honestly, China, do you think we'll *ever* get our book back?"

"Honestly? I don't know. I hate to confess to failure, but I know *I'm* not going to get it back for you. I guess it depends on whether you can persuade the board to announce that it's been stolen so that dealers and collectors and museums can at least be on the lookout for it."

From their glum faces, I guessed that they didn't think there was much of a chance of that.

CHAPTER SIXTEEN

For centuries, ritual smudging has been used to banish ghosts and other negative energies. In churches, priests burned myrrh and frankincense, for instance, to produce a purifying and protective smoke. Shamans often burned tightly wrapped and bound bundles of herbs, such as lavender, rosemary, white sage, yarrow, and rue. Twigs and leaves of certain trees can be used, as well, such as juniper, cedar, eucalyptus, and hemlock. If you feel the need of a little special protection, these may work for you.

Ruby Wilcox
"Using Herbs in Your Personal Rituals"

As it turned out, our sleepover wasn't much of a party, either.

We gave it the old college try. I made hot chocolate and popped some popcorn in the microwave. Jenna — who laughingly called us "ghostbusters" and said that we needed some special protection against intruders from the spirit world — had made a couple of smudge bundles with rosemary, yarrow, and lavender from Sunny's garden and juniper and hemlock from the nearby trees. She lit the bundles in a copper bowl, let them burn for fifteen or twenty seconds, and then gently blew out the flame, allowing the orange embers to produce a fragrant smoke.

We settled on Jenna's bed with the popcorn and hot chocolate — Jenna in flannel PJs, I in McQuaid's old black T-shirt — and talked about ourselves. I told her about Thyme and Seasons and Ruby and our tea room and catering service, and about McQuaid and the kids. She told me about her plan to finish her master's degree by the end of the fall term and look for a library job with an emphasis on book conservation.

"I'd rather spend my time writing but I know I'll need a day job," she added.

"You don't want to stay here?" I asked.

She shook her head. "I love working with Dorothea and I'm learning a *lot* about organizing a library and cataloging and conserving old books. And of course, living and working here is giving me time to finish the novel and complete my thesis. But this place is too isolated. I need *people*."

"I can understand that," I said. "Do you think Dorothea will stay?"

"I think she might, but only if the board becomes more supportive. She thinks Sunny's library has great potential. And I'm sure she's right."

I scooped out the last handful of popcorn. "Well, whatever happens, I hope you'll let me know when your novel is published. I want to see how you've answered our questions about Elizabeth. Did she kick Alexander out? Did she become a midwife? What did she do with the rest of her life?"

Jenna laughed. "You'll get one of the very first copies, I promise." She rubbed her eyes. "The Hemlock ghost made sure I didn't get much sleep last night and I'm about pooped out. I'll get your sheet and some blankets and a pillow and we can make up your bed."

"Speaking of the ghost," I said as we pulled out the sofa bed, "what's our plan? If it shows up, I mean?"

"Maybe we won't need a plan," Jenna said. "Maybe, since the truth about Sunny's death is out in the open, her ghost can rest in peace."

I tucked in the sheet. "But what if the ghost isn't Sunny's ghost? I mean, not Sunny's spirit. What if it's somebody — something — else?"

"Not Sunny's ghost?" She spread out a blanket.

"Claudia Roth told me that the ghost was here before Sunny died. In fact, Sunny herself seems to have been on good terms with it. According to Claudia, she enjoyed using it to scare visitors — to keep them from coming back." I eyed Jenna. "It sounded sort of like a . . . well, like Sunny having a pet ghost."

"Pet ghost?" Liking the sound of that, Jenna pursed her lips. "Actually, that makes me feel a little better. The idea that it was the ghost of Sunny really spooked me." She shuddered. "Rose said that after they took Sunny's body away, there were gallons of blood on the floor upstairs."

"Gallons?" I frowned. "But there are only five or six quarts in the average human body."

"Well, okay, not gallons." Jenna plumped up the pillow and handed it to me. "But she said they had to rip up the carpet, and when they did, they found it had already soaked into the floorboards. If this was Sunny's ghost banging around upstairs, I couldn't help imagining it dripping with blood." She shuddered. "And I'm the sort of person who

447

passes out cold when she has to get blood drawn."

I put the pillow on the bed. "And if it isn't Sunny?"

She straightened up, thought for a moment, and added, "If it's only a dusty old Carswell ghost who's been hanging around this place for a century or so, I suppose I might learn to live with it." She put her hand on my arm. "But I'm glad you're here just the same, China. You give me courage."

"For the sake of argument, let's say it's a dusty old Hemlock House ghost who likes to move things around and make a little noise," I said. "What's the game plan?"

Jenna produced a couple of flashlights and a broom. "I guess if we hear anything upstairs, we'll go up by the back staircase and . . . well, take a look. See what's happening. Chase a ghost."

She gave a deprecating little laugh. "Just listen to me. When I heard those noises in the dark last night, I got so scared I started hyperventilating and I . . . I couldn't stop. I had to put my head down and hold my breath to keep from fainting. Now you're here, and the lights are on and I'm sooo brave."

"I understand the flashlights. Good idea." I frowned at the broom in her hand. "But *this*?"

"I wouldn't know what to do with a gun. A knife seemed awfully . . . well, primitive, not to mention bloody." Another shudder. "I thought of holy water, but I didn't know where to get it."

"A broom isn't primitive?"

"It was handy. I saw it in the kitchen when I went to get the flashlights, and I just grabbed it." She laughed, then sobered. "Really, China, I hope you don't think I was hallucinating last night. Or just being silly."

I patted her hand. "My friend Ruby thinks that houses can soak up some of the strong human emotions that are spilled in them. That they're like . . . well, like batteries. They take a charge and hold it. Then a certain kind of personality comes along and plugs into that charge and brings it to life. Not to physical life, necessarily, but to . . . well, to psychic life. If that makes any sense," I added. "Ruby tells it better than I do."

Jenna was watching me closely. "What kind of personality?"

"Intuitive people, like Ruby. Empathic people. People who relate to other people easily — who get in touch with the way others are feeling, especially if the feelings are strong." As I spoke, I thought that Jenna was a lot like Ruby — intuitive, empathic, relatable. Elizabeth Blackwell had been dead for two-and-a-half centuries, but Jenna understood her deeply and intuitively, as if she could slip into Elizabeth's skin.

"I . . . see," Jenna said, into the pause. "So I'm sort of like an . . . an energizer? An activator? An agent? I come along and plug into Hemlock's psychic circuits and bring them to life?"

"Something like that, maybe. Ruby really does explain it better."

"Well, it describes a lot of what I've been through in my life," Jenna said. "Someday I'll come to Texas and ask Ruby to explain it to me." She yawned. "But for now, I'm dead on my feet. I think it's time for bed."

My eyelids were drooping too, so we crawled into bed. Jenna left a nightlight burning and there was a clock with a bright digital face on the table beside her bed. But the room was mostly dark and comfortably warm and I fell asleep as soon as I pulled the blankets over me.

I didn't get to sleep for more than a couple of hours, though. I was awakened from an especially nice dream of McQuaid by Jenna, crouching beside the sofa, grasping my arm in the dark. She was wearing a fluffy red shawl over her purple flannel PJs,

450

and pink bunny slippers with floppy ears on her feet. Over her shoulder, the digital clock showed that it was 2:45.

"Wake up, China," she whispered. "I heard a door closing upstairs. Footsteps. And a thump — a couple of thumps. Something . . ." She swallowed, clutching. "Something's up there. Moving around. Listen."

If Jenna had been determinedly brave before we went to sleep, she was definitely frightened now. Her fingers on my bare arm were trembling and her breath was ragged. Her face was shadowed, but there was enough light to see that her eyes were huge, the pupils dilated.

I sat bolt upright, listening. For a moment, I heard nothing but the surrounding silence and her uneven breathing.

Then I heard it, a series of irregular thumps. *Thump-thump-kathump-thump.* It sounded as if it could be in the room overhead, or maybe in the wall. Jenna's fingers dug into my arm.

"Is that your ghost?" I thought of Annie, who doesn't thump. She occasionally rings a bell, but most of the time she just likes to make herself felt. She's a presence with an attitude.

"It's a coffin, China." Jenna's whisper was edged with hysteria. "Something is dragging

451

a coffin across the floor upstairs." Her breathing was getting faster and more un-even.

I remembered that Dorothea had said that Jenna could be something of a drama queen and that she liked to play at being fright-ened. Was that what was happening here?

"It doesn't sound like a coffin to me," I said crisply. "It's not heavy enough. And stop hyperventilating. You don't want to pass out."

"Oh, yes, I do," she said fervently. "I would *love* to pass out. If I did, I'd have an excuse for missing whatever happens next." She took another couple of deep, fast breaths and closed her eyes as if inviting herself to collapse. After a moment, still upright, she opened her eyes. In a small voice, she asked, "What happens next?"

I swung my legs off the sofa and slipped my bare feet into my sneakers. "Well, you can stay here and faint if you want." I reached for the white terry bathrobe I'd brought from my room. "I'm going to see what's making that noise." I slipped my cell phone into my bathrobe pocket and grabbed my flashlight and the broom that was lean-ing against the wall.

"But you can't go up there by yourself," Jenna wailed dramatically. "And you can't leave me here all alone. I'm *scared.*"

"Then I guess you'll have to come with me." I shrugged into my bathrobe and knotted the belt around my waist. "Bring your flashlight."

She made a woozy little moan, but after a moment she did what I asked, and the two of us made our way to the door. Cautiously, I pulled at it. It didn't seem to want to open, almost as if something were out there in the hall, holding it. Something that didn't want us to leave this room.

Taking a breath, I tugged at the door even harder. It gave just a little, then opened so quickly that I flung out an arm and took a step backward to keep from falling.

The darkness in the hallway was as thick as molasses and the air had an odd, heavy quality, as though it were compressed. It smelled of stale dust and musty carpeting. It was cold, too. Icy cold. It must be twenty degrees colder than Jenna's room, I thought, remembering something Ruby had told me about researchers finding measurable temperature drops where psychic activity was going on.

I paused in the doorway to get my bearings, Jenna close behind me. I looked left, toward the staircase, where I could see the tall window at the end of the hall, a mysterious gray rectangle of moonlight in the utter darkness. Somewhere close by, I heard the skitter and patter of little feet. Rats, maybe.

But there was something else. Something that rustled. Or whispered, like the sound of many distant voices. Or just . . . waited, its breath fading in and out of the darkness, barely audible but darkly menacing.

Jenna heard it too, and whimpered. "There's something out here, China." She put an urgent hand on my arm. "Please. Let's not —"

But we had come this far and I wasn't going back. "You stay," I said. I stepped out into the hall and glanced to the right — and my breath froze in my throat.

Coming toward us in the darkness was a shimmering figure. Cloaked in luminous white gossamer, sheer, fluid, shape-shifting, it seemed to float above the floor.

Behind me, Jenna saw it too. She gave a small shriek. "No! Oh, no! Please, no. I . . ." Her knees gave way. Holding onto the door jamb, she slid to the floor.

I couldn't breathe. My heart seemed to have stopped and I could taste the acrid terror at the back of my throat. The whispers grew louder as I turned toward the apparition. Brandishing my broom, I aimed my flashlight full on the place where its face would be, if it had a face.

It did, although its owner had flung up an arm to shield her eyes from the bright light.

"Dorothea!" I exclaimed, feeling weak-kneed myself.

"Oh, good. You have a flashlight," Dorothea said in her usual voice. "The batteries went out on mine." She caught sight of Jenna. "Jenna, dear, why in the world are you sitting on the *floor*?"

Jenna's eyelids fluttered. "I . . . think I fainted," she said unsteadily. "I thought you were the ghost."

"Ridiculous," Dorothea said. "I am *not* a ghost."

Obviously. But she had certainly looked like one.

"You heard what we heard?" I asked.

"I heard something," Dorothea said in a sensible, all-business tone. "I didn't know what it was, so I decided I'd better go have a look, in case the wind broke a window somewhere." She shivered and pulled her white negligee around her. "I didn't realize it would be so *cold,* though. I should have put on something warmer." She frowned at me. "What are you doing with that broom?"

"It was handy," I said, feeling a little silly.

"I see," she said. She held out a hand to Jenna. "Get up, Jenna. That floor is cold."

Jenna took her hand and got slowly to her feet, but her face was the color of pale cheese and she swayed. Any pretense to being brave about the ghost had vanished. Drama queen or not, she was clearly terrified, and I could hardly blame her. The sight of the figure in that white negligee floating down the hall had knocked the breath out of me.

"Jenna, you are white as a sheet," Dorothea said with motherly concern. She put her arms around her and said, "You're trembling. You should be in bed, my dear."

Jenna leaned into Dorothea's embrace. "I'm afraid . . . to stay by myself," she murmured incoherently. "Please don't leave me."

"We were on our way to have a look, too," I said, trying to make my voice sound normal. And if we didn't go soon, we were likely to miss whatever it was.

On second thought, that might actually be a good idea. Who were we, to imagine we could face this . . . this thing? If it had been haunting this place for decades, the three of us weren't going to make it leave. Not with a broom and a couple of flashlights.

At that moment, we all heard it again. The oddly irregular thumping noise.

"Yes," Dorothea said, very quietly, "*That's*

what I heard."

It still seemed to be coming from over-head, or from the walls. But I knew that wasn't the force that was out here in the hallway. No, this was something else, more of a sensation than a sound, hovering over us, brushing against us, raising the hair on the back of my neck and goosebumps on my arms. A dark something. Ominous. Full of menace.

And then, from somewhere in the depths of the house, we heard the slow, hollow reverberation of a distant gong: *one two three.* As its last dull note eerily shivered and dissolved, Jenna swallowed a frightened moan and her face seemed to grow even more pale. She was trembling visibly. Her terror was palpable.

"There, there, dear," Dorothea said sooth-ingly, tightening her arms around Jenna. "It's just that old brass clock in the sitting room — the one that came from India. Nothing to be frightened of."

But her voice cracked. Around us, the blackness grew heavier and blacker, seem-ing to pulse with echoes of the gong. My heart was rattling around inside me as if it had come loose from its moorings. I could feel myself being infected by Jenna's fear.

I cleared my throat, tried to speak, then

tried again. "If we're going, I guess we should go."

Dorothea gave me an encouraging smile. "You go first, with the flashlight. And the broom. Jenna and I will be right behind you."

I could have argued, but I didn't. I turned and started down the hall toward the faintly luminous window. Jenna was close behind me, shuffling along in her bunny slippers, clutching my bathrobe belt as if she were afraid that if she let go of me, I would disappear — or *she* would. Dorothea was beside her, a firm arm around her waist, as if she thought Jenna might faint again.

A fine team of stalwart ghostbusters *we* were, I thought, and was swept by a half-hysterical impulse to giggle.

But none of this was the slightest bit funny. Something — some sort of corporeal creature and quite substantial, by the sound of it — was making that noise upstairs. But something else — something that whispered, something inexplicably dark and terrifying — had hovered over us. There was no telling what we might find on the third floor, where two suicides and a murder had taken place. It was no laughing matter.

"I think we should all go back," Jenna whispered faintly. "Sorry to be such a wuss, but can we please . . . go back?"

"We'll just go as far as the staircase," Dorothea said, in her reassuringly normal tone. "And then we'll decide."

It seemed to take forever, but when we got to the door that opened onto the circular staircase, I took a deep breath, grasped the knob, and pulled it open, reaching for the light switch, on the wall to the right of the door. I flicked the switch but nothing happened. I flicked it again. Nothing.

"Damn," I muttered. In front of me, the stairway was a giant black well. Somewhere down the stairs I thought I heard an odd bumping sound and I stepped forward onto the landing, directing my flashlight beam downward. But the utter darkness swallowed up the thin thread of trembling light.

Behind me, Dorothea made an impatient noise. "The electricity must be off again. If it isn't back on by morning, Joe will have to —"

But whatever she was about to say was blanketed by the sudden wild cry that echoed up the stairs, followed immediately by a series of soft thuds and louder bangs. And then a moan, and another, and then silence. This was no ghost. Something — and someone — had fallen down those narrow steps.

I didn't stop to think. Flashlight in one hand, the other on the iron railing, I clattered down the stairs. Above me, Dorothea cried out, "Oh, China, please be careful! That stair, it's *dangerous*!"

And then there it was, at the foot of the staircase, silent and unmoving. A sprawled figure wearing a black parka and black ski mask, arms flung out, jeans-clad legs at odd angles. I knelt down. I could barely see the face, but enough to recognize her. It was Claudia Roth.

And off to one side, on the floor, lay one of those rolling luggage bags, wheels up, one wheel broken. The suitcase had tumbled down the stairs and split open along the zipper, and I could see what was still fitted snugly inside.

It was a large brown leather book with silver corners and a pair of ornate silver clasps.

CHAPTER SEVENTEEN

Queen Anne's lace is a favorite of people who like to forage for edible foods. As a biennial, this wild ancestor of the garden carrot produces leaves and roots in the first year; in the second year, it produces flowers and seeds. You can mince the fresh leaves and add them to salad or soups. The roots are best harvested in the spring or fall of the first year when they are tender; second-year roots become woody. The peeled flower stalk has a carroty flavor and may be eaten raw or cooked. The flower itself makes a flavorful jelly or a pretty garnish. The ground seeds are spicy. However, if you're pregnant, you should avoid eating any part of this plant. The seeds have been used for centuries as a morning-after contraceptive, and a decoction of the root can produce uterine contractions and cause a miscarriage.

And foragers, please beware! You must

take extra care to be sure that what you are harvesting is wild carrot and not its deadly lookalike, poison hemlock. Crush a few leaves. If they smell like fresh carrot, you're safe. If they have a foul odor, leave it alone. This is serious stuff, folks, so pay attention. Mistakes with this plant have cost lives.

"Anne's Flower"
China Bayles
Pecan Springs Enterprise

I turned the shop door sign to open and went back around my sales counter.

"So what happened next?" Ruby was leaning against the counter, staring at me, her eyes round. I had just given her an abbreviated version of the events at Hemlock House. "Claudia wasn't *dead,* was she?"

"Just concussed," I said. "But she's lucky she wasn't hurt worse. Those stairs really are dangerous, especially in the dark. The med techs and the deputies took her to the hospital for observation. The doctor said the concussion was mild and that she would be her usual self in no time." I grinned. "To quote Jenna, 'No loonier than usual.' I drove her home the next day. She was anxious about her parrots."

It was a bright and balmy April morning

in Texas. I had gotten home the evening before and was glad to be back behind the counter of my shop, surrounded by the familiar Thyme and Seasons sights and scents. The crisp, clean smell of lavender blended with an exotic orange ylang-ylang that wafted through the open door of Ruby's Crystal Cave. The big antique hutch was stocked with herbal vinegars, oils, jellies, teas, and potpourris. The corner cupboard displayed herbal soaps, shampoos, and bath herbs. Beside it, the bookshelves were filled with cookbooks and gardening books. Handcrafted wreaths and swags hung on the walls, along with bundles of dried yarrow, sweet Annie, larkspur, statice, and tansy. Through the window behind the counter, I could get a glimpse of the rack of potted herb seedlings for sale — parsley, sage, thyme, fennel, more — and larger pots of shrubby herbs: lavender, rosemary, and bay.

I sighed happily. The trip had been an interesting experience. I had enjoyed the people and the mountains and even the snow. But I was glad to be *home.*

Ruby pushed up the sleeves of her trippy psychedelic sweater. "So it was Claudia Roth who actually stole the *Herbal,*" she mused, shaking her head. "How many of the other books did she steal? Was Jed Conway fencing her thefts on the internet, too?"

"She didn't steal it," I said. "In fact, the book never left Hemlock House. It was hidden in the secret room."

"You're kidding." Ruby blinked. "A secret room! Like the one in that old Mary Roberts Rinehart mystery?"

"Sort of." I opened the cash register drawer and began checking to make sure there was enough change for today's business. "Not nearly as spooky, though. It was only about the size of a large walk-in closet with floor-to-ceiling shelves, hidden behind a bookcase in Sunny's third-floor bedroom. The bookcase swung out on little rollers — that was the noise Jenna thought was a coffin being dragged across the floor. Inside the closet, the shelves were full of books Sunny had stashed there, maybe to keep them for herself. Or to keep them out of Jed Conway's clutches."

"And Claudia Roth knew about this secret room?"

I opened a roll of pennies and dumped them into the cash drawer. "Claudia Roth knows about a lot of things, as it turned out. After all, she was one of the family. She and Sunny were closer than anybody knew.

464

Anybody but Rose Mullins, that is — and Rose wasn't about to share that information with outsiders, like Dorothea and me." I closed the cash register and checked to make sure that the credit card system was on and ready to go.

"Rose is the housekeeper — right?"

"Right. After Dorothea arrived to take over the library, Rose told Claudia that the Hemlock House board couldn't decide what they wanted to do with Sunny's library. Dorothea had been hired to catalogue and evaluate it, and then it might be sold. Which wasn't exactly true, but Rose *thought* it was."

"So Claudia decided she had to do something."

"Exactly." I began straightening the small display of herb seeds on the counter beside the cash register. "She was convinced that it was her duty to protect the thing that Sunny held most precious: the Blackwell *Herbal.* So she went to Hemlock House one weekend when Rose told her that Dorothea and Jenna would be gone. She moved the book from the display case in the library up to Sunny's secret room." I relocated an envelope of basil seeds from the parsley section up next to the bee balm, where it belonged. "She was doing what she thought Sunny

465

would want her to do. She was keeping the *Herbal* safe."

"But if that was her motive, what made her change her mind? Why did she try to take it away? In the middle of the night, too."

"That was . . . well, it was my fault," I said ruefully.

"Your fault?"

I opened the laptop behind the counter and turned it on. "Afraid so. The morning after I arrived, I quizzed Rose about the secret room. I even asked if she'd be willing to help me hunt for it. My questions made her nervous, and when she talked to Claudia, she mentioned that a stranger — that was me — was asking about the room. Claudia and I had a common bond when it came to parrots, but she saw through my cover story and thought she saw more than that. She thought I wanted the *Herbal*."

"So she figured the safest place for the book was her parrot sanctuary." Ruby shook her head. "But she had to go and fetch it in the middle of the *night*?"

"Well, she could hardly do it in the daytime, when everybody was around," I said. "Actually, it was her second attempt to get the *Herbal*. She had come the night before, but she couldn't get the bookcase to open the way it should — that was the noise that scared Jenna and prompted her to ask me to sleep in her room. So Claudia came back the next night, with tools. She was concerned that the book might get wet in the snow, so she brought the wheelie. Unfortunately, one of the wheels broke. That was the weird thumping noise."

Ruby frowned. "But didn't you say that her house was more than a mile away? Surely she didn't expect to drag a loaded wheelie all that distance, even if the wheel hadn't been broken."

"That lady is eminently resourceful," I said. "She drove her snowmobile."

Ruby looked skeptical. "And nobody heard it? Those things are *loud.*"

"She cut the engine a hundred yards from the house and walked the rest of the way. I think she might have gotten away with her plan if the sliding bookcase hadn't slipped off its rollers. That's what woke Jenna. Dorothea, too."

There was a loud *mrrrrow* and Khat, our fawn-colored Siamese shop kitty, stalked through the door to the tea room and jumped onto the sales counter. "Hello, sweetie," I said, stroking his lovely seal-point ears. "Miss me?"

Khat flicked his dark tail dismissively. Like

most Siamese, he disdains any show of affection unless he thinks it will get him an extra helping of kitty food. I laughed. "As long as somebody fed you, you probably didn't even know I was gone," I told him.

"So is what Claudia did a *crime*?" Ruby asked. "Is she going to get into trouble with the law for hiding that book?"

"The sheriff is threatening to charge her with obstruction," I said. "But I doubt he'll go to the trouble. The *Herbal* is back where it belongs, undamaged, and he has his hands full with Jed Conway and Socrates-.com. He'll give Claudia a stern lecture, clear the theft, and that will be the end of that. She has also promised Dorothea that she won't come back — not at night, anyway."

"Jed has been arrested?"

I opened the little cupboard behind the counter and took out the broom. "Yep. Chief Curtis has charged him with offering two stolen prints of Redouté's *Lilies* on Socrates.com, and there will be additional charges when they figure out what's what. Jenna is going through all the listings on the website in an effort to match them with items that are missing from the library. Jed had better start looking for a lawyer."

"And the foundation's board?"

"Good news." I smiled. "They've commended Dorothea for getting the book back. And agreed to her proposal for climate control, an alarm system, and an additional person to help with the cataloging. I think they're beginning to take their work seriously at last."

Ruby sighed. "And the story of the ghost of Hemlock House — it was Claudia Roth all along?" She sounded disappointed.

I hesitated. "I didn't say that," I said slowly. I shivered, thinking of the intense cold and the powerful dark energy I had felt when I stepped out into the hallway. "There's something there. A ghost, a spirit, a force — whatever it is, it's been there for years. I don't think it's going away anytime soon. And I'd just as soon not know what it is."

The bell over the shop door chimed gently. I looked up, expecting to see the door open and the first customer of the day step inside. But there was no one there — at least, no one that I could see.

Ruby smiled. "That's Annie," she said. "She always likes to have the last word, you know."

RESOURCES

Background material for this book, including recipes, suggestions for further reading, and some notes on Elizabeth Blackwell's *A Curious Herbal* are available on Susan's website: https://susanalbert.com/hemlock-book-28/

ABOUT THE AUTHOR

Susan Wittig Albert

Growing up on a farm on the Illinois prairie, Susan learned that books could take her anywhere, and reading and writing became passions that have accompanied her throughout her life. She earned an undergraduate degree in English from the University of Illinois at Urbana and a PhD in medieval studies from the University of California at Berkeley. After fifteen years of faculty and administrative appointments at the University of Texas, Tulane University, and Texas State University, she left her academic career to write full time.

Now, there are over four million copies of Susan's books in print. Her best-selling mystery fiction includes the Darling Dahlias Depression-era mysteries, the China Bayles Herbal Mysteries, the Cottage Tales of Beatrix Potter, and (under the pseudonym of

Robin Paige) a series of Victorian-Edwardian mysteries with her husband, Bill Albert.

Susan's historical fiction includes *The General's Women,* a novel about the World War II romantic triangle of Dwight Eisenhower, his wife Mamie, and his driver and secretary Kay Summersby; *Loving Eleanor,* a fictional account of the friendship of Lorena Hickok and Eleanor Roosevelt; and *A Wilder Rose,* the story of Rose Wilder Lane and the writing of the Little House books. She is also the author of two memoirs: *An Extraordinary Year of Ordinary Days* and *Together, Alone: A Memoir of Marriage and Place.* Other nonfiction titles include *What Wildness Is This: Women Write about the Southwest* (winner of the 2009 Willa Award for Creative Nonfiction); *Writing from Life: Telling the Soul's Story;* and *Work of Her Own: A Woman's Guide to Success off the Career Track.*

Susan is an active participant in the literary community. She is the founder of the Story Circle Network, a nonprofit organization for women writers, and a member of Sisters in Crime, Women Writing the West, Mystery Writers of America, and the Texas Institute of Letters. She and her husband

Bill live on thirty-one acres in the Texas Hill Country, where she gardens, tends chickens and geese, and indulges her passions for needlework and (of course) reading.

The employees of Thorndike Press hope you have enjoyed this Large Print book. All our Thorndike, Wheeler, and Kennebec Large Print titles are designed for easy reading, and all our books are made to last. Other Thorndike Press Large Print books are available at your library, through selected bookstores, or directly from us.

For information about titles, please call:

(800) 223-1244

or visit our website at:

gale.com/thorndike

To share your comments, please write:

Publisher
Thorndike Press
10 Water St., Suite 310
Waterville, ME 04901